Loon Chase

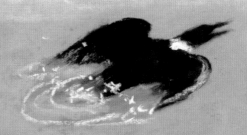

By Jean Heilprin Diehl
Illustrated by Kathryn Freeman

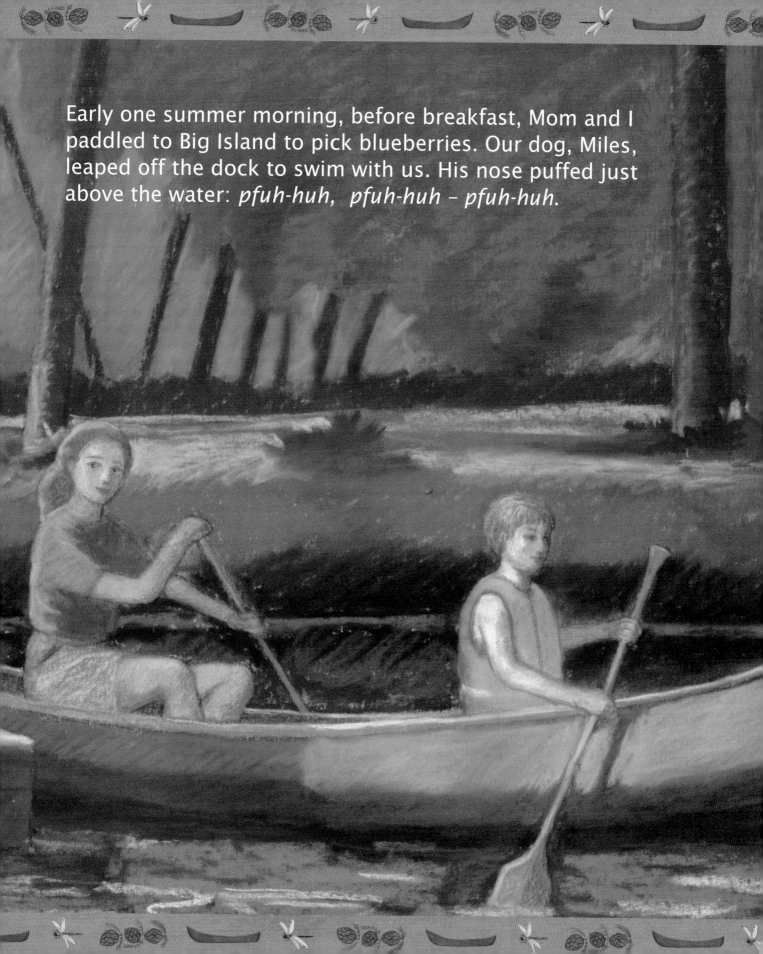

Early one summer morning, before breakfast, Mom and I paddled to Big Island to pick blueberries. Our dog, Miles, leaped off the dock to swim with us. His nose puffed just above the water: *pfuh-huh, pfuh-huh – pfuh-huh.*

Miles loved to swim. He could dog-paddle faster than I could paddle a canoe.

I made a triangle with my arms and the neck of my wooden paddle, dipped the paddle into the lake, and pulled—just like Mom had taught me.

"Can I go out to the island by myself soon?" I asked.

Mom just smiled. I could tell that it wouldn't be long until she said, "yes."

At the end of the lake, by the mill, a loon and two loon chicks were swimming. Loons were rare birds, and seeing them was as exciting as watching a shooting star. There were so few left in the world, and it was against the law to hurt one. I was glad that they were far away, though. Miles was a bird dog; he wasn't mean, but he just had to chase every bird he saw.

"*Pfuh-huh—pfuh-huh.*" His nose sprayed silvery drops. Luckily, Miles was too busy swimming to see the loons.

At Big Island, I stood in the canoe picking berries while Mom held the boat steady. Now we were busy, so we didn't notice when Miles stopped sniffing around in the bushes and swam away.

Sound carries a long way over water. Before we saw Miles again we heard, "*Pfuh-huh—pfuh-huh, pfuh-huh—pfuh-huh.*" The sun bounced so brightly off the lake that we had to squint to see him, out in the middle, his black head pointed straight toward three tiny specks—the loons.

I tossed the berries I had in my hand into the bucket. We jabbed our paddles onto the rocks to push off. We had to stop him.

Miles was our family pet. He played ball, slept on a dog bed and ate out of a bowl, but when he saw a bird, something came over him. He had never been close to catching one in our yard. These loons were on the water though—and two of them were babies!

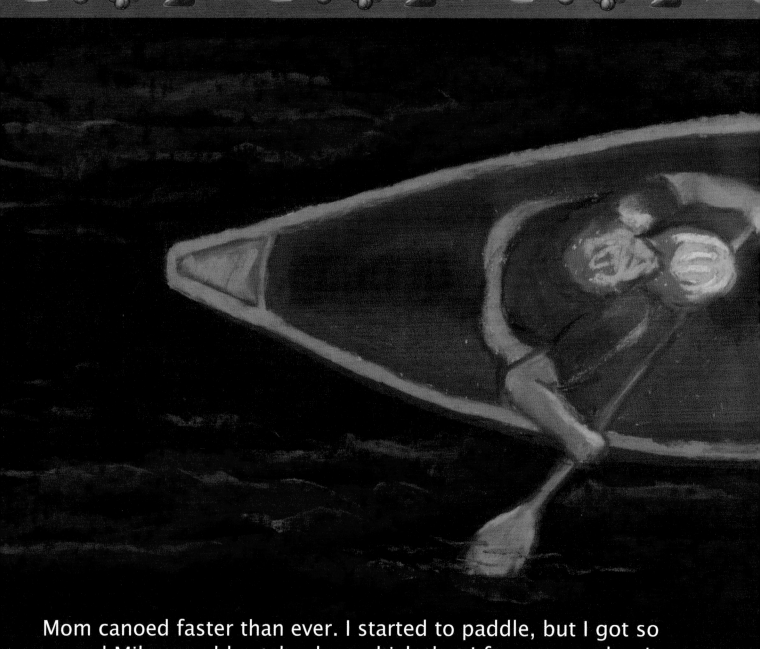

Mom canoed faster than ever. I started to paddle, but I got so scared Miles would catch a loon chick that I froze up and quit. While the boat raced along, I held my paddle on my lap like a useless stick. A dragonfly flew up and hovered over the blade.

"I need your help if we're going to head him off," Mom said. So I pushed at the dark water again. It felt as thick as chocolate icing.

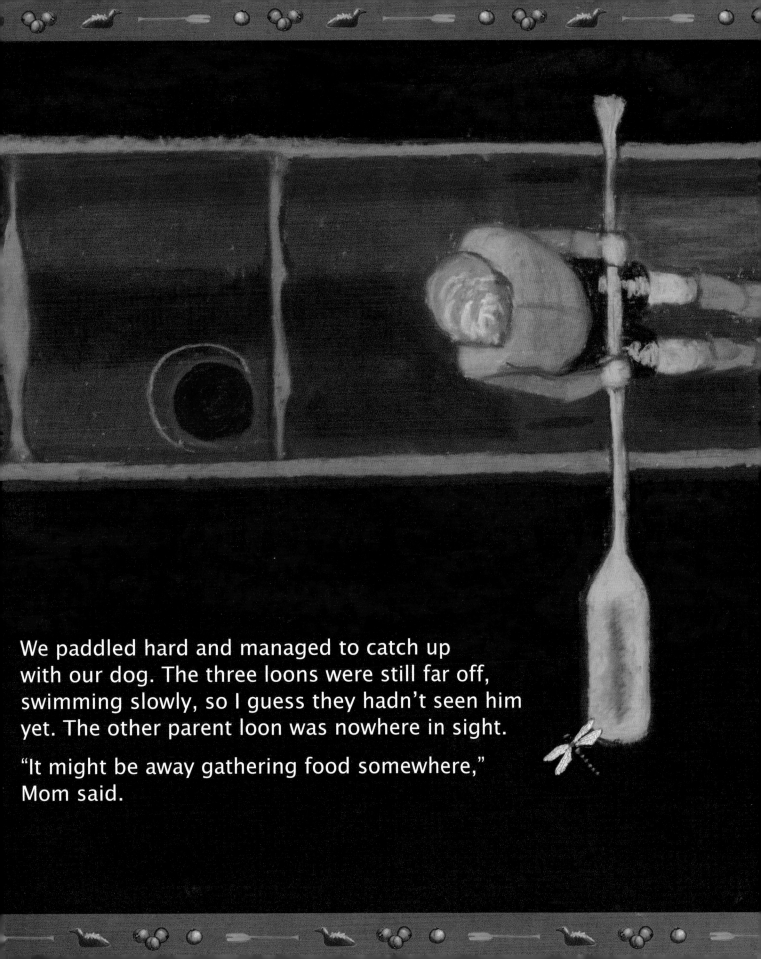

We paddled hard and managed to catch up with our dog. The three loons were still far off, swimming slowly, so I guess they hadn't seen him yet. The other parent loon was nowhere in sight.

"It might be away gathering food somewhere," Mom said.

She turned the canoe so it crossed Miles' path, but he swam around the boat. She tried prodding him with her paddle, to point him in a different direction. He ducked and came up near me at the bow. I reached out to grab his collar—and missed.

"Miles!" I yelled. He swam off.

"Get my paddle!" Mom shouted behind me. In the confusion, it had slipped from her hands.

I pushed and pulled with my paddle and somehow yanked the canoe close enough for Mom to reach in and grab hers. By the time we turned the boat back toward the loons, Miles had almost reached them.

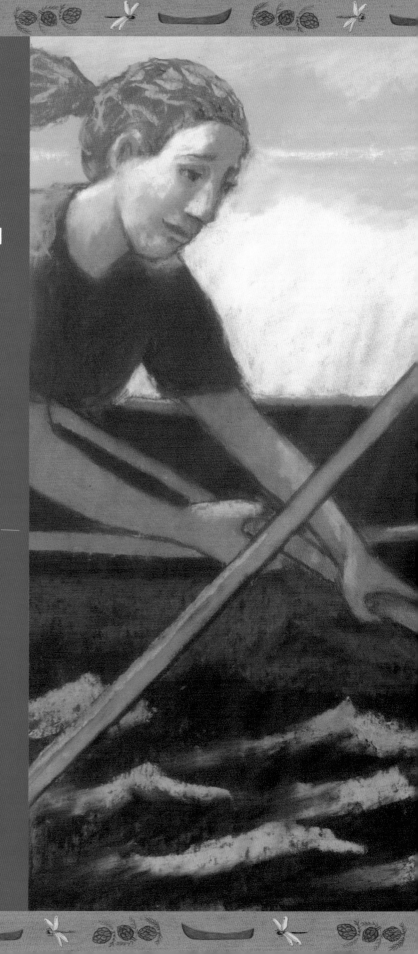

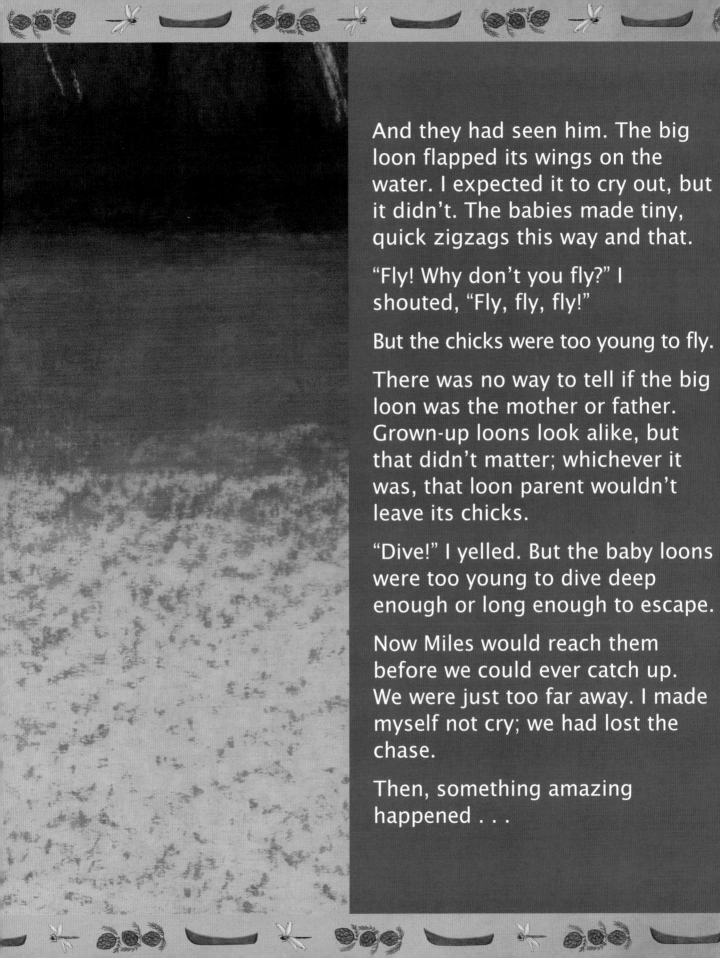

And they had seen him. The big loon flapped its wings on the water. I expected it to cry out, but it didn't. The babies made tiny, quick zigzags this way and that.

"Fly! Why don't you fly?" I shouted, "Fly, fly, fly!"

But the chicks were too young to fly.

There was no way to tell if the big loon was the mother or father. Grown-up loons look alike, but that didn't matter; whichever it was, that loon parent wouldn't leave its chicks.

"Dive!" I yelled. But the baby loons were too young to dive deep enough or long enough to escape.

Now Miles would reach them before we could ever catch up. We were just too far away. I made myself not cry; we had lost the chase.

Then, something amazing happened . . .

The big loon rose up in the water. It flapped its wings and splashed its webbed feet as though it were walking on the lake. Below, down in the water, the dog's head looked very small. The bird spread its huge wings between Miles and the babies. Its feet began to dance, faster and faster. Water flashed up in the sun and foamed white, like a fountain in the middle of the lake.

Whoosh—Miles lunged at the loon. The water splashed up even higher. What was happening?

Wait!

Miles was turning back.

He was swimming toward our canoe! That loon looked delicate and beautiful, but on the water it was fiercer than our dog.

The loon was swimming too—in the opposite direction, as if the dog were still chasing it. We couldn't see the chicks.

When Miles passed us, we could see that there was nothing in his mouth except bubbles. We followed him. He climbed out of the lake, shook off, and lay panting on the dock, "*Heh-heh heh-heh heh-heh*."

Mom clipped the leash back onto his collar.

"I want to go out by myself and make sure the chicks are okay," I said.

She looked at me carefully.

"All right," she said. She would watch me and hold Miles.

I steered back to Big Island. Alone in the canoe for the first time, I wasn't scared, just disappointed not to find the loons on the other side of the island or in the cove.

From the dock, Mom waved and pointed to where we had picked blueberries.

There they were: two big loons now, and—yes—the two chicks between them.

I stopped paddling and let the canoe float. One of the parents dropped its head forward under the water and dove without a sound or a ripple.

A few inches from the canoe, it came up again. I heard nothing. It just appeared. It was so close to me that I could have reached out and touched it.

Well, I knew—I just instantly knew: this was the loon Miles had chased.

It was twice as big as it had looked from far away—bigger than any duck. The tip of its beak was thin and as sharp as the point of a knife. Its black was the deepest black; it's white, pure white. And, it looked like it was wearing a necklace. It was hard to believe that no one had painted that exact pattern on its feathers.

The loon looked at me with its red eye and did not move. Had it come up in this spot on purpose, or was the loon as surprised as I was?

We stared at each other, for what felt like several minutes. Then, just as silently as it had arrived, the bird again dove and was gone.

After dinner that night, Mom and I sat on the dock to look for shooting stars. At our feet, Miles lay curled up—fast asleep. When the loons cried out in the dark, he was too tired to hear them.

Mom and I listened. Those weird loon voices called to each other like sad laughter. Then one of the loons whisked through the moonlit air, close to the surface of the lake. It looked like a black bowling pin with a spear-shaped tip as it flew—out of the wild and back into the night.

For Creative Minds

Loon Fun Facts

A loon is a large water bird that looks something like a duck, but is not related to a duck at all. Loons belong to a family of ancient birds, at least 20 million years old. The best-known species is the common loon (*Gavia immer*). The common loon is the state bird of Minnesota.

Loons spend almost all of their lives on water, and come on land only to mate, build their nest, and to incubate their eggs.

Scientists think loons may live as long as 30 years. *Who do you know who is about 30 years old? Does that seem old to you? Is that a long time for a bird?*

The common loon is famous for the black and white pattern of its summer feathers, and its many eerie, unmistakable calls.

Loons eat small fish, insects, snails, crayfish, frogs, and salamanders.

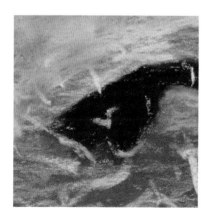

Underwater, loons almost always use their feet to move, not their wings. *What parts of your body do you use to swim?*

Loons' webbed feet (adapted for swimming) are set so far back on their bodies that it is difficult for them to walk on land.

Loons are able to fly at speeds of 60 to 90 miles (96.5 to 145 km) per hour. *Many cars on a highway drive about 60 miles (96.5 km) per hour. If a loon flies at 60 miles (96.5 km) per hour, how long does it take to fly five miles? What is five miles from your house or school? How long does it take you to drive those five miles? Walk? Ride a bike?*

While most birds have hollow, sponge-like bones, making their skeletons light, loons have solid bones. To lift their heavy bodies into the air, loons need a long runway, sometimes several hundred yards of water surface.

Loons have been known to dive to depths of more than 100 feet. They usually dive for about a minute at a time to hunt for food. How long can you hold your breath? How deep can you dive in a swimming pool?

Male and female adult loons look alike, though the male is often a little bigger.

Common loons weigh between 8 and 15 pounds (3.6 to 6.8 kg) and get larger in size as you go from west to east (Maine has larger loons compared to the west or Midwest.) *Math activity: find something in the house or classroom that weighs 10 pounds or 5 kilograms (bags of flour, a few books).*

They are 28 to 35 inches (71 to 90 cm) long with a wingspan of an adult being up to 58 inches (147 cm) wide. Math activity: use a yard stick to see how long a loon is and how wide the wingspan is. Use chalk to draw how big a loon is on the driveway, a quiet street, sidewalk, or playground.

Loon Life Cycle

Put the common loon life-cycle events in order to spell the scrambled word.

Loon pairs are territorial during the breeding season which means they defend an area around their nest and young, chasing other loons away if they come too close. Sometimes these chases lead to intense fights between the birds. Loons usually pair off with the same partner each year, but not always.

N

Common loons spend summers on lakes in the Northern United States and Canada. Loons migrate each season, flying back from their winter, ocean homes usually to the same lake.

I

They build their nests right at the shoreline because they need to slip on and off the nest without being seen by predators. Sometimes people will float an artificial nesting platform for a loon to nest on, which is especially useful on lakes where dams artificially raise or lower the water level each year.

C

Loon parents keep their chicks in a sheltered "nursery" area of the lake until they are three to four weeks old. Their feathers turn from downy brown to gray, and gradually the young loons swim in a larger part of the lake.

T

In winter, they live on the ocean along the Pacific coast, all the way to Mexico, and along the Atlantic coast, south to Florida and the Gulf of Mexico. Look at a map and identify where Loons spend the summer and winter. *Do they live in your area?*

S

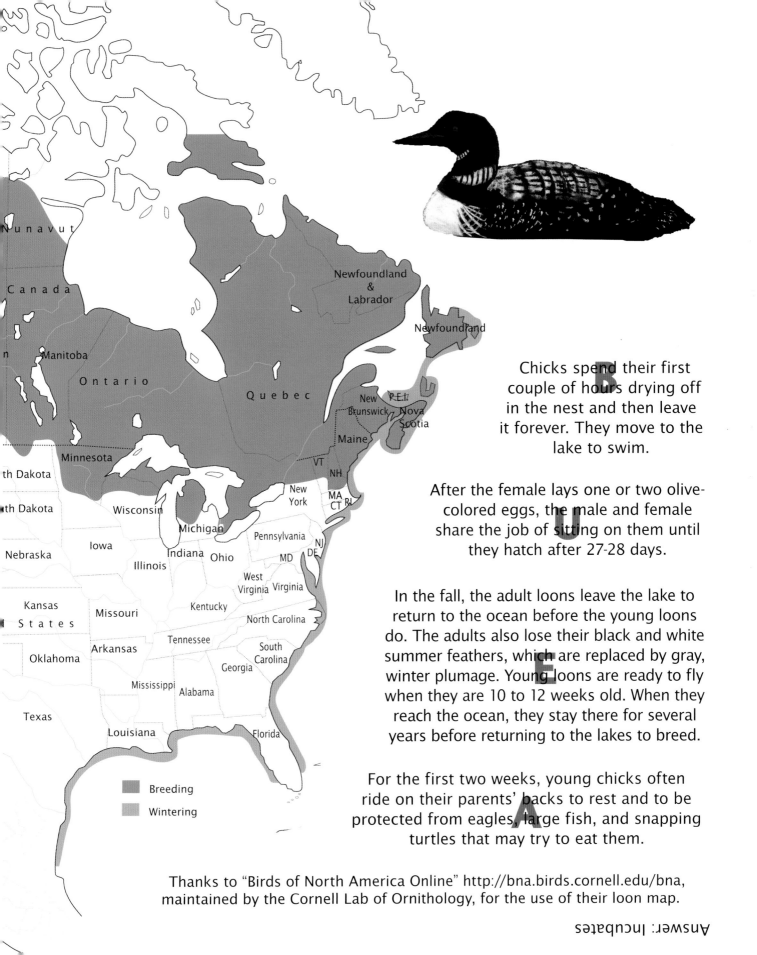

Chicks spend their first couple of hours drying off in the nest and then leave it forever. They move to the lake to swim.

After the female lays one or two olive-colored eggs, the male and female share the job of sitting on them until they hatch after 27-28 days.

In the fall, the adult loons leave the lake to return to the ocean before the young loons do. The adults also lose their black and white summer feathers, which are replaced by gray, winter plumage. Young loons are ready to fly when they are 10 to 12 weeks old. When they reach the ocean, they stay there for several years before returning to the lakes to breed.

For the first two weeks, young chicks often ride on their parents' backs to rest and to be protected from eagles, large fish, and snapping turtles that may try to eat them.

Breeding
Wintering

Thanks to "Birds of North America Online" http://bna.birds.cornell.edu/bna, maintained by the Cornell Lab of Ornithology, for the use of their loon map.

Answer: Incubates

This book is dedicated to the memory of Miles—JHD & KF

The author and illustrator donate a portion of their royalties to the Loon Preservation Committee (www.loon.org).

Thanks to Harry Vogel (LPC) and to the staff of the Maine Audubon for reviewing the"For Creative Minds" section and verifying its accuracy.

Publisher's Cataloging-In-Publication Data
Diehl, Jean Heilprin.

Title / by Jean Heilprin Diehl ; illustrated by Kathryn Freeman.

[32] p. : col. ill. ; cm.

Summary: A mother and son enjoy a peaceful canoe trip until their dog's instinct to chase birds adds excitement to the trip. Includes a "For Creative Minds" section.

ISBN: 978-0-97649438-6 (hardcover)
ISBN: 978-1-60718116-3 (pbk.)
Also available as eBooks featuring auto-flip, auto-read, 3D-page-curling, and selectable English and Spanish text and audio
Interest level: 004-008
Grade level: P-3
Lexile Level: 670

1. Loons --Fiction. 2. Dogs --Fiction. 3. Animal defenses --Fiction. 4. Canoes and canoeing --Fiction. I. I Freeman, Kathryn. II. Title.

PZ7.D5725 Lo 2006
[E] 22   2005931000

Manufactured in China, January, 2010
This product conforms to CPSIA 2008
Second Printing

Sylvan Dell Publishing
976 Houston Northcutt Blvd., Suite 3
Mt. Pleasant, SC 29464

Blogger
Beyond the Basics

Customize and promote your blog with original
templates, analytics, advertising, and SEO

Lee Jordan

PUBLISHING

BIRMINGHAM - MUMBAI

Blogger
Beyond the Basics

First published: April 2008

Production Reference: 1230408

Published by Packt Publishing Ltd.
32 Lincoln Road
Olton
Birmingham, B27 6PA, UK.

ISBN 978-1-847193-17-9

www.packtpub.com

Cover Image by Vinayak Chittar (vinayak.chittar@gmail.com)

Credits

Author

Lee Jordan

Reviewer

Narayan Bhat

Senior Acquisition Editor

David Barnes

Development Editor

Ved Prakash Jha

Technical Editor

Dhiraj Chandiramani

Copy Editor

Sumathi Sridhar

Editorial Team Leader

Mithil Kulkarni

Project Manager

Abhijeet Deobhakta

Indexer

Monica Ajmera

Proofreader

Angie Butcher

Production Coordinator

Aparna Bhagat

Cover Work

Aparna Bhagat

About the Author

Lee Jordan is an avid user of Blogger, Twitter, and other useful web applications. She designs interactive customer service portals, enterprise-level websites and other web-based applications and writes web content and user guides. She applies over ten years of experience designing and writing for the web to developing interactive, user friendly web sites and writing technical guides to popular web technologies. This is her second book with Packt Publishing. Get Blogger tips and download source code on her companion web site to this book at http://bloggerbeefedup.blogspot.com.

A big thanks to my daughter Celeste who practiced her reading skills by looking over my shoulder, and editing my writing. Her cheerful suggestions kept me motivated.

An Innocent Drinks smoothie or ten is owned to David Barnes. His vision for the book, and constructive feedback kept me focused and helped me through the rough spots.

About the Reviewer

Narayan Bhat is passionate about wandering the Internet and Blogging.

Table of Contents

Preface   1

Chapter 1: All Blogs Are Not Equal   7
  Meet Georgia Peach, Fanatical Fruitier   7
  The Way She Blogs Now   8
  What's Out There   10
    Cooking with Amy   11
    Meeblog   12
    BoingBoing   14
    Innocent Drinks   15
  What They Share   16
  Time to Plan   16
  Defining Goals   16
    Attract More Readers   17
    Reinforce her Brand, Build a Community   22
    Sell More Fruits, Explore New Revenue Opportunities   22
    Measure and Improve   23
  Summary   24

Chapter 2: Customize and Create Templates   25
  Choosing a Theme   25
  Presentation—It's About the Visual Things   26
  Changing Blogger Templates without Code   27
  Use the Test Blog   27
  Customizing Page Elements   27
    Managing Page Elements   29
    Editing the Header Page Element, Title, and Description   30
    Replacing the Header Image   33
    Changing Blog Templates   37
    Changing the Fonts and Colors   41
    Choosing High Contrast Text Colors   43
    Matching the Font to the Blog   45

Choosing an Effective Layout — **49**
The Usual Suspects — 49
Pruning the Template Code — **51**
Designing the Visual Look — 52
Preparing to Style the Post Content Block — 53
Adding a Custom Variable Tag to the Template — 53
Displaying an Image Next to the Title of Each Post — 55
Adding Background Images to Post Text Blocks — 57
Spicing up the Sidebar — 59
Styling the Footer Section — 61
Styling the Header Section of the Template — 63
Adding Polish to the Template with Style(s) — 65
Creating Visual Interest with Backgrounds and Borders — 65
Creating a Three-column Template — 67
Preparing to Modify Your Current Template — 68
Tweaking Template Images — 71
Summary — 75

Chapter 3: Social Bookmarking — **77**
How Social Bookmarking Works — **78**
Submitting Posts without Bookmarks — 78
Sharing Posts by Email — 81
Adding Bookmarks to Blogs — **83**
Choosing the Right Bookmarks for Your Blog — 83
Deciding Which Bookmark Services to Use — 85
Using Simple Text Link Bookmarks — 86
Adding Social Bookmark Buttons — 89
Offering Multiple Bookmarks with One Button — **92**
Adding Dynamic Counters to Bookmark Links — 94
Adding Multiple Counter Scripts Simultaneously — **96**
Attracting Readers with Links — **102**
What People are Tagging — 102
Planning an Article — 103
Building an Audience with Regular Posts — 105
Summary — **106**

Chapter 4: Joining the Blogosphere — **107**
Backlinks, Trackbacks, & Pingbacks — **107**
Configuring Backlinks — 107
Why You Need Backlinks — 108
Trackbacks Added Automatically — 110
Viewing Multiple Backlinks — 110
Being a Backlinker — 111
Maintaining Backlinks — 111

Using a Trackback Service	113
Trackbacking Non-Blogger Blogs	116
Blogrolls	**119**
Setting up Blogrolls	120
Caring for Blogrolls	124
Linkbaiting Bloggers	**124**
Attract Attention	124
Find a Unique Story Angle	124
Create Controversy	125
Technorati and Other Blog Networks	**125**
How Blog Networks Work	126
Summary	**128**
Chapter 5: Using Widgets	**129**
Adding a Blogger Page Element Widget	**129**
Widgets Your Readers Want	**132**
Adding a Custom Third-party Widget	132
Adding Interactive Third-Party Widgets	136
Interacting with Visitors Using Chat	136
Social Network Badges	139
E-commerce with Blogger	143
Using Product Sales Widgets	143
Offering Products as an Amazon Affiliate	143
Providing PayPal Service on Your Blog	146
Blogger and Third-Party Widgets	**151**
Crafting Custom Blogger Widgets	**152**
Anatomy of a Widget	157
Choose Your Widgets Wisely	**158**
Picking the Right Widgets	158
Widget Matching Matrix	158
Ways to Pick Widgets	159
Planning for Future Widgets	**159**
Using Experimental Widgets	160
Summary	**165**
Chapter 6: RSS and Atom Syndication	**167**
How Site Feeds Work in Blogger	**167**
Choosing a Feed Protocol for Your Blog	168
Multiple Feed Protocol Icons Confuse Visitors	168
Discovering the Post URL of Your Blogger Blog	168
Grabbing Feeds with Safari	171
Managing Blogger Feeds	**171**
Basic Feed Settings	172
Advanced Feed Settings	173

Redirecting Feeds	175
Promoting Your Blog with Feed Chicklets	178
More Ways to Publicize Your Feed with FeedBurner	180
Updating Google Sitemaps for Redirected Feeds	182
Give Visitors the Feed They Need with SmartFeed	183
Notifying Services with PingShot	183
Label Specific Feeds	**183**
Offering Feeds by Label	183
Measuring Feed Success	**185**
Showing Your Success with FeedCount	185
Using FeedBurner Stats	186
Adding Outside Feeds to Your Blog	**187**
Test Driving Blogger Subscription Links	**189**
Making it Easy for Visitors to Add Your Feeds	189
Subscription Links versus FeedBurner Redirect	191
Summary	**192**
Chapter 7: Making Money with Ads	**193**
Eating a Google AdSense and Blogger Sandwich	**193**
Setting up Google AdSense for Your Blog	**194**
Creating AdSense Ads with Blogger Page Elements	194
Using Custom AdSense Ads	198
Considering Your AdSense Options	198
Designing Your AdSense Ads	199
Putting YouTube Videos to Work with Video Units	203
Before You Begin	203
Managing Video Unit Players	206
AdSense for Search	207
Adding a Custom AdSense for Search to Your Blog	207
Setting up Referral Ad Units	212
Why Not to Use Referrals	215
Getting the Most Out of AdSense Ads	**216**
Managing Ads in AdSense	216
Using Advanced Reports	217
Generating Reports	217
Viewing Reports	218
Using AdSense Filters	219
Monetizing Blog Feeds with FeedBurner	**221**
Ways to Monetize	221
FeedBurner Ad Network (FAN)	221
Displaying AdSense Ads with FeedFlare	222
Managing AdSense Content Ad Units in FeedBurner	225
Discovering Other Advertising Programs	**225**
Amazon Affiliate Ads	225
Project Wonderful	229

BlogAds 229

Summary **229**

Chapter 8: Measuring Site Performance with Google Analytics **231**

Setting up Analytics **232**

Time for Action!—Activating Google Analytics **232**

Adding Tracking Code without Editing Your Template 234

Administrating Google Analytics **235**

Managing Website Profiles 235

Adding Additional Profiles 235

Managing Users with Access Manager 236

Preparing to Add a User 236

Editing Existing Users 238

Deleting Users 239

Controlling Data with Filters 239

Setting up Filters 239

Understanding Regular Expressions 241

Processing Data Using Custom Filters 242

Types of Custom Filters 244

Managing Ad Campaign Metrics **246**

Tracking Campaigns 246

Tagging Campaign Items 246

Experiencing URL Builder 246

Identifying Campaign Tags 248

AdWords Integration **248**

Analyzing Keyword Effectiveness 249

Driving the Reports Dashboard **250**

Navigating the Dashboard 250

Using the Left Menu of the Dashboard 250

Exploring the Main Dashboard Overview Section 251

Customizing the Dashboard Overview 251

Viewing Reports 253

Analyzing Reports 255

Emailing Reports 256

Evaluating Performance with Goals **258**

Tracking Performance with Goals 258

Editing Goals 261

Improving Your Blog with Google Analytics **262**

Analyzing Navigation 262

Exploring the Navigation Summary 262

Entrance Paths 263

Optimizing your Landing Page 263

Examining Entrance Sources 264

Discovering Entrance Keywords 264

Interpreting Click Patterns 264

Understanding Site Overlay	265
Summary	**266**
Chapter 9: Search Engine Optimization	**267**
Seeing a Blog through Search Engine Goggles	**268**
Performing a Search—Which Blogs Rank High	268
What High Ranking Blogs Do Right	269
Using Tools to Evaluate a Blog	270
Using the Google PageRank Button	272
Discovering Search Engine Reach Using Tools	273
Improving Search Engine Rank with Web Standards	274
Validating Your Blog Template	274
Blog SEO Checklist	277
Planning Improvements	**278**
Creating a List of Improvements	278
Ten Ways to Optimize a Blog for Search Engines	279
Wearing a White Hat	279
Developing Improvement Strategies	280
Prioritizing Improvements	280
Optimizing Your Blog for Search Engines	**281**
Optimizing On-site	281
Seeding the Blog Title & Description with Keywords	281
Allowing Search Engines to Find Your Blog	282
Fertilizing Content with Keywords	284
Optimizing Image and Video Posts for Current Searches	284
Submitting Rich Media Content for Indexing	286
Improving Template Validation	286
Optimizing with Off-Site Techniques	287
Adding a Blog to Google Webmaster Tools	288
Adding a Sitemap using Google Webmaster Tools	289
Communicating with Search Engine Spiders	291
Understanding User-Agent Behavior in Robots.txt	293
Measuring Optimization Success	**293**
Evaluating the Impact of Improvements	294
Tools and Resources	**294**
Maintaining Your SEO Status	**295**
Controlling the Destiny of Your Blog	295
The Secret to Search Engine Attraction	295
Search Engines Crave Rich Media Content	296
Why Search Engines Care about Rich Media Content	296
Summary	**296**
Chapter 10: Website Integration	**297**
Adding Website Navigation	**298**
Preparing to Add Navigation	298
Creating a Multi-Level Menu for a Blog	302

Using Widgets on Your Site to Share Your Blog   **308**
  Publicizing Blog Articles with Headline Animator   309
  Publicizing Your Blog with SpringWidgets   312
  Adding Twitter Updates to Your Website   317
Integrating the Look of Your Blog & Website   **321**
  Using the Same Fonts   321
  Choosing the Same Colors   323
Using Blogger with a Custom Domain   **324**
  Deciding How to Publish Your Blog   325
  Publishing to a Current Domain Using FTP   326
    FTP Errors and Solutions   328
  Using a New Custom Domain   329
    Purchasing a New Custom Domain   329
Summary   **331**
Index   **333**

Preface

This book actively immerses you in going beyond the default Blogger blog. Descriptive tutorials help you take action and learn to customize Blogger templates, add and create your own widgets, use social bookmarking tools, optimize your blog for search engines, attract more readers, play nice with other bloggers, understand Google Analytics, and make money with your blog.

As a bonus, you will also learn many delicious fruit recipes and have access to a rich array of images, code, and tips for your blog.

What This Book Covers

Chapter 1 will help you start by comparing a default Blogger blog with top blogs. You will meet Georgia and her organic fruit company *Fruit for All*. Georgia's blog will be our example throughout the book. Developing a wish list of the features and design elements for her blog will include an overview of the many types of features and online tools used by bloggers.

Chapter 2 will help you plan and customize your Blogger template to give your site its own look. This will include the blog post, sidebar, header, and footer areas of the blog. Tweaking the template will include quick fixes such as fonts, colors and background images and then cover more complex tasks, including adding a third column to your design.

Chapter 3 covers the types of social bookmarking and network tools, along with the most popular sites. Promoting your site using social bookmarks and using related widgets adds interactivity. You will use social bookmarking techniques with your blog and apply them to different parts of your blog. Blogger and third-party tools are customized and integrated into your blog.

Chapter 4 is all about being an active citizen of the Blogosphere. You will set up Blogger link backs, use tools to make it easier for other bloggers to link back to you, and learn ways to attract other bloggers to your blog.

Chapter 5 covers the best widgets for Blogger. Widgets are small, self-contained programs that can help you build a community, provide rich content, show and sell products, and make money. They give you more choices for how you can use your blog. You will not only add Blogger and third-party widgets to your blog, you will create your own custom widgets. Picking the right widgets for your blog is covered by widget type and function.

Chapter 6 will help you make the most of Blogger's feed syndication. You'll learn how to make it easy for people to subscribe, use tools like Feedburner to promote, measure and share your feed, and go beyond basic feed syndication with widgets and optimization tips.

Chapter 7 covers advertising as a source of revenue for your blog. Using Google AdSense and other popular programs, you will select ad formats, customize widgets, and place ads on your blog. Rich media formats including YouTube AdSense units are explored.

Chapter 8 covers the ways to measure the performance of your blog using Google Analytics. You'll start with installing Analytics code on your blog and learning how Analytics is useful for Blogger blogs. This chapter is full of active tutorials on getting the most out of Google Analytics, including how to use regular expressions to create custom filters. Understanding and analyzing the reporting features of Analytics is also explored.

Chapter 9 focuses on optimizing your blog for search engines. Create site maps, understand the cryptic syntax of robots.txt, and learn tips specific to how search engines crawl and rank blogs. Taking action with checklists and techniques designed to get you started in five minutes or less.

Chapter 10 integrates your blog with your main website or any other site or blog you already have. You will add dynamic universal navigation, match the fonts and colors of your blog to other sites, add content from your blog to an external site, and learn multiple ways to use a custom domain for your Blogger blog.

Who is This Book for

The book is aimed at current users of the Blogger platform who want to get the most out of Blogger, and people who use a different blogging platform and are planning on switching to Blogger. Blog owners who promote their own services, expertise, and products, and want to increase their blog's success by pushing the limits of what Blogger can do will get the most out of this book.

This book doesn't require any specific knowledge of Blogger or the related technologies: RSS, CSS, HTML, and XML. Everything you need to know to grow beyond the basics is covered in this book. The companion website to this book, `http://bloggerbeefedup.blogspot.com` includes free resource images and content.

Conventions

In this book, you will find a number of styles of text that distinguish between different kinds of information. Here are some examples of these styles, and an explanation of their meaning.

There are three styles for code. Code words in text are shown as follows: "Every link used within the Blogger template begins with `<a expr:href`."

A block of code will be set as follows:

```
#navigation ul
{
  background: none;
  width:400px;
  padding: 0;
  margin: 0;
  float:right;
  font: bold 80% Verdana;
}
```

When we wish to draw your attention to a particular part of a code block, the relevant lines or items will be made bold:

```
h2.date-header
{
  color:$datecolor;
  margin:1.5em 0 0.5em;
}
```

New terms and **important words** are introduced in a bold-type font. Words that you see on the screen, in menus or dialog boxes for example, appear in our text like this: "clicking the **Next** button moves you to the next screen".

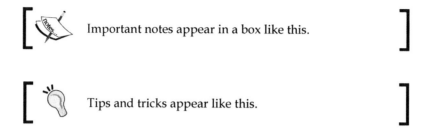

Important notes appear in a box like this.

Tips and tricks appear like this.

Reader Feedback

Feedback from our readers is always welcome. Let us know what you think about this book, what you liked or may have disliked. Reader feedback is important for us to develop titles that you really get the most out of.

To send us general feedback, simply drop an email to feedback@packtpub.com, making sure to mention the book title in the subject of your message.

If there is a book that you need and would like to see us publish, please send us a note in the SUGGEST A TITLE form on www.packtpub.com or email suggest@packtpub.com.

If there is a topic that you have expertise in and you are interested in either writing or contributing to a book, see our author guide on www.packtpub.com/authors.

Customer Support

Now that you are the proud owner of a Packt book, we have a number of things to help you to get the most from your purchase.

Downloading the Example Code for the Book

Visit http://www.packtpub.com/files/code/3179_Code.zip to directly download the example code.

The downloadable files contain instructions on how to use them.

Errata

Although we have taken every care to ensure the accuracy of our contents, mistakes do happen. If you find a mistake in one of our books—maybe a mistake in text or code—we would be grateful if you would report this to us. By doing this you can save other readers from frustration and help to improve subsequent versions of this book. If you find any errata, report them by visiting http://www.packtpub.com/support, selecting your book, clicking on the **let us know** link, and entering the details of your errata. Once your errata are verified, your submission will be accepted and the errata are added to the list of existing errata. The existing errata can be viewed by selecting your title from http://www.packtpub.com/support.

Questions

You can contact us at questions@packtpub.com if you are having a problem with some aspect of the book, and we will do our best to address it.

1
All Blogs Are Not Equal

There are so many features and tools you can use to power your Blogger blog. It can be difficult to decide where to begin. By the end of this chapter you will have learned to plan a blog that visitors will love to interact with.

Blogs are approachable and look great, casual or dressed up, just like a good pair of jeans. We're going to have fun exploring many ways to make default Blogger blogs better. This chapter will focus on getting your feet wet with our tutorial blog. We're going to:

- Explore the benefits of customizing a Blogger blog.
- Look at great blogs to decide what features and tools to use.
- Stake out a new direction for our blog, *Fruit for All.*
- Figure out how to make sharper blogs.

Let's meet Georgia, the owner of *Fruit for All* — a company specializing in shipping high quality fruits and southern hospitality.

Meet Georgia Peach, Fanatical Fruitier

Georgia grew up on a small farm. She would sneak bites of freshly harvested strawberries packed in sugar from the family freezer. She began to share her passion for fruits when she opened her first fruit-stand on the Main Street in a small North Georgia town. Word quickly spread about her fresh local fruits and exotic finds. Chefs from Atlanta and the surrounding countys begged her to save specific lots for them, or to find them a particular type of fruit. Georgia made contact with suppliers all over the world in her quest for unusual and delicious fruits.

She was worried though that only the elite were lucky enough to enjoy the treasures she found. What if there could be a way regular people like herself who shared her love for fruits could have fresh fruits delivered right to their door? It was then that *Fruit for All* was born.

Georgia provides fresh, seasonal fruits grown organically by local farmers. Her customers are fruit lovers from all over the globe. Whether they crave peaches or papayas, they know she will ship them the highest quality fruits from eco-friendly sources. She doesn't just want to sell fruits to people, she wants to develop a personal connection, and bring the "fruit-stand experience" to her customers in the comfort of their homes.

The Way She Blogs Now

Georgia's blog is a celebration of fruits and a business blog. She wants it to be a fascinating blog for fruit lovers. Her typical customers are not just "foodies"; they are "fruities", in search of exotic fruits or high quality staples such as strawberries.

She currently uses her blog to share the fruits she has for sale and also for recipes on fruits, including household remedies and unusual uses for fruit. Her suppliers and the growers are also mentioned, wherever possible.

Georgia found Blogger easy to set up and began using it to get messages out to interested customers. She would love to make her blog play a bigger role in her marketing. She's using a default template she chose when she created her blog. It doesn't look bad, but it doesn't reflect her company's unique personality.

She thinks she has readers, but doesn't know how many. All she has to go with are the comments they leave. She wants to use the blog to foster a community of customers. But, at present, not many are emailing her and she also finds the blog comments limited. She has noticed some increase in business since she launched the blog, but not as much as she was expecting.

She posts regular updates, but doesn't know which are the most popular. If she knew the topics that excited her readers the most, she could focus more on information relevant to them. Do they want more recipes on cherry sauces, or the best fruits for holiday breads? She needs a way to find out.

We will take Georgia's default Blogger blog and transform it into a blog worthy of a benevolent global fruit shipping empire. This business will be a great testing ground for all the advanced work we want to do. When we are done, we will have a professional blog and a greater knowledge of fruits. Georgia's current blog is shown in the following screenshot. It can also be found at (`http://fruitforallbefore.blogspot.com`). Let's take a look at it now and see what areas need improvement at first glance.

The default blog has many areas we can improve. The contrast between the text color and the background color on the side bar and the main content sections need to be increased for readability. The blog looks too generic to be taken as a serious source of knowledge on fruits. We will increase the visual impact of the blog by changing the colors, images, and the basic blog template in Chapter 2—*Customize and Create Templates*.

First time visitors might struggle to understand the purpose of the blog. There is no description explaining why Georgia is blogging, who her audience is, or what topic the blog is focused on. Georgia will need to clearly explain what her blog is about to new visitors to gain their trust and encourage potential sales. We will explore many ways to do this throughout the book.

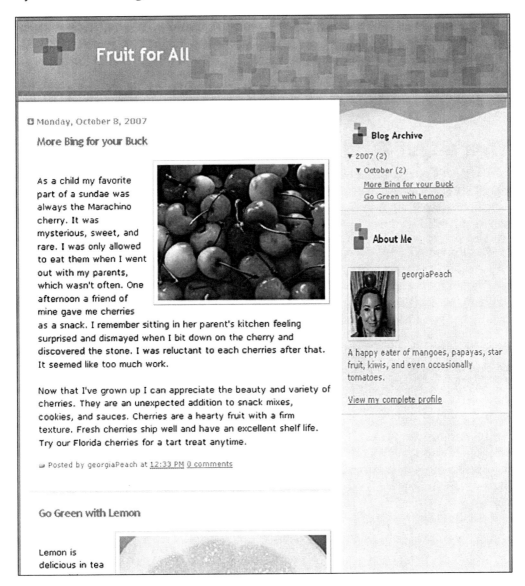

The blog is not currently using anything but the basic default page elements that were included with the template. She feels it looks like every other blogspot blog. The only elements that stand out here are her image displayed in the profile page element on the sidebar, and the images of fruits used in her posts. There are no social bookmarks. The only way users can respond to her blog is through comments. The **Subscribe to: Posts (Atom)** link is hidden at the footer of the site. New visitors looking for the familiar orange feed symbol or RSS/XML/Atom links on the side bar or under each post may miss it.

The blog uses the default image header from the template Georgia selected when the blog was created. The block images on the sidebar also do not match the content. Georgia thinks the gray sidebar color is too boring and the gray wave doesn't really fit the template. She wants to keep the white background and dark text for her posts.

Now, we have a basic grasp of what is lacking on the default blog. We are ready to explore what other bloggers are doing to make their blogs stand out.

What's Out There

There is a lot Georgia can do to make her blog stand out. Georgia wants to build a blog that is as tart and sweet as her fruit. Customizing her blog will attract more readers, turning them into regulars, building a community, and thus selling more fruits to all, while reinforcing the *Fruit for All* brand.

She decides to take a look around the blogosphere and make a list of the features and tools she likes the most. Georgia begins exploring Blogger blogs using the **Next Blog** link. The following screenshot shows the standard Blogger navigation bar, called the "Navbar", used by bloggers to search, flag, explore, post, and customize Blogger blogs. Clicking the **Next Blog** link will cause a recently updated random blog to appear.

The *Blogs of Note* site http://blogsofnote.blogspot.com/ is a monthly selection of Blogger blogs suggested by the Blogger team. Exploring them will give Georgia examples of engaging content and template styles from a wide pool of other bloggers who use the Blogger platform. Blogs of note from October 2007 to December 2007 can be seen in the following screenshot. They cover a range of topics from paintings to primates.

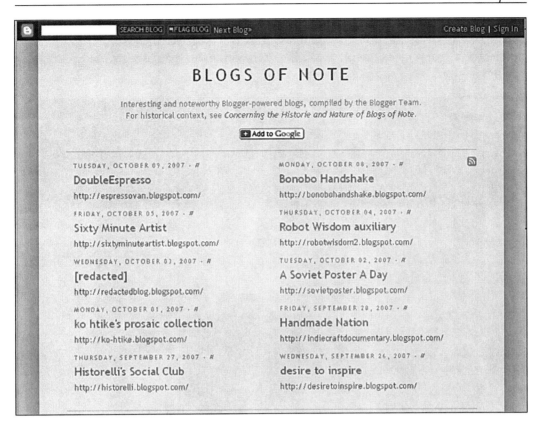

Cooking with Amy

Georgia finds the *Cooking with Amy* blog (`http://cookingwithamy.blogspot.com`) that features a variety of navigation paths, search, cool photos, and delicious recipe ideas. It uses an image, instead of a logo, for the top header section. The **About Me** section has been replaced with an **About** link describing the purpose of the blog. Readers can still choose to read her profile by clicking on **Read my profile** link under **Who's Amy?** A **Search** box is next on the left sidebar. This is an easy to reach location for anyone who wants to search the blog. The **Get Cooking!** link contains multiple drop-down boxes organized by recipe type. Visitors can easily drill down to the recipe they are looking for with minimal clicks. The posts use eye catching images that illustrate the contents of the post.

Georgia decides that her blog is a mix of both personal sharing and industry news. Amy is both a cook and a writer. So the blog gives her the freedom to discuss topics she is interested in and is an active example of her writing and cooking skills. Her self promotional tools include a special **Syndicate this site** block on the left menu and a social book marking button at the bottom of every post. This is where visitors expect to find them. Unlike Amy's blog, Georgia's blog buries the feed subscription link in the footer of the blog. In Amy's blog we can see the header image, the about page element, the link to her profile, her blog search, drop-down site navigation, and a sample post.

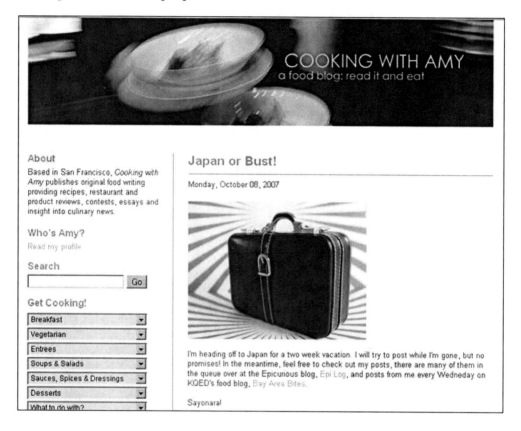

Next, Georgia takes a closer look at other popular blogs. She wants to know if the tools and features they have match their apparent business objectives, and if she can discover any best practices to follow for her own blog.

Meeblog

She is a fan of *Meeblog* (http://blog.meebo.com/), Meebo's company blog. The Meebo logo is used with the word "blog" added to better identify the page. Text site navigation links are displayed in the upper right section of the top header. The **search** box below the site links adds balance to the right side of the header. The **pages** block on the right sidebar leverages the ability of blogs to incorporate static pages, making it double up as the Meebo corporate site. Georgia is inspired by the **where are you?** block. Would her customers benefit from a map that showed the source locations of her fruit? The **top 10 meebo fans** list looks like a nifty way to encourage readers to link back, or spread the word about Meebo. Georgia wonders if she can do something similar for her own site to help build community. Scrolling down, she notices the *Flickr* (`http://www.flickr.com`) photo widget. She could display seasonal fruit or popular fruit selections, maybe even start a photo group for fruit enthusiasts, on *Flickr*.

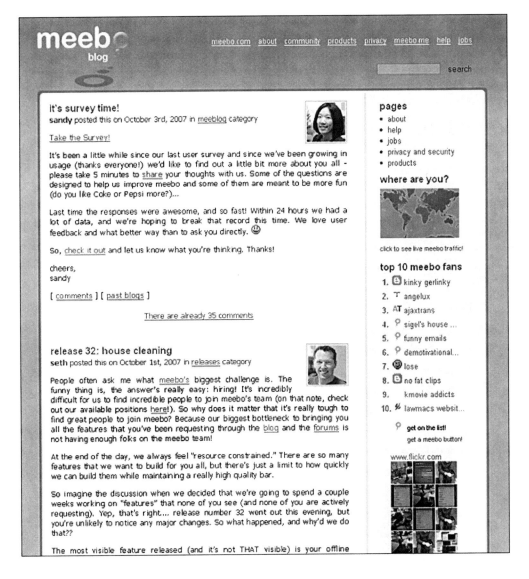

The business objective of Meeblog is to communicate news about Meebo with current and potential users, retain current users, and spread the word about the Meebo chat tools. Its focus is the Meebo site. She thinks that their use of branding is strong. Georgia thinks that the blog does a good job of retaining current users, but thinks that they could do more with social book marking and syndication to spread the word about Meebo.

Georgia does not have her blog set up to channel traffic from her blog to her commercial site. We'll take this step with her in Chapter 10, integrating her blog and her commercial site together. Next, let's look at an example of a blog integrated with multiple sites that successfully uses advertising. BoingBoing's blog has a strong personality that is carried across all its related sites.

BoingBoing

The *BoingBoing* blog (`http://boingboing.net`) shares quirky, interesting articles submitted by readers and makes income from merchandise and prominent site ads. The site's plain white background showcases horizontal site navigation, easy printing for posts, relevant ads, and a standard two-column blog layout. We can see the strengths of the blog in the following screenshot. The site has logo-based links for all three related sites above the top menu bar.

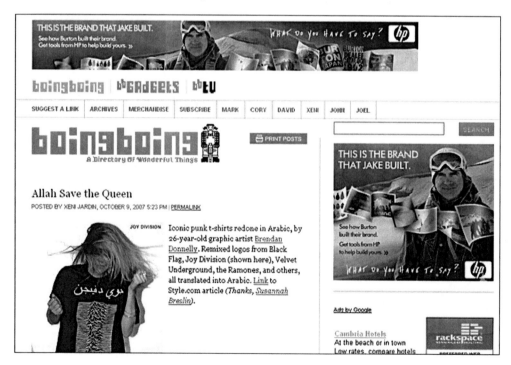

The main logo for the BoingBoing blog is placed below the menu. The strong color provides high contrast and makes it stand out, even with multiple flash ads enveloping the site content. Georgia decides that using banner ads might drive users away from her site. The **SEARCH** block is in an easy to spot location, just below the main menu. She makes a note of the color coordinated text ads on the rightside bar, a **Don't Miss** block of suggested posts and a block for **Recent Comments** by users. She finds the **Subscribe** buttons for the RSS, podcasts, and emails, buried at the

bottom of too many, front page, blog posts. Visitors can click on the **Subscribe** link on the top menu, but that adds a click. The **Suggest a Link** menu item makes it easy for visitors to send content and promote their blogs. Georgia wonders if ad revenues really help pay for the site.

All the blogs we've looked at so far are two-column blogs. There are many successful three-column blogs. Georgia's favorite is the *Innocent Drinks Daily Thoughts* blog (`http://innocentdrinks.typepad.com/`). This blog, of a commercial fruit smoothie company, manages to be fun and professional at the same time.

Innocent Drinks

The *Innocent Drinks* blog team makes carefully structured use of a three-column layout. We can see in the following screenshot that they have positioned their logo in the standard top left position with overall site navigation taking up the top right side.

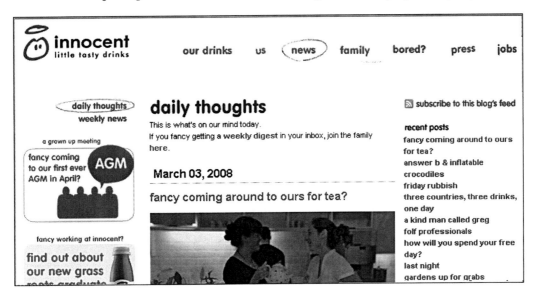

Upcoming events and new products are featured in the left column of the blog. Posts take up the center column. The right side contains elements commonly seen on blogs. A subscription link is featured in the top right, followed by a list of recent posts, recent comments, and links to social network groups they participate in. Georgia notes they are using *Flickr* groups (`http://www.flickr.com/groups/bigknit2007/`) to share photos of their community projects. Continuing down the right column are other blogs by the innocent drinks team: a **monthly archive** block, **categories** for blog posts, and a **Search** box. There are a rich collection of elements on the blog for visitors to explore. Georgia may want to share her own community projects on *Flickr* (`http://www.flickr.com`) or through other social networking sites in the future.

We've seen blogs with their own answers to how blogs should look and function over the last few pages. Looking at each one, we have narrowed down what features are most important for a successful blog.

What They Share

Georgia discovered that all the most popular blogs she looked at shared several best practices. The blogs used a strong color difference between the text and background, usually dark text over a white or pale background color. All the more popular blogs Georgia looked at used search and clean column-based layouts. Both Meebo and BoingBoing had site navigation menus and features to encourage visitors to interact. Each blog used strong logos or other visual imagery to create an environment that visitors would remember and associate with the site.

Time to Plan

Now that Georgia knows what's out there in the blogosphere, she needs to define her goals and decide how she can use the *Fruit for All* blog to achieve them. Georgia puts pen to coffee shop napkin and begins to brainstorm.

Defining Goals

First, she begins to draw a visual mind map of the many goals she has for the site. The word "fruit blog" is placed in an oval in the center. Then she draws a line branch for each idea and connects it to the center oval or another idea. When she is done, she has a network of ideas to pull and organize her goals from.

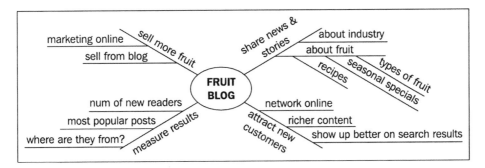

She then takes the main ideas from the mix and creates a list of the biggest goals for her blog. She will use these to guide her decisions. Whenever she thinks she is losing focus, Georgia can refer back to the list and the idea map.

Georgia's big goals are:

- Marketing her business online
- Attracting new customers
- Sharing stories and news about fruits and the fruit growers' industry
- Measuring the results of her blogging efforts

With her list of goals in hand, Georgia excitedly shares her ideas with us, over some tasty cornbread pancakes with cherry sauce. "High on sugar and the chance to work on a fun project", we agreed to help sharpen and shape up her blog. We take Georgia's list of goals and use them to make an outline of requirements for her blog. This way, we can match her business objectives to the tools and features that will bring them to life.

Attract More Readers

We decide that the two core issues before Georgia are: bringing more readers to the site and turning them into repeat readers. There are many ways to resolve these issues. We will help Georgia customize her blog using the following methods:

Bringing Them In

Georgia needs to work on how she is going to bring visitors to her blog. Using a strategic combination of rich content, search engine optimization, social networking, and integration with her main site will draw in new visitors.

- **Link bait content**: Georgia knows that people like novelty. She can increase traffic, and other peoples' links to her site by providing content that will interest a broad audience. She can use the top ten lists of most exotic fruits, surprising ways to present or prepare dishes with fruits, and captivating photographs of fruits. Georgia is considering running a regular poll where readers try to guess which fruit is represented in an enlarged photograph. Blogger's poll page element will give her a quick way to do that. Her goal is to have potential readers visit at least once. We'll focus on choosing and installing widgets in Chapter 5. Different captivating widgets will be covered by type, throughout the book.

- **SEO**: Georgia isn't sure which search terms are attracting people to her blog. Emphasizing the search terms in her content will help improve the search engine rankings of her blog. Using and participating in social networking sites such as Digg, Reddit, and Facebook will also increase her rankings as other people begin to link to the blog. She can also use targeted keywords in her post tags, titles, and within the post content. After doing a Google search for "target keywords", Georgia discovers that very few people use the keyword phrase "exotic fruit". Everyday, thousands of people are looking for a fruit basket or a particular fruit by name. We will look through the maze of SEO in Chapter 10.

- **RSS Feeds**: Georgia's feed is tucked away at the bottom of her blog where only industrious visitors can find it. Many of her visitors may not be Internet savy and may not know to click on the orange feed icon in the browser window when they visit her site. Adding a subscribe page element to the sidebar of her blog and subscription links under each post will make it easy for all her visitors. We'll do that and more, when we burn her feed in Chapter 6.

- **Integrate the blog to the Fruit for All e-commerce website**: Georgia will freshen up the content of her main site and give visitors reasons to visit frequently, with the latest posts from her blog featured on her website. The blog and the main site will be linked together using different navigation methods. Georgia will share specials and news that are instantly updated on both sites. We will meet Georgia's main *Fruit for All* site and figure out different ways to integrate it with her blog in Chapter 10.

- **Social networking and book marking**: Georgia already has Facebook, Digg, and Reddit accounts, but doesn't provide links to them from her site. We will show her how to add widgets such as badges, add social bookmarks to her blog so that others can share it, and come up with a plan to contribute links to Reddit and Digg.

Facebook

Georgia can get more out of Facebook by adding more details to her profile, joining groups, sharing photo albums, and adding events. She should add a Facebook badge to her page, and perhaps a link back to Facebook in relevant posts. She can use Facebook to network too.

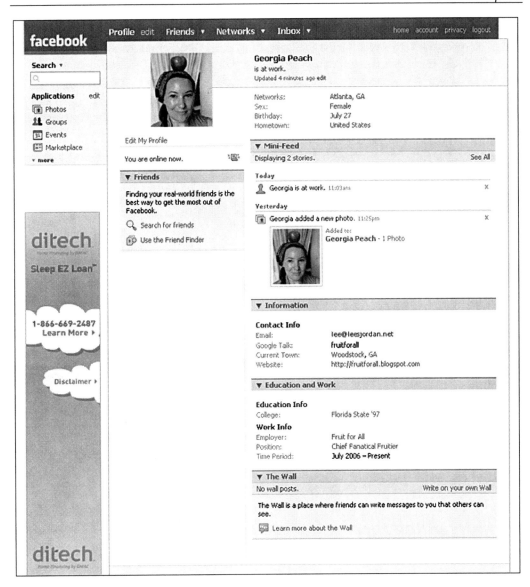

Reddit

Links to news and sites of interest are sorted on category, how new they are, and how "hot" the topic is. Georgia can vote links up and down and submit her own. If a link she submits becomes popular, she will gain a reputation in the community. Reddit also has the flexibility to adjust the links displayed to readers based on how they vote. Georgia should set aside time to regularly submit articles she finds and her own content to Reddit.

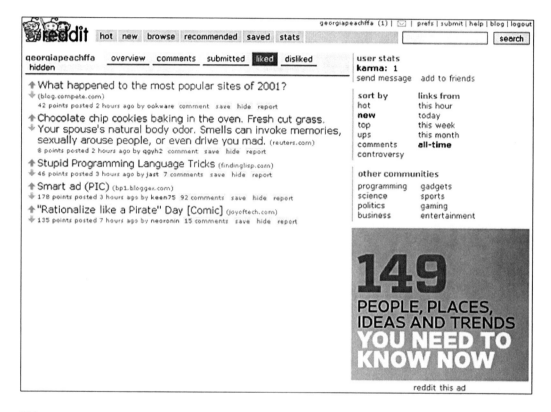

Digg

In Dingg Links to news and interesting sites are added and voted on by readers. Georgia needs to add her blog and Facebook links. She can network and find other people who share her passion for fruit and share links she finds. Digg can create a "big circle of submission", as readers to her blog increase her posts are more likely to be submitted to Digg by her readers. As more Digg visitors come to her blog from Digg, she will have more readers. We will help Georgia add a Digg bookmark button to her blog posts in Chapter 3.

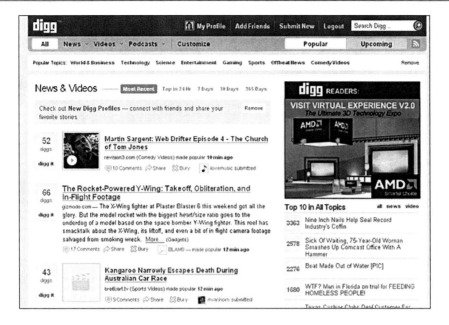

Submitting news makes Georgia part of the social network of fellow foodies. The more interesting the links she submits, the more likely that new readers will visit her blog. She fills out a simple form after logging in to the Digg site whenever she has a link to submit.

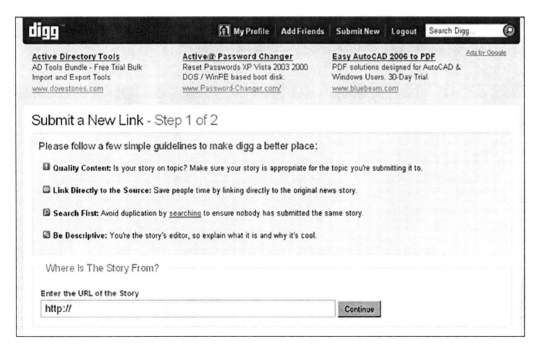

We will explore social networks and book marking for blogs in depth, in Chapter 3. Being a good neighbor in the blogosphere, including trackbacks, blogrolls, and networking with other bloggers, will be covered in Chapter 5.

Georgia wants to do more than just attract people to her blog. She wants to build awareness for her company and share it with a community of other people who share her passion for organic fruits.

Reinforce her Brand, Build a Community

The more recognizable her blog is, the easier it will be for readers to describe her blog to others. She wants it to be welcoming and fun-filled, where visitors can go and try the latest fruits and maybe find a reliable recipe for blackberry cobbler. Let's look at some ways to make her blog more memorable:

- **Site fonts and colors**: Use fonts that are easy to read and match the friendly tone of the blog. The colors will be high in contrast to the background and match the *Fruit for All* logo.

- **Customized template with logo and navigation**: Georgia wants a funny but professional look for her blog. She wants to use bright colors for accents, while keeping the post text and links readable. She is going to use the colors from her current logo and the same menu structure as her main site, to keep all the *Fruit for All* sites consistent in look and feel.

Customizing the default Blogger template and building our own unique template for the *Fruit for All* blog will happen in Chapter 2. We will start with the layout and design ideas, and then build a homegrown Blogger template.

Sell More Fruits, Explore New Revenue Opportunities

Georgia needs to expand on how she communicates with readers and experiment with new ways to encourage sales.

- **Set up RSS feeds, Feedburner** (http://www.feedburner.com): Visitors can subscribe to feeds directly from the *Fruit for All* blog or discover the posts through feed searches and Feedburner ads. Google's recent acquisition of Feedburner creates even more possibilities for advertising and providing ad space.

- **To share time sensitive specials and information, Twitter** (`http://www.twitter.com`): Short updates in text format keep messages short and to the point. Georgia can update Twitter from her Gmail account or online at the Twitter site. She can add a Twitter "badge" to her blog to share up to the minute specials and news. Georgia will explore using Twitter badges and other third-party widgets in Chapter 5.

- **Offer online payment, such as Paypal** (`http://www.paypal.com`) **or Google Checkout** (`https://checkout.google.com`): Georgia can increase impulse sales by adding checkout buttons to posts and the main menu of her blog.

- **Promoting her blog to the world by advertising with Adsense** (`http://www.google.com/adsense/`), **Project Wonderful** (`http://www.projectwonderful.com/`), **or by using Google Adwords** (`https://adwords.google.com`): Georgia can place relevant ads on her own blog that may provide side revenue for her business. She thinks readers might appreciate being able to buy cookbooks or see ads about cooking gadgets that complement her fruits. Third-party affiliate systems such as Amazon Associates (`https://affiliate-program.amazon.com/`) could provide additional ways to increase revenues, while providing useful content. We will work with Georgia to see how advertising systems can bring in additional revenue and promote the *Fruit for All* blog in Chapter 7.

Measure and Improve

Georgia wants to know who is visiting the blog, the sites they come from, and what their favorite posts are. She also wants to collect information about the general effectiveness of her blog.

- **Google Analytics** (`http://www.google.com/analytics`): Georgia should use the graphing tools and other features to determine more about her visitors and see what she can do to improve her blog and main site.

- **Feedburner** (`http://www.feedburner.com`): Feedburner provides many great measurement tools. Google's buyout of Feedburner may alter the services and tools offered in the future.

We will explore the above options to measure and improve Georgia's blog in Chapter 8 and Chapter 9.

Summary

In this chapter, we've met Georgia Peach and her fanatical fruit business. We've seen that she has a lot of options on how to use her blog. She will have to go beyond the standard Blogger blog to reach her goals. To go further, she needs to:

- Customize her blog template with her company logo, colors, and attitude.
- Participate in and add social networking widgets and bookmarks to her blog.
- Turn visitors into regular readers with RSS, and offer regular high quality content updates.
- Measure her progress, and continue to improve using tools such as Google Analytics and Feedburner.

In the next chapter, we'll see exactly how to do all this and more on our Blogger blog. We'll build our own exciting custom Blogger template.

2
Customize and Create Templates

Georgia Peach has reviewed what she wants to do with her blog. Now she is ready to start by fixing the visual appearance of her blog. Georgia says the default blog is boring. She wants an exciting new look that fits her company.

Making a custom template is like throwing a party, which involves some planning to be a success. We have to decide the theme, food, drinks, decorations, guest list, location, and invite the guests before we can have the party. To create a custom template we need to decide on a theme and then prepare a layout to act as the location on which we will hang our presentation elements such as images, fonts, and colors.

You will learn how to use Blogger and design techniques to modify an exciting custom template. Specifically, in this chapter we will:

- Learn to change default templates without coding.
- Plan the visual presentation and behind-the-scenes layout of the template.
- Find resources for images, fonts, and codes on the Internet.

Choosing a Theme

"I have lots of ideas about how the template should look", Georgia announces, "bright groups of fruits, some of it floating in the background…".

A template is more than just pictures; it also organizes and presents the contents of a blog in a meaningful way. Let's start by deciding the theme for the blog.

Themes help us focus on our goals. The theme will help us make decisions about the look and feel of the template. We can use the theme to:

- Set the tone of the blog to be friendly, whimsical, serious, or formal.
- Use existing logos and other company materials for color palettes, tone, and image assets.
- Guide our choice of fonts.
- Limit the color palette.
- Choose an artistic direction for images.

Georgia's company has a friendly, open personality with an emphasis on high quality fresh fruits. The images, fonts, colors, and text used on her blog should reflect her company's fresh and funny personality. We also want to use the existing logos, fonts, and colors, wherever they fit.

Presentation—It's About the Visual Things

The presentation or visual assets of the template should be separate from the layout structure. The visual assets include logos, background gradients, illustrations, and any other images that are part of the template. They leave a visual impression that readers will remember. We will leverage the visual impact of the blog to serve the following purposes:

- Attract visitors
- Enhance the message of the blog
- Build the brand by using the logo, fonts, and colors of the company

Georgia agrees that she wants her blog to reflect her company's values of quality and service, without being stuffy. The images should be funny and whimsical. The colors used on the blog should be pulled from the company's logo or should complement them.

 The fewer colors used in a design, the more professional and unified it looks. Limit your color choices and the focus will be on your logo and content.

The blog will use white as a background for large bodies of text and accent colors of green, red, yellow, and dark grey. `Sans serif` fonts such as `Arial` will be used for the body of the blog.

Changing Blogger Templates without Code

Georgia wants immediate changes made to her blog. She wants to experiment with fonts and colors to narrow down what she wants to use on the custom blog.

"This reminds me of the time I bought a bunch of generic shipping supplies when my printer messed up my custom order", she tells us as she logs into her blog, "My shipments of fruits looked nice, but I missed the custom colors and designs".

There are many changes that can be made to a blog without code. Let's see what we can do to make changes to Georgia's blog right away. We will edit the page elements, experiment with moving them around, and make changes to the basic fonts and colors of the blog.

Use the Test Blog

Let's create a new blog (`http://fruitforalltest.blogspot.com/`) to test the template changes before we apply them to our live blog. It's always a good idea to have a test site. Even though Blogger has many places to preview changes, it is better to work on a test site so that changes aren't made accidentally and go, live on a production site.

Customizing Page Elements

The exact same template of *TicTac* by *Dan Cederholm*, is on the test site. Georgia clicks the **Customize** link on the Blogger navigation bar at the top of her screen to bring up the **Page Elements** section under the **Layout** tab.

"Can I drag my **Blog Archive** and **About Me** page elements to the left side as I can't seem to do it on this screen?", asks Georgia.

The current template Georgia is using only allows page elements to be added to the footer or to the righthand side of the layout. Choosing a default template with a sidebar on the left hand side will allow her to add page elements on the left. If she wants the ability to add page elements to either side of the blog on the **Page Elements** screen, she will need a three-column template. We will create a three-column template later on in this chapter. You can see the **Page Elements** screen in the following screenshot, which displays all the areas where page elements can be added to the blog. The navbar and header page elements at the top are **static**. Chapter 10—*Hacking the Template,* will allow us to add an additional navigation block. Adding widgets to the footer section of the blog is done by clicking the **Add a Page Element** link in the **Page Elements** block at the bottom of the layout.

We can see that the **Blog Archive** and **About Me** page elements have already been added by default to the right side of the template layout. The elements can be dragged and dropped, up and down, to change their order. The **Blog Posts** page element is another static page element. The **Blog Posts** element can be configured by clicking the **Edit** button. It cannot be moved to a different area of the layout without altering the template.

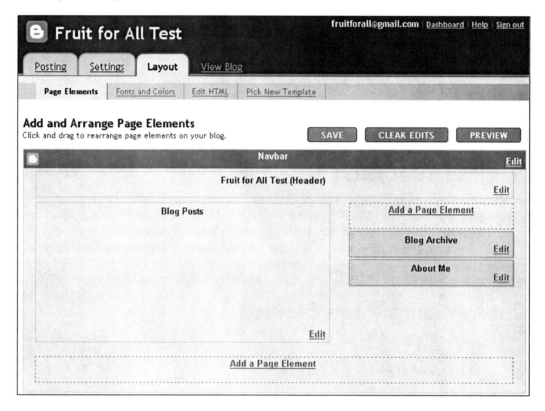

Each blog has a default layout. Most Blogger templates have page elements on either the left or the right side of the **Blog Posts** page element. These left and right columns are commonly called **sidebars**. Hopefully, in the future, they will change it so that all default blog templates allow you to rearrange the page elements exactly where you want them.

"Well, I chose this template originally since the sidebar is on the righthand side. What other things can I do here?" asks Georgia.

Managing Page Elements

We can edit the page elements we already have, add more, and remove the ones we don't want. All the page elements are managed the same way. To edit or remove a page element, first click the **Edit** link on that element. Elements are added by clicking the **Add a Page Element** link in one of the layout blocks. We can see the **Add a Page Element** block on the right sidebar and one at the bottom of the layout area for the blog footer.

Time for Action!—Editing the Navbar Page Element

The navbar is the top page element. You may have noticed it above your blog and the blogs of other people who use Blogger. The color of the navbar can be changed to any one of the four color schemes: **Blue** (the default), **Tan**, **Black**, or **Silver**.

1. Log in to Blogger (`http://www.blogger.com`) and click the **Layout** link. Click the **Edit** link in the **Navbar**. The **Navbar Configuration** screen will appear as shown in the following screenshot. Note that each color choice has a radio button to the left.

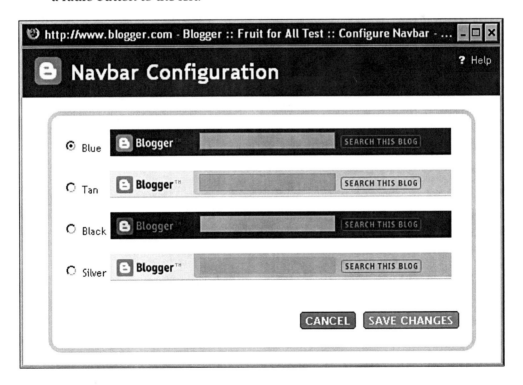

2. The first option, **Blue,** is selected by default, but **Silver** will match our template better. We can always select a different color.

3. Click the **SAVE CHANGES** button to save the new navbar color. You will have the option to view the blog when you return to the main **Page Elements** screen.

4. The navbar is now a neutral color that won't distract visitors from the blog. That was a very quick and easy change with drastic results. The navbar now looks like part of the template. The blog already looks much more professional. We can see the results of our change in the following screenshot:

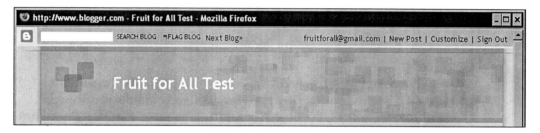

What Just Happened?

When we clicked on the **Edit** link of the **Navbar** page element, we were able to change the appearance of the navbar above the blog. When a different color theme was selected, and saved for the navbar on the **Configure Navbar** screen, Blogger processed the setting change. Visitors viewing the blog from that point on saw the silver navbar at the top of the screen, above the blog header.

Editing the Header Page Element, Title, and Description

We can change the title of the blog, the description, and even place our own image in the header section of the blog. Adding images can be tricky with some of the templates. We will experiment to see how different templates display images and text placed in the header area.

Time for Action!—Changing the Header Text

If you have created your blog on the spur of the moment, you may not have taken the time to create a description. Adding a brief description will make it easier for potential readers to find your blog. Let's change the blog title and add a description.

1. First click on the **Edit** link for the **Header page** element. A **Configure Header** window pops up just like the one shown in the following screenshot. Note that there are separate text fields for the **Blog Title** and **Blog Description**. There is also an area to add an image to the **Header**, from either your computer or from a link on the Internet.

2. Open the edit window by clicking on the **Edit** link in the **Header** page element.

3. The **Blog Title** field displays the current title of the blog. We'll add **Seasonal and shipped to you!** at the end of the title text.

4. The **Blog Description** can hold a paragraph about the blog, such as, **A delicious test of high quality seasonal fruits! We ship organic seasonal fruits of the highest quality directly to your door**.

5. Click the **SAVE CHANGES** button to save the text edits made to the **Header** page element.

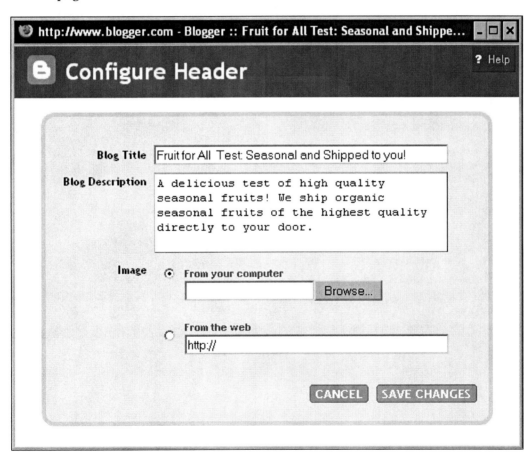

What Just Happened?

The **Configure Header** screen form accepted the text we typed and then passed it to the Blogger site code for processing. When we changed the **Blog Title** and **Blog Description** using the **Configure Header** screen, Blogger responded by changing the settings for the blog in the template and the site code.

Think carefully about what you include in the **Blog Description**. It should contain keywords to help potential readers find you. It should also be as short as possible and should be different from the **Blog Title**. Many people use this space for a tagline, or a short message about the purpose of the blog. Let's view the blog to see the changes we have made so far:

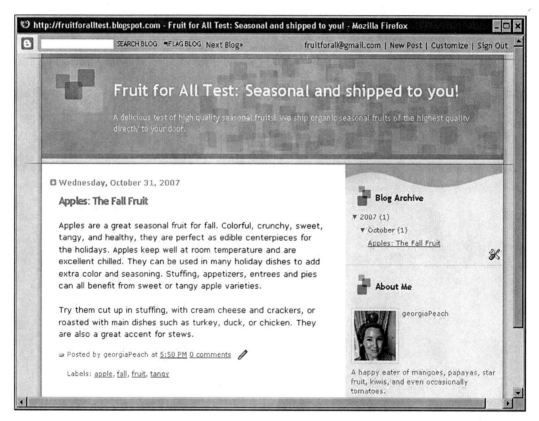

The **Blog Title** is a little long, but very descriptive. We could probably cut the descriptive text down to make it more effective. We decide to leave it for now since we can always change it later.

> You can also change the **Title** and **Description** from the **Settings | Basic** page.

Replacing the Header Image

Georgia likes being able to change the **Header** text, but wants to add her own image too. She wants to discover whether the **Header** image in the template can be replaced from the **Configure Header** edit screen, and we have agreed to give it a try. We have an image to experiment with the exact height and width of the image in the blog template. The height and width can sometimes be found by right-clicking on the image while viewing the blog. Most default templates are background images. So the best way to discover their height and width is by logging into Blogger, clicking on the **Layout** link, selecting the **Edit HTML** tab and then scrolling to the template code for the `#header-wrapper` style.

Time for Action!—Adding an Image to the Header

We're going to add an image to the header of our blog by editing the Header page element. We will upload an image file from our computer using the form within the **Configure Header** window. You should have an image optimized for use on the web ready to go. A sample image is available in the code folder for this chapter at (`http://bloggerbeefedup.blogspot.com`).

1. Log in to Blogger and click on the **Layout** link in the **Dashboard** to open the **Page Elements** page. Then click the **Edit** link in the blog header to open up the **Configure Header** window.

2. Select the radio button option next to **From your computer** then click the **Browse** button to choose an image. We'll use the image ffa_header_orig.gif from our Chapter 02 code files. A yellow triangle with an exclamation mark will be displayed as the file is uploaded, just like the one seen below. If it takes more than a minute, cancel the action, and then try to upload the file again.

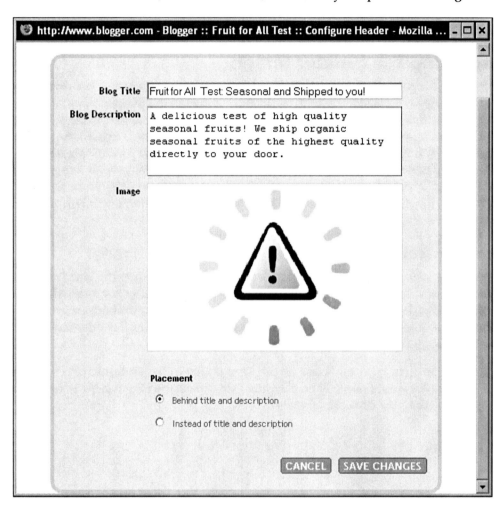

3. Once the file is uploaded, you will see a copy of the image you have just uploaded in the **Configure Header** window.

4. You can decide whether you want the image to display **Behind the title and description,** or **Instead of the title and description** by selecting your choice from the **Placement** radio group. The following screenshot shows a preview of the image with the placement of the image set to **Instead of title and description**.

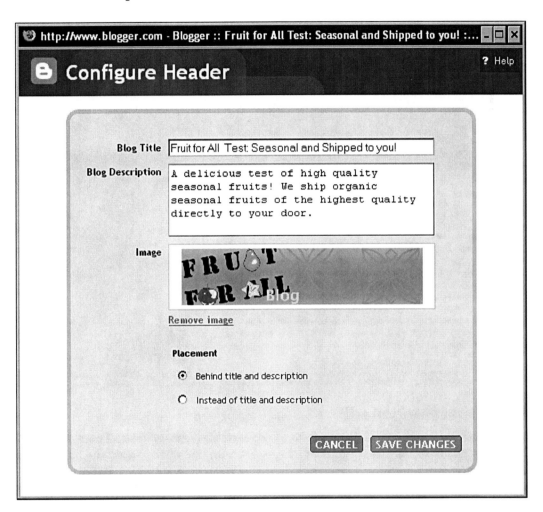

5. Click **SAVE CHANGES** and then clear your browser's cache. If you do not clear your cache, you may not see the changes you have made. Click **View Blog** to see what has happened. An example of how it looks now is shown in the following screenshot.

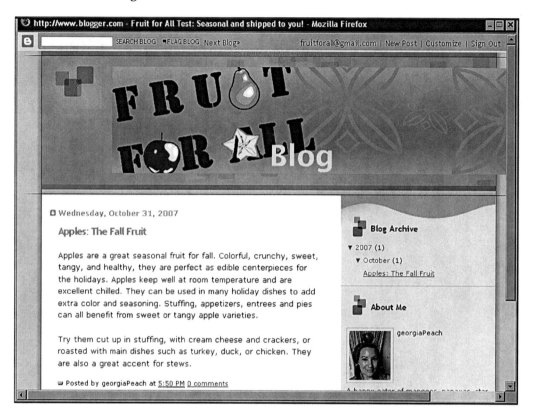

What Just Happened?

Whoa! That did not go well. Take a look at the results above. Instead of placing the image exactly over the other template image, the template code caused the new image to display over to the right. This was not the effect we were going for. Before you upload an image, check the size of the `header-wrapper`. It can be found by navigating to **Layout | Edit HTML** and then scrolling down the template code in the **Template** text area box. A logo or other visual element will work best here if you don't want to take the time to match the size of the `header-wrapper`. You can resize the image you want to use with an image tool like Ifranview (`http://www.irfanview.com/`). The only way to accurately replace the header image used in the *TicTac* template is to edit the HTML code. We'll tinker with the code later in the chapter.

Changing Blog Templates

Some templates are more suited for custom header images than others. Let's see the effects of changing with a different template. The best template for customization is currently the Minima template. It has no template images or other add-ons that can get in the way.

Time for Action!—Picking a Customizable Blog Template

Let's make things easier on ourselves by picking a template that is easier to customize. One quick word of warning—you will lose all your current page element widgets, unless you back up the current template first. You can then copy and paste them back into your new template.

1. Go back to the **Layout** tab and click on the **Pick a New Template** menu item. We'll try a simpler template this time. The **Minima** template is very clean. There are no extra images on this one.

2. Click on the **Minima** template image. A box will appear around the template image. The original version of **Minima** is chosen by default. Click the **SAVE TEMPLATE** button to finish switching templates. You can use the following screenshot as a guide while navigating the **Pick New Template** window:

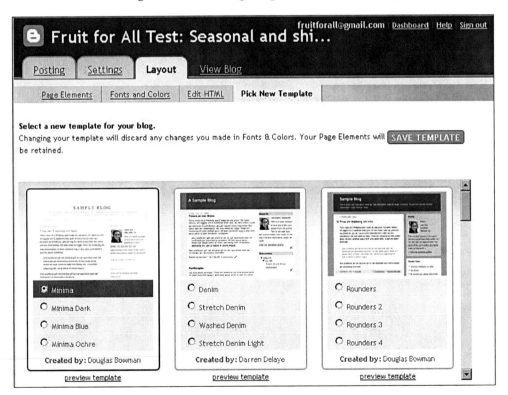

3. Now let's view the blog and see if a new template makes a difference. Well, it looks like the new template helped. It doesn't quite fit in the borders of the header. Georgia thinks reducing the image width will make it fit.

 You may not experience the same results we did. Blogger is constantly updating it's code. If your header fits perfectly using the Minima template, you can skip the next steps.

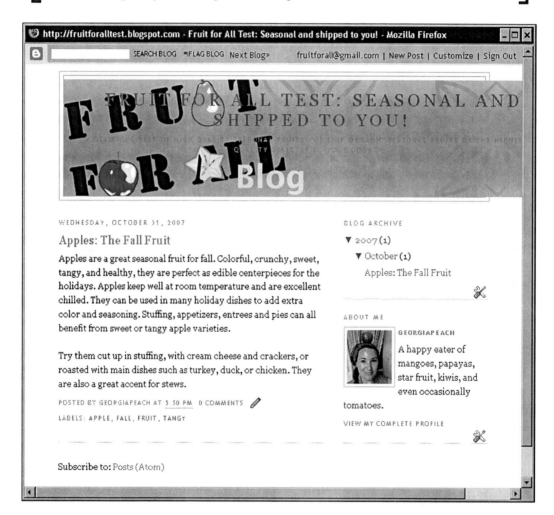

4. The header section of the **Minima** template is 660 pixels wide. Using an image that is 652 pixels wide should fit better. Let's try this once more. Upload the image named `ffa_header.gif` from the code folder. Your settings on the **Configure Header** window should be the same as those shown in the following screenshot.

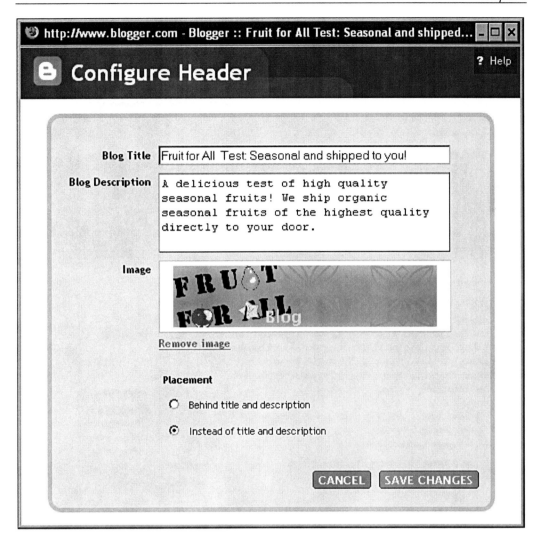

5. The **Placement** should be set to **Instead of title and description**. Click **SAVE CHANGES** and view the blog. You can see an example of how it would look in the next screenshot.

What Just Happened?

When we selected a different template that did not have links to external images, we gained more control over the look and feel of our blog.

"Looks like we just needed a simpler template to pull it off. I knew it could be done", says Georgia proudly as she hands us glasses of homemade raspberry lemonade.

You can keep the same template if you check the width of the header in your template code or resize the image to match the width. If you are in a situation where the template you are using has too many graphical elements and you would rather start with a clean template, use Minima.

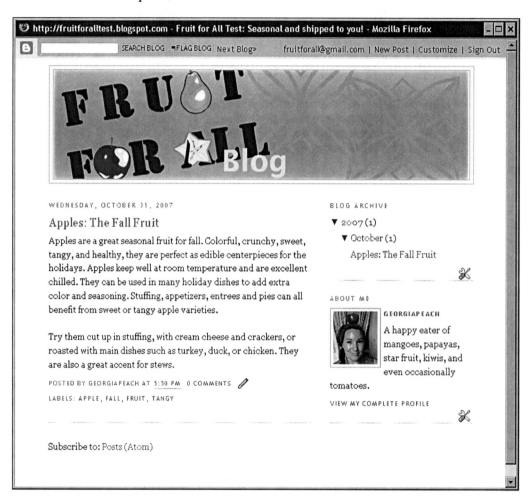

"Can we do something about that text?" asked Georgia, squinting at the new template. "I want to use the same text that we had on the other template."

Luckily for us (and Georgia) the fonts used in the template can be changed from the **Fonts and Colors** section under the **Layout** tab.

Changing the Fonts and Colors

"I hope this is as easy as you said it's going to be," sighs Georgia, "getting the new header image to work was almost as painful as picking wild blackberries."

The good news is the **Fonts and Colors** section is very visual and easy to use. The bad news is… "I knew it," Georgia grins, "what's the catch?"

…the font choices are limited to six main web safe fonts. If you want to use other fonts, you'll have to specify them in the template code. We'll cover how to do that later in this chapter.

Time for Action!—Picking Colors with the Fonts and Colors Editor

The **Fonts and Colors** editor is easy to use once you get used to it. The template items whose color can be changed are listed in the menu box on the left side of the screen. Three different palettes help you keep track of the current color palette of your blog. Let's try changing colors to get comfortable with the editor.

1. Log in to Blogger and select **Layout** from the **Dashboard**. Choose the **Fonts and Colors** tab under the **Layout** tab. Once you've clicked on the **Fonts and Colors** menu item, you will see a list box on the left and a color picker on the right, as shown in the following screenshot.

2. Click on the **Page Background Color** item in the list menu. You will see the current color is in a small square just to the left of the item name. Pick a different color by selecting a color chip from one of the three menus: **Colors from your blog**, **Colors that match your blog**, or **More Colors**.

3. When you are done with the customization of colors, click the **SAVE CHANGES** button, clear your browser's cache, and view your blog.

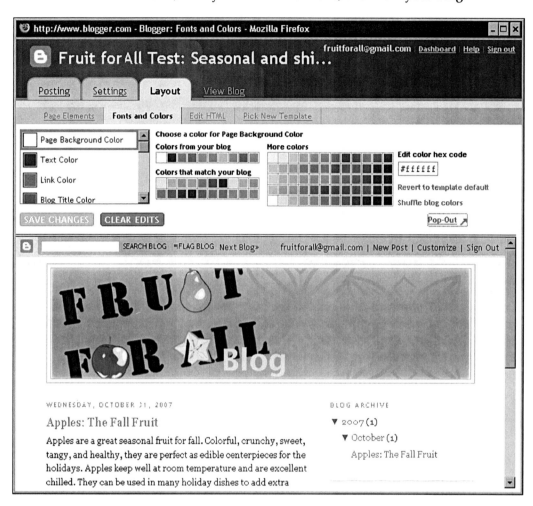

What Just Happened?

When you highlighted a listed item in the left menu, and then selected a different color choice from one of the three color menus, the color values also changed within the template code. Each item listed in the left menu has its own variable defined in a tag at the top of the template. We will edit those variable tags next and add our own new tags later in this chapter.

Choosing High Contrast Text Colors

Soft, blended colors for text may look great in glossy magazine ads, but they don't work well for blogs. We'll pick a darker text color that will be easier for visitors to read. You can pick a color by selecting the color boxes, but that limits you to what Blogger shows you. Did you notice the **Edit color hex code** box to the right of the color blocks? It shows an alphanumeric code for any color you pick. It specifies a specific color from the RGB color palette using a pound (#) symbol followed by a combination of six alphanumeric characters. The RGB color palette is represented by two characters for red, two for green, and two for blue. This system of characters is known as the **hexadecimal color code** or hex code for short.

Time for Action!—Changing the Text Color Using Hexadecimal Code

When deciding on a template for this book, I chose high contrast colors that would show up well in print for all the text. We're going to choose high contrast colors to make reading the blog easier on our visitor's eyes.

1. Highlight the **Text Color** item in the list box. The hex code field on the right now displays the hexadecimal code of the soft dark grey color, `#333333`.

2. A darker color is what we need. Highlight the characters in the **Edit color hex code** text field and Type `#000000`, and then hit the `Enter` key on your keyboard. The overall text color for the blog has now been changed to black. A preview of the change is displayed instantly, in the preview window below the editor.

3. Repeat the steps for any other text colors you want to change. Georgia chooses a red (`#cc0000`) for the sidebar title and text color, and a green (`#73a92b`) that matches the header for the links. She changes the **Visited Link** color to a dark green (`#1B703A`) so that readers can quickly see the links they have already followed.

4. Click the **SAVE CHANGES** button to finalize the edits. Clear your browser's cache and then view your blog.

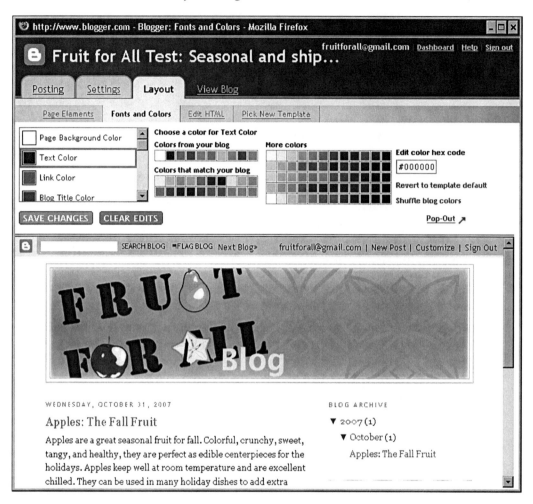

What Just Happened?

When you entered a new color for the **Text Color** in hexadecimal format, Blogger processed the hexadecimal code and displayed the new color choice in the list menu, the **Colors from your blog** menu, and within the blog preview pane. Once the color choices were saved, the **Text Color** variable tag in the template was set to a new value.

The contrast is much better now. If readers want to print a recipe or other interesting posts, the text will show up better on paper, too.

[Click the **Pop-Out** link to see the **Fonts and Colors** editor in its own window. It will be easier to check the changes on the blog as you work.]

Matching the Font to the Blog

When she was done playing with the font colors in the editor, Georgia commented, "changing the colors wasn't hard at all; it was actually fun. I liked seeing the colors change in the preview window below the editor."

You can preview the font changes too, scroll down the list menu and we'll show you.

Time for Action!—Changing Template Fonts with the Fonts and Colors Editor

It may be a little confusing having the colors and fonts of the blog on the same list, but that's where they are. Scroll down the combo box to find the areas of the blog where the font can be changed. Let's make a few changes to the current font settings to get a feel of how it works.

1. Start by highlighting the font item in the list menu on the left. The **Text Font** item is first. So, we'll go ahead and select it.

2. The editor will now display the different font choices under the **Font Family** heading. The default text for this template is **Georgia**. **Verdana** has a more modern, casual look. Select the radio button next to **Verdana** by clicking on it.

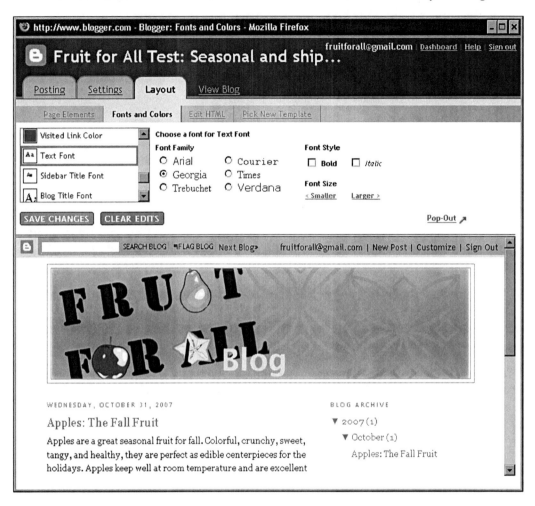

3. The visual look of the blog is improving. The content text could be easier to read. Choosing a bold **Font Style,** and a larger text size will change the look even further. Go back to the **Fonts and Colors** section under the **Layout** tab to continue editing the fonts. You can see a preview of the changes while you work, as shown in the following screenshot:

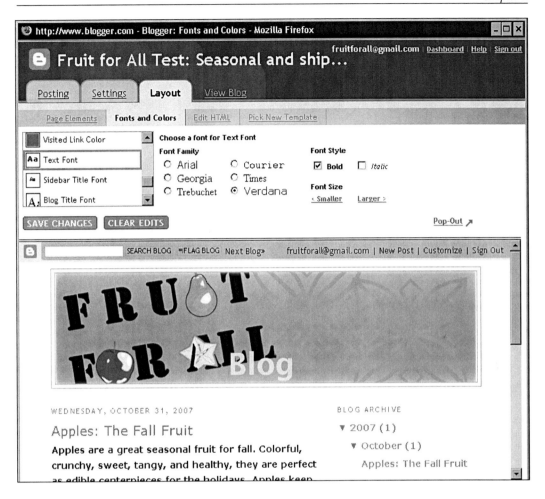

4. We continue to change each item, using **Verdana** for larger blocks of text and **Georgia** for the **Sidebar Title**, **Blog Description**, and **Post Footer**. We also add bold styling to the **Sidebar Title** so that it has more weight and looks like a proper heading.

5. With our work done, we save our changes, clear the browser's cache, and view the blog. We may want to remove the **Bold** (**Font Style**) from the **Text Font** later, but for now, let's keep it. We can always change it back later. The results of our changes can be seen in the following screenshot:

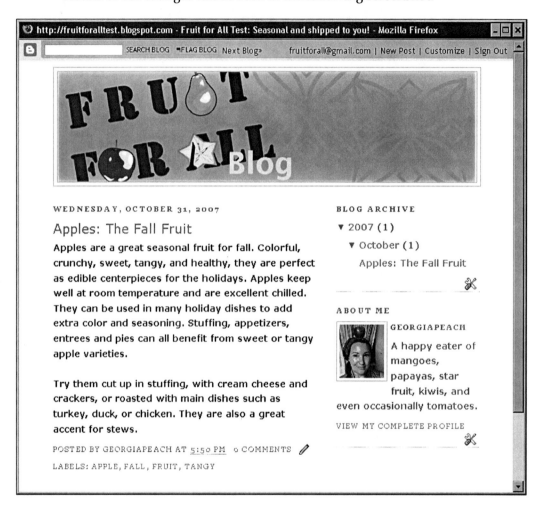

What Just Happened?

When we edited the fonts using the **Fonts and Colors** editor, Blogger saved our changes in the site code. It also updated the values of the variables in the template code. Each item listed in the left side list menu of the editor, both fonts and colors, has a corresponding variable tag in the template.

"It's amazing," exclaims Georgia as she views the changed blog, "it looks so different and we didn't have to mess around with the template code at all!"

We'll be able to do even more, once we begin editing the template. The **Edit HTML** section is next on the **Layout** tab, but before we tackle it, we need to finalize the layout and design.

Choosing an Effective Layout

We need to choose an effective layout for our blog. Georgia has already told us that she prefers the sidebar on the right. We will also need to add a bottom navigation section with links to her main site and room for social bookmarks. Blogs have a very specific layout structure. They have a top header section for ads, logos, and descriptive text, a sidebar on the left or right (and sometimes on both sides), and a main content area with posts commonly organized by date. Four layouts are commonly used with blogs.

The Usual Suspects

The good news is that there are already several main layouts used for most blogs. We will make sketches of several different ones and pick the ones that will be most useful for us. A layout is like a simple blueprint for a house. It shows the different sections of the template and where they are located in relation to each other. We want a layout to contain:

- The individual blog posts.
- A sidebar with plenty of width for most widgets. We'll add a second sidebar when we create a three-column template. Additional sidebars give you greater flexibility with your layout. The Blog posts column can be in the middle, between the sidebars, like a sandwich. Experienced bloggers prefer placing the Blog posts element on the left with both sidebars at the right, for maximum search engine optimization benefits.
- A header container for the logo, taglines, and any other buttons or top elements.
- A navigation section for links to the archives and other parts of the blog as well as the corporate site. This will either be directly under the header section or on the sidebar.
- A footer containing alternate navigation, any legal news, links, or other items.

Time for Action!—Making Sample Sketches

We can visualize our choices better by making several sample sketches. You can use any tool you like, including a paper napkin, but tools like Photoshop and Irfanview help with measuring pixels and getting exact color matches.

1. Open up Photoshop or any other image editing tool, or use Post-its, note cards, or a piece of copy paper.

2. Start by drawing four boxes. They can be exactly to scale (1024 pixels in width by 768 pixels in height) or roughly drawn. We're just using them as guides and they don't have to be exact.

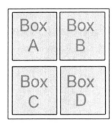

3. Draw a horizontal line about 1/4th of the way down the four boxes. It should take up no more than 200 pixels. You can use the duplicate layer trick in Photoshop to use the same line for all the boxes. This will contain the header.

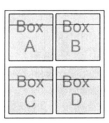

4. Now draw a vertical line about 1/3 of the way in on the left side of Box A and on the right side of Box B. Draw a vertical line on the left and then the right side of Box C. Place a second horizontal line about 200 pixels in height under the header of Box D, just to be different.

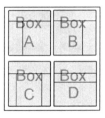

5. Footer sections are the final area we will add to our layouts. Draw a rectangle, about 30 pixels in height at the bottom of all the boxes. Footers should be tall enough to display at least one line of text or row of buttons.

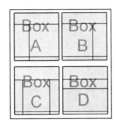

What Just Happened?

We now have four boxes. Any of these would work fine for a blog. Which one will display the *Fruit for All* blog best? We show our sketches to Georgia to get her feedback.

After looking at all the four sketches, she admits, "I would like the sidebar to be on the right like the default blog. The layout of Box B looks more like a magazine."

The right sidebar stands out from typical website layouts that use a left sidebar. It will also place more emphasis on the blog posts. Now that we are sure about our layout, it's time to start editing the template code.

Pruning the Template Code

We will be editing the template code in this section. Printing a copy of the code is a good way to examine the existing code and gives you a reference to prop up next to your computer as you work. Log into Blogger and click on the **Layout** link in the **Dashboard** to open the **Page Elements** sub tab of the **Layout** tab. Click on the **Edit HTML** sub tab of the **Layout** tab. The template code goes on for pages and pages. Print out a copy of the code and see for yourself. Don't panic, we will attack the code, one section at a time. We will start with the most common content block. This "inside out" method is a common technique used when designing sites.

Backup your original template before you make any changes. Click the **Download Full Template** link on the **Edit HTML** sub tab of the **Layout** tab to backup the template. Save the original in a backup folder. This way, you can always revert back to the original.

Designing the Visual Look

Remember when we made all those changes to the template without code? We changed the fonts, colors, the look of the header, and even the default template. We're going to combine those changes with Georgia's images to create a stylish custom template.

Here is our goal: a sharper, sweeter template for our blog:

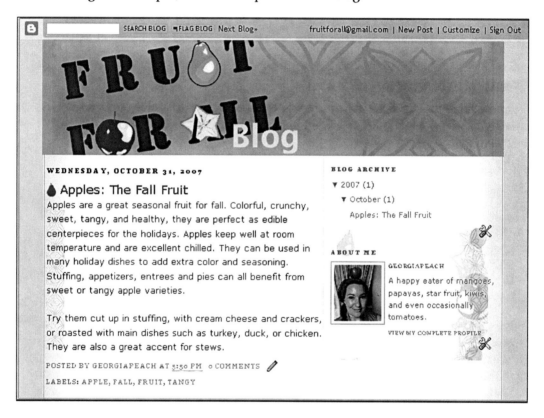

It looks very different from the basic Minima template, doesn't it? We will be adding background images, gradients, custom icons, and changing the position of different elements of the template.

 You can download the entire sample template and image package in the code download section of the book's companion website: http://bloggerbeefedup.blogspot.com/.

Preparing to Style the Post Content Block

The blog post is the most basic content element. The decisions we make here will flow outward to influence the design of the rest of the blog.

1. Go to the **Layout | Edit HTML** link. The entire current template code can be downloaded by clicking the **Download Full Template** link.

2. You will be prompted to open or save a copy of the xml file onto the hard drive of your computer. Save it to a backup folder.

 Use comments /**/ to make notes to yourself as you make changes. This is a great way to jog your memory later, months down the road. Click the / forward slash key and then enter the asterix symbol * twice. Type the comment between the asterix symbols and then finish the comment block with another forward slash.

3. Open the file up using a text editor or an html editor such as HTML Kit (http://www.htmlkit.com/), Arachnophilia (http://www.arachnoid.com/arachnophilia/), or Dreamweaver (http://www.adobe.com). Any html editor that has a line count feature will help you, since the blogger template files are several pages in length.

4. You can also edit the template 'in situ' within the template code box and use the **Preview** button to see the changes. If there is an error, you can immediately correct the code and click **Preview** again. If there is no error on preview, you can save the changes. Off-site template editing carries the risk of having too many errors to locate and correct, which can be a daunting task, even for a professional.

We will start working on the sections of the template that affect the blog posts area of the blog.

Adding a Custom Variable Tag to the Template

First we will add a variable tag to control the color of the date in the post. Variable tags are always placed at the top of the template code document. The date color needs to be individually controlled, since red is too distracting. We will change it to dark gray.

Time for Action!—Darken the Post Date

Variable tags give you greater flexibility while customizing your template and editing it in the future. The date post is a standard part of all blog posts. Making a variable to change the color will save you from editing it directly within the template in the future.

1. Type the following into the top section of the code:

```
<!-- change date color to a dark gray -->
  <Variable name="datecolor"
     description="Date Header Color"
           type="color"
        default="#ccc"
          value="#333333">
```

2. Now that we have declared a new variable to control the color of the date, we need to add it to the CSS class `h2.date-header`. It can be found at the top of the `Posts` section:

```
/* Posts */
h2.date-header
{
   margin:1.5em 0 0.5em;
}
```

3. Add a line for the color with our new `datecolor` variable directly below the opening curly brace:

```
h2.date-header
{
   color:$datecolor;
   margin:1.5em 0 0.5em;
}
```

4. Click the **SAVE CHANGES** button. The date color on the blog has changed from a dark red to grey. Readers will still be able to see the date, but it will no longer clash or distract from the title of the post.

5. From now on you can change the date color on the **Fonts and Colors** page.

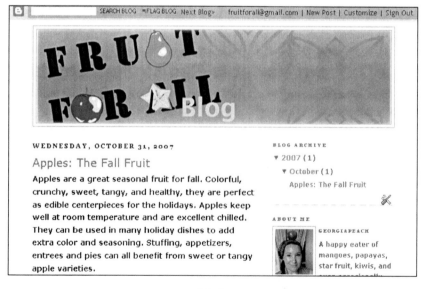

What Just Happened?

When we added a new variable tag named `datecolor`, we made it possible to make changes to the color of the date on the blog using the **Fonts and Colors** editor in the future. When we set the value of the `datecolor` variable tag to #333333, we also created a `default` value of #333. This was a shorthand version of the same color. The default attribute will enable you to reset the variable to the original value, using the **Fonts and Colors** editor.

 You may have noticed that we didn't create a variable to change the font of the date. You can give that a try on your own, now that you know how to create your own variable tags.

Displaying an Image Next to the Title of Each Post

Now that we've warmed up by adding our own custom variable tag, we are ready to start adding images to our template. Let's add an image to the post title. This will cause an image to display next to the title of each blog post.

Time for Action!—Adding an Image to the Post Title

Now let's add a decorative image to the `Post Title` class, to draw reader's eyes to the post. We'll also change the title color to dark green.

1. Click the **Layout** link on the Blogger **Dashboard and** then the **Edit HTML** link under the **Layout** tab. Scroll down the code window under the **Edit Template** section of the **Edit HTML** screen until you see this code block:

    ```
    .post h3
    {
      margin:.25em 0 0;
      padding:0 0 0 3px;
      font-size:140%;
      font-weight:normal;
      line-height:1.4em;
    }
    ```

2. Increase the padding on the left side of the text from 3px to 20px:

    ```
    .post h3
    {
      margin:.25em 0 0;
      padding:0 0 0 20px;
      font-size:140%;
      font-weight:normal;
      line-height:1.4em;
      color:$titlecolor;
    }
    ```

3. Time to add the background image that will sit to the left of the post title. Insert the following code just below the color, as shown:

```
color:$titlecolor;
background:url(http://www.leesjordan.net/images/test_templates/
                  green_pear.gif) no-repeat 0 0;
```

This image and several bonus ones are in the code folder for download at `http://bloggerbeefedup.blogspot.com/`.

4. Finally, we change the hexadecimal color code in the `titlecolor` variable tag:

```
<Variable name="titlecolor"
    description="Post Title Color"
          type="color"
       default="#c60"
         value="#3f7e1f">
```

5. Click the **SAVE CHANGES** button. The title of the posts now has a little image pizzazz and a color that better matches the logo as we can see in the following close up screenshot:

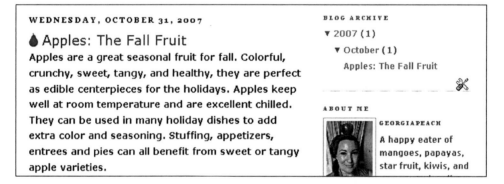

What Just Happened?

Changing the padding of the `.post h3` class made room for the background image to the left of the post title text. When we added the background image to the `.post h3` class, we instructed the template to display the image to the left of every post title. Since we were already in the template code, we went ahead and changed the color of the `titlecolor` variable to match the new background image.

If you add new images to your template, you will need to find a place to store them online. There are many online image hosting services such as Picasa (http://picasa.google.com/), Flickr (http://www.flickr.com), and Photobucket (http://www.photobucket.com), or you can upload the images to your own web host if you have one. Create an account at any of the sites above, upload your images, and copy down their links. They should look similar to this sample link: http://....... which should look like this sample link: (http://www.leesjordan.net/images/test_templates/post_background6.gif).

Adding Background Images to Post Text Blocks

We are almost done styling the post section. Next, we need to change the text of the posts from bold back to a normal font weight. We will then see how a background image looks behind the posts.

Time for Action!—Editing Post Text Styles

Adding a background image will give each post a little extra flair and visually set the posts apart from the rest of the blog. You can use the steps below and replace the image with any other image you want to use.

1. Scroll to the variable tag section of the template code until you see the bodyfont variable. Change the value from normal bold to normal normal:

   ```
   <Variable name="bodyfont"
       description="Text Font"
               type="font"
           default="normal normal 100% Georgia, Serif"
             value="normal normal109% Verdana, sans-serif">
   ```

2. We are going to place a subtle decoration in the background of the post text. Add the text in bold to the .post p class:

   ```
   .post p
   {
     margin:0 0 .75em;
     line-height:1.6em;
     background:url(http://www.leesjordan.net/images/test_templates
                     /post_background6.gif) no-repeat 0 0;
   }
   ```

3. Save your changes, clear your browser's cache, and take a look at the blog now:

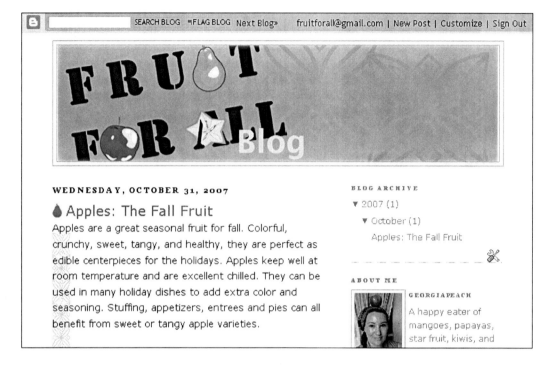

What Just Happened?

When we added the background image to the `.post p` class, we instructed the template to display the image underneath the paragraph text of each post. The post section now has a custom look. The background image behind the post may be difficult to see in print. It is meant to subtly bring attention to the post without making the text difficult to read. So, it is ok if it is very faint.

Now that we have styled the post section of the Blogger template, we can build on what we have learned and work outwards to the rest of the template. Blogger templates use a combination of XML tags, XHTML tags, and CSS styles. If you are not sure what a color will look like, you can use an online color tool, or any image editing program. Most HTML editors also have color pickers.

There are many online sites where you can create color swatches for your template. Here are a few of my favorites:

Color Hunter lets you upload an image and uses it to build a swatch of colors:

`http://www.colorhunter.com/`

Transparent color generator:

`http://apps.everamber.com/alpha/`

VisiBone groups colors by shade:

`http://www.visibone.com/colorlab/`

Spicing up the Sidebar

The sidebar of the template needs a background image and a few text tweaks. When we are done, it will have a more attractive and polished appearance.

Time for Action!—Editing the Sidebar Styles

We are going to edit the sidebar class in the CSS portion of the template. As always, backup your current template before you start modifying the template.

1. Scroll down to the sidebar section in the template code. We are going to add a background property to the `.sidebar` class. Add the text shown in bold below into the template code:

```
.sidebar
{
  float:right;
  font-size:85%;
  line-height:1.5em;
  color:$sidebartextcolor;
  background:url(http://www.leesjordan.net/images/test_templates/
                    sidebar_bg.gif) no-repeat 0 0;
  word-wrap:break-word;/* fix for long text breaking sidebar float
                    in IE */
  overflow:hidden;/* fix for long non-text content breaking IE
                    sidebar float */
}
```

2. Increase the size of the sidebar title font from 78% to 82%.

```
<Variable name="headerfont" description="Sidebar Title Font"
         type="font"
     default="normal normal 78% 'Trebuchet MS',
             Trebuchet,Arial,Verdana,Sans-serif"
     value="normal bold 82% Georgia, Times, serif">
```

3. We almost forgot to remove the dotted border underlining each sidebar element. The `.sidebar.widget`, `.main.widget` class controls the margin, padding, and borders around widgets or page elements contained in the sidebar and the main area of the template. Set the `border-bottom` of the class to `none` as shown in the example:

```
.sidebar.widget,  .main.widget
{
  border-bottom:none;
  margin:0 0 1.5em;
  padding:0 0 1.5em;
}
```

4. Save the changes to the template, clear your browser's cache, and view the blog. It should now display images underneath the content of the sidebar as seen in the following screenshot:

What Just Happened?

Adding barely two lines of code has spiced up the sidebar. A copy of the background image can be found in the code folder. The background image defines the space around the sidebar and anchors it visually to the rest of the template.

Georgia says, "The background image on the right is made up of fruit images from the logo. Reusing these images makes it look balanced."

Speaking of balance, we also need to add a footer section to our template.

Styling the Footer Section

The footer of the blog can contain site links, social bookmarks, and other information like `BoingBoing.net` does. It can also contain traditional links to a privacy policy, contact information, and copyright information. We will add those traditional links as part of the integration between Georgia's company site and her blog in Chapter 10. The height of the footer should be equal to one row of text or small images. When readers scroll down the page of the blog, they will be able to follow any links to other sites that we have or recommend the blog on social networking sites without having to scroll back up to the top of the page.

Time for Action!—Editing the Footer Styles

Editing the footer styles will involve pasting links into a **HTML/JavaScript** page element. This is a good technique for adding typical footer items like privacy notices and links to your main site or other sites associated with your blog.

1. Log in to Blogger and click on the **Layout** link under the **Dashboard**. The **Page Elements** sub tab under the **Layout** tab will then be displayed by default. The **Minima** template has a bottom section reserved for footer content. Click the **Add a Page Element** link at the bottom of the layout box.

2. Click the **Add to Blog** link under the **HTML/JavaScript** page element to select it on the **Choose a New Page Element** screen. The **Configure HTML/JavaScript** form will open in a pop-up window.

3. Leave the **Title** field blank on the form. Click in the **Content** field of the form, leaving it set to the default editor view.

4. Add the links to Fruit for All's main blog, for Packt Publishing, and bookmark links for Digg and Reddit. We can always add more links later:

```
<a href="http://packtpub.com/">Packt Publishing</a>
<a href="http://fruitforall.leesjordan.net/">Fruit For All</a>
<a href="http://www.digg.com/"><img alt="Digg!" width="80"
        src="http://digg.com/img/badges/80x15-digg-badge-2.gif"
        height="15"/></a>
```

```
<script>reddit_url="fruitforalltest.blogspot.com"</script>
<script language="javascript"
            src="http://reddit.com/button.js?t=1"></script>
```

5. Remember to leave space between the links for better readability. Click the **SAVE CHANGES** button, clear the browser cache, and then view the blog. The **HTML/JavaScript** page element will now exist at the bottom of the **Page Element** layout area.

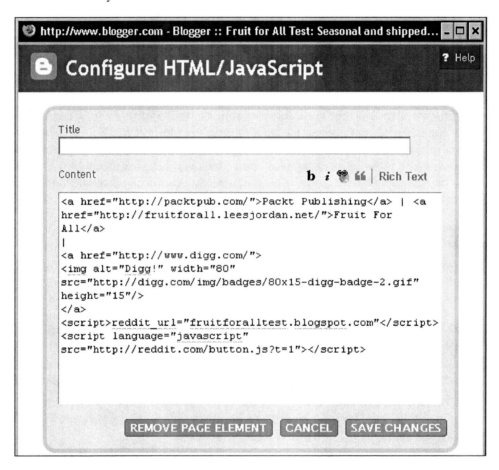

What Just Happened?

When we added an HTML/JavaScript page element to the footer section of the layout, our own custom sets of links were added. We used this page element, instead of a link list, to control the display of the links in a horizontal row. We will add more site links to the footer in the next chapter, when we discuss *Social Bookmarking* and also in Chapter 10, while integrating the *Fruit for All* blog with the corporate web site.

The set of footer links are now displayed at the bottom of the blog, as seen in the following screenshot:

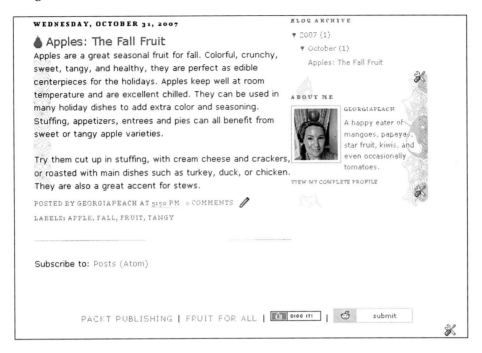

Styling the Header Section of the Template

Georgia is worried that we have forgotten about the header section of the template, "It doesn't stretch across the screen like I wanted it to," she says, moving the palms of her hands together and far apart to demonstrate, "what can we do about that?"

The header section of the template needs to be edited to make it look like we want it to. We will remove the border around the header area and then add a new and wider header image.

Time for Action!—Editing the Header Styles

Let's continue editing the template. If you've come straight to this example you'll need to log in to Blogger, click the **Layout** link of your blog under the **Dashboard**, then click on the **Edit HTML** sub-tab under the **Layout** tab. Scroll down the template code until you see the #header-wrapper div tag.

1. Increase the width of the #header-wrapper to 680 pixels, set the margin to zero and the border to none:

    ```
    #header-wrapper
    {
    ```

```
    width:680px;
    margin:0;
    border:none;
}
```

2. Now that the outer box of the header container is styled, we can modify the `#header` div, the box that contains the image. Set the margin property as shown below, the `border` to `none` and the `background` to a medium green (`#82d645`), to pad the header image:

```
#header
{
    margin:0 0 0 2px;
    border:none;
    text-align:center;
    color:$pagetitlecolor;
    background:#82d645;
}
```

3. Save the changes to the template, clear your browser cache, and view the blog to see the results.

What Just Happened?

The header is now properly aligned in the template. The following screenshot shows the centered header image with the old Minima borders removed. The wider header section frames the top of the blog:

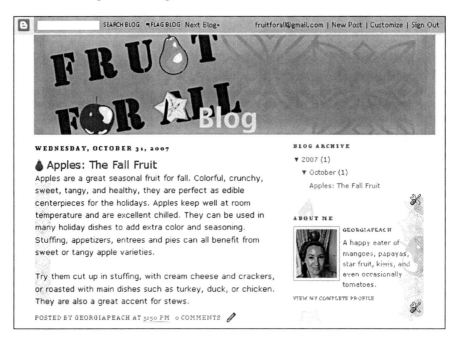

"The template is still missing something," Georgia tells us, "I'm not sure what, but the blog looks too flat, and the sidebar doesn't look separated from the posts."

She's right. The blog could use some additional graphical tweaks and improved positioning. We are ready to work on the larger container styles that control the sidebar, main content, and overall blog structure.

Adding Polish to the Template with Style(s)

The settings for the background of the blog, including the invisible box around it, the content area, and the other page elements, are contained in the **Outer-Wrapper** section of the template code. We are going to manipulate the containers in that section of the template to add more visual interest to the blog.

Creating Visual Interest with Backgrounds and Borders

Adding a soft gradient and border to the background of the entire blog will give it a visual punch. The Outer-Wrapper section of the template contains positioning blocks for the main content areas of the blog. This includes the divs for the blog post area, sidebar, and footer. This is where we will place a background image for the whole blog.

We first have some unfinished business with the sidebar-wrapper div of the template. A border on the left side of the sidebar will separate it visually from the main content area. We will also go ahead and add positioning elements. After that, we will add the background image to the Outer-wrapper.

Time for Action!—Adding Backgrounds and Borders

We're going to continue editing the CSS styles within the template code of the blog. Make sure you backup your template before continuing. When we are done with the steps below, the entire blog will have a gradient background and a border separating the sidebar from the blog posts area.

1. Open up the template code and find the Outer-Wrapper section. Add a light yellow border to the left side of the sidebar-wrapper div as shown:

   ```
   #sidebar-wrapper
   {
     width:240px;
     padding-left:10px;
     border-left:#ffffcc thin solid;
     float:left;
   ```

```
word-wrap:break-word; /* fix for long text breaking sidebar
              float in IE */
overflow:hidden; /* fix for long non-text content breaking IE
    sidebar float */
}
```

2. It's time to add a gradient background image to the blog. Increase the `width` of the `outer-wrapper` div to `680`. Then set the `margin` to `0 auto 0`. Remove the `padding` property. The `background` image will repeat horizontally down the page. Add it just below the `font` property.

```
#outer-wrapper
{
  width:680px;
  margin:0 auto 0;
  text-align:left;
  font:$bodyfont;
  background:url(http://www.leesjordan.net/images/test_templates/
                  blog_bg.gif)repeat-y;
}
```

3. Now that we have it styled, we need to format the `main-wrapper` div so that the posts will line up properly in the layout. Add a `padding-left` property element and set it to `5px` to move the post over towards the right:

```
#main-wrapper
{
  width:410px;
  padding-left:5px;
  float:left;
  word-wrap:break-word; overflow:hidden;
}
```

4. The background color for the entire template is controlled by the `bgcolor` variable tag. Change it to a light green color (hexadecimal code #d1edd):

```
<Variable name="bgcolor"
   description="Page Background Color"
          type="color"
        default="#fff"
          value="#d1edbb">
```

 You can learn more about XHTML, XML, and CSS at `http://www.w3schools.com/`. Their Try-It Editor shows changes to code snippets in real time.

What Just Happened?

The template has been customized for greater visual impact and usability. We changed fonts and colors, working from the inner content styles to the larger div blocks controlling the whole template.

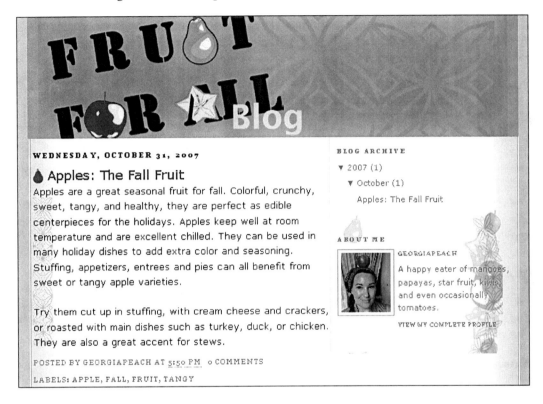

Two-column templates are easy to modify in Blogger. The real challenge is to create a three-column template where you can use multiple sidebars. To keep things simple, we will alter a basic Minima template. You can add the other background images after adjusting the padding and margins.

Creating a Three-column Template

We will alter the CSS styles of the template to control the positioning of the template sections. New div tags will then be created and placed to give us a location to add page elements.

If you are using a classic Blogger template, visit the *Random Bytes* blog for a quick and easy three-column template tutorial: `http://weblensblogs.blogspot.com/2006/02/build-three-column-blogger-template.html`.

The newest version of Blogger templates are carefully formatted with closing tags for all tag elements and strict use of HTML tags; a human way of saying they are processed as well formed XML.

 You can learn more about HTML, XHTML, and XML at `http://www.w3schools.com/`.

Have you been struggling to change your default two-column blog template to a more flexible three-column one? You can do it in 15 minutes or less with a little math and some copy and paste skills. Back up your current template before you begin making any changes. If you are already using Minima, you're in luck. It is the easiest Blogger template to customize. We're focusing on converting more recent Blogger templates, sometimes referred to as **Blogger Beta** templates.

Preparing to Modify Your Current Template

Making room for an additional sidebar is going to require an increase in the width of the `#Outer-wrapper` and the `#Header-wrapper` div styles. We'll use a formula, since the width of the wrapper styles in your blog might not match the width of my blog.

Find your ideal width using the following formula:

First find the `extra padding` by subtracting the `main-wrapper` and `sidebar-wrapper` width from your `outer-wrapper` width:

```
extra padding = outer-wrapper width - (main-wrapper width + sidebar-
                wrapper width)
```

A template with default Minima widths would look like this, when applying the formula:

```
extra padding = 660 - (410 + 220)
extra padding = 30
```

Template width formula:

```
outer-wrapper= main-wrapper width + (sidebar width x 2) +
                                              extra padding
```

The math for a default Minima blog template width formula should look like this:

```
outer-wrapper = 410 + (220 x 2) + 30
outer-wrapper = 860
```

Now we know the overall width of the template and can apply it.

Time for Action!—Building a Three-column Template

We're going to add a second sidebar by copying the current one, pasting the copy after it, and then making adjustments to the new sidebar style. We will then make changes to the tags within the template.

1. Log in to Blogger and click the **Layout** link under your blog **Dashboard**. Select the **Edit HTML** sub tab under the **Layout** tab. Scroll down the template to find the styles #Header-wrapper, #Outer-wrapper, and any other styles with the same width and replace it with our new outer-wrapper width.

2. Copy the current sidebar-wrapper style set and paste it below the closing bracket of the sidebar-wrapper tag. Rename the second sidebar-wrapper tag to sidebartwo-wrapper. The two sets of styles should now look like the ones shown below:

```
#sidebar-wrapper
{
  width:220px;
  float:$endSide;
  padding-left:3px;
  word-wrap:break-word; /* fix for long text breaking sidebar
          float in IE */
  overflow:hidden; /* fix for long non-text content breaking IE
      sidebar float */
}

#sidebartwo-wrapper
{
  width:220px;
  float:$startSide;
  padding-right:3px;
  word-wrap:break-word; /* fix for long text breaking sidebar
          float in IE */
  overflow:hidden; /* fix for long non-text content breaking
          IE sidebar float */
}
```

3. It's time to add a new sidebar div tag to the XML tag portion of the template. Add the new tag directly after the closing div tag for the `crosscol-wrapper` div. Type the following set of tags just below that closing `crosscol-wrapper` div and before the `main-wrapper` div.

```
<div id='sidebartwo-wrapper'><b:section class='sidebar'
    id='sidebartwo' preferred="'yes'"></b:section></div>
```

4. Your newly added tags should be placed like the tags shown below:

```
<div id='content-wrapper'>
<div id='crosscol-wrapper' style=""><b:section class='crosscol'
 id='crosscol' showaddelement='no'/></b:section></div>
<div id='sidebartwo-wrapper'><b:section class='sidebar'
    id='sidebartwo' preferred='yes'></b:section></div>
<div id='main-wrapper'></div>
<!--other tags including the sidebar-wrapper go here followed by
the closing content-wrapper div>
</div>
```

5. Save the template. Now we can add widgets to the new sidebar. Click on the **Page Elements** sub tab under **Layout,** and drag individual page elements over to the new sidebar. An example of how the page elements screen should now appear is shown in the following screenshot.

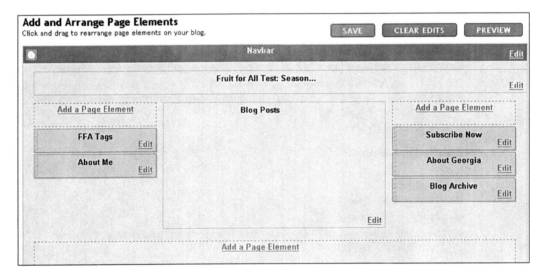

6. Click the **SAVE** button, clear your browser's cache, and view the results. You can see the new sidebar on the left, and the original sidebar on the right in the following screenshot of the blog:

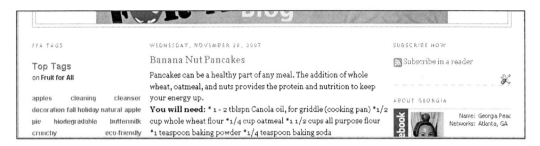

 Place both sidebars to the right of the blog posts page element, by typing `float:left;` for the `sidebar-wrapper` and `float:right;` for `sidebartwo-wrapper`.

What Just Happened?

When we edited the template styles and XML tags, we instructed Blogger to display an additional sidebar on the blog and to allow page elements to be added to it. Moving the existing page elements to the new sidebar by dragging and dropping them on the page elements screen helped control where they were displayed on the blog.

You can experiment by placing the sidebar in other locations such as, directly under the `main-content` ending div tag or below the ending div tag of the original sidebar. Once you start experimenting, you will discover more ways to layout the page elements on your blog.

Tweaking Template Images

We need to change the width of the header image to match the new widths of the other styles in our template. The old header image was 650 pixels. We need to resize it to a width of 850 pixels. It is also possible to let Blogger resize the image for you. Remove the old image from the **Configure Header** screen, then upload it again with the **shrink to fit** checkbox selected.

Time for Action!—Editing the Header Image Width

We're going to go through the process of editing an image within an image editing program, saving it for the web, and then uploading it to our blog.

1. Open up Irfanview or your favorite image editing program. Skip ahead to the next step unless you are using Photoshop. If you are using Photoshop, click on **image | mode | RGB** to edit an image ending in .gif. If you are using an image with a format of .png or .jpg, you can go right for resizing the image.

2. Next, open up the **Resize** feature (Ctrl + R in Irfanview). In Photoshop this can be done with the shortcut ctrl + alt + I. Uncheck the **constrain proportions** checkbox, click **OK**, and check out the results. Irfanview has a large number of options on its **Resize/Resample Image** screen. Select the **Set new size** radio option, uncheck the **Preserve aspect ratio** checkbox, and then type the new width. Click the **OK** button to save the changes. You can see a **Resize/Resample Image** screen within Irfanview in the following screenshot:

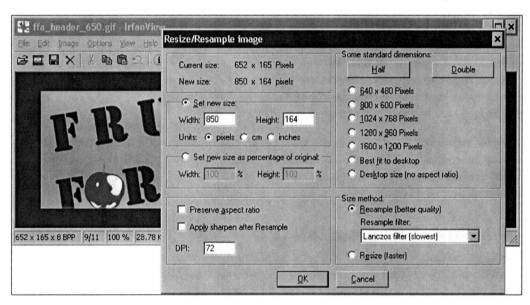

3. Save the newly edited image as ffa_header_850.jpg by typing the s key on the keyboard to save in Irfanview, or by selecting **File | save for web** (ctrl + alt + shift + s) in Photoshop and specifying it as a .jpg file set at quality of 80 or less.

4. While saving with Irfanview, it is important to select the correct file type from the **Save as type:** drop-down menu in the **Save Picture As** window. The default file type is bitmap (.bmp). Once you choose the **JPG – JPG/JPEG** format, a dialog box pops up allowing you to choose how much you want to compress the image and whether to keep the image data. Click on **Save** after making your selections on the **Save Picture As** window. An example is shown in the following screenshot:

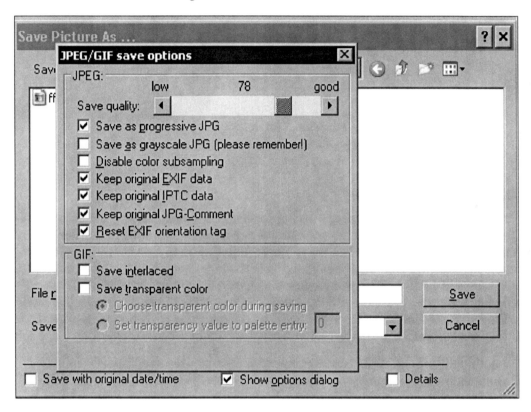

5. Now, it is time to replace the old header image with the one we just modified. Log in to Blogger and click the **Layout** link under the **Dashboard**. Click the **Edit** link in the **Header** page element. Remove the old header image and upload the new one by selecting the radio option next to **From your computer:** and then click on the **Browse** button to locate the file. If you are using a file from a website, select the radio option next to **From the web,** and type the full URL to the image location in the text field.

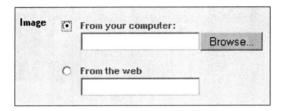

6. Click the **Save Changes** button, clear your browser's cache, and view the template

What Just Happened?

When you removed the old image and uploaded a new one, the image was floated in the header of the template. The resize function within the default Blogger templates is not always predictable. When we went through the trouble of resizing the image manually, we increased the effectiveness of the image uploading tool and optimized the image for the web. The image uploading tool pulled the current width of the template's #header-wrapper div style and automatically attempted to size the image to the width set there. Changing the padding and margins of the template would allow for additional control over alignment of the image within the header.

If you think the image looks too **stretched** you may have to open up the original file you used while creating your header, increase the canvas size of the image, and play with modifying the background. Most header images look fine with a little distortion. Too much space around the image may be due to extra margins or padding. Go to the **Edit HTML** sub tab and scroll down to the #outer-wrapper and #header-wrapper styles. Play with the margin and padding attributes of those styles until you are satisfied with the results.

Summary

Georgia now has a custom Blogger template for her blog that matches her company's logo, colors, and personality.

- We began by editing the default Blogger template.
- We chose a layout to lay the foundation for the new template.
- The page elements of the blog were then styled using CSS and Blogger tags.
- Custom images were added to the template.
- All the parts were combined together for a complete look.
- A third column was added to the template to make room for additional page elements.

Next we will explore how Georgia can use *Social Bookmarking* to attract more readers and spread the word about her blog.

3
Social Bookmarking

Blogging is not done in a vacuum. We are all looking for ways to attract readers and share our message. Social bookmarking will help you find new readers and measure successful posts. The features of social bookmarking sites are in constant evolution. Currently they can be broadly categorized into three types:

- **User generated news**: The main goal is to increase visits by getting on the front page of a site like Digg or Reddit. This will increase traffic to a site by huge amounts for anywhere from a few minutes to a day. Sites unprepared for the avalanche of hits often choke on the visitor overload. This is commonly known as the *Slashdot effect* (`http://www.slashdot.org`); a popular technologies site whose readers have broken many a site under the crush of their visits.

- **Circle of friends sharing**: When posting to Facebook (`http://www.facebook.com`), Twitter (`http://www.twitter.com`), Flickr (`http://flickr.com`), or a blog, the user knows that the main purpose of these sites is sharing content with friends and people. When a user shares a link with a friend, a slight increase in traffic may occur (unless the user is a "celebrity" blogger with thousands of followers). Focusing on such groups would be more effective for smaller blogs.

- **Online bookmarks**: Readers use these sites to manage their bookmarks online. Links can be public, and may even serve the public interest, such as "How To". Most people see these sites as a welcome alternative to trying to export or duplicate bookmarks across multiple browsers or computers. Adding links to these sites will increase the chance of first time readers becoming regulars. Examples include del.icio.us (`http://del.icio.us`), Furl (`http://www.furl.net`), and Ma.gnolia (`http://ma.gnolia.com`).

How Social Bookmarking Works

Social bookmarking works because people share information they find online with each other. The different features that social bookmark services such as online bookmarks, categories, and rss feeds provide make it easier for people to find sites that interest them in new and sometimes unpredictable ways. People are connected to each other through these services, forming social and interacting networks, helping others find information, and spreading the word about sites they enjoy.

Submitting Posts without Bookmarks

Bookmarks are convenient for readers and bloggers. Submitting articles and posts manually is extra time and work for a reader. Making it easier for them by linking the post title and URL automatically encourages readers to submit posts spontaneously. Let's recommend a site to Reddit (`http://www.reddit.com`) without using bookmarks. Reddit is a popular online bookmark and user-generated news service.

Time for Action!—Become a "Bookmarker"

1. Navigate to `http://www.reddit.com` and click the **submit** link at the top of the screen.

2. You will be redirected to the register or login screen. A username and password are all that is needed. Enter a username into the **username** box. You can enter an email address such as `fruitforall@gmail.com` into the **email** text field. Type a password into the **password** box and again into the **verify password** box.

3. You can choose to have the site remember your login for you by clicking on the **remember me** checkbox. After reviewing the privacy policy and user agreement pages, place a check in the box next to **I understand...**. Click on the **create account** button after the form has been filled out as shown in the following screenshot:

4. Find an interesting article to submit. We will submit the latest post on the (`http://cookingwithamy.blogspot.com`) blog. An example of the post being submitted is shown in the following screenshot. Copy the URL and the title of the post into a text editor such as Notepad (Windows) or Textpad (Mac).

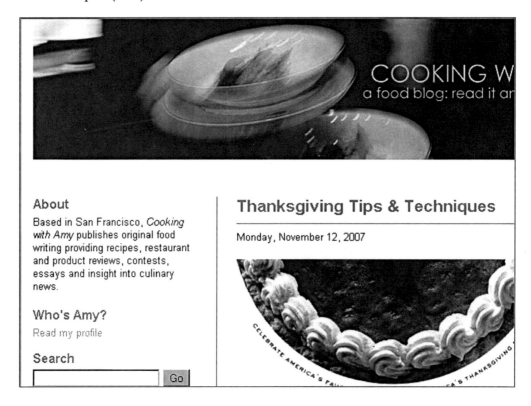

5. Log in to Reddit and click the **submit** link. Enter all the data manually, as shown in the following screenshot. Click the **submit** button. The link has now been shared.

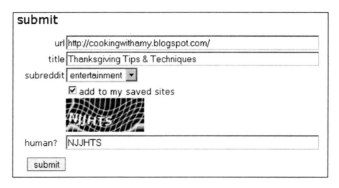

What Just Happened?

It took three steps to add one link to Reddit. That did not include the time spent finding the site we wanted to submit. Then we had to log in to the bookmarking service and go to the submit form. We had to copy all the submission information ourselves and then enter it all manually into the bookmarking site form. The URL had to be entered correctly. If we had made a mistake while typing, the process would have taken longer and been more frustrating. It took a minute or two instead of the few seconds a bookmark would take. Now let's see how social bookmarks are a useful addition to our blog. They save the readers' time and make it more likely that new readers will impulse bookmark.

Sharing Posts by Email

A common way for visitors to share posts and articles they like is to email them to other people. Blogger has an *Email Post to a Friend* feature. Using features that make sharing posts more convenient for visitors will increase the exposure of your blog. This is a small subset of a type of marketing known as **viral marketing**, where readers spread your message for you from one person to another.

"How hard is it to turn on this feature?" asks Georgia as she navigates the blog. "I'd like to try it. Then my readers will have an easy way to share my posts!"

Time for Action!—Turn On Email Posting

1. Log in to the blog, click the **Settings** link, and navigate to the **Basic** sub tab link.

2. Scroll down the list to **Show Email Post links?** and select **Yes** from the drop-down list as shown in the following screenshot:

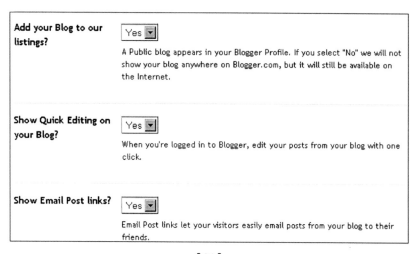

3. Click on **Save Settings**. Now it's time to test the feature.

4. View the blog and click on the small email icon below the post. The **Email Post to a Friend** screen will appear.

5. The sender will need to enter his name and email address and the email address of the person he wants to send the post to. The **Message** box, which is not a required field, can contain any notes from the sender. A sample of the post content is displayed at the bottom of the screen. Click the **Send Email** button to send the message.

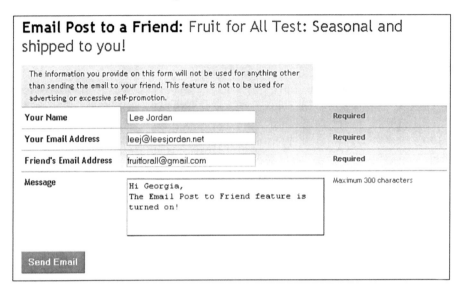

6. An email will be sent to the address **fruitforall@gmail.com,** and a success screen is displayed with a link back to the blog, as shown in the following screenshot:

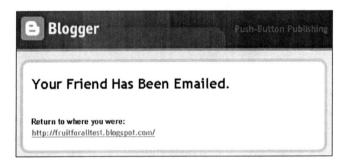

7. The submitter will be able to return to the blog using the link under **Return to where you were** on the confirmation screen.

What Just Happened?

When you logged into the blog and turned on the email post links feature, **The Email post** link setting in the blogger template was set to "show". The icon for the Email-Post-To-A-Friend feature was then visible under each blog post. Clicking on the icon brought up a new screen with a form that prompted the submitters to enter the email information for themselves and their friends. The code displayed the post at the bottom of the screen, automatically. The friend is then sent an email with a link to the post.

Adding Bookmarks to Blogs

Social bookmarks can be displayed on blogs as text links, buttons, or as dynamic mini-widgets showing the number of submissions. Adding bookmarks to blogs is a task that ranges from simple cut and paste to custom coding. We will first choose the social bookmarks and then explore several different techniques to add them to our blog.

Choosing the Right Bookmarks for Your Blog

Blogs that focus on specific topics or points of views stand out from thousands of other blogs and attract a more regular following. The social bookmarks you choose should fit the subject and tone of your blog. A technology blog would most likely have bookmarks to Digg (`http://www.digg.com`), Slashdot (`http://http://www.slashdot.org`), and Reddit (`http://www.reddit.com`).

"There are so many social bookmarking services out there," says Georgia. "How do I pick the ones that are right for my blog?"

Earlier, we had defined three broad types of social bookmark systems. You could just choose whatever bookmark sites you see your friends using. But you're smarter than that. You are on a mission to make sure your blog post links will show up where readers interested in your topic congregate. Listed below are the most popular and useful social bookmark systems and networks.

Popular Social Bookmarking Sites:

Name/Link	Symbol	Type	Description
Del.icio.us http://del.icio.us		Online Bookmarks	The most popular social bookmarking site across all types of users. Provides many categories. Most useful for bloggers who post tutorials and "How To" articles.
Digg http://www.digg.com		User Generated News	Users submit links of articles to Digg and rate them. Can search, filter, and browse. Primarily a collection of technology links, with popular news and culture.
Blinklist http://www. blinklist.com	blinklist	Online Bookmarks	Easy tools to display bookmarks on social network pages or blogs, auto-fill description fields, import bookmarks from competing sites, use of thumbnails.
Furl http://www.furl. net/	LookSmart FURL	Online Bookmarks	Site with a mature set of features including exporting, site caching, and metadata.
Yahoo My Web 2.0 http://myweb2. search.yahoo.com/	Y	Circle of Friends, and Online Bookmarks	Not very focused on one audience, categories shaped by users.
Flickr http://www.flickr. com	flickr	Circle of Friends	Social bookmarking for images. Sort, browse, search, and categorize images in ways that can be listed. Interest groups and metadata may lead people to your blog. Best for blogs that use images as a major part of content.

Name/Link	Symbol	Type	Description
YouTube http://www.youtube.com/	**You Tube**	Circle of Friends, Online video storage, and Site Bookmarking.	Visitors' rates, categories, tags, and watch videos on many subjects. A useful site for video "How To", including recipes, troubleshooting, decoration, and artistic techniques. Best for cutting edge blogs or blogs about visual topics.
Reddit http://www.reddit.com		User Generated News	Users vote submitted links up or down. Has a very general article, but also "Hot" and "Popular" categories.
Twitter http://www.twitter.com	twitter	Circle of Friends	Users give short updates and share links
StumbleUpon http://www.stumbleupon.com/	su	Online Bookmarking	Browse and search bookmarks and add your own. Uses a toolbar widget with browser. Categorized collection of site links.
Ma.gnolia http://ma.gnolia.com	magnolia	More feature rich than Del.icio.us, same type	Rate links with a five star system, browser bookmarklet, thumbnails, and page caches.

There are many social bookmarking sites out there. If you are just starting out, submitting to a site like Reddit can't hurt. But don't be disappointed if users don't flock to your site right away. Start with sites that categorize content and encourage visitor interaction. If users can search a social bookmarking site by category, tag, or by browsing, they are more likely to find you.

Deciding Which Bookmark Services to Use

Is your blog a "niche" blog like Georgia's, or one with broader appeal that falls into a general category, such as a technology blog? If your audience is more likely to find you through specific tags, searches, or by browsing user generated categories, services offering finely categorized community driven features are the best fit. Many of these services also provide RSS feeds based on categories or tags their users show interest in.

Georgia's best bets are del.icio.us, StumbleUpon, Facebook, Twitter, and Reddit.

Having trouble deciding? Pick two or three services, and then submit posts you write for several weeks. Make sure the posts offer "How To", commentary on new products, or industry news that readers will find useful. We will cover the details of "killer" content later in this chapter. Review the results of your efforts to see if the services attracted readers or increased the hits of your blog. Remove the service with the worst results and add a different one.

The "Circle of Friends" services operate differently from the *User-News* and *Online Bookmark* services. They are usually added as third-party blog widgets, which we will explore in Chapter 5—*Using Widgets*. We will focus now on different ways to add the online bookmark type of site to our blog.

Using Simple Text Link Bookmarks

The most basic type of social bookmark is a text link. Currently the bottom of each post on Georgia's blog contains only a comments section. Georgia wants readers to be able to click a link to recommend one of her posts, instead of submitting them manually to the bookmark service.

Time for Action!—Adding Bookmarks as Text Links

Backup the current Blogger template, as discussed in Chapter 2—*Customize and Create Templates*.

1. Log in at `Blogger.com` and click the **Layout** link on the **Dashboard**. The **Page Elements** sub tab is opened by default. Click on the **Edit HTML** sub-tab of the **Layout** tab. Click on the **Expand Widgets Template** checkbox. Scroll down to this line: `<p class='post-footer-line post-footer-line-2'>`.

2. We type a list of bookmark links just above the `<p class='post-footer-line post-footer-line-2'>` line in the template code:

```
<!-- social bookmarks -->
<ul id="postsocial">
  <li>
    Bookmarks:
  </li>
  <li>
   <a expr:href='"http://del.icio.us/post?url=" + data:post.url +
              "&amp;title=" + data:post.title' target='_blank'>
              del.icio.us</a>
  </li>
  <li>
   <a expr:href='"http://www.stumbleupon.com/submit?url=" +
              data:post.url + "&amp;title=" + data:post.title'
```

```
                       target='_blank'>StumbleUpon</a>
      </li>
      <li>
        <a expr:href='"http://reddit.com/submit?url="
                     + data:post.url + "&amp;title=" + data:post.
                     title' target='_blank'>Reddit</a>
      </li>
      <li>
        <a expr:href='"http://www.blinklist.com/index.
                     php?Action=Blink/addblink.php&amp;Url=" +
                     data:post.url + "&amp;Title=" +
                     data:post.title' target='_blank'>BlinkList</a>
      </li>
    </ul>
  <!-- end social bookmarks -->
```

3. Add the following css styles to the page just below the closing bracket of
   the .post p class:

```
#postsocial
{
  float:left;
  width:95%;
  margin:0;
  padding:2px 2px 2px 2px;
  list-style:none;
  background:#d1fbb2;
}
#postsocial li
{
  float:left;
  margin: 1px;
  padding:0;
  font-size:80%;
}
#postsocial a
{
  float:left;
  display:block;
  margin:0;
  padding:2px 2px;
  text-decoration:none;
  border:1px solid #f0f0ff;
  border-bottom:none;
  background:#ffffff;
}
#postsocial a:hover
{
  border-color:#727377;
  background:#d1fbb2;
}
```

3. **Save** the changes. The links should be displayed just below the comment's block. Hovering over a link with your mouse should cause a gray border and green background to display. The rest of the time the links should have a white background.

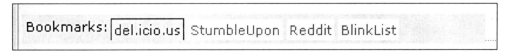

4. It is time to test the links and make sure that they work the way we expect them to. They should cause a new window to open with the **URL** and **description** (title) already populated. Click on the **del.icio.us** link to test the results:

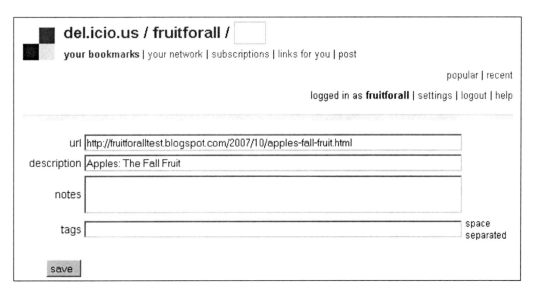

What Just Happened?

When we loaded the blog after making the changes, we saw a group of simple button links across the bottom of each post. These were generated by the lines of XHTML tags containing each bookmark link. Each item in the bookmark list was contained in a tag like this one:

```
<a expr:href='"http://del.icio.us/post?url=" + data:post.url +
        "&amp;title=" + data:post.title' target='_blank'>
        del.icio.us</a>
```

Every link used within the Blogger template begins with `<a expr:href`. This beginning portion of the link tag identifies the tag as a link to the template code. The tags contain reference attributes such as `data:post.url` and `data:post.title`, which will automatically gather the title and label information of the posts so that the reader can easily submit the post to the bookmark service. The example tag above is saying, display the link del.icio.us. When it is clicked, grab the description and URL of the blog post and automatically populate the information into the submit form on the del.icio.us site. Each tag link may look slightly different, depending on the required format for the bookmark service.

Take it Further—Bookmark Link Scavenger Hunt

The links for over 20 popular sites are included in the code folder on this book's companion site. Most of the bookmark service provide text links you can modify to fit the blogger link tags. Find the submit link of a bookmark service you use and convert it using the tag format shown above.

If you get stuck, seven of the most popular sites are already formatted for you in the `pop_textlinks.html` file in the code folder of this book's companion website located at `http://bloggerbeefedup.blogspot.com`. We've added text links and they look fine. Many blogs use them. You can add your own background images to social bookmark links. They can look like buttons or have other attention grabbing backgrounds.

Adding Social Bookmark Buttons

"The text links work," Georgia says, as she examines the new bookmarks on the blog, "but actual buttons would look more professional."

Graphical button links are easier to spot among all the comment links and other information at the bottom of a blog post. Using buttons will give readers a quick visual cue to submit the post if they have enjoyed it.

Time for Action!—Adding Bookmark Buttons to Posts

1. Collect the bookmark images to add to the template. Most bloggers collect the icons from the bookmarking service sites, resize them, and store them on Photobucket (`http://www.photobucket.com`), Google pages (`http://pages.google.com`), Flickr (`http://www.flickr.com`), or their own domain. We will be using button icons stored at `http://www.leesjordan.net`.

2. Select the **Expand Widget Templates** checkbox. Type the following code into the template, replacing the text link code we entered previously:

```
<!-- social bookmarks with image buttons -->
 <ul id="postsocial">
  <li> Bookmarks: </li>
  <li>
    <a expr:href='"http://del.icio.us/post?url=" + data:post.url +
                "&amp;title=" + data:post.title' target='_blank'>
                <img alt='Save to Delicious' src=
                'http://www.leesjordan.net/social/
                delicious.gif'/></a>
  </li>
  <li>
    <a expr:href='"http://www.stumbleupon.com/submit?url=" +
                data:post.url + "&amp;title=" + data:post.title'
                target='_blank'><img alt='Stumble It!'
                src='http://www.leesjordan.net/social/
                stumbleupon.gif'/></a>
  </li>
  <li>
    <a expr:href='"http://reddit.com/submit?url=" +
                data:post.url + "&amp;title=" + data:post.title'
                target='_blank'> <img alt='Submit to
                Reddit'src='http://www.leesjordan.net/social/
                reddit.gif'/></a>
  </li>
  <li>
    <a expr:href='"http://www.blinklist.com/index.
                php?Action=Blink/addblink.php&amp;Url=" +
                data:post.url + "&amp;Title=" + data:post.title'
                target='_blank'> <img alt='Save to Blinklist'
                src='http://www.leesjordan.net/social/
                blinklists.gif'/></a>
  </li>
 </ul>
<!-- end social bookmarks -->
```

3. **Save** and view the blog. We can see how they look on the blog in the following screenshot:

4. Test the links to see if they work as expected. Click the **StumbleUpon** button (the second button in the row) to submit Georgia's post.

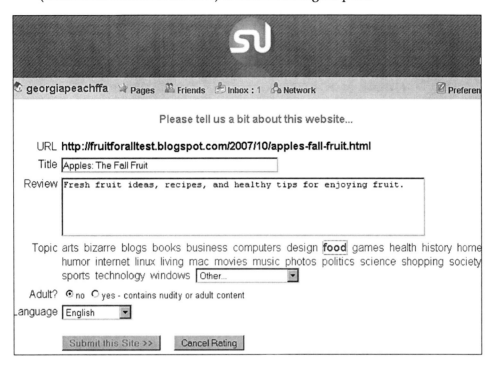

What Just Happened?

We added image links instead of text links this time. The most important thing to remember is to decide where to host the bookmark links. The image links can be found on the bookmark service sites, but you will not have control over the size of the image. Self hosting on a free site such as Flickr, Photobucket, or Google pages is the best option if you don't have a web space. Don't forget to change the image link code shown below to match your hosting service.

```
<img alt='Save to Blinklist'
    src='http://www.leesjordan.net/social/blinklists.gif'/>
```

The button link tags contain special link references that collect dynamic information from the bookmark service. When a button is clicked, the attributes in the tag are used to automatically populate the title and the URL for the reader.

Many of the popular social bookmark icons, as well as a Photoshop .psd file of the button background, are in the code folder of this book's companion website. Other icons can be found on the bookmark service sites themselves. You can use a simple image editor to shrink the icon down to 16 pixels by 16 pixels.

Adding buttons gives the site a more homemade feel, but it is time consuming to hunt down the links to the different services on the social networking sites. Wouldn't it be great if there was a third-party service out there that did the gathering for you? AddThis (http://www.addthis.com) offers a multi-bookmark widget popular with many bloggers.

Offering Multiple Bookmarks with One Button

Using a widget like the one offered by AddThis frees you to spend your time blogging. You can choose to show all the main bookmark networks or pick and choose from an extensive list. We'll configure the widget and then install it on our blog.

Time for Action!—Offering Multiple Bookmarks with AddThis

1. Register at the AddThis (http://www.addthis.com) site. Georgia has already created an account for *Fruit for All*.

2. The **AddThis Social Widget Builder** screen has multiple options to customize the widget code. Choose the **Bookmarking widget** option from the **Which kind of widget?** drop-down box. Select the style of bookmark button you want to use. We will choose the second one. The **on a Blog** option should be selected for **Where?** Choose **Blogger** for the **Blogging Platform** and then click **Get Your Free Button>>** for the code.

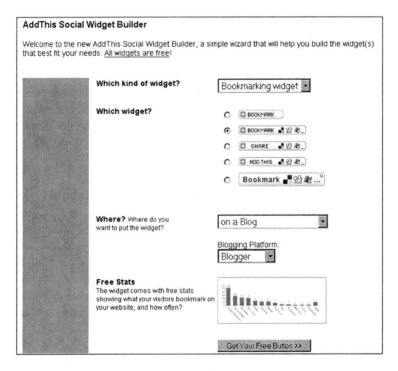

3. Next, AddThis will provide you with the code. Copy the code from the site or type the code below in place of the button links, above the `<p class='post-footer-line post-footer-line-2'>` tag in the template code:

```
<!-- AddThis Bookmark Post Dropdown BEGIN -->
<div>
  <script type='text/javascript'>addthis_url='<data:post.url/>';
              addthis_title='<data:post.title/>';
              addthis_pub='fruitforall';</script>
  <script src='http://s7.addthis.com/js/addthis_widget.php?v=12'
          type='text/javascript'></script>
</div>
<!-- AddThis Bookmark Post Dropdown END -->
```

4. **Save** the template changes and view the blog. Try hovering the cursor over the **Bookmark** button to see whether the list of bookmarks appears.

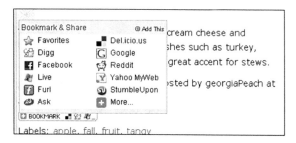

5. The button looks great. We need to test an icon to see how AddThis submits posts. Click the **Del.icio.us** icon to bring up the submission window.

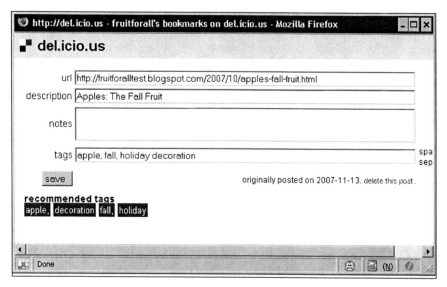

6. The **URL**, **description** (title), and **tags** were auto populated for us. Taking a note of the recommended tags will help us label future posts, and will guide us in adding more labels to the current post.

What Just Happened?

The AddThis button replaced our group of social bookmark buttons. When the visitor hovers their cursor over the button, a list of social bookmark icons appear. The visitor also has the option to choose from social bookmarks not listed in the main group. A new window opens with a submission form for the service we selected. After the form is filled out, AddThis collects statistical data for us and displays it graphically on our AddThis account page. The icons displayed on the button can be changed on the AddThis site.

You can't predict which bookmarks your visitors use. Using a multiple bookmark aggregator such as AddThis keeps your posts free of bookmark clutter while giving visitors more bookmarking choices. There are other options as well. ShareThis (`http://www.sharethis.com`) has recently released the latest version of its multiple bookmark service, which includes tracking. It is available at `http://sharethis.com/publisher/`.

Adding Dynamic Counters to Bookmark Links

Showing counters on social bookmark icons is becoming popular. Dynamic counters are offered by bookmark services Reddit, Del.icio.us, Ma.gnolia, and Digg. Bookmark services are adding their own counters every day.

Readers can quickly see if a post has already been submitted to a service and can vote to increase or decrease the popularity of the post while still at the blog. We will add the popular del.icio.us dynamic bookmark and examine the features it offers. We will then explore and then explore using Feedburner Flare (`http://www.feedburner.com`) to show multiple counters easily.

Time for Action!—Adding Dynamic Links with Counters to Posts

1. Navigate to the **Edit HTML** screen on the blog, and click the **Expand Widget Templates** checkbox.

2. Type the following block of code directly above the `<p class='post-footer-line post-footer-line-2'>` tag in the template code, deleting any existing social bookmark code we added before:

```
<script type="text/javascript">if (typeof window.Delicious ==
        "undefined") window.Delicious = {};
        Delicious.BLOGBADGE_DEFAULT_CLASS = 'delicious-
        blogbadge-line';</script>
<script src="http://images.del.icio.us/static/js/
        blogbadge.js"></script>
```

3. **Save** the template, and view the blog to see the changes. An example of how it should look now is shown in the following screenshot:

4. Are there any differences between the information captured using this bookmark and others? Let's test the bookmark and find it out. Click on **bookmark this** on the del.icio.us button and review the results:

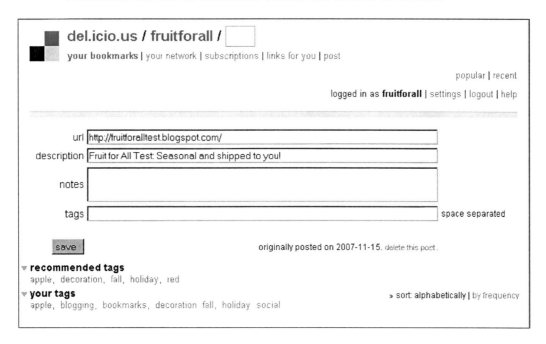

5. The bookmark does not display the actual post title and post URL. We will need to customize it to display that information when the reader submits the post.

What Just Happened?

We inserted a ready made counter bookmark script from the del.icio.us site into our template code. The first JavaScript code snippet will check to see if a link to del.icio.us already exists. If it does not, a special default CSS class is set to control the appearance of the badge. The code is shown for reference below:

```
<script type="text/javascript">if (typeof window.Delicious ==
        "undefined") window.Delicious = {};
        Delicious.BLOGBADGE_DEFAULT_CLASS =
        'delicious-blogbadge-line';</script>
```

Calling the code controlling the badge counter is done with the final script tag. It links to an external JavaScript file stored at the del.icio.us site.

```
<script src="http://images.del.icio.us/static/js/blogbadge.js">
        </script>
```

The script counts how many times readers have recommended the blog site to del.icio.us using their own script counter. The number shown will increase each time the site is bookmarked by someone on del.icio.us.

Adding Multiple Counter Scripts Simultaneously

What if we want to display multiple scripts for different bookmarks or social networking services? Adding them individually can be very frustrating with Blogger's current syntax for post titles and URLs. We can also do it the easy way and have the bonus of automatic feeds and site statistics using a service such as Feedburner (http://www.feedburner.com).

Time for Action—Add Multiple Counter Scripts with Feedburner Flare

1. Log into Feedburner (http://www.feedburner.com) and click on the **MyFeeds** link at the top of the page. Choose the **Optimize** tab and select **FeedFlare** from the left menu. Select the checkboxes next to each service you wish to add. You can choose to show some services on the site or the feed only. Checkout the items you will be able to see in the following screenshot:

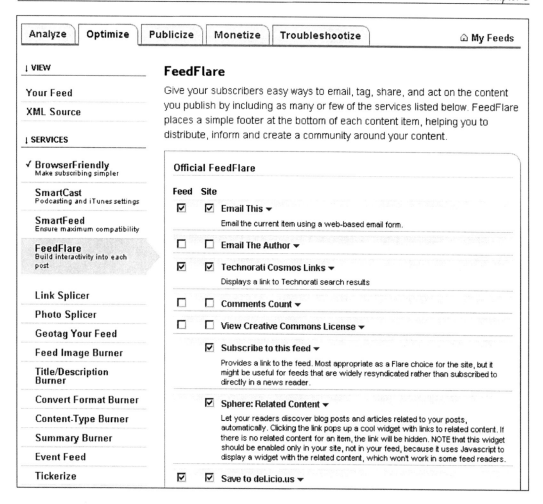

2. As we scroll down the list we will be able to see more services. We need to check the boxes next to Technorati, Digg, and Delicious. The **Personal FeedFlare** section will remain blank until we add a new flare. Reddit is not listed under the **Official FeedFlare** section as a service. So we will add it by typing in a link to an XML file found while clicking **Browse the Catalog**. Later on, when you have extra time, check out the catalog for many other FeedFlare choices. Go ahead and type this URL into the **Personal FeedFlare** textbox: `http://dmiessler.com/feedflare/reddit.xml`.

After clicking the **Add New Flare** button, the service will show up under the **Personal FeedFlare** section as shown in the following screenshot:

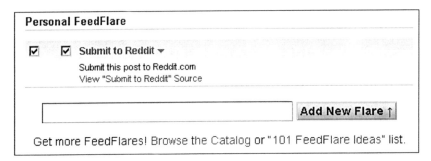

3. After selecting the **Reddit service** checkbox, scrolling down further will reveal the **FeedFlare Preview/Ordering** section. Drag and drop links into the order you wish to appear on the blog and the feed. When we are done, the service links will be in alphabetical order. Activate FeedFlare by clicking the **Activate** button at the bottom of the screen.

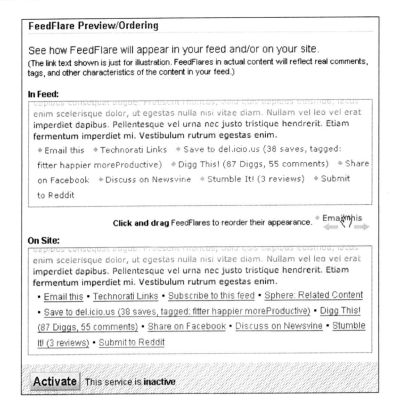

4. A success message appears at the top of the screen indicating that the feed was updated. Now, we are ready to add the FeedFlare code to our blog.

5. Scroll down to the bottom of the screen. A new drop-down option, **Get the HTML code to put FeedFlare on your site** has appeared. Select **Blogger** from the drop-down list. A new window will automatically open with the codes and instructions.

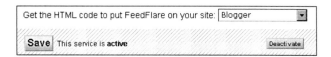

6. The new window contains basic instructions and codes which we can copy and paste into our blog. Scroll down and copy the code in the text area box under the **Editing Blogger "Layouts"** heading. Now, we need to paste it into our template code.

7. Just like with the other buttons and bookmark links before, we will click the **Edit HTML** link under the **Layout** tab of our blog, select the **Expand Widget Templates** checkbox, and paste the code just above the second post footer line `<p class='post-footer-line post-footer-line-2'>`. The code should look like:

```
<!-- social bookmark dynamic badges -->
  <script charset='utf-8' expr:
  src='"http://feeds.feedburner.com/~s/FruitForAllTestSeasonal
  AndShippedToYou?i=" + data:post.url' type='text/javascript'/>
<!-- end dynamic badges -->
```

8. Save the changes and view the blog. It may take a few minutes for the links to show up, since Feedburner processes them. Clear your browser's cache. Closing and restarting your browser may also help. The block of links will appear in an ordered set below the comments area. Counters will appear after the post has been submitted to an individual bookmark service. You can see an example of the links in the following screenshot:

Try them cut up in stuffing, with cream cheese and crackers, or roasted with main dishes such as turkey, duck, or chicken. They are also a great accent for stews.

0 comments Links to this post Posted by georgiaPeach at 8:50 PM

Email this • Technorati Links • Subscribe to this feed • Save to del.icio.us (1 save) • Digg This! • Share on Facebook • Discuss on Newsvine • Stumble It! (1 Reviews)

Labels: apple, fall, fruit, tangy

9. It's time to test the FeedburnerFlare code. Click the **del.icio.us** link to submit the post and view the results. The individual post title and URL are sent to the submission form just like we had intended. A copy of the submission form is displayed in the following screenshot:

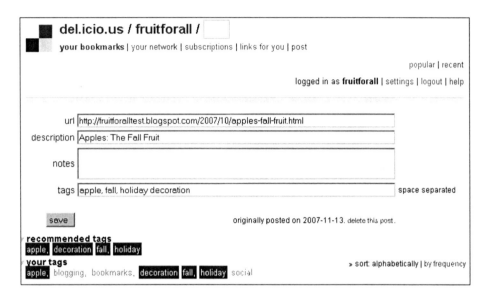

What Just Happened?

Using the del.icio.us Tagometer badge reveals to us that the information submitted was the general site title and description, and not the post title and post URL that we wanted. We took the easy route and installed multiple bookmark links with counter functionality using the FeedburnerFlare tool.

We selected the bookmark services we wanted and then activated the tool. The code for all the bookmark services was gathered by us. Once the FeedburnerFlare tool was successfully activated, we were able to copy an expression tag specifically designed for blogger:

```
<script charset='utf-8' expr:src='"http://feeds.feedburner.com/~s/
          FruitForAllTestSeasonalAndShippedToYou?i=
          " + data:post.url' type='text/javascript'/>
          </script>
```

Notice the `expr:src` attribute, which is a part of the syntax for blogger's XML template code. It converts a normal script containing link data into a tag specifically designed to be used in the template code. FeedburnerFlare tracks and updates the bookmark links using special dynamic code that communicates with the API (Application Program Interface) of each bookmark service. Every time a user submits a post to one of the bookmark services, the individual counters increase by one.

Visit the Feedburner forum (`http://forums.feedburner.com`) for more tips, common questions, and techniques.

Attracting Readers with Links

Georgia's blog is all about fruits. She has discovered that this is still a very broad topic. Creating interesting content that will attract new readers (also known as **link bait**) is vital to marketing her blog and her company. How can she figure out the different topics that visitors are really interested in? She can discover what content is spreading among people like a virus, by doing a little research.

What People are Tagging

Georgia is eager to create her own viral content. She wants to know what sort of "fruity" content people are most likely to bookmark. Searching `http://del.icio.us` for the tag "fruit" gives us the following results:

We see some expected results including recipes for making fruit salad and picking fruits. We also found several commercial sites offering fruit baskets and fruit drinks. Practical articles about fighting fruit flies and fruit labels also appeared in the results. Based on the results, it appears people are interested in sampling free fruits, protecting the fruit they have, and looking for new ways to enjoy fruits. Georgia now has more article ideas and additional related tags to search on. It is time to use the research to create an interesting content article.

Planning an Article

The goal is to create an article that a wide number of people might find useful, as well as attract visitors who would not normally go to a fruit related site. The content should deliver exactly what the title promised: *five interesting ways to use lemons to "clean green" every day*. Users will recommend the content they like. Taking care to match the content to the title also builds visitors trust. They will see you and your site as more reliable, which will build a positive relationship and encourage repeat visits.

Keywords should be used for the labels attached to the post. The labels are also known as "tags" in social bookmarking. They are the keywords and search terms people use to identify information, including blog posts, images, podcasts, and videos. Users can also subscribe to news feeds of labels. Any type of content posted to the web can be tagged.

We are going to perform the following tasks:

- Detail five ways to "clean green" in the content of the blog post.
- Use keywords as labels.
- Upload a descriptive image that matches the content.

Time for Action!—Create a Killer Article

Georgia decides to start with a more general article that will be useful to those looking for environment friendly alternatives for cleaning products. She writes a post focusing on using lemons for household cleaning.

1. Create a new post and enter the text **Five Reasons to Go Green with Lemons** in the title area.

2. Type the following text into the content portion of the post:

   ```
   Tart, bright, and shaped like a smile, the simple lemon is useful
   for a variety of purposes including decorating, cooking, and
   cleaning. Lemon is delicious in tea or a tall icy glass of
   lemonade. It adds tart zest to many dishes, even pancakes. Lemon
   ```

is also an eco-friendly household cleanser. Here are five ways to use this cheerful fruit every day.

- ° **Making Lemon Buttermilk:** Add a teaspoon of lemon for every 1/4 of milk to curdle milk for cooking. I use this method whenever I make pancakes.

- ° **It can be used instead of vinegar for windows.**

- ° **The acid in lemons is very effective at removing tough stains from stove tops.**

- ° **Using it as a drain cleaner is a biodegradable way to clean the kitchen pipes without using harsh chemicals. Drop three tablespoons of baking soda into the sink drain, then squeeze one cup of lemon juice onto the powder. It creates a chemical reaction with the soda, causing a fizzing that is fun to watch!**

- ° **Don't throw away the lemon rinds:** Use the drained lemons as cleaning pads. Sprinkle baking soda into the sink basin. Turn the lemon skins inside out so the fleshy inside will touch the surface of the sink. Scrub away until it shines.

The natural fresh scent the lemon leaves behind is a pleasant byproduct. Add a little lemon to your cleaning routine to go green.

3. Upload an attractive image that fits the content. We will use this closely cropped image of a cut lemon:

4. Publish the post. We aren't done yet. The labels need to be added to the post.

5. Open up the new post for editing and type the following keywords into the labels text entry field of the new post: lemons, environmental, environment friendly, lemonade, remove stains, biodegradable, green clean, lemon, tea, yellow, tart, fruit.

6. Are the labels we just assigned to the post effective? Do searches contain the phrases "lemon" and "eco-friendly cleaning"? The results show that we could have also used the following tags in the labels section of our post: howto, lemon tips, cleaning, organic, home, eco, sustainability.

What Just Happened?

When we created the title we used keywords to identify, clearly and briefly, what the post was about. Potential readers will often click a searched link based on the title alone. People interested in finding out more ways to clean using simple and effective natural products will be tempted to click the descriptive title.

We used the actual content in the post as a source for our keyword labels. This is an easy way to find meaningful keywords to use as labels. Next, we checked a couple of the keywords on the del.icio.us site to see if we found results related to our own post topic. We also used this opportunity to gather other labels to add to our own post. Labeling posts properly directly affects the easiness of potential readers to find your blog posts.

Feed readers, sort and present blog posts not just to people but to news aggregator services, search engines, and other web-based services. Discover the keywords potential readers use while searching for bookmarks and information by using services such as del.icio.us for research. Using keywords as labels will increase your chances of positive site traffic.

All social bookmarking sites have some type of labeling or tagging system. Visitors will be more likely to use the labels you want them to if you provide the labels with your posts.

Building an Audience with Regular Posts

Readers prefer sites that update on a regular basis. It is important to pick a post schedule and stick with it as much as possible. You will be seen as a more reliable source by posting consistently.

How do we pick one for Georgia's blog? Many blogs update every day. If there is no dedicated person, whose only job is to blog, it can be difficult to meet that expectation consistently. Many company blogs update once a week on a scheduled date, or rotate responsible bloggers. Special notices or updates would occur whenever there is time sensitive information to share.

Time for Action!—Develop a Post Schedule

Let's break it down as a chart. Create two columns on a piece of paper. Write "**Types of information**" in the column on the left and "**How often to post**" in the column on the right. Make a list of the different types of information you are posting on your blog. Are you focusing on only one type? The more time sensitive the information, the more frequently you should post.

Here is an example of a post schedule for different types of content:

Types of information	How often to post
Urgent news (Topics might include politics, Internet security, and celebrity gossip)	Several times a day
Online diary and daily progress log	Daily
Company news and weekly feature articles	Weekly
Longer, and more complex magazine style articles	Monthly

If you are using a feed service or if your users use a blog tracking service, keep in mind that updates that appear too frequently may overwhelm readers or cause them to "burn out" on the blog. The more time sensitive the information, the more often you should post. Weekly is a good place to start for most company blogs. Readers will get used to reading the blog once a week consistently. Georgia should start posting once a week, using Twitter (`http://www.twitter.com`) for sporadic news updates the rest of the time.

What Just Happened?

When you filled out your own post schedule chart, you set a deadline for regular posts. Whether daily, weekly, monthly, or once an hour, you committed yourself to posting consistently. Evaluating the types of content that were the most urgent gave you the chance to step back and have the content dictate the schedule.

Summary

Now you know how to add social bookmarks to your blog and focus your posts to attract readers. We explored the different ways to add bookmarks, how to choose the social bookmarking sites that are right for your blog, how to do social networking, and shape blog content into tasty morsels for visitors.

4
Joining the Blogosphere

It's possible to enjoy short term success without being part of the Blogosphere. But if you want to drive traffic to your site continuously over the long term, you need to join and participate in the Blogosphere. The **Blogosphere** is used either in admiration or in irritation by bloggers to talk about all blogs as a whole. We will explore the main tools which bloggers use to communicate with each other, attract other bloggers to our blog using different techniques, and become part of a blog network.

Backlinks, Trackbacks, & Pingbacks

Backlinks, Trackbacks, and Pingbacks are all different tools you can use to see who is linking to your blog posts. You can measure the success of your blog by the link relationships created with these tools. Blog networks, such as Technorati, use link relationships to rank blogs. The popular blogging platform, Wordpress, displays the links and partial posts created on other blogs that mention and link back to a Blogger's post. These specialized commentaries are called **Trackbacks**. Blogger has its own tool called Backlinks that you can use, as it is similar to Trackbacks. We will take a look, under the hood of Backlinks and see how they work, how to set them up, and learn how to make them an effective part of our blog.

Configuring Backlinks

You can configure Backlinks in Blogger in just two steps. Default Blogger templates already have Backlink code included. It just needs to be turned ON. Once the service is activated, it will scan blogs for links referring back to your blog.

Time for Action!—Activating the Backlinks Service

Activating backlinks is a simple, three step process. Follow these directions to activate the backlinks service:

- Log in at `Blogger.com` and click the **Settings** link under your blog title. Under the **Settings** tab, click on the **Comments** sub-tab and then scroll to the **Backlinks** radio button setting.

- Click **Show** so that Backlinks will be visible to visitors. Select **New Posts Have Backlinks** from the **Backlinks Default for Posts** drop-down box.

- Click **Save Settings** to finalize the change.

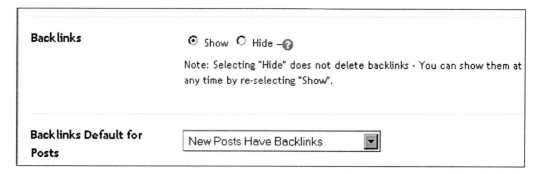

What Just Happened?

When we set the **Backlinks** option to **Show** from **Hide**, we made any backlinks that already exist or will exist in the future visible to our visitors. They are not deleted or added by using this setting. Note that it is also possible to choose whether new posts should have Backlinks or not. Turning Backlinks ON gives other bloggers an additional incentive to post, since more potential readers will be attracted to their sites.

Why You Need Backlinks

Tracking information such as, who has linked to your posts and is posting about your site will help you measure your success and your network with others. This is how the Blogger feature Backlinks works. It tracks the links made to posts automatically when it is turned ON, similar to the Trackbacks feature found in most blogging software. Let's compare Backlinks, Trackbacks, and Pingbacks:

	Backlinks	Pingbacks	Trackbacks
How it works	Protocol scans and sends information back to your blog when another person links to your post or blog, no matter what tracking tool they have set up. A summary of the information can be seen by your readers when the Backlinks feature is set to "Show" in your settings.	When a blogger links to your post, a signal is sent back to your blogging software. Your site code sends a return signal to verify whether the other site exists. The physical link is confirmed as live and valid. A physical link must exist.	Linking to your post, a blogger's site sends a signal back to your blog with basic information about their referring post. Readers can then follow the new connection made between your blogs. Does not require a physical link between the sites.
Advantage	Sends site name, URL, snippet of Backlink post, author, and date.	Less prone to spam attacks due to signal check.	Sends site name, URL, and post information. Most popular link back method.
Disadvantage	Person linking to your blog must use a Trackback or Backlink feature. You may have to submit your own trackbacks manually or by using a third-party tool, such as Haloscan.	Sends only URLs of sites which are pinging and being pinged. A person linking to your blog must use a Pingback feature.	A person linking to your blog must use a trackback feature or similar script.
Blogger feature?	Code unique to Blogger.	User can turn ON pings in settings.	Can be sent using a third-party site such as Haloscan.

Trackbacks Added Automatically

When a blogger, using Wordpress or another blog platform, links to your post, his or her response will appear under the **Links to this post** section of your post as backlinks automatically. Google indexes blogs continuously. So while it may take a few minutes, or even a few hours, their backlinks should appear like the one shown in the following screenshot:

November 20, 2007 7:07 PM 🗑

Post a Comment

Links to this post

▼ Natural refreshment and cleaning

Georgia mentions in her post
http://fruitforalltest.blogspot.com/2007/11/5-reasons-to-
How to use lemons in envionmentally friendly and healthy
ways. Lemons are also inexpensive.
Posted by leej07 at November 20, 2007 7:11 PM

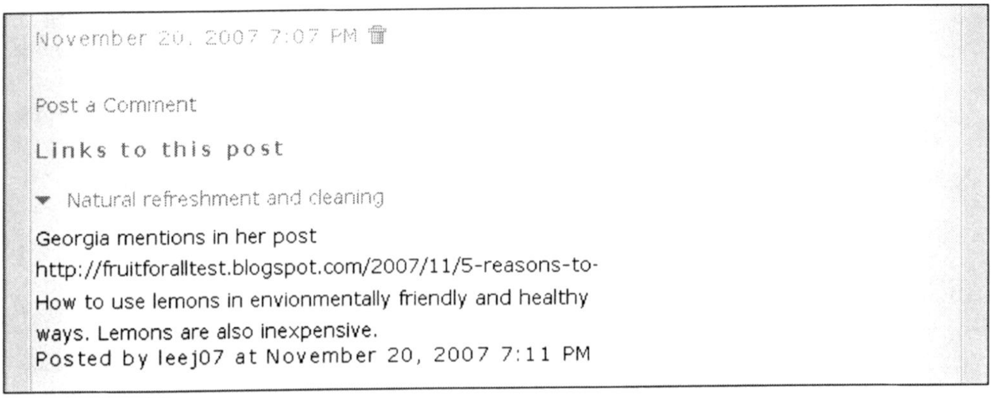

Clicking on the title of the blog article that the other person had posted will take you to their original post. It lists the user, time, and a post snippet. You don't need to worry about your posts not receiving backlinks from other blogs. One less technical detail to fret about!

Viewing Multiple Backlinks

Open up a browser and visit the Official Google blog (`http://googleblog.blogspot.com`). We are going to see what a list of backlinks looks like. Scrolling down to any of the posts, we can see a **Links to this post** text link. Click on it to find the possible backlinks visible for a post. You can go directly to individual post page shown in the following screenshot by typing the URL `http://googleblog.blogspot.com/2007/11/custom-search-goes-global.html#links` into your address bar.

The individual page of the post displays all the backlinks as a list of links, as shown in the preceding screenshot. When we click the tiny arrow next to a backlink, the details of the backlink will be displayed. Clicking on the title of a backlink will take us to the actual blog or site.

Being a Backlinker

Backlinking to other blogs increases your chances of being frequently backlinked. Visit other blogs and comment on them in your own posts by adding your own viewpoint or additional information. If you reach out to them first, you might be surprised to know how many times other bloggers visit your blog and also link back to your posts.

Maintaining Backlinks

Backlinks are added to your posts automatically once they are set up. But you need to make connections with other bloggers to encourage more traffic to your blog by finding new blogs to visit. Make it a habit to visit and post a selected number of blogs you like and want to share with your readers. You will see your readership and link relationships grow.

Time for Action!—Backlinking to a Blogger Blog

Blogger gives you multiple ways to create links back to blogs. This one is a little extra work, but will introduce you to the process so that you can get a strong grasp of how it works.

1. Click on the **Title** to view the full post. For example: the post we are Backlinking to is `http://zoeb-organic-weekly.blogspot.com/2007/11/ eco-friendly-wallets-by-db-clay.html`. Click on the **Create a link** text link under the **Links to this post** section on the individual post's page. In the following screenshot, we can see the **BlogThis** screen that appears when the link is clicked.

2. You are able to choose your blogs to post to from the drop-down list at the top of the BlogThis window. The **Title, Link,** and a link to the original post in the content window are added for you.

3. Type your blog post content and then click on **SAVE AS DRAFT** to save, or on **PUBLISH,** to publish your post.

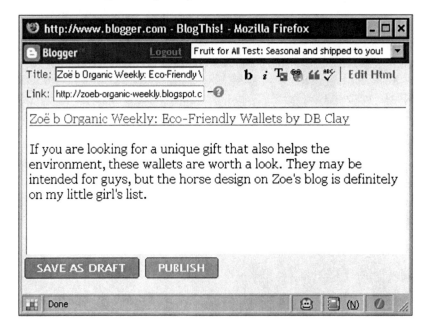

4. Your new post will show up on your site as a blog post and on the original Blogger site as a backlink, as shown in the following screenshot:

LINKS TO THIS POST

▼ Zoë b Organic Weekly: Eco-Friendly Wallets by DB Clay

Zoë b Organic Weekly: Eco-Friendly Wallets by DB Clay If you are looking for a unique gift that also helps the environment, these wallets are worth a look. They may be intended for guys, but the horse design on Zoe's blog is definitely ...
POSTED BY GEORGIA AT NOVEMBER 20, 2007 10:22 PM

GREEN BLOGS

Haute Nature

Eco Fabulous

Green Fertility

Live Paths

Organic Baby NZ

Green Parenting

What Just Happened?

When you visited a different Blogger blog, you were able to create a post and link back to the blog using Blogger's BlogThis form. Entering the details of your post and then publishing the post caused Blogger to send a message to the backlinked blog informing it of the backlink. The Blogger code scanned and automatically updated the post you linked to with your backlink information.

You can also insert a BlogThis Bookmarklet in your Google Toolbar. This will help you to blog about blogs that do not have a link under their posts. See: `http://betabloggerfordummies.blogspot.com/2007/11/backlinks-with-bob-and-alice.html`.

Using a Trackback Service

Third-party trackback services such as Haloscan, offer customized features for bloggers. If you want more control over your backlinks, using a trackback service may be right for you. Additional features include managing comments, trackback forms, and a forum to swap ideas with other members.

Time for Action!—Adding the Haloscan Trackback Service

Haloscan will give you a central place to manage you backlinks. Adding this service will also give you access to many of the features of Haloscan:

1. Navigate to the Haloscan site (`http://haloscan.com`) and sign up for their free service.

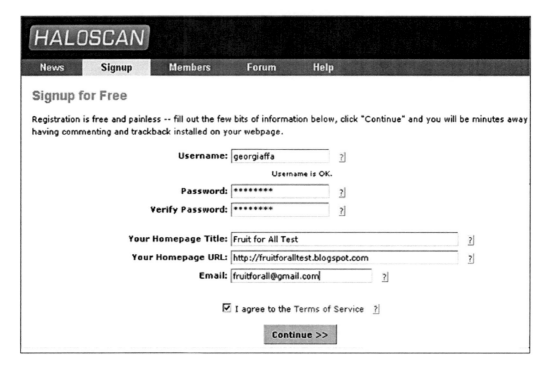

2. After your membership is confirmed, log in to the Haloscan service. You will see a small link labeled **Put this widget in your site**. Click on it to see the code for the widget appear in the window, as shown in the following screenshot:

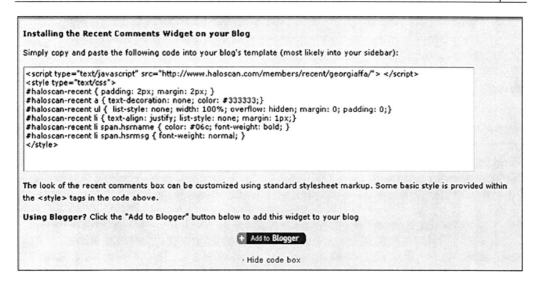

Installing the Recent Comments Widget on your Blog

Simply copy and paste the following code into your blog's template (most likely into your sidebar):

```
<script type="text/javascript" src="http://www.haloscan.com/members/recent/georgiaffa/"> </script>
<style type="text/css">
#haloscan-recent { padding: 2px; margin: 2px; }
#haloscan-recent a { text-decoration: none; color: #333333;}
#haloscan-recent ul {  list-style: none; width: 100%; overflow: hidden; margin: 0; padding: 0;}
#haloscan-recent li { text-align: justify; list-style: none; margin: 1px;}
#haloscan-recent li span.hsrname { color: #06c; font-weight: bold; }
#haloscan-recent li span.hsrmsg { font-weight: normal; }
</style>
```

The look of the recent comments box can be customized using standard stylesheet markup. Some basic style is provided within the <style> tags in the code above.

Using Blogger? Click the "Add to Blogger" button below to add this widget to your blog

⊕ Add to **Blogger**

· Hide code box

3. Since we're using Blogger, click the **Add to Blogger** button to see what happens.

4. Haloscan automatically creates a custom page element widget for us, and takes us to the screen to configure the widget. We can choose the blog to apply it to. The new widget is titled **Recent Comments**. You can type in a different title if you want to.

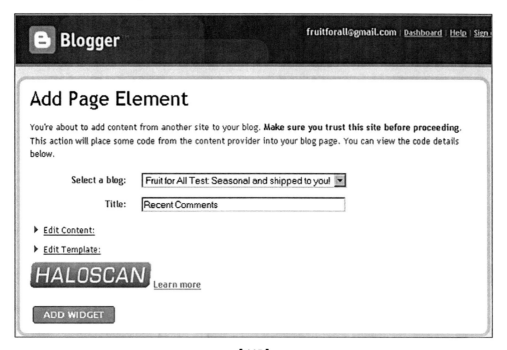

5. We can drag and drop the new page element to arrange it on the blog template. The free version will list all recent comments to the blog in the sidebar.

What Just Happened?

When we signed up for the Haloscan service, we included the URL of our main blog. Haloscan used scripts to gather a list of our blogs and then automatically added information about them on our membership page. When we clicked the **Add to Blogger** link, we had the option to add the Haloscan widget code ourselves or use their integration feature to have Haloscan create a custom page element for us. We were able to edit the new page element and add it to our blog.

Any time a reader comments on one of our posts, it will show up in a link list in the sidebar of the blog. Readers are more likely to comment if they see other comments. You will be able to easily manage comments for backlinks using your Haloscan account.

Trackbacking Non-Blogger Blogs

It can be frustrating when you write an article about a post on a different blog, and that site doesn't list it as a trackback. Wordpress blogs do not automatically pick up backlinks from Blogger blogs. Using Haloscan's link back service will ensure that your posts show up as a trackback.

Time for Action!—Trackbacking with Haloscan

You will need to create an account with Haloscan and have the links ready for you to trackback. Storing them in a text file or using Google's Notebook (`http://www.google.com/notebook/`) browser tool keeps your links close at hand.

1. Log in to Haloscan and click on **Members | Manage Trackback | Send a Trackback Ping**. Fill out the trackback form as shown in the following screenshot. Be very careful to fill out the full Trackback URI for Wordpress blogs. It is usually the individual post page with an additional **/trackback** added at the end:

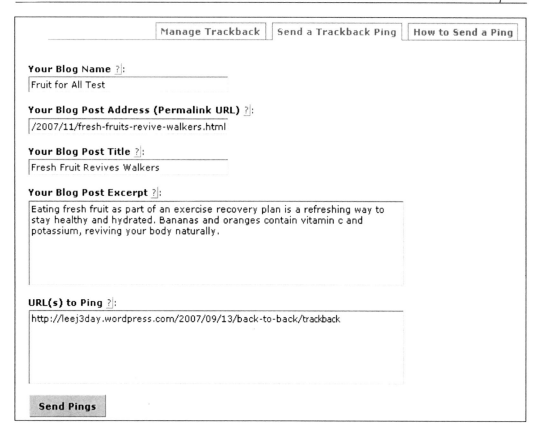

2. After you have sent the ping, a success message will be displayed:

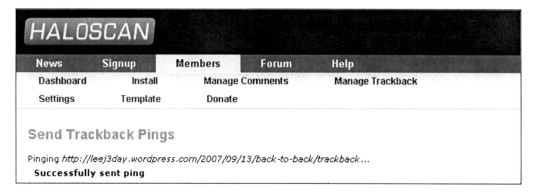

3. You can then go check the other blog for your trackback. We can see the trackback we sent on the Wordpress post in the following screenshot:

One Response to "Back to Back"

1 Fruit for All Test   edit this on November 21, 2007 at 7:48 pm

Fresh Fruit Revives Walkers

Eating fresh fruit as part of an exercise recovery plan is a refreshing way to stay healthy and hydrated. Bananas and oranges contain vitamin c and potassium, reviving your body naturally.

 You can also send multiple trackbacks of the same post, just by listing them on the Haloscan form. This saves time if your article mentions several blog posts.

What Just Happened?

We filled out the form with our blog URL, post title, post URL, and an excerpt from our post. We then added the addresses we wanted to ping in the **URL(s) to ping** box. We took extra care to enter the full trackback URI (Uniform Resource Identifier) for the original post where we want our trackback to appear.

Haloscan then processed our request and sent a trackback ping to the Wordpress blog in a format that it recognized. Our trackback was accepted by the blog and added underneath the post. The original poster and any of her readers could then see our response to the post and visit our post on our blog. Traffic will be sent to the original blog from our site and vice-versa.

Blogrolls

Listing other blogs on your site in a more permanent blogroll list is another way to build link relationships with other bloggers. Adding links that relate to the topic of your blog is easy to do with Blogger. Taking a look at the **Official Google Blog** (`htttp://googleblog.blogspot.com`) is one way of using a blogroll:

More Google Blogs

AdWords API blog
AdWords Retail Tips
AJAX Search API blog
Analytics 日本版 公式ブログ
Android Developers Blog
Blogger Buzz
Blogger Buzz (Español)
Blogs of Note
Blogs of Note (Español)
Custom Search Engine blog
Google AdSense China Blog
Google Analytics blog
Google Base blog

Google uses a blogroll to show a list of links to other Google blogs the reader can visit. Blogrolls can be used to organize link lists when you want to have multiple groups of links on your blog. Now that we have an idea of what they look like, let's set one up.

Setting up Blogrolls

Georgia is looking for her first set of blogroll links. She decides to do a search for "organic fruit" on Technorati to see what other fruit blogs out there look like. After performing her search she sees the following results:

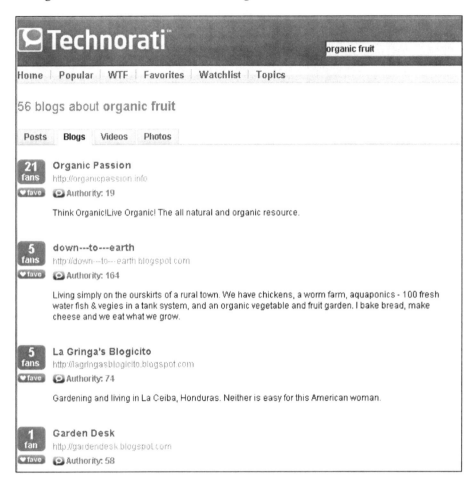

She finds three blogspot blogs in the top five of her results. She will check the links and if they are a good match for her blog, she will prepare to add them to her new blogroll.

Some blogging platforms include a list of sample blogs for you, called a **blogroll**. Blogger gives you the minimum number of page element widgets possible in the default templates: a profile and a blog archive. The designers of Blogger decided that you could choose whether to add a list of links or not. Let's use a link of a page element to add our own blogroll.

Time for Action!—Adding a Blogroll Widget

Blogger has a page element that can be used for creating a list of links for any purpose, including a blogroll. We are going to configure the **Link List** of a page element as a blogroll.

1. Log in at Blogger.com and click the **Layout** link under your blog title on the **Dashboard**. Navigate to the **Page Elements** sub-tab by selecting it. Click the **Add a Page Element** link on the sidebar portion of the **Page Elements** screen.

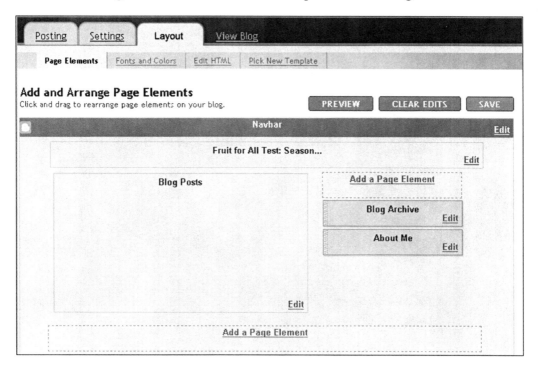

2. The **Choose New Page Element** window will pop-up. Click **ADD TO BLOG** below the **Link List** widget. The **Configure Link List** window will replace the **Choose New Page Element** window.

3. Using the dynamic **Configure Link List** form shown in the following screenshot, create a title for the list. Leave the **Number of links to show in list** box blank for now, so that all links we add are displayed. Select **Sort Alphabetically** from the **Sorting** drop-down box.

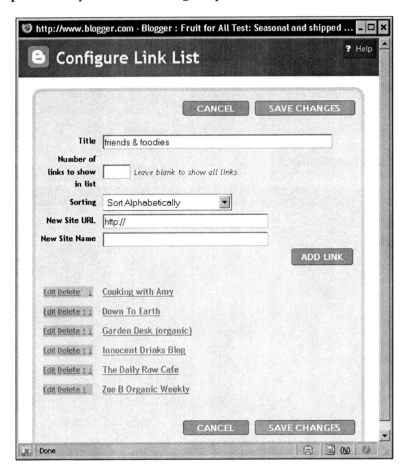

4. Add each link one at a time, entering first the URL, then the name that will appear to visitors, and then click on **ADD LINK**. The newly added link will appear at the bottom of the window. Once multiple links are added, you can edit, delete, or reorder them.

5. When you are finished with adding links, click the **SAVE CHANGES** button, clear your browser's cache, and view the blog to see the new list. An example of how it will look is shown in the following screenshot. Notice the links are arranged alphabetically below the title of the page element.

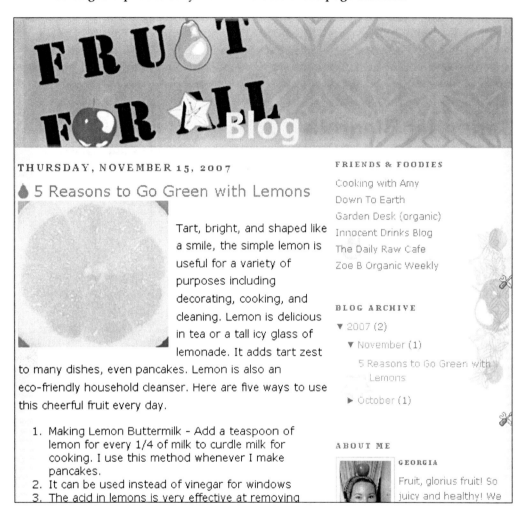

THURSDAY, NOVEMBER 15, 2007

5 Reasons to Go Green with Lemons

Tart, bright, and shaped like a smile, the simple lemon is useful for a variety of purposes including decorating, cooking, and cleaning. Lemon is delicious in tea or a tall icy glass of lemonade. It adds tart zest to many dishes, even pancakes. Lemon is also an eco-friendly household cleanser. Here are five ways to use this cheerful fruit every day.

1. Making Lemon Buttermilk - Add a teaspoon of lemon for every 1/4 of milk to curdle milk for cooking. I use this method whenever I make pancakes.
2. It can be used instead of vinegar for windows
3. The acid in lemons is very effective at removing

FRIENDS & FOODIES

Cooking with Amy
Down To Earth
Garden Desk (organic)
Innocent Drinks Blog
The Daily Raw Cafe
Zoe B Organic Weekly

BLOG ARCHIVE

▼ 2007 (2)
  ▼ November (1)
    5 Reasons to Go Green with Lemons
  ► October (1)

ABOUT ME

GEORGIA

Fruit, glorius fruit! So juicy and healthy! We

What Just Happened?

When we added each link, it became a part of our link list widget. After we saved the changes, the new widget was added to the blog template. You can add or manage your new blogroll widget by returning to the layout template view and clicking the edit button. The **Configure Link List** window will then appear. If you've added the wrong link or gave it the wrong URL or title, you can change the blogroll link as easily as using the edit or delete links next to each item. The links on the list can be moved up or down by clicking on the arrows shown next to them in the **Configure Link List** window.

Caring for Blogrolls

Sooner or later, a blogroll needs tending, just like a garden. Dead links should be weeded out, and new links should be added to keep it fresh. Nurture your blogroll. Choose links to blogs that relate to your topic. Recommend links that you enjoy visiting or reading to your own visitors.

Linkbaiting Bloggers

Enticing bloggers with creative and sometimes deceptive links or content, also known as **Linkbaiting**, is a popular technique. The term is often used to describe misleading ways of luring bloggers. But like any technique, it is a tool that can also be used positively. You can see the same technique used by magazines and newspapers to attract readers.

Bloggers are always hungry to add more content to their blogs. Creating content with other bloggers in mind will increase traffic to your blog and build link relationships. You can attract their attention with unique story angles or controversies, or provide content-rich articles, which they can mine for their own blogs.

Attract Attention

Other bloggers will find a unique response to a story or a controversial viewpoint hard to resist. How can you take an average story and look at it another way?

Find a Unique Story Angle

Explore a hot topic from a different perspective. There were many stories about the iPhone when it first came out; almost all of them were rave reviews. There were very few articles that took the time to discuss what it was like for different segments of the population. Did senior citizens find the iPhone easier to use than regular phones, because of the touch screen and friendly interface? If other bloggers are all sounding alike, looking for a new twist or approach to a topic will make you stand out.

Create Controversy

Take a stand on an issue important to your readers. Blogs are opinionated by their very nature, unlike newspaper articles which attempt a more neutral approach. Be an advocate of the underdog, or take a stand on an issue that resonates with you.

For example, Georgia could write a post "Big fruit industry squeezes organic farms", about how local organic fruit farms are being fined by the city and county governments in water restricted areas, while big fruit industry farms are unaffected.

Provide Richer and Deeper Content

Bloggers turn to each other for inspiration and sources for content. In a blogosphere cluttered with short summary posts, a blog providing rich content is as welcome to other bloggers as a slice of chocolate cheese cake topped with fresh strawberries.

Here are two ways to encourage other bloggers to read and share your posts:

- Writing about complex topics
- Creating serial articles

Let's talk about these techniques in a little more detail.

Writing about Complex Topics

Bloggers spend a lot of time scouring the Internet for complex stories to dissect and explain to their readers. Creating posts about complicated topics that other bloggers can summarize, share on user generated news services, and their own blogs, will expose your blog to more potential readers.

Creating Serial Articles

Keep readers coming back for more with articles that span several posts. This is a technique popular with newspaper journalists. Other bloggers will have a dependable source of frequently updated content to pull from for their own posts. Readers who visit your blog will be encouraged to read multiple articles, create more traffic, and more potential ad revenue or product sales.

Technorati and Other Blog Networks

Blog networks expose your blog to more readers through recent update lists, category sorting, and most importantly by ranking your blog against other blogs. Technorati is the best known and the most popular of the bunch.

How Blog Networks Work

The higher your rated link relationship or popularity is, and the more the exposure you get from blog networks, the higher your own traffic will be. More bloggers will visit your blog when it is listed on a blog network. The blog networks benefit through increased ad revenue when more visitors come to their site.

Time for Action!—Exploring Technorati

To fully explore Technorati, you'll want to sign up for an account. Signing up for a Technorati account is easy.

1. Click on the **Join** link from the home page (http://technorati.com) or navigate to http://technorati.com/signup/. Choose a member name, enter your email address, and choose a password. Place a check on the box next to **I agree to....**Finally click on the **Join** button to finish signing up.

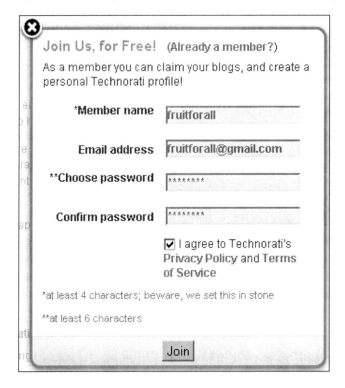

2. You will then be redirected to the member page. Note that you can view lists of top posts, blogs, videos, and photos by popularity, topic, searching, or become mesmerized by the newly updated list on the main page.

3. Technorati ranks blogs by member votes and link relationships. When a member likes a post, blog, video, or photo, they can mark it as a **fave**. Each item has a box next to it displaying the number of members who voted it a fave as **fans**. The authority of the item is calculated by Technorati based on the number of links to it from other sites. This affects its ranking. We can see an example of this in the following screenshot:

4. The **Organic Passion** blog has 21 fans and an **Authority** of 19. It is the top search result on Technorati under blogs for **organic fruit**.

What Just Happened?

Joining Technorati gives you another way to connect with other bloggers and measure the success of your blog. Users of Technorati can find content in multiple ways: based on searches, topics, popularity, and by content type. We saw that Technorati ranks blogs, using not just user rankings, but also link relationships. The more other bloggers use your site as a reference, the higher is your blog's authority rating.

Technorati displays the number of fans, the title of the blog, the URL, the authority rating, and a brief description of the blog. Technorati is unique as compared with many other network sites. It has separate category rankings for posts, blogs, videos, and photos which give you multiple ways to gain exposure for your blog.

Summary

Bloggers are attracted to blogs in a manner different from other Internet users. They gain reputation on sites and in the blogosphere by responding to a constant stream of information. We got a grip on backlinks, blogrolls, and other tools that bloggers use to create link relationships in the blogosphere. Next, we will work on more creative ways to add useful tools to your blog, including slide shows, polls, video clips, and third-party widgets to publicize your blog.

5
Using Widgets

Widgets help you interact with customers better and attract people to your site. They hook readers with rich, tasty, interactive content, and compel them to tell their friends too about your blog. We will explore how widgets can help improve your customer service, add rich media content to your site, and increase revenue.

We are going to explore the widgets, group by group, have a little fun, and see what we can do with them. We've already covered adding social bookmarking widgets in the previous chapters, so that this time, we'll give our full attention to all the other types of widgets out there.

Adding a Blogger Page Element Widget

Blogger comes with a variety of page element widgets easy to add to your layout. You can add the widgets to any part of the layout where you see an "Add a page element" block. Adding Blogger widgets isn't rocket science. To start, let's go over the basics of adding a page element widget.

Time for Action!—Add a Photo Slideshow Widget

The **Slideshow** page element widget in Blogger can display photos from popular sites such as Flickr, Picasa, and Photobucket. Any service that can transmit information about your image files in an XML feed format can also be used in the slideshow.

1. Log in to your Blogger blog and click the **Layout** link under your blog on the **Dashboard**. You will be taken to the **Page Elements** area under the **Layout** tab by default. Under the **Page Elements** area, click the **Add a new Page Element** link located on the sidebar.

2. A new window will open with a list of Blogger page element widgets. Click the **ADD TO BLOG** button under the Slideshow widget. The following screenshot shows how the **Slideshow** page element widget appears on the **Choose a New Page Element** screen.

3. This widget has many options to choose from. Type **Current Specials** in the **Title** box. After you enter a title, you will need to select a photo service. The choices are **Picasa**, **Flickr**, **Photobucket**, and **other source**. Choose **Flickr** from the drop-down box.

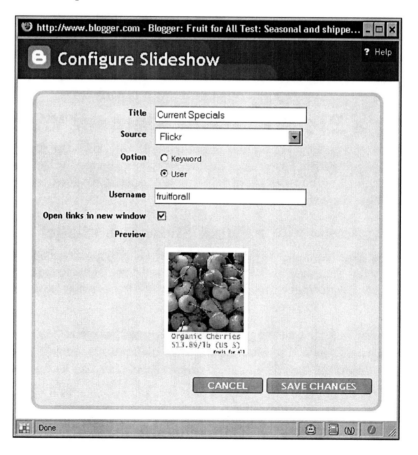

4. We are going to pull images directly from Georgia's *Fruit for All* Flickr account; so select the **User** option. Next, we type the **Username** for her Flickr account.

5. Check the **Open links in new window** box. The **Preview** pane at the bottom has been changing while we make our choices. Pretty cool, huh? Save the changes, and the widget is done. We can now see the slideshow on the right side of the blog.

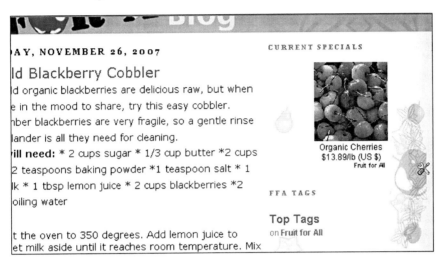

What Just Happened?

When we added the Slideshow widget, there were a lot of options to choose from. The source we chose dynamically changed the form. We could have chosen a Picasa Web Album, a Photobucket keyword slideshow, or a feed from another source instead of a Flickr slideshow. Choosing a user gave us the ability to specify a particular person's collection of Flickr photos. The keyword option would have given us no control over what photos would appear in our stream.

Setting the photo links to open in a new window will keep our blog open, making it easier for readers to get back to it. The photo links will open up the public page of the Flickr account. The widget can be edited or deleted by clicking the **Edit** link on the **Layout** screen. You can drag and drop the widget to a different position too.

Users can easily control the slideshow by hovering their cursor over it. They will be given the options to pause, go forward, or backward in the slideshow.

Widgets Your Readers Want

There are four types of widgets. You've got social bookmarking widgets, community, e-commerce, and multimedia. Your readers may not know that they want a widget, but you can tell by the questions and comments you get. The following chart shows how you can respond to your visitors' needs with widgets. We are also going to create our own custom widget later in the chapter. It's not as hard to do as it sounds. We're going to have a whole lot of fun doing it.

Reader	You	Widget Type
I want to chat online with you about my order…	No Problem! I have a meebo me (http://www.meebo.com) chat widget here on the blog. Go ahead and ask. I'll answer you, even if I'm using Yahoo, and you are using AIM.	Community
Can you show me how to make Skillet Apple Crisp?	Yes! Take a look at my YouTube (http://www.youtube.com) video on the right side of the blog posts.	Multimedia
Where can I buy a skillet?	Cookware items are right here on the Amazon product block.	E-commerce
When will the Florida oranges be available?	You can follow my Twitter (http://www.twitter.com) messages here or at the Twitter site.	Community
I love those recipes. Can I add them to my blogspot blog?	Sure. Click the add to Blogger icon on the sidebar.	Community
So you have photos and prices for your fruit?	Check them out on the Flickr slideshow.	Multimedia

Widgets are most useful when they fulfill a need you or your readers have. Can you think of a recent feedback from your own readers that you can turn into opportunities? Blogger contains a lot of default page element widget blocks and they are adding new ones all the time. Now that you know the basics of adding a Blogger widget, you are ready to try a third-party widget, like the Twitter badge on the chart above.

Adding a Custom Third-party Widget

Third-party widgets can be pasted into the **HTML/JavaScript** page element in Blogger. Many of them require only being able to copy and paste. Your blog will look better and more professional if you know how to customize your badges and other widgets.

As other people may be looking for you by email address or name on community sites, try using the same one every time while promoting your blog.

Twitter text updates add a more personal feel to your blog keeping it fresh with time sensitive news. You can send text messages using the Twitter website, your IM, or by phone. Twitter has badges you can use on your blog to show your most recent text message updates. Sending a brief message to Twitter will update any other site where you have a Twitter badge installed. They tend to look like buttons or clip on badges and are usually rectangular or square-shaped.

We're using Twitter as it is popular, easy to use, and has a growing list of third-party support applications including GoogleTalk. You will be able to easily keep friends, and visitors updated on what you are doing wherever you are. Let's add a Twitter badge to our blog so that we can share time-sensitive updates about news or specials.

Time for Action!—Add a Twitter Badge

We will create a free Twitter account, and then build a custom badge on the Twitter site. Then we will install the badge on our Blogger blog as a page element widget.

1.   It's very easy to sign up for Twitter, if you haven't already. Choose a username and an email address that will lead people back to your blog. Georgia used **fruitforall** as her Twitter username. Give them your name, email address, username, and you're on.

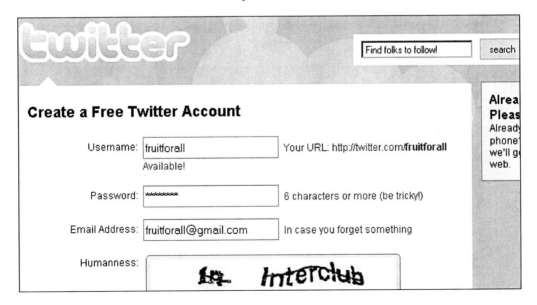

2. Start adding updates by typing into the big text box under the **What are you doing?** heading. You are limited to 140 characters. Each update is date and time stamped. After you click the **update** button, the message will appear below the **update** box as shown in the following screenshot:

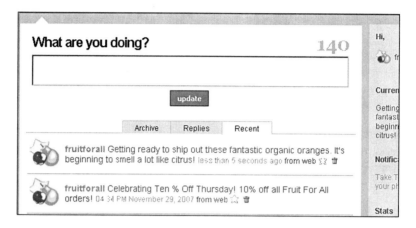

3. The badges can be found at `http://twitter.com/badges/`. Choose **Blogger** from the list. You will be redirected to a Twitter badge wizard page. Twitter will show us a dynamic view of our badge on the right while we make changes.

4. We are choosing to show only the latest text update by selecting **1** from the **Number of updates** drop-down list. We can change the title of the badge from **Twitter Updates** to **What's Happening** by typing our new title in the text field. Click the **Add to Blogger** button to launch the Blogger page element installer.

5. A custom page element window will appear with the Twitter badge already configured. Select the blog you want to use from the **Select a blog** drop-down list. If you have changed your mind about the title of the badge, you can change it too. We are keeping the title we chose in the previous step. Click **ADD WIDGET** to add the badge to your blog.

Add Page Element

You're about to add content from another site to your blog. **Make sure you trust this site before pro** This action will place some code from the content provider into your blog page. You can view the cod below.

Select a blog: Fruit for All Test: Seasonal and shipped to you!

Title: What's happening:

▶ Edit Content:

▶ Edit Template:

Learn more

ADD WIDGET

6. We can now see the Twitter updates on the sidebar of the blog. The Twitter badge uses the font and colors set in our template. The time the message was posted is displayed directly below the text. Did you notice the **follow me on Twitter** link? Visitors can impulsively add you to the list of people they follow on Twitter.

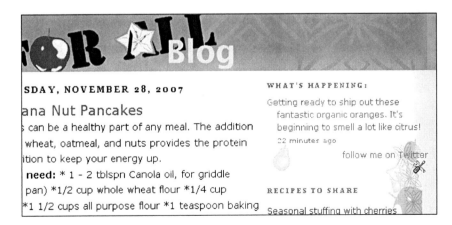

What Just Happened?

Adding a Twitter badge made us cooler and more in touch with our readers. Now you can send updates to Twitter using IM, SMS, or the Twitter site. The messages will then display on the Twitter site, and you have placed a Twitter badge everywhere. Readers of the blog will see instant text bites, making it ideal to announce specials, site issues, or other brief updates. If you want, you can customize your Twitter page and brand it with your own colors or background image. Take a look at other Twitter blogs for some fun ideas.

Adding Interactive Third-Party Widgets

Giving your readers the option to interact with your blog opens up a whole new way for them to communicate with you. The blog becomes more interactive, and you become a real person to them. You will be able to respond quicker to feedback about posts. Readers who are members of the same social networking site you use can add you to their network of friends. Your live interactions with your readers will build loyalty and turn them into repeat readers.

Interacting with Visitors Using Chat

You can talk to your visitors in real time when they visit your blog, instead of waiting for comments, and have a log of your conversations with a chat widget. Talking to visitors who have different chat clients is no problem using the meebo me widget. This free tool gives you an easy way to add customer service to your blog.

Time for Action!—Installing a MeeboMe Chat Widget

Before you begin installing the meebo me widget, you must have an account with Meebo. After you have a Meebo account you can customize and install the **meebo me** widget just as we are about to do now.

1. Log in to Meebo (www.meebo.com) and click the **meebo me** link on the home page, or you can use this link http://www.meebome.com.

2. Time to choose a title for our widget. Type **Let's talk fruit** in the title box. We are going to display Georgia's name in the **Display name** box. The following screenshot shows the numbered progress buttons above the widget form. The title of the widget and the display name of the primary user are also shown on the form located on the left side of the screen.

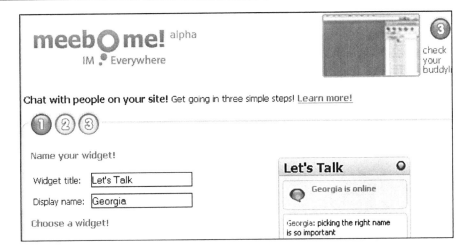

3. Choose the widget size by selecting **small** from the **Choose a Widget!** radio option. Note that you can also set a custom size for the widget. The following screenshot shows the different options for size and color, and also the preview of the changes to the right of the widget form, as you make your selections.

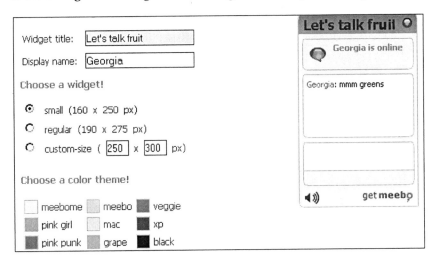

4. Click the **Customize it...** link under the color themes to change the colors on other areas of the widget. We can now see the **Custom Colors** editor. Let's change the title text to a higher contrast color, such as yellow. Click on the block of color next to **Title Text**. A color picker will appear. Select light yellow and then click the **Next** button to continue. You can even enter a hexadecimal color value in the **rgb** box, instead of using the color picker.

5. The **Congratulations** page is the last step of the meebo me widget. We have now finished creating our widget in Meebo. Time to copy the widget code, which should look like this:

```
<!-- Beginning of Meebo me widget code.
     Want to talk with visitors on your page?
        Go to http://www.meebome.com/ and get your widget! -->
<embed src="http://widget.meebo.com/mm.swf?pAqaziaNYZ"
       type="application/x-shockwave-flash" wmode="transparent"
       width="160" height="250"></embed>
```

6. Grab the widget code, log in to Blogger, and click the **Layout** link under your blog on the **Dashboard**.

7. You should now be on the **Page Elements** sub-tab under the **Layout** tab. Click the **Add a New Page Element** link on the sidebar. Paste the code into a Blogger **HTML/JavaScript** page element and then save it. Try chatting for a while. We can see it in action in the following screenshot:

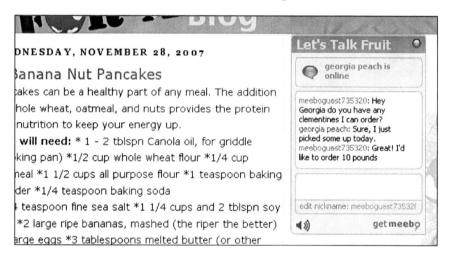

What Just Happened?

When we added the meebo me widget, we actually embedded the link to a small flash application. The widget showed up in your Meebo Buddy window as a new group. Immediately after, visitors were able to begin chatting with you.

You must be logged into Meebo to use the widget to interact with others. Meebo widgets can be maintained at the Meebo website. Click on the **meebo me** widget link on the home page after you log in. A new window will appear in the middle of your screen like the one shown:

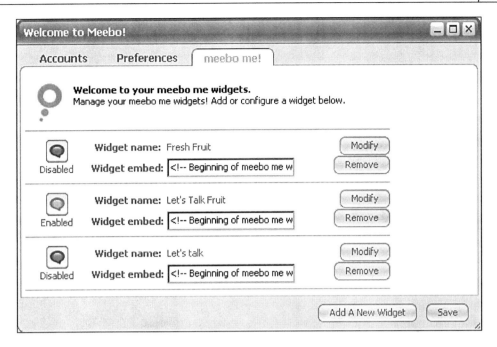

You can disable and enable widgets using the buttons on the left side of the screen. You can also modify, remove, or create widgets using the buttons on the **meebo me!** tab.

Social Network Badges

Social networks give you another way to market your blog, and connect you with readers. Your blog can share your social network information with badge widget. You can even use it in place of the **Profile** widget on Blogger. You can use a Facebook badge in its default format or customize it to display a profile image and other Facebook Items. Let's make it look more like the Blogger **Profile** page element widget.

Time for Action!—Mimicking a Blogger Profile with a Facebook Badge

You can choose from the many different blocks of information to customize what is displayed on your Facebook badge. Using this badge instead of the default Blogger profile page element will give you greater flexibility on the information you share about yourself with your readers.

1. First you need a Facebook account. Log in to Facebook (`http://www.facebook.com`) and go to the badges page (`http://www.facebook.com/badges.php`) to see your own badge. It is automatically created for you with default settings. The `JavaScript` version is the one we will use on the blog. If you didn't want to use the `JavaScript` version of the badge, you could grab the `image` version instead.

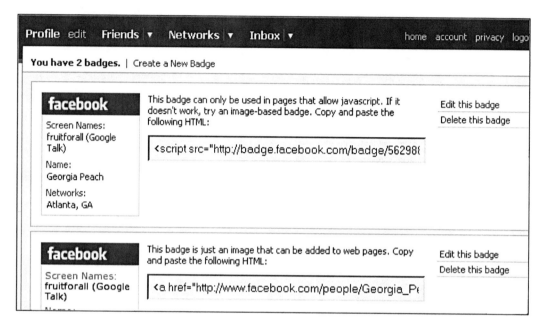

2. Click **Edit this badge** to open up the **edit** screen. You can customize the layout, format, and items that display on the badge. Select the **Horizontal** layout to change the shape of the badge from vertical to horizontal. Next, choose the **JavaScript** format of the badge. The **Profile picture**, **Name**, and **Networks** have been selected on each of the **Items** drop-down box, as shown in the following screenshot. You can add additional items by clicking the **Add Item** button. When you are done with editing the badge, click the **Save** button.

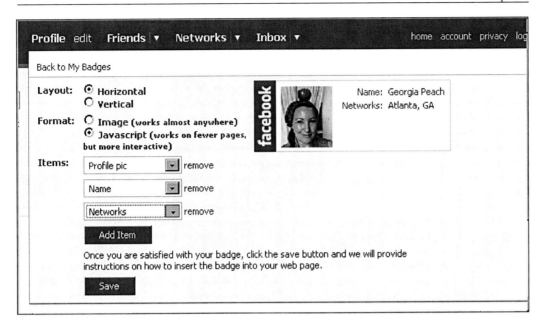

3. The revised badge screen will appear with an update success message. The code for the badge will be displayed next to the badge in a text field.

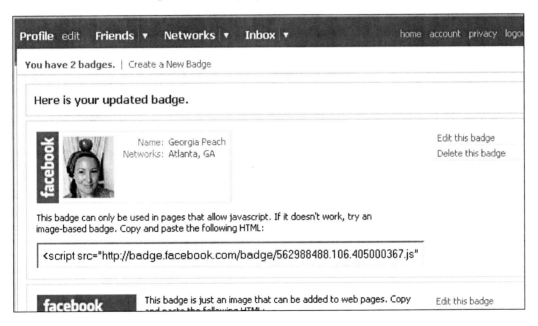

4. We are happy with the changes for now, so it is time to copy the code. It should look similar to the code shown below:

```
<script src="http://badge.facebook.com/
        badge/562988488.106.405000367.js"></script><noscript>
<a href="http://www.facebook.com/people/
    Georgia_Peach/562988488">Georgia Peach's Facebook
    profile</a></noscript>
```

5. Log in to Blogger, go to the **Layout | Page Elements** screen and add a new **HTML/JavaScript** page element. Paste the copied code into the content box on the page element's configuration screen. We have given it the title, **About Georgia**, using text similar to a typical profile.

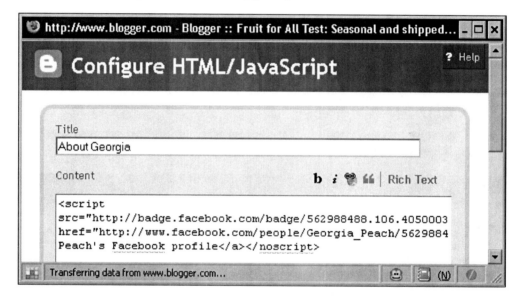

6. The **Facebook** badge will now appear on the blog. The wide format is just small enough to fit the sidebar of the blog. Remember, you can edit the items displayed on the badge anytime by logging into Facebook and visiting their badges page.

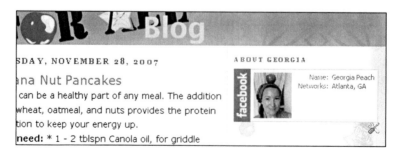

What Just Happened?

Your Facebook account contains a lot more information about you than a Blogger profile does. When we created the Facebook badge, we were able to customize the items we wanted to display. To make it look more like a Blogger profile, we displayed a portrait image, name, and the Facebook networks that Georgia belongs to. Clicking on the image or Facebook logo will take people directly to Georgia's Facebook page.

E-commerce with Blogger

Having a way to sell your own products from your blog or bringing in additional income is a must have for professional bloggers. Business owners and freelancers know the readers who like your blog, and are more likely to purchase a book, t-shirt, or organic fruit gift basket on impulse, given the opportunity. Products for sale are usually displayed on the left or right sidebar of a blog. E-commerce tools such as PayPal and Amazon Affiliate widgets can be used with Blogger. There are many more, but adding them usually follows the same process.

Using Product Sales Widgets

The easiest way to sell items on your blog is by using product sales widgets. You can sell products offered by other companies as an affiliate member and gain a small percentage of each sale. Selling your own products using PayPal or specialized widgets from Amazon is another option.

You will need an account with the e-commerce site you are participating with before you can add their widgets to your blog. We'll start with Amazon Affiliates and then graduate to using Paypal with our blog. Google Adsense and other advertising programs are also useful. Jump to Chapter 7 of this book to learn more about using them with your blog.

Offering Products as an Amazon Affiliate

I'm sure you've seen those Amazon product blocks on blogs. Amazon has an affiliate product network. It offers many different styles of widgets and types of products that can be customized to your content niche. Let's add one to our blog.

Time for Action!—Add an Amazon Affiliate Widget

Using an Amazon Affiliate widget requires you to first join their Affiliate program. Open a web browser and type in the URL `https://affiliate-program.amazon.com`) to sign up.

1. You must become an Affiliate member to use the service. Fill out the form and then review the terms of service. Continue to the widget screen.

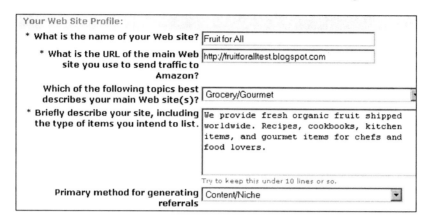

2. There are several different options to choose from: **Product Links, Recommended,** and **Omakase.** Don't worry if none of them seems to fit you. Once you have created your account, there will be many more types of widgets to choose from. We will try the third option, **Omakase.** It will automatically serve products to our blog that match the topic and content of our posts.

3. There are a lot of choices here on the widget creation screen. First, we need to set our options under **Select Template Style**. We are going to show **Amazon. com** as a logo. We want people to see samples of the delectable fruit that Georgia has for sale. So, choose **Show product images** from the **Product Images** drop-down box.

4. Select a smaller **Banner Size, 120x240**. Choose **New window** for **Clicked Link to Open in**. The colors of the widget can be customized on the right under **Select Template Colors**. We change the **Border color** to lighter grey, and the **Link color** to bright green.

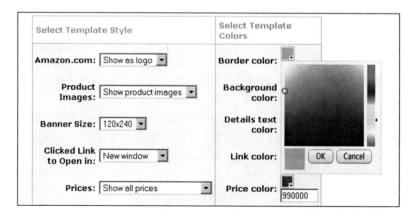

5. After customizing the widget, scroll further down the window and copy the code. It should look similar to this:

```
<script type="text/javascript">
<!--amazon_ad_tag="fruitforall-20"; amazon_ad_width = "120";
         amazon_ad_height = "240"; amazon_ad_link_target
         = "new"; amazon_color_border = "CCCCCC";
         amazon_color_link = "23CB33";//--></script>
<script type="text/javascript" src="http://www.
         assoc-amazon.com/s/ads.js"></script>
```

6. Log in to Blogger and paste the code into an **HTML/JavaScript** page element. After saving the new page element, you may want to drag and drop it until it is positioned where you wanted it. View the blog to see the results:

What Just Happened?

When you signed up for the Amazon Affiliate program, you were given a wide range of widgets to choose from to add product sales to your blog. Omakase was a good place to start to get a better feel for how the program works as we didn't have to do any work adding product links or keywords.

After choosing our widget options, we copied the code snippet that hooks the Affiliate network to our blog. If we had not used the code snippet, the program information would not have shown up on our blog, and the widget would not be active.

There are many other types and styles of product widgets to choose from. A sample is shown in the following screenshot:

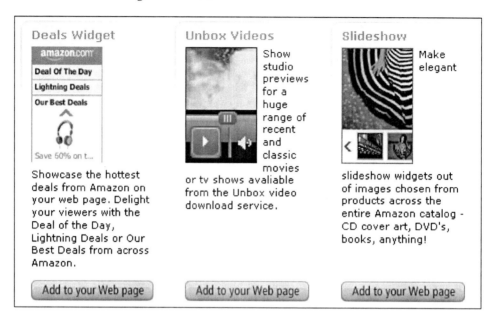

If you are promoting a book or want to limit sales to specific items, choose one of the **Product Links** widgets. The basic process for adding them to your blog is the same. Click the **Add to your Web page** button, and you will be taken to a configuration screen similar to the one we just worked thorough.

Providing PayPal Service on Your Blog

You can accept payments, donations, and even run a mini-storefront on your blog with a PayPal account. As of the publishing date of this book, the storefront widget is still in beta, but it is so slick and easy to set up that it will revolutionize the way people promote their products online.

Time for Action!—Create a PayPal Storefront Widget

Let's add a PayPal storefront widget to our blog. We will customize the look of the widget and choose what to sell in the store. Then we will add the storefront widget to our blog.

1. Go to the Storefront site for PayPal (`http://storefront.paypallabs.com`). Verify your PayPal account. Click the **Create a new storefront** button to begin creating your own storefront widget.

2. Modify the storefront by selecting from a set of themes and colors. The themes are wallpaper borders for your widget. A bright green color that should match Georgia's blog is shown in the following screenshot. Create a **Badge title** for the Storefront. Typing **Fresh Organic Fruit** causes the text to appear in the preview window on the right at the top of the widget. A **Store logo** can be added by pasting or typing the link to a logo image. It must not be wider than 60 pixels and larger than 35 pixels.

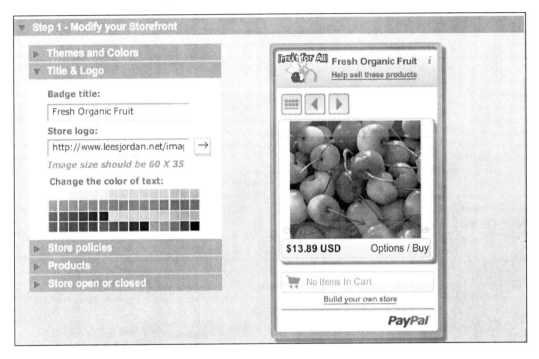

3. Next, add **Store Policies** and other legal information by clicking the arrow to the left of the menu item. Storefront items are added in the **Products** section. Enter a **Title** for the product and then set the **Price**. The **Price** is entered in the field to the right of the **Title**. You can change the **Currency** shown using a drop-down menu at the top of the screen. By default, U.S. currency is chosen.

4. Information entered in the **Product description** field will display detailed information about the product. Enter the URL of the product image in the **Picture of product** text box and click the arrow button. If the image is found by the storefront code, it will display the image on the top.

5. Each item can have a minimum of zero quantities of itself available. The quantity available can be set by clicking the **Inventory** sub-tab. Additional items are added by copying the previous ones using the plus sign button.

6. Now it is time to update the widget and publish it. Click the **Update your Storefront** section to expand it. Next, click on the **republish your storefront** link. Now, since we are using Blogger, select the second radio button under **How do you want to publish your storefront?**

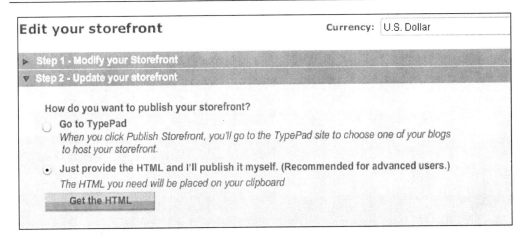

7. The HTML code is automatically pasted onto your clipboard after the **Get the HTML** button is clicked. Paste the HTML code below into a Blogger **HTML/JavaScript** page element:

```
<object classid="clsid:D27CDB6E-AE6D-11cf-96B8-444553540000"
     codebase="http://download.macromedia.com/pub/shockwave/cabs/
           flash/swflash.cab#version=7,0,19,0" width="215"
           height="355">
    <param name="movie"value="http://storefront.paypallabs.com
           /store/portablestore.swf?store_id=
           c8e92de08900012aff17000d60d4b7b8"/>
    <param name="quality" value="high"/>
    <param name="FlashVars" value="store_id=
           c8e92de08900012aff17000d60d4b7b8">
    <param name="allowScriptAccess" value="always"/>
    <param name="allowNetworking" value="all"/>
    <embed allowScriptAccess="always"
        allowNetworking="all"
        src="http://storefront.paypallabs.com/store/
           portablestore.swf?
        store_id=c8e92de08900012aff17000d60d4b7b8"
        quality="high"
        pluginspage="http://www.macromedia.com/go/
                getflashplayer"
        type="application/x-shockwave-flash"
        width="215"
        height="355"></embed></object>
```

8. When you paste the code into the **Content** box, it should look like the following screenshot. The code block will cause scroll bars to appear to the right and bottom of the **Content** box.

9. Save the changes and view the coolness of your new slick PayPal storefront.

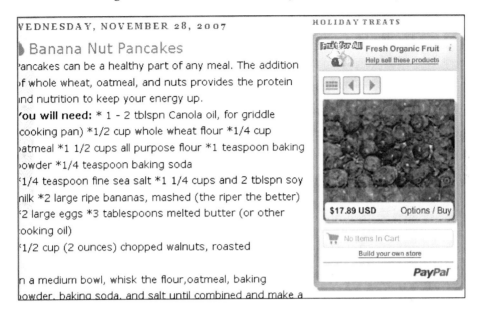

What Just Happened?

When we signed up for a PayPal storefront account, we were given the ability to create a customized storefront widget to paste in our blog or any other site. We entered information into a series of sections. We added images of the products by typing in the URL where they were stored online. The widget gave us an easy way to present our products for sale in a professional and maintainable way.

After the code was copied to a Blogger page element, the product image, price, options, and a shopping cart were instantly displayed to visitors. The products could be viewed as a group, or individually, using buttons above the product image.

This service is currently in beta. It is not a stable production tool. Before using a service like this, it is important to have store policies, shipping, and other business practices already set.

Blogger and Third-Party Widgets

Now, you must be wondering about the differences between Blogger page element widgets and third-party widgets. Using one or the other kind on your blog is not "good" or "bad". Be aware of the risks and use widgets that are the best fit for your blog.

Blogger widgets:

- Are always being created and added to the Page Elements chooser.

- Are easy to add.

- Require no code.

- Are tested by the Blogger team.

- Can be tested in Blogger's draft version of blogs at `http://draft.blogger.com`.

Third-party widgets:

- Provide services that Blogger widgets do not provide.

- Are interactive with multiple blog platforms (such as Twitter).

- Require ability to copy or paste and possibly do minor code entry.

- Are not tested (use at your own risk).

- May contain ads or links to the creator or a sponsor site.

Third-party widgets are useful because they add additional features and functionality to Blogger blogs. Blogger provided widgets are safer but are fewer in number and limited in features. Choose your widget sources carefully and give them a test run first. You'll also want to talk to other bloggers about the widgets they are using and get their opinions too.

We've explored many different widgets available directly from Blogger and third-party widgets from other sources. After trying many different widgets, there will eventually come a time when you will want to make one of your own. In the next section, we will build a custom widget and examine what functions different tags used in Blogger page element widgets perform.

Crafting Custom Blogger Widgets

You can set it up so that other people can add your custom widget to their blogspot blog. We will walk through the steps of creating a basic custom widget. We will then explore the anatomy of a widget.

Georgia wants to make it easy for visitors to add links of her recipe posts to their own blogs. She wants a widget that will automatically launch a page element installer, and then display the widget on the user's preferred blog.

Time for Action!—Create an Add Recipes Widget

It's time to create our own Blogger page element that other Blogger users can install on their own blog.

1. Log in to Blogger and click the **Layout** link next to your blog. Click the **Add a New Page Element** link in the sidebar of your **Layout,** on the **Page Elements** section under the **Layout** tab.

2. Select **HTML/JavaScript Page Element** from the **Choose a New Page Element** screen. Give the widget a descriptive title such as, **Add recipes to your blog**. Next, we will add our widget content wrapped inside a form. You can see a preview of how the custom page element form will look after the code is added in the following screenshot:

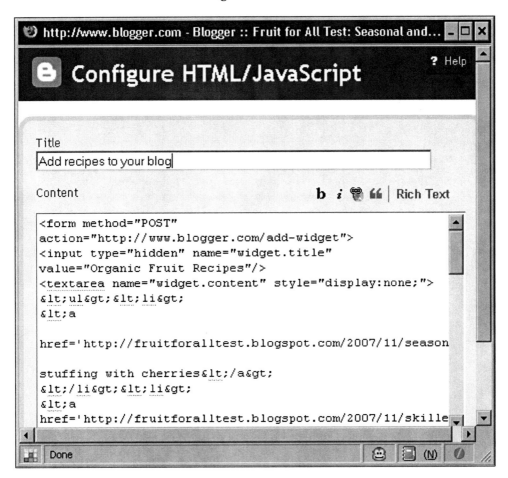

3. The form contains a list of all the recipe posts in Georgia's blog. Visitors can add the list to their own blog, once we are done. Paste the following code into the content portion:

```
<form method="POST" action="http://www.blogger.com/add-widget">
<input type="hidden" name="widget.title" value="Organic Fruit
        Recipes"/>
<textarea name="widget.content" style="display:none;">
            &lt;ul&gt;&lt;li&gt;&lt;
        a href='http://fruitforalltest.blogspot.com/
            2007/11/seasonal-cherry-stuffing.html'&gt;
            Seasonal stuffing with cherries&lt;/a&gt;&lt;
            /li&gt;&lt;li&gt;&lt;
        a href='http://fruitforalltest.blogspot.com/
            2007/11/skillet-apple-crisp.html'&gt;
            Skillet Apple Crisp&lt;/a&gt;&lt;
            /li&gt;&lt;li&gt;&lt;
        a href="http://fruitforalltest.blogspot.com/
            2007/11/wild-blackberry-cobbler.html'>Wild
            Blackberry Cobbler&lt;/a&gt;&lt;/
            li&gt;&lt;li&gt;&lt;
        a href='http://fruitforalltest.blogspot.com/2007/11/
            5-reasons-to-go-green-with-lemons.html'&gt;Natural
            householdcleanser&lt;/a&gt;&lt;/
            li&gt;&lt;li&gt;&lt;
        a href='http://fruitforalltest.blogspot.com/2007/11/
            banana-nut pancakes.html'&gt;Banana Nut
            Pancakes&lt;/a&gt;&lt;/li&gt;&lt;/ul&gt;
</textarea><input type="hidden" name="widget.template"
            value="&lt;data:content/&gt;"/>
        <input type="hidden" name="infoUrl"
            value="http://fruitforalltest.blogspot.com"/>
        <input type="hidden" name="logoUrl"
            value="http://www.leesjordan.net/images/
                fruitforall_logo.gif"/>
        <input type="hidden" name="widget.template"
            value="&lt;data:content/&gt;"/>
        <input type="image" src="http://www.blogger.com/img/
            add/add2blogger_sm_b.gif" name="go"
            value="Add Recipe Widget"/>
</form>
```

4. Save the changes, clear your browser's cache, and view the custom widget. Note that the list of recipes is hidden from the visitor until they add it to the blog.

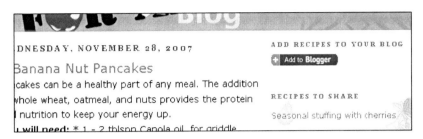

5. A separate widget titled **Recipes to Share** shows how the recipe widget will look once it is installed. Click the **Add to Blogger** button and choose a different blog from the page element wizard that pops up. The user can change the **Title** if they want to. Notice the *Fruit for All* logo is displayed on the widget.

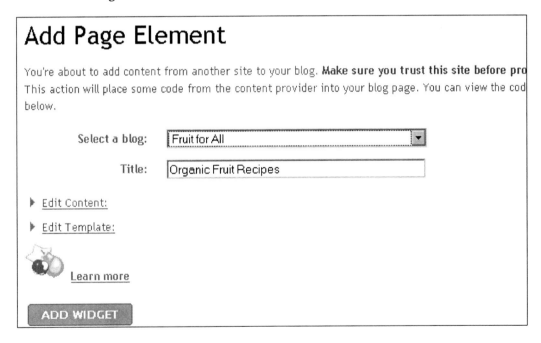

6. After the user clicks the **Add Widget** button, it will appear on their blog. View the results. The other blog now shows a list of recipes. Clicking on any item on the list will take them to the **Fruit for All** test blog.

What Just Happened?

We added a custom widget that included a form for readers to install the widget on their own Blogger blog. We began by opening up a **HTML/JavaScript** page element. The purpose of the page element was to contain our custom content code and display a portion to the visitor. The form contained a post action to Blogger's add-widget system. When the visitor clicked the **Add to Blogger** button, the data contained in the form was sent to the add-widget system and returned as a custom page element widget. The user could then add to a blog they selected.

The default title of the widget was contained in an input field with a value set by us. The value was then displayed as the default title after the form was processed. The actual content of the recipe widget was wrapped by a text area tag set. The list of recipe articles were formatted with the opening and closing brackets converted from < and > to < and > respectively. The double quotes usually used around a page link were converted to single quotes. This had to be done before the list was added to the form.

The remaining tags contained links back to the original blog, the logo of the blog, and the **Add to Blogger** submit button.

Now that we've experimented with a custom widget, let's dissect the different parts of a typical Blogger widget. Understanding the anatomy of a Blogger widget will help you build your own widgets. You will also be able to view the widget code of the third-party widgets and make an informed decision about whether they will do what you want.

Anatomy of a Widget

The great thing about using the page elements widgets in Blogger is that you can avoid putting too much directly into your template code and separate presentation from code. Keeping third-party JavaScript and HTML code out of your template makes maintaining your blog easier. Let's take a look at the tags you need to know while creating your widgets. The following table shows typical form tags used in widgets and what they do.

Blogger Widget Form Tag	What it does
`<form method="Post" action="http://blogger.com/add-widget">`	Sends the form information to Blogger's add-widget system for processing.
`<input type="hidden" name="widget.title" value="Organic Fruit Recipes"/>`	Sets the title of the widget.
`<input type="hidden" name="infoUrl" value="http://fruitforalltest.blogspot.com"/>`	Contains a link back to the original creator of the widget. Can be a specific page explaining the widget.
`<textarea name="widget.content" style="display:none;"></textarea>`	Contains the content of the widget. Can be any container form element or a link to an external file.
`<input type="hidden" name=" widget.template" value="&lt;data:content/&gt;"/>`	Describes the type of data contained in the widget.
`<input type="hidden" name="logoUrl" value="http://www.leesjordan.net/images/fruitforall_logo.gif"/>`	Displays the URL source path of your site logo or icon (optional).
`<input type="image" src="http://www.blogger.com/img/add/add2blogger_sm_b.gif" name="go" value="Add Recipe Widget"/>` or: `<input type="submit" name="go" value="Add Recipe Widget"/>`	Can display a plain submit button, or Add to Blogger button.

The main advantage of creating a custom widget is that users can then add it to their own blogs. Another example to try is a "Link to this blog" widget. Although, the content tag can theoretically contain any type of HTML tag as long as it is not an `<html>`, `<head>`, or `<body>` tag. The form tags seem to work best.

Choose Your Widgets Wisely

Way back in Chapter 1 of this book, we identified the kinds of widgets we thought would work best with Georgia's blog. Widgets should be a natural extension of your blog, like a stepping stool used to reach fruits higher up a tree. Readers will react to your blogs content, including the information that displays in your widgets.

Picking the Right Widgets

The blogger chooses the widget; the widget should not be choosing you, unless you are a teen-aged hero using widgets instead of wands. Always think, "How can this widget help me?" When you find one that interests you, remember your readers. They are the audience for the widget. Which widget can you add to make their experience at your blog better?

Widget Matching Matrix

Making a grid is a quick way to match widgets to blogs. You can see right away which widgets are most likely to work for you. The following matrix is a general guideline of what kinds of widgets are used by what types of blogs. Feel free to "break the rules" and choose a widget you think is right for your blog.

Blog type	Community badge (Twitter, Facebook)	Chat or other live interaction	Slideshow/Video	PayPal/ e-commerce
Personal	X		X	
Special Interest	X		X	X
Professional Expert	X		X	X
Small Business Blog	X	X	X	X
Corporate		X	X	X
Arts/New Media	X	X	X	X

Visitors already have a picture in their head of what the different types of blogs should look like. They expect a "corporate" or a "professional expert" blog to look clean, not busy, or packed full of widgets. Anything goes for "art" blogs. Use your widgets in moderation. This doesn't mean that they have to be boring. The colors, fonts, and images you choose will add visual excitement and set the stage for the content to shine.

Ways to Pick Widgets

There are hundreds of widgets out there. Deciding between them can be frustrating, and nerve wracking. The great thing about widgets is that you can always replace them if they aren't working out. You have the power to decide which ones best reflect the personality and purpose of your blog.

- **The Experiment**: Choose one widget of each type and try them out for a month. Then decide, of the three, which has worked out the best, and which one was the worst? Drop the one you like the least and add a new one.

- **Follow the pain**: Identify the areas of the blog that are causing you the most pain. Is it communication with visitors? Loss of revenue? Or lack of supporting content such as photos or videos?

- **The Widget Party**: Which widgets do you gravitate to? Imagine you are at a party where there are different widgets in each room. Which one would you go to first? Is there one you would avoid?

- **Prioritize**: Based on the focus of your blog and the scope of your blog, pick ten widgets that you would like to use. Sort them using the bottom up method. Would you choose number ten over number nine? If yes, then number nine takes the number ten spot and widget number ten moves up. Do this until you have worked your way all the way up the list. Now comes the hard part. Cross out the bottom five. Of the remaining five, are they all the same type? Will it make sense to use all of them at once on the blog? If not, choose only three from the top five.

- **Don't go shopping hungry**: Decide what type of work needs to be done by widgets before you start looking through the Blogger page elements list or searching the Internet for widgets. This is the technique we used for Georgia. We did look around to see what others were doing, but we had a good idea early on as to what kinds of widgets we wanted to use on her blog.

- **Let your readers choose**: Put up a poll asking your readers which widgets they liked or would like to see on the blog. The responses might surprise you.

There are no black and white answers for this issue. You can always remove a widget if it is not working out. I am hoping that in the future Blogger will introduce a way to disable widgets without fully removing them.

Planning for Future Widgets

There are a lot of cool new page elements that Blogger will be introducing, and many of them may even be out by the time this book is published. Blogger has a system specifically set up for testing new page element widgets. You can even test them out on a draft version of your blog.

Using Experimental Widgets

Visit the official Blogger draft site (http://bloggerindraft.blogspot.com) to catch up on the latest news for draft sites. Notice the blueprint pattern. That is a visual indicator that you are on a draft site. Now go to http://draft.blogger.com. You can now play around in draft versions of your blogs.

Time for Action!—Adding a Google Gadget to draft. blogger.com

Let's visit the draft version of a blog and try working on a new page element that is just a draft.

1. Navigate to the draft.blogger.com site. You will see your **Dashboard** with a checked blue background and a special Blogger logo. You should see all the blogs that you have associated with your Blogger profile. The actual items you see may vary, since this is a test version of Blogger.

2. Click the **Layout** link next to your blog to navigate to the **Page Elements** section of your blog. Click the **Add a Page Element** link to launch the **Choose a New Page Element** screen. Look at all the new choices! The following screenshot shows the **Choose a New Page Element** screen in the draft version of Blogger. Select the **Gadget** widget to choose from a whole array of Google Gadget widgets.

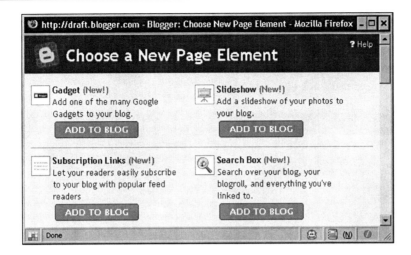

3. The **Add a Gadget** screen has a list of the **Most popular** Google gadgets to choose from the one's that are displayed by default. There is a left menu to choose widgets by category, or a search can be performed. Scroll down to see quite a long list of potential gadgets for your blog.

4. Let's do a search for `Organic`, and see what results we get. Three choices appeared in our results. The results are shown in the following screenshot. We also have the option to search again for other gadgets. Click the **ADD** button on the right of the **realfoodfinder.com** gadget title to add the realfoodfinder gadget to the blog.

5. We can customize the title and size of the gadget if we want to. The **Title** is set to **realfoodfinder.com** and the **Height** is set to **200px** in the **Configure Gadget** screen shown in the following screenshot. Keep the height of the gadget smaller than your sidebar to avoid breaking the layout of the template. Click **SAVE CHANGES** to add the gadget widget to Georgia's blog. It will put a small, searchable map on our blog.

6. Click the **Preview** button from the **Layout** screen to see the Google Gadget widget on Georgia's draft version of her blog. Do not click the **View** button. It will take you to a live version of your blog. You can see how the map widget looks in the `draft.blogger.com` version of the blog in the following screenshot. Note that the visitors can search the map for locations.

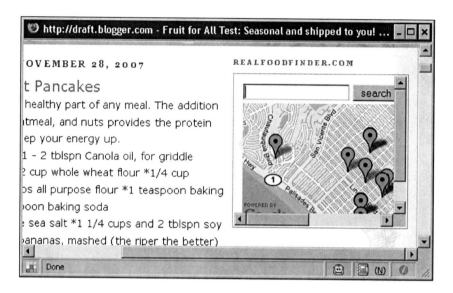

What Just Happened?

You just added an experimental widget to your draft blog! Now you can test it and see if you like it, even before it goes live to the public. The draft site gives you the freedom to experiment with new Blogger features before they go live, and to give feedback to the Blogger team. As the draft sites are test sites, they are subject to changes at any time. They are not a stable production environment.

When we clicked the **Add a New Page Element** link on the **Layout** screen of our draft blog, we saw new widgets, some of which were still being tested. When we added the Google Gadget page element widget, we were given a large amount of choices for our draft blog. The screen also contained many ways to sort gadgets, including category, newness, search, and most popular. Once we chose a widget, the process was the same for any other widget. We had the option to customize the title and size of the widget.

Once we added the widget to our draft blog and previewed it, we could see that it contained ugly scrollbars, and did not fit well with the width of the sidebar. It did add a whole new way for visitors to interact with our blog, at least in the future.

Summary

You've learned about the types of widgets, when they are useful, and how to choose the ones that fit your blog. You know how to configure, and install many different types of widgets. You can even create your own custom widgets to share with other blogspot bloggers. Whether you blog for fun, or have a professional blog, there are Bloggers and third-party widgets to make interactions with your visitors a more exciting and effective experience.

So far, in this book, we've added widgets for social networking, e-commerce, interactive chat, and even custom widgets. The one area that we haven't yet explored is feed syndication. In the next chapter, we will make it easier for visitors to find and subscribe to our blog's feed, and use a variety of tools to share our blog in syndicated formats.

6

RSS and Atom Syndication

Feed syndication is the biggest thing to happen since email. It gives people the freedom to choose from a variety of content subject and sources. Instead of wading through a list of websites, they can read summaries of site updates at their leisure once the information comes to them. Bloggers use RSS and Atom feeds to automatically transmit their content. Syndication gives Bloggers flexible ways to handle their content:

- **Track**: Find out which services are consuming post content.
- **Measure**: See the number of visitors and subscribers visiting a post, and then drill them down by content item.
- **Serve**: Deliver content in different syndication formats, accessible to mobile devices and traditional Internet platforms.

How Site Feeds Work in Blogger

Site feeds are an important feature of blogspot blogs. When site feeds are turned ON, visitors can subscribe to feeds collected from the content of your blog posts and comments. A feed reading service then sends the title, a short description, author, and date or time stamp as an XML file to a website, application, or mobile device from where the subscribers can then read the information at their own leisure.

Blogger blogs have three types of feeds that you can directly control within Blogger: Blog posts, Blog Comments, and Per-Post Comment feeds. You can turn them all off or choose to transmit the full content of an individual feed, its short description, or nothing at all. The fourth type of feed is label feeds. We will look at them later on in this chapter.

Choosing a Feed Protocol for Your Blog

There are two feed protocols popular with blog visitors. Both of them use XML to wrap content and deliver it as feeds. If you prefer one over the other, or if you know that your audience does, you can specify the feed protocol.

- **Atom**: It is officially known as **Atom Syndication Protocol**. It is a popular feed protocol, and it is the one used for Blogger feeds by default.
- **RSS**: The popular definition is **Really Simple Syndication**. No one actually agrees on what it stands for. It is usually the first acronym to come to mind when people think of feed syndication. It is actually a protocol, the way Kleenex is the name of a brand of tissue.

Multiple Feed Protocol Icons Confuse Visitors

Choose one protocol, RSS or Atom, and go with it. You've visited blogs and other sites with multiple feed buttons. The average person only finds them confusing. Many people have sophisticated feed reader services that can detect the types of available feeds and capture them automatically. You can also redirect your blog feeds to a third-party service, and let it serve feeds to your visitors and the world at large.

Discovering the Post URL of Your Blogger Blog

Modern browsers such as Firefox, Internet Explorer 7, and Safari make it easy to add feeds directly to the browser. We will use Firefox, as we have done throughout the book. Let's see it in action by grabbing a feed of all the posts of the blog. We'll then add it to the browser as a bookmark.

Time for Action!—Grabbing a Feed Post URL

Blogger automatically processes each of your blog posts and serves them as part of a posts feed. Knowing how to grab this feed manually will make it possible for you to use this and other feeds on your blog, in page elements and third-party widgets.

1. Type the following URL into your browser window: `http://fruitforalltest.blogspot.com/feeds/posts/default`. If you prefer RSS to Atom, type this, `http://fruitforalltest.blogspot.com/feeds/posts/default?alt=rss` into the address bar of your browser, instead of the first URL. Note the orange icon that appears in the address bar.

2. Firefox and Internet Explorer browsers will open up a bookmark dialog window like the one shown in the following screenshot. You can change the title of the bookmark in the **Name** text field. Select your preferred folder from the **Create in** drop-down menu. Click **OK** to add a bookmark of the feed to your browsers' window.

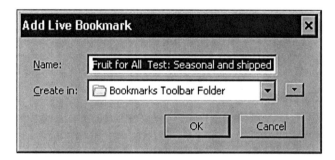

3. To display the bookmark toolbar in Firefox, click on **View | Toolbars | Bookmarks toolbar**. Now you can see the *Fruit for All* bookmark with an orange feed logo in the bookmark toolbar, as shown in the following screenshot:

4. You want to click the feed bookmark and see what happens, don't you? Clicking on the feed will cause a drop-down list of recent feed titles to appear as shown in the following screenshot. We can see all the available blog posts that currently exist in the posts feed.

5. When you click on the title of a feed, the original post will display in the browser window. You also have the option to open all the posts in a series of tabs using the **Open All in Tabs** choice.

What Just Happened?

The default feed for blog posts is currently a hidden feature in Blogger. Knowing how to grab the post feed will enable us to offer it in a widget to visitors and grab the URL to use it with other services such as FeedBurner (http://www.feedburner.com).

When we typed the URL of the default blog posts feed, we sent a request to the browser to make a bookmark. Firefox responded by prompting us with an **Add Bookmark** pop-up. The bookmark, also known as a bookmarklet or "chicklet" is then added to the bookmark toolbar of the browser. Many sites offer bookmarks you can drag and drop onto your toolbar with your mouse. We will create our own later on in this chapter.

Most modern browsers include some method for gathering and reading syndication feeds. Internet Explorer 7, Firefox, Opera, and Safari display feeds for users, but they don't work exactly the same.

Grabbing Feeds with Safari

Everyone out there using Safari browsers are now saying, "That's not how it worked for me". Safari redirects you to a special feeds page instead of creating a bookmark. You can still add the feed as a bookmark from the following screen by clicking on the plus [+] symbol. This is what the feed URL will look like in Safari:

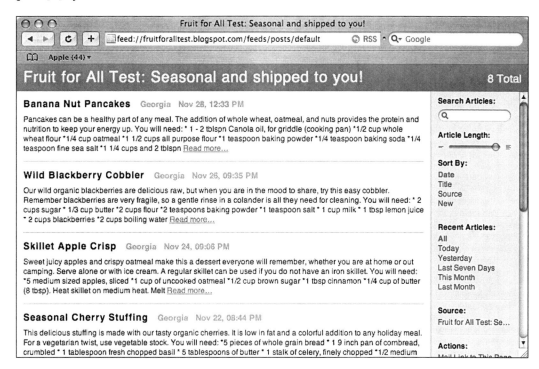

The Safari browser has its own tools for managing feeds, which are beyond the scope of this book. When you type the feed URL, it converts from **http** to **feed** and displays a portion of each post along with the title, author, and date.

Managing Blogger Feeds

You just took the first baby steps of managing feeds when you grabbed the feed URL. Site feed management is done with several simple forms in Blogger. Feed management is currently limited to turning feeds on/off, redirection, and minor customization. Blogger may upgrade or improve the feed management features in the future, since Google has recently acquired FeedBurner (http://www.feedburner.com).

Basic Feed Settings

The basic setting page for managing Blogger feeds is very simple. Your options are limited to managing all feeds as a group, entering redirect URLs, and adding footer blog post feeds. When you don't want to worry about the details of what the individual blog feeds display, this is the page to use.

Time for Action!—Managing Basic Site Feed Settings

Let's examine the default **Basic Mode** of the **Site Feed** options in more detail. The **Basic Mode** on the **Site Feed** section is limited to three options: **Allow Blog Feeds**, **Post Feed Redirect URL**, and **Post Feed Footer**. We'll set the basic **Site Feed** options to allow full blog feeds.

1. Log in to Blogger and select the **Settings** link next to your blog on the **Dashboard**. You will now be on the **Basic** sub-tab under the **Settings** tab. Click on the **Site Feed** sub-tab to begin managing your blog feeds.

2. The **Allow Blog Feeds** option controls the blog feeds as a group. It must be set to **Full** for the **Post Feed Footer** option to display content in the feed.

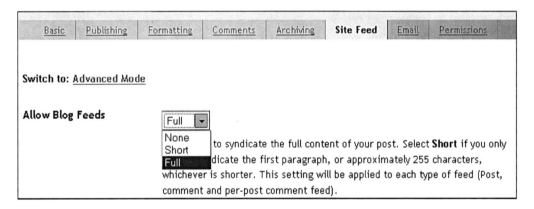

What Just Happened?

When we set the **Allow Blog Feeds** setting to **Full**, we instructed Blogger to process the feeds on our blog to display the full content of each feed. Choosing **Short** would have set the feeds to display only content from the first paragraph or 255 characters. Setting it to **None** would deactivate syndication of all feeds from the blog posts, blog comments, and per-post comments.

Advanced Feed Settings

Blogger gives you more control over the settings of your individual blog site feeds in **Advanced Mode**. Are long comments cluttering up your feeds? Do you need to syndicate only the first paragraph of your blog post feed, but want to display all the per-post comments in full? The **Advanced Mode** settings will give you those choices. The **Basic Mode** is displayed in the **Site Feed** section, by default.

Time for Action!—Configuring Advanced Feed Settings

Let's configure the **Site Feed** settings for our blog in **Advanced Mode**. Click the **Switch to: Advanced Mode** link to display the **Advanced Mode** options. Now, we are ready to manage our site feeds using the advanced feed features in Blogger.

1. Navigate to the **Settings | Site Feed | Advanced Mode** page. We will set the **Blog Posts Feed** to **Full.** The entire content of the post will now be displayed in the feed, including an optional footer that we will add in the next step. Set the **Blog Comment Feed** to **Short** so that only the first paragraph or 255 characters is displayed. Choose **None** to remove the individual **Per-Post Comment Feeds** from syndication.

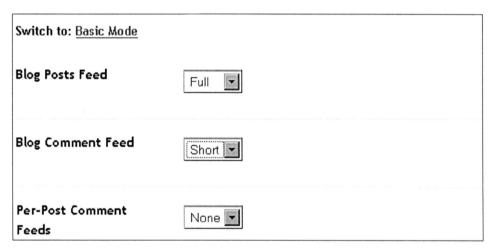

2. Skip past the **Redirect URL** option for now. It is part of an example we will discuss later in this chapter. It's time to place content in **Post Feed Footer**. Content in this box could be an ad, a teaser text about the blog, or could be used to enter other details. Basic HTML tags can be used here. Type the following text into the block: **<p>Ads would appear here</p>**.

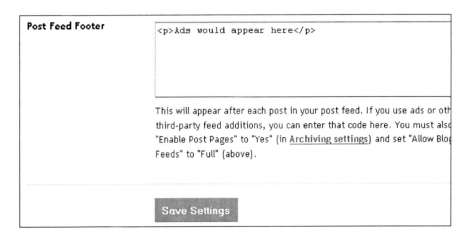

3. Remember to visit the **Archiving** section under **Settings** and **Enable Post Pages**. This creates a unique page for each post. Click the **Save Settings** button to finalize the changes.

4. Clear your browser's cache. Now, it's time to find out the look of our blog as a syndicated feed. Using Google Reader (`http://reader.google.com`), we can view our blog feed. Here's how it looks to someone who has added the feed to their Google Reader:

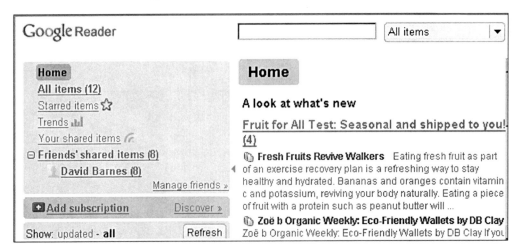

5. We can see the blog title, post titles, and a summary of each post. Whenever a new post is added, the feed will be updated and the post will be available in a syndicated format for the syndication tools to grab.

What Just Happened?

When we switched to **Advanced Mode**, we opened up more ways to control the appearance and syndication choices of our three site feeds. Earlier, with the **Basic Mode**, we could only control the feeds as a group. Using **Advanced Mode** we were able to turn off individual feeds by setting them to **None**. Selecting **Short** limited the display of a feed entry's text to a paragraph or 255 characters. We could also opt for a **Full** text version, enabling us to leverage the **Post Feed Footer** for ads or additional information.

The **Short** option will be useful to any blogger who is aiming his or her content at visitors using mobile devices. Smaller screens demand summaries of content for easy navigation. The drawback of the **Short** option is that you cannot, currently, include a post feed footer.

Redirecting Feeds

Redirecting your blog feeds gives you new ways to manage and promote your blog. Blogger makes it easy to redirect your blog feeds to a third-party service such as FeedBurner. You will need an account with the service.

 The log in for FeedBurner is currently separate from other Google tools. In the future, it may become possible to get logged into FeedBurner automatically, once you log in to Google.

Before you can redirect the feed, you need to know the correct path for the feed given to you by the feed service. What this means is that you will use the Blogger feed path, we grabbed earlier in this chapter, to create an individual feed account in FeedBurner. When we do that, FeedBurner will give us a new FeedBurner URL to use while redirecting our Blogger feed. Let's go through the process, step-by-step.

Time for Action!—Configuring Feed Redirects

We're going to add our Blogger feed to FeedBurner, also known as burning. Think of it as a process similar to burning files from your computer onto a DVD disc. Once we burn the feed, we will take the new feed URL provided by FeedBurner and redirect our site feed to that URL.

1. Log in to FeedBurner (http://www.feedburner.com) and click on **My Feeds,** if you are not already on the **My Feeds** page. Begin by adding the address of your feed. Enter the URL of the blog feed into the **Burn a feed** field and click the **Next** button. This is the same URL we used at the beginning of the chapter: http://fruitforalltest.blogspot.com/feeds/posts/default.

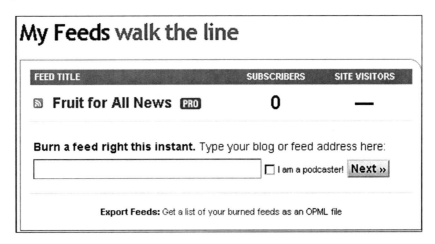

2. Choose the type of syndication for your blog. The default syndication type for Blogger blogs is Atom. If you want to serve multiple syndication types, don't worry. FeedBurner has a tool for that. Click **Next** to continue the set up.

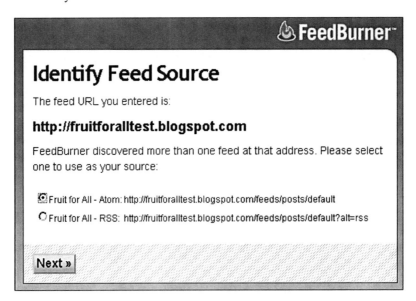

3. Continue through the set up, choosing **Activate Feed** and then **Next,** until you are back to the **My Feeds** section of the site. Click the **Edit Feed Details** to view information about your feed. You will need a copy of the FeedBurner feed address for your blog. We can see that the **Feed Address** for our blog is `http://feeds.feedburner.com/fruitforalltest`.

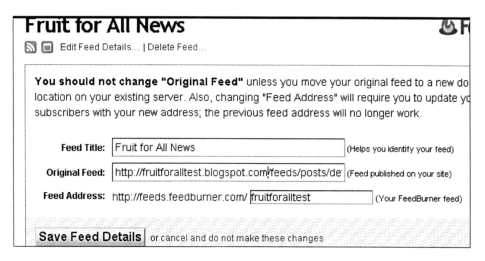

4. Go to your blog and navigate to the **Settings | Site Feed** section. Enter the FeedBurner address in the **Post Feed Redirect URL** field and click the **Save Settings** button. The URL has to be entered as shown in the following screenshot:

What Just Happened?

FeedBurner processed the URL of your blog and created a new URL pointing to the FeedBurner formatted version of your blog. When you used the redirect feature in Blogger, by pasting the FeedBurner feed URL, you instructed Blogger to send all requests for feeds of your blog content to FeedBurner.

Every time a new post is created, the content is sent to FeedBurner and wrapped with FeedBurner's own code. The content can then be packaged and served up as different syndication formats and content formats including posts by email.

Promoting Your Blog with Feed Chicklets

Getting the word out about your blog is a lot easier when visitors can subscribe to a feed easily. The little orange icons, popularly nicknamed "chicklets" after a type of chewing gum, are a quick way for new visitors to subscribe to a feed of your blog. The easier you make it for new visitors to enjoy your content, the more likely they will become frequent readers.

Blogger does not currently display feed icons on blogs by default. You can add your own orange chicklet icon using FeedBurner. In just a few short steps, you'll have a feed subscribe icon on your blog without using any code.

Time for Action!—Adding FeedBurner Chicklets

Since we've already redirected our feed to the FeedBurner service, we'll use FeedBurner's subscribe feed chicklet feature to add a feed subscription icon to the sidebar of our blog.

1. Now, it's time to activate the chicklet feature of FeedBurner for our Blogger blog. Go back to the FeedBurner site and click on the title of your feed under **My Feeds**. The management screen for the feed appears. Click the **Publicize** tab.

2. The **Chicklet Chooser** link is on the left menu. Click it to open up the chooser screen. Select the small orange feed icon as shown in the following screenshot, and then scroll to the bottom of the screen to activate the widget installer tool.

3. Copy the code if you want to add it to your template. We have covered the steps for adding a code in Chapter 3. Let's try a different route and add the chicklet to the blog as a page element widget. Select **Blogger** from the **Use as a widget in** the drop-down list and click the **Go!** button.

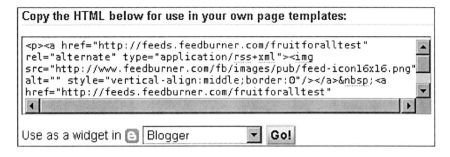

4. If you are logged into your blog, FeedBurner will open a custom page element widget form in a new window. Select the blog and change the default title from **Subscribe Now: standardSmall** to **Subscribe Now**. Click the **ADD WIDGET** button to save the widget and add it to the blog.

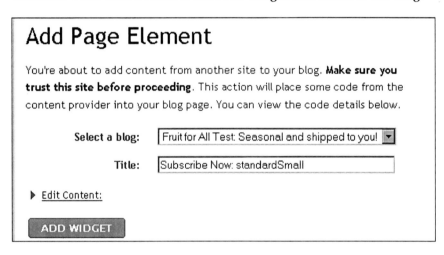

5. We can see that a new orange feed icon has been automatically placed in the sidebar at the top of the other sidebar page elements. When visitors click the **Subscribe in a reader** link, they will be taken to the FeedBurner page for the blog, where they will have a wide range of web-based feed readers to choose from.

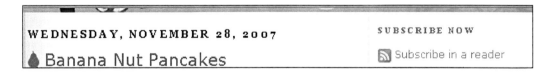

What Just Happened?

When you used the redirect feature in Blogger, you made it possible to gather site statistics, manage your feed in new ways, and to syndicate your blog to a wider range of feed readers and people. The **Chicklet Chooser** tool in FeedBurner made it possible to quickly add a subscribe button and link it to your blog where visitors can easily find it.

More Ways to Publicize Your Feed with FeedBurner

Did you know FeedBurner has multiple ways to publicize your feed? We could write a whole book on FeedBurner (and we may have to), here are the coolest tools you will want to try:

- **BuzzBoost**: Make your feed readable without a feed reader. BuzzBoost converts the feed content into HTML.

- **Email Subscription**: Your subscribers can receive updates to your feed content by email instead of a feed reader.

- **Headline Animator**: Showcase your recent feed content with a flashy headline graphic.

All these tools are easy to set up from the **Publicize** tab. They also optimize your feed by providing your blog in multiple content formats and delivery methods.

Time for Action!—Adding Headline Animator

Let's go ahead and use the most glamorous of the tools mentioned above to add a flashier way for visitors to enjoy our blog feeds.

1. Log in to FeedBurner.com and click on the **Publicize** tab. Click the **Headline Animator** option to begin with. Keep the **Clickthrough URL** option unchanged for now. Select a **Theme** size for the headline animation box. We are placing it in the sidebar, so let's make it **180 * 100, white**.

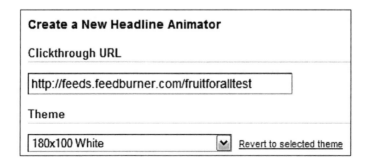

2. You can scroll all the way to the bottom of the screen and select **Blogger** as your blog and click **Next**, or you can customize the colors and look of the widget. Let's change the **Title** color to bright green. Click on a color next to the item.

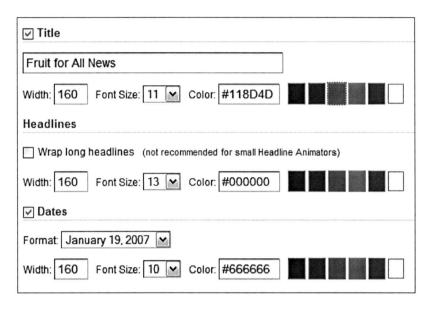

3. When you are satisfied with the results, click on the **Activate** button. Then select **Blogger blog** from the **Add to** drop-down list and click the **Next** button.

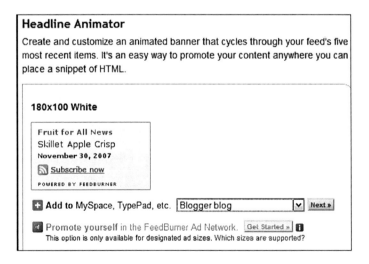

4. It's time to make a couple of choices and let the installer do the walking. We can see a preview of our subscribe box. Everything looks fine. We'll leave the **Grab this** box checked. It will display a link below our subscribe box that visitors can click on to make their own feed box. Click the **Add to Blogger** button to continue.

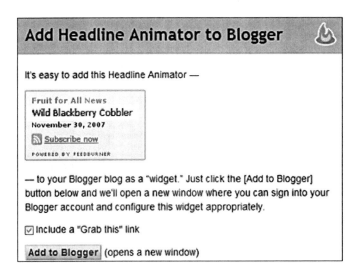

5. Change the title of the widget on the configure window that pops up to **Fruit for All News** and click the **ADD WIDGET** button. Let's see how it looks on the blog:

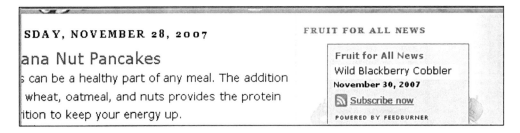

Updating Google Sitemaps for Redirected Feeds

After redirecting your blogspot blog, you may notice problems with the Google's Webmaster Sitemap tool. The fix is very simple. Log in to your Webmaster tools page (`http://www.google.com/webmasters/tools/`) and submit the following URLs with the format `http://yourblog.blogspot.com/atom.xml` and `http://yourblog.blogspot.com/rss.xml` to Google Sitemaps. Here is an example of the format to use:

```
http://fruitforall.blogspot.com/atom.xml or
http://fruitforall.blogspot.com/rss.xml
```

If you have auto discovery tags in your template from a previous feed redirect work around, you will want to navigate to the **Template** tab and edit the template code. You can update the tags manually with the new redirect code mentioned in the previous **Time for Action!** section.

Give Visitors the Feed They Need with SmartFeed

Are you worried that visitors may be turned off if they can't access your feed using their preferred protocol? SmartFeed comes to your rescue! Turn on the SmartFeed feature offered by FeedBurner to send the version of your feed that subscribers want. SmartFeed converts your feed to the correct type without any work from you.

People use a wide variety of feed reading services, also known as "user-agents", to find and collect feeds that interest them. SmartFeed supports over fourteen different types of user-agents. Using SmartFeed makes your blog much more syndication friendly to your visitors and the feed services they use.

Notifying Services with PingShot

FeedBurner can automatically publicize the content that you post to feed collector services, also know as aggregators, search engines, and any other service out on the Internet looking for public feeds. To activate **PingShot**, log in to `Feedburner.com`, click on the **Publicize** tab, and check the box next to **PingShot** on the left menu.

Label Specific Feeds

Sometimes, visitors don't want to subscribe to all your posts feeds. They would prefer to subscribe to posts that fit specific labels or categories. You can add this feature to your blog with a little ingenuity. Feeds can be grouped into label-specific feeds by using the Blogger API syntax. This is easier than it sounds.

Offering Feeds by Label

The way you type the label feed URL is crucial to your success in sharing it with users in an easy to use widget. Let's get familiar with the proper format first. Type blog post URL followed by `/summary/` then a `/-/` and finally the label name, like this:

```
http://fruitforalltest.blogspot.com/feeds/posts/summary/-/bananas
```

If you are using Firefox, you will be prompted with a bookmark label to add to your browser. This is similar to the example we saw at the start of the chapter. You need to give your readers a prettier interface and an easy way to find the feeds without typing in the labels. Let's create a widget that displays the label feeds and links to them.

Time for Action!—Specifying Feeds by Label

Let's add subscribe links for several different labels: Bananas, Dessert, and Organic Fruit. We'll list each link in a **Link List** page element so that our visitors can subscribe to them.

1. Log in to Blogger and click on the **Layout** link of your blog under the **Dashboard**. Click the **Add a Page Element** link in the sidebar section of the **Layout** area under the **Page Elements** sub-tab. Select a **Link List** page element from the **Choose a New Page Element** screen.

2. Enter a name for your list of labels. We're using **Subscribe by Label** for **Title** as shown in the following screenshot. Type the number **3** in the **Number of links to show in list** text field. Select **Sort Alphabetically** from the **Sorting** drop-down list.

3. Begin by adding the following links in **New Site URL**:

   http://fruitforalltest.blogspot.com/feeds/posts/summary/-/ bananas, http://fruitforalltest.blogspot.com/feeds/posts/ summary/-/Dessert, http://fruitforalltest.blogspot.com/feeds/ posts/summary/-/Organic_Fruit

4. The following screenshot shows the **Configure Link List** page element screen. Notice each link is added, one at a time. The links can be sorted and edited once they are added.

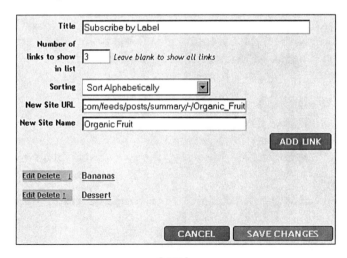

5. Add a title for each URL in the **New Site Name** field. Click **ADD LINK** to continue adding links. When done, click **SAVE CHANGES** to finish the widget.

6. The widget is displayed as a simple link list on the sidebar of the blog. Clicking on a link will prompt a bookmark or take the user to a feeds page, depending upon which browser he or she is using. You can see an example of how it should look in the following screenshot:

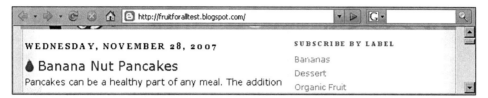

What Just Happened?

When we created a widget to pull all the feeds with a specified label, we made it possible for visitors to subscribe to feeds by interest. Hopefully, in the future, Blogger will offer new ways to easily offer feeds by post labels. If a link in your subscribe by label page element is not working, you may have accidentally misspelt the label. To show all links by default, leave the **Number of links to show in list** option empty.

Measuring Feed Success

Comments and site hits are traditionally used to measure blog success. Syndication provides a larger audience and better ways to measure how a blog is doing. FeedBurner contains many ways to analyze your feed. Log in to FeedBurner and click on the **Analyze** tab to take advantage of the graphs and other statistical data about your blog.

Showing Your Success with FeedCount

When you want to show off your circulation statistics, FeedCount can help display your feed count in the number of readers with a simple JavaScript widget that you can grab from the FeedBurner **Publicize** page. Showing your FeedCount gives your visitors a real time indicator of how popular your feed is. It raises the value of the blog to visitors, since others like it enough to add it to their list of feeds.

When you are just starting a blog, or have a small following, showing the FeedCount may only reflect negatively on your blog. If you know that you have many frequent visitors, but your FeedCount is low, showing the FeedCount and encouraging them to add your blog may help boost the count, since they can easily measure the number of new feeds with you.

Using FeedBurner Stats

FeedBurner statistics are a free service. If you have a FeedBurner account, you can use **Feed Stats** to visually measure the activity of your feeds, including the range of syndication, which content items are actually read and how much, and how it all relates to the circulation of your feed. The TotalStats premium service is now a free feature. It contains detailed information about subscriber base activity and content popularity.

- **Reach**: It measures the percentage of your blog's subscriber base reading and clicks on feed items. People don't always read an individual feed item they have subscribed to. Viewing the reach of your blog gives you insight into what titles and contents subscribers are drawn to.

- **Item Popularity**: It measures the success of individual feed items. You can view graphs and other information to see how your posts are doing on a daily basis. You will quickly be able to measure whether a post topic is well liked.

We can see an example of the statistics for **Item Use** in the following screenshot. FeedBurner **Feed Stats** displays the number of visitors and the dates visually in a graph. Note that we can export the statistics in Excel (xls) and CSV formats for further reporting.

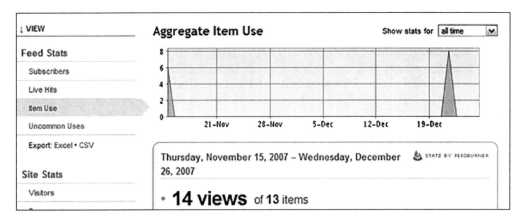

So far in this chapter, we've focused on ways to use the feeds from your Blogger blog. There are times when you'll want to make other feeds available on your blog. We'll explore ways to do this in the next section.

Adding Outside Feeds to Your Blog

Adding more feeds is handy if you have multiple blogs which you want to promote, or if you want to provide other feeds that you think your visitors will enjoy. Blogger provides a simple page element form that you can use to display up to five feeds in a widget block.

Time for Action!—Adding a Feed Using Blogger Page Elements

Let's add an external feed using Blogger's **Feed** page element. We'll select the page element and provide it with the URL of a feed, which we have collected using our browser.

1. Log in to Blogger and click on the **Layout** link next to your blog. Add a new page element to your blog under **Layout | Page Elements** and choose the **Feed** page element.

2. Time to enter the URL of our external feed. Type `http://feeds. feedburner.com/innocentdrinks` or your favorite external feed into the **Feed URL** text field. Click the **CONTINUE** button after the feed address has been entered. The configure page will reload with additional settings.

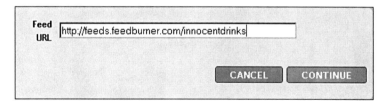

3. We can change the **Title**, the number of items to **Show**, and choose whether to display the item dates and authors. A preview of the feed is displayed in the **Preview** box. We also have a chance to change the feed URL, if it is not the one we expected. Check the **Item dates** box and then click the **SAVE CHANGES** button.

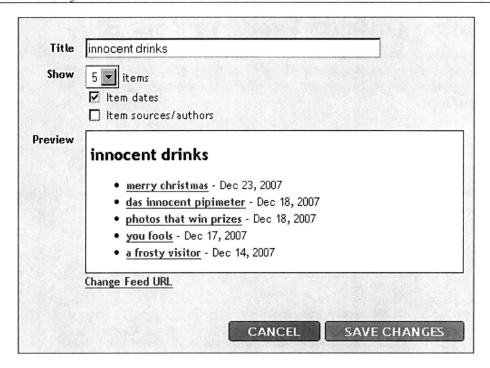

4. Now let's see what the feed looks like. The five most recent posts and dates are displayed below the title of the feed. Note that the colors and fonts of the feed now match with the ones set in the template of our blog.

What Just Happened?

When we added the feed URL to the **Feed** page element, it stored the URL and put in a request for the five most recent feeds. The feeds were then wrapped and displayed as a list on the sidebar of our blog.

To find the correct feed URL, you will need to visit a site that contains a feed, click on the feed subscribe link and then copy the link that is displayed in the address bar of the browser window. Sometimes, subscribe links are listed using different icons, including "XML", "RSS", and "Subscribe".

You have to know the URL of the feed and enter it in the correct format. Most feeds either begin with an address similar to or have an address similar to the one shown: `http://feeds.someadddress.com/myfeed` or `feeds://someaddress.com/myfeed/`.

Looking for a Blogger widget that will make it easier for visitors to subscribe to your blog? The Blogger team has been hard at work on the subscription links page element for you.

A disadvantage of the method we just tried is that only the post titles are shown. If you want to show some post content, use the **Add Content with RSS Feeds** method described on the Beta Blogger for the Dummies site:

`http://betabloggerfordummies.blogspot.com/2006/10/add-content-with-rss-feeds.html`

We've used page elements to add external feeds to our blog and used FeedBurner to redirect our blog feeds and add additional features to our blog. The disadvantage of using FeedBurner was that we had to hack our template to add subscription links under each post. Blogger has a solution to that very issue with a new page element widget called **Subscription Links**.

Test Driving Blogger Subscription Links

We had earlier used FeedBurner to provide an easy way for visitors to subscribe to our blog. If you don't want to use FeedBurner, but still want an easy way for visitors to subscribe to your blog feed without hacking your template, then the new **Subscription Links** widget is for you.

Blogger has made offering your blog feeds to visitors easier with the **Subscription Links** widget. This widget is in Blogger draft as of December 2007. The available feed reader services include those most popular links with Blogger users.

Making it Easy for Visitors to Add Your Feeds

Visitors can now add your blog to their feed reader or iGoogle home page with two clicks. We can make this possible by adding a page element widget to the sidebar of our blog. We have to choose the feed readers we want to display and different blog feeds we want visitors to be able to subscribe to.

Time for Action!—Using the Subscription Links Widget

We'll add the **Subscription Links** page element from the draft version of our blog. Then, we will configure it by choosing the feed delivery services that we want to display to our visitors.

1. First you should be logged into `http://draft.blogger.com`, to access the experimental page elements. (Note: Once this feature is live, it will appear in your regular list of Blogger page elements.) Log in to Blogger on the draft. blogger.com site and then click on the **Layout** link. Click on the **Add a New Page Element** link on your layout sidebar to open the page element list.

2. Choose the **Subscription Link** page element. It should look similar to the following screenshot:

3. Configure the page element. Check the boxes next to the feed services that you want to display next to your blog. We'll choose all of them for this example. Click **Save Changes** to finish adding the page element to the blog.

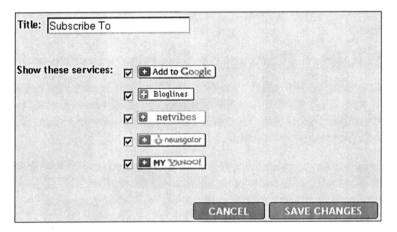

4. Clear your browser's cache and then view your blog. An example of how it will look is shown in the following screenshot. Note that visitors can also choose to **SUBSCRIBE TO** the **Posts** or **All Comments** feeds. Hovering the mouse over a button expands it to show all the feed buttons that we had chosen, while configuring the page element.

What Just Happened?

When we added the **Subscription Links** page element to our blog, we made it possible for visitors to easily choose from multiple feeds and feed readers. We can quickly change the available feed reader choices by editing the page element from the **Template | Page Element** screen. If you set the **Posts** feed or **All Comments** feed to **None** on the **Site Feed** page, they will not appear when this page element is active.

Subscription Links versus FeedBurner Redirect

The big advantage of using subscription links, instead of a FeedBurner redirect, is that it automatically displays all available feeds from our blog in the drop-down list. Using FeedBurner, we would have to add feeds for blog comments and per-post comments separately. We will also avoid using a third-party tool from an outside source.

You should choose to use FeedBurner if you want additional tools to measure and market your blog. For example, Blogger does not give you a count of your subscribers or graphical reports like FeedBurner does. Since FeedBurner has been acquired by Google, we should see more improvements and changes that allow Google's many tools to work together.

Summary

We've explored different ways to make our Blogger feeds available for users. We can now:

- Measure, redirect, and track our blog using a third-party tool, such as FeedBurner.
- Manage our blog feeds with Blogger.
- Add outside feeds to our blog.

Providing feeds opens up new ways for us to publicize our blog and share content with others. We can also add convenience for our readers and hopefully turn them into regular readers when they subscribe to our feeds.

Next, in Chapter 7, we will monetize our blog using Adsense and e-commerce tools, such as PayPal. We'll add and use PayPal's new storefront tool to sell products on our blog and also explore affiliate programs, such as Amazon Affiliates, to bring in additional potential revenue.

7
Making Money with Ads

Bloggers like you make money with ads everyday. You've seen a lot of other blogs with ads and have thought about using ads to bring in extra revenue for your blog. Knowing about the different types of ads and how to set them up effectively will make your ads appealing to visitors and increase your potential revenue.

We're going to uncover the mysteries behind:

- Setting up Google Ads on your blog
- Increasing revenue with FeedBurner
- Managing your ads
- Getting the most out of your AdSense ads
- Discovering alternative sources of ad revenue

Eating a Google AdSense and Blogger Sandwich

They go together like strawberry jelly and peanut butter. Google's ownership of AdSense and Blogger is a big benefit for blogspot bloggers. It is in Google's best interest to continue to make improvements to how these tools work together. So, you can expect to see great integrations between the two in the future. To keep up with the latest changes to AdSense, visit or subscribe to the Inside AdSense blog (`http://adsense.blogspot.com`).

A big advantage to using Google tools is that when you are logged into Gmail, the login information is passed to sites such as AdSense, and they automatically log you in when you visit them. You can also rest easier knowing the motto of the Google testing team—*If it ain't broke, you're not trying hard enough* (`http://googletesting.blogspot.com`). This team puts in their best to ensure that the different Google sites play nicely with each other.

AdSense isn't your only advertising revenue option. There are many other similar advertising networks out there. We will check out several of them at the end of this chapter. Let's warm up our ad display skills by digging into AdSense.

Setting up Google AdSense for Your Blog

AdSense is the easiest advertising program to set up for your blog. The integrations between AdSense and Blogger make setting up a basic AdSense ad block a painless process. If you don't already have an active AdSense account, Blogger will give you a chance to create one when you select the AdSense page element.

Creating AdSense Ads with Blogger Page Elements

Google funds all their cool projects such as Blogger from selling ads. So naturally, there is a page element widget you can use to display AdSense ads on your site. You will have to give Blogger a portion of your ad revenue in exchange for the simplicity of using the AdSense page element. Think of it as a convenience fee.

Time for Action!—Using the AdSense Page Element

Before you begin, you need to decide where you want the ads to go on the template. Our current choices using the template layout section under the **Page Elements** sub-tab are the right sidebar and the footer area of the page. Let's put a set of ads on the right sidebar.

1. Log in to Blogger and click the **Layout** link next to your blog in the **Dashboard**. Navigate to the **Layout | Page Elements** area and click **Add a Page Element** on the right sidebar. Select the **AdSense** page element from the list of page elements and click **ADD TO BLOG** to begin configuring the ad block.

2. Instead of the usual page element configuration screen, you will see a window explaining the AdSense program. It contains a sign up form at the bottom of the screen. Before you start configuring the AdSense widget, you will need to sign in to AdSense or create an AdSense account. If you don't have an AdSense account, enter your **Email address** and click the **CREATE ACCOUNT** button. An example of the create account form is shown in the following screenshot. As Georgia has already created an account, we can click on the **Sign in** link to continue setting up our ad block.

> Already have an AdSense account? Sign in.
>
> Identity
>
> **Email address**   fruitforall@gmail.com
>
> Language
>
> **Blog language:**   English
> Please tell us the language in which your blog is published.
>
> **Email language:**   English (US)
> Please tell us which language you prefer for email correspondence.
>
> CREATE ACCOUNT

3. Clicking the **Sign in** link loads a new screen. There is a link at the top to create an AdSense account. They sure are persistent! Type the email address, and postal code associated with your AdSense account into the text fields as shown in the following screenshot. That's right, not your Blogger information, your AdSense account information. If they are the same, great, one less detail to worry about. A phone number can also be used instead of a postal code. Click the **SIGN IN** button to continue.

> **AdSense Email**   fruitforall@gmail.com   *Specify the email address of the AdSense account.*
>
> **Postal Code**   30188   *Specify the postal code of the AdSense account, if any.*
>
> — or —
>
> **Phone Number**   ‎   *Specify the last five digits of the phone number associated with the AdSense account, if any.*
>
> SIGN IN

4. Now it is time to configure the ad. The **Ad Unit** ad type is the default for the AdSense page element block. It can serve both text, and image ads. As we're putting this ad block on the sidebar, we select the narrower **160 x 600 Vertical Wide Banner** from the **Format** drop-down list.

5. We select **Blend Template** from the **Colors** drop-down list. Displayed below the **Colors** drop-down list is a group of colors that should work with our own template colors. Moving from the top to the bottom of the group, let's blend the ad colors with the template by clicking on the hexadecimal color boxes, choosing white (**#ffffff**) for the **Background**, black (**#000000**) for the **Text**, and dark green (**#1b703a**) for the **Url** and **Title**. We can view a **Preview** of the ad block while making the changes. Now we are ready to save our settings and view our new ad block.

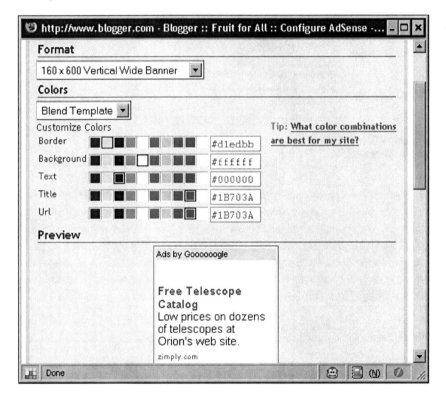

 Google recommends the following ad format sizes for maximum effectiveness: 300 width x 250 height, 336 wide x 280 height, and 160 width x 600 height.

6. Hey, it's looking mighty nice! The colors are a seamless complement to the blog, but different enough to stand out. We will have to decide if we want the ad block as the top item on the sidebar or not. Moving it around the sidebar can be done by dragging and dropping the page element box on the **Layout** screen.

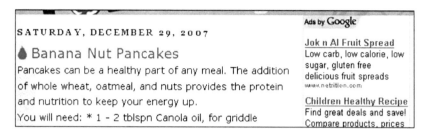

What Just Happened?

When you chose the AdSense page element, you activated a feature that is integrated with Google's AdSense advertising network. A sign in screen was presented to tie your preferred AdSense account to the blog. You can have only one AdSense account per bank account. Blogger is serious about reporting potential income from ad revenue to tax authorities. You can use the same AdSense for multiple sites. Signing in using the Blogger page element does not permanently tie your AdSense account to your blog. Changing the AdSense account or publisher id can be done by editing the page element.

Once you were successfully logged in, the actual configuration screen for the AdSense page element appeared. You probably noticed that the AdSense page element is limited to **Ad Unit** (text and image) ads for now. The ad format choices for that ad type were also restricted. To add other types of Google ads, we need to create custom ads on the AdSense site and paste the resulting code into an **HTML/JavaScript** page element. We will do that later in the chapter. We were able to select different sizes of ads, referred to as formats by Google. We also had the option to select from a set of color palettes, or customize our look. Blogger gave us a real-time preview of how our ad block would look. When we were satisfied, we saved the page element. This sent a message to AdSense to receive authorization from us.

Your email box should have contained a message similar to "Google AdSense Verification for blogger.com", with a link to authorize the sharing of code and performance information. This is a handy security feature in case someone else decides to hijack your blog for their ads.

We've tried setting up an AdSense ad the easy way. Now it's time to dig deeper into AdSense and explore the different flavors of ads we have to choose from. You can stick to the default Blogger AdSense page element. But, as you will see in the next section, you would be severely limiting the ways your blog can earn revenue through ads.

Using Custom AdSense Ads

AdSense provides many additional types of ads besides the light weight version of AdSense content units currently available in Blogger. You can even entertain your visitors with rich multimedia content while displaying ads using video units.

AdSense ads are useful and popular. They are:

- **Customizable**: There are more choices as compared with the Blogger AdSense page element.
- **Flexible**: There is a choice of many different ad products and formats.
- **Transferable**: The same ads can be shown on multiple sites.

Each ad product type can be edited to match the theme, and content of your blog. Some of them, such as the video unit ads, allow you to specify certain content categories, or sources. Others automatically customize the categories of ads they display, based on the content of your blog.

Considering Your AdSense Options

There are more text ads available with AdSense. There are many AdSense product types and each one of them has a different way of earning revenue with ad placement. To see samples of the ad formats visit: `https://www.google.com/adsense/static/en_US/AdFormats.html`.

Here is a breakdown of your options:

- **Link units**: It provides only Text Ads.
- **AdSense content units**: It provides text and image ads. The image ads may be animated.
- **AdSense for search**: It provides a search box for your site and the web. You can earn revenue when visitors click an ad on the search results page.
- **Referrals**: It displays only ads from Google or Google partners. You can earn a little extra when visitors click on a referral ad.

- **Video unit ads**: It provides flexible ways to add additional multimedia content and revenue to your blog.
- **Mobile ad units**: It provides ads that visitors can interact with from their mobile phones.

The maximum number of AdSense for content ad blocks on a site is three. After you choose an ad product you will need to design how it will look on your site.

Designing Your AdSense Ads

You have a lot of control over how your ad blocks look. The colors and sizes can be matched to fit your blog's template and build your visitor's trust. AdSense color palettes contain colors for your ads that go well together. You will be perceived as a professional who happens to support the blog with ads.

Time for Action!—Creating a Custom AdSense Ad Block

Let's create our own customized ad block. We'll choose the format, colors, and advertising channels we want, and then place the ad on our blog using a HTML/JavaScript page element.

1. Log in to your AdSense account and select the **AdSense Setup** tab. First, we need to decide an ad product to add to our blog. We are going to place this ad in the footer of our site. Choose the **AdSense for Content** link by clicking on the product title. Select the **Ad unit** ad type, choose **Text only** from the drop-down list, and then click the **Continue** button.

2. It's time to customize our ad. The **Format** should be wide, since it will be on the bottom. Select the **468 x 60 Banner** from the **Format** drop-down list. This shape will fit the bottom section of the blog.

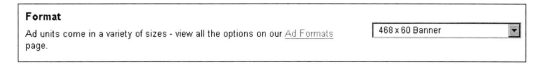

3. Google has pre-designed color palettes to choose from, as well as a customizable list of color choices for each element of the ad. We can see an instant preview of our ad directly below the **Colors** description while making the changes. Let's start with a color palette and customize it. Select the **Seaside** color palette from the **Colors** drop-down list. Enter (**#ccffcc**) into the text field next to the **Border** color. This will match the background of the edges of the blog. Change the **Title** link text to the darkest green (**#11593c**) by selecting it from the color box.

4. The final step in configuring the actual look of the ad is to choose the shape of the corners of the ad and the display, if no ads are available. Select **Slightly rounded corners** from the **Corner Styles** drop-down list. Under the **More Options** section, select the **show public service ads** radio button. Click the **Continue** button to move to the next step.

5. Now, we will create a custom ad channel. Click the **Add new channel** link at the bottom of the screen. You will be prompted to enter a name for the channel. Type **banner for footer** and click the **OK** button. The channel will appear in the **All channels** box. Click the **Continue** button to make a name for the ad.

6. Now it's time to name the ad. The name will be seen only by us and not by our visitors. So, we can describe it uniquely, in a way that makes sense to us. Let's name it **468 x 60 footer banner**. This name identifies the size of the ad and its location.

7. Now, its time to get the custom ad code. Paste the code into the content area of an **HTML/JavaScript** page element, and then click on **SAVE SETTINGS** to finally set up the custom ad.

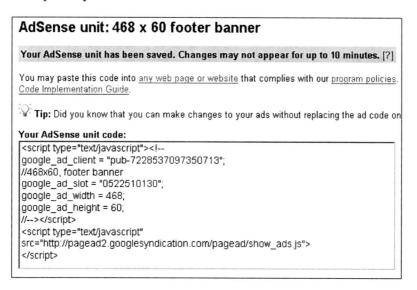

Enjoy a cup of tea or your favorite beverage—you've earned it! While you are relaxing, take a look at how nice the custom ad appears. It does look right at home, doesn't it?

What Just Happened?

When you began the steps to create a new AdSense content ad, Google created a unique id for the ad, assigning it a `google_ad_slot` number. Once you have chosen a format for the ad, you have locked the ad block into that size and presentation. To change the format after running the AdSense wizard, you will have to create a new ad.

After choosing the format, you were able to change the colors and border shape of the ad box, which gave you finer control over the look of the ad block. The ad box should be high in contrast, enough to visually grab the eye without using colors that are too bright, or different from the blog template. The text should be dark, and the background white, or any light color. Reverse that on blogs with dark backgrounds, unless you want your ads to really go unnoticed.

Next, you told Google to set up a unique tracking channel for reporting the ad. You noticed that you could create up to five different channels for the ad, tracking color changes or other performance related items. Think of channels as labels for the ads on your site. They are not the titles or the names of the ad, but are similar to blog post labels, which help describe a blog post, but not the title or the content. These labels are unique identifiers while viewing reports in AdSense. There are actually two types of channels: the custom channel that we set up a few days ago and the URL channels. URL channels help you compare sites with each other in your AdSense reports. We'll talk about channels in detail a little later, since it's a confusing topic.

Now, the ad itself has been set up, but has not been named. Just like Pinocchio, it needs a name before it can go out into the world as a real ad. We'll give it a descriptive title that includes the size and location of the ad to enable easy management when our ads are placed in a table along with several other ads.

After all the hard work you put in slogging through the wizard, you are finally rewarded with the code snippet for your blog. Google has taken all your form input throughout the wizard steps, processed it, and presented you with a block of code. This code contains your publisher id, containing your publisher id, the ad slot id, the size of the ad block, and a link back to AdSense to process and serve the ads. The biggest payoff for going to all this trouble is that now you can post this ad on all your sites, not just on your blog.

When you paste the code into an HTML/JavaScript page element in Blogger, the first set of JavaScript tags contain the basic details about the ad block. The second set contains a link to Google's ad syndication system.

 If you already have ads setup, you can paste the code into your blog using the HTML/JavaScript page element.

Putting YouTube Videos to Work with Video Units

You have already shown videos on your blog. Let's put them to work, to provide additional content, and to increase your ad revenue.

Before You Begin

You will need the following, before you begin setting up video units on your blog:

- YouTube account
- AdSense account
- An activated link between the two accounts

To link your YouTube account with your AdSense account, log in to AdSense, and click on the **Video units** product. You will be redirected to the YouTube site. You will then be presented with YouTube's **Create Account** form. YouTube has already populated the form with the email address from your AdSense account. Every field is required. Fill it out, agree to the terms of use and privacy policy, and click the **Sign Up** button. You will be asked to confirm your AdSense account. Enter the last five digits of the **Phone Number** associated with your account, and the **Zip or Postal Code**. Click the **Submit Confirmation** button. An example of the confirmation screen is shown in the following screenshot:

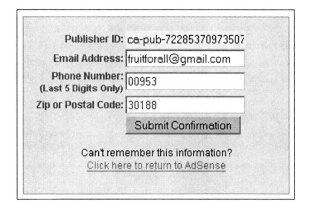

The screen will refresh and display a message congratulating you on joining the AdSense and YouTube account in linkage. Now let's add a video unit to the blog.

Time for Action!—Adding Video Units

We will customize a video player for our blog, and then add it to our blog using the **HTML/JavaScript** page element. In the future, it is possible for Blogger to have a video unit AdSense page element. Remember you'll need an active AdSense and YouTube account, before you begin.

1. Sign in to your AdSense account (http://www.google.com/adsense). Click the **AdSense Setup tab | Get ads** and then select the **Video unit** product. AdSense will redirect you to the YouTube site to begin customizing the video unit.

2. Type a unique **Player Name** and **Description** for the video unit player. Georgia has recommended not to name her video units.

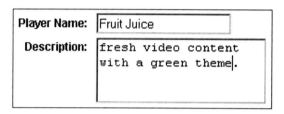

3. Now for the fun part. Design your player by customizing the colors and layout. Let's click on the green theme to create a colorful and an eye-catching video player.

4. Here's the important part, so be careful. We can either display content that is automatically targeted at our blog, or we can pick and choose our content from different content providers and categories. Select the **Automated Content** radio button, and then add the keywords **organic fruit, recipes, cooking, how to cook**, and **eco-friendly** to the **Hints** text field.

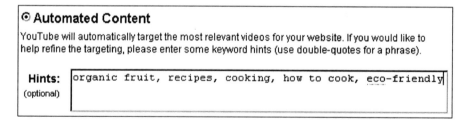

5. Now we need to choose a size for our player. Currently, none of the sizes offered are small enough for most Blogger sidebars. We may want to place it at the top or bottom of our blog for now. Select the **Mini** player size.

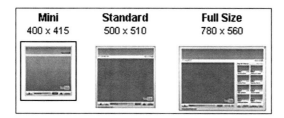

6. It is time now to grab the code. Click the **Generate code** button. Copy the code snippet that appears, and paste it onto the **HTML/JavaScript** page element. The code should look similar to the following example:

```
<div id='vu_ytplayer_
            vjVQa1PpcFP5OnXAjtXF7UdXj1B0lnHkvBVWuN4lzzo='>
<a href='http://www.youtube.com/browse'>Watch the latest videos on
                                    YouTube.com</a></div>
<script type='text/javascript' src='http://www.youtube.com/cp/
vjVQa1PpcFP5OnXAjtXF7UdXj1B0lnHkvBVWuN4lzzo='></script>
```

7. The videos should begin showing up as soon as the code is added to our blog. Go ahead and watch a few of the videos to see if they fit. An example of the player in the footer area of the blog is shown in the following screenshot:

What Just Happened?

When we linked our AdSense and YouTube accounts together, we were able to show YouTube video units on our blog to increase the potential ad revenue. Customizing the YouTube video player gave us control over the size and appearance of the player to match the look of our blog in a better way. When we were done with creating the player, we were given a block of code to add to a page element on our blog. Once we pasted the code onto the page element, the code retrieved the file information, and then served up YouTube videos and ads to our blog.

The tracking code within the code block communicates with AdSense, keeping track of all clicks on ads shown within the specialized YouTube player.

 It's okay to watch the videos occasionally, but don't click on the ads. Clicking the ads of a video unit is a violation of the AdSense policies.

Managing Video Unit Players

All the players you have created will appear in a list as shown in the following screenshot. You can edit the colors and content of the player by clicking the **Edit Player** button. The edit screen for the player works in a similar way as the creation screen. You can also create new players or remove a player. Remember, you will not be able to change the size of the player once it is created. The mini player also still seemed really big for our blog. Hopefully, we will see even smaller players in the near future.

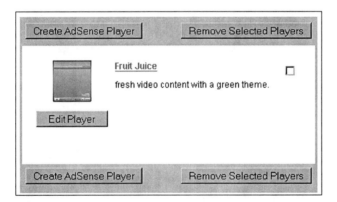

Why this, instead of the Blogger video bar page element? Though the video bar is cool, currently it does not integrate with AdSense. Another product found on AdSense that isn't available as a source of ready revenue is AdSense for Search.

AdSense for Search

Your Blogger blog comes with a Google search tied for searching within your blog, but that isn't going to help you make any money. As long as you limit your AdSense blocks to three or less, you can use a custom AdSense search block in your blog. There are many advantages of adding one to your blog. Here are the top four advantages:

- Adds up to three URLs for integrated SiteSearch
- Google pays you when visitors click on search result ads
- Adds a useful feature for visitors that give them another reason to return
- Helps building visitor's trust

Whatever reason you have for wanting to add an AdSense search block, you'll find it easy to set up. Let's go ahead and work on setting one up for our blog now.

Adding a Custom AdSense for Search to Your Blog

Before you begin trying to add AdSense for Search to your blog, you should have an AdSense account, ready to use. Look earlier in the chapter for details about how to do that. Once you have an AdSense account, you will need to decide which type of search to add. You have two choices currently: **Google WebSearch** and **Google WebSearch + SiteSearch**. The second option is the best choice when you want to enable visitors to find information that might be buried deep within old posts. Let's go ahead and add a **Google WebSearch + SiteSearch** block to our blog.

Time for Action!—Setting up AdSense for Search

We're ready to add an AdSense for Search block to our blog. We'll pick the search block, configure it, and then add it to our blog using an **HTML/JavaScript** page element.

1. Log in to AdSense. Click the **AdSense for Search** product link on the **Get Ads** page. A brief overview of the product will be displayed. Click the **Get Started** button to begin the setup wizard.

2. Choose the **Search Type** you want to use on your blog. We want our visitors to search the web as well as our blog. So, select the **Google WebSearch + SiteSearch** radio button. Type the URL of your blog: **http://fruitforall.blogspot.com**.

○ **Google WebSearch**

Allows users to search the web directly from your site

⦿ **Google WebSearch + SiteSearch**

Allows users to search the web or the specific site(s) of your choice

Enter up to three URLs for SiteSearch:

http:// `fruitforall.blogspot.com`

http:// `                    `

http:// `                    `

3. Configuring the **Search box style** directly controls how the search box will look on your blog. Select the **Google Logo** radio button under **Logo type**. Select the **Logo above text box** field and the **Search button below text box** field. Leave the **Background color** and **Length of text box** settings unchanged.

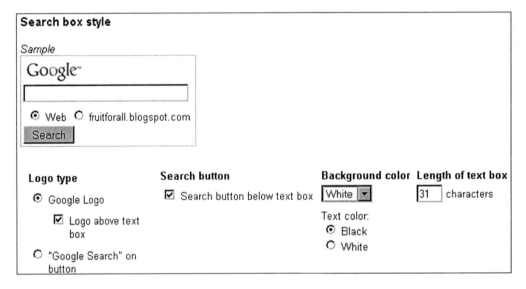

4. Review the **More options** section at the bottom of the screen. Google should have automatically selected the correct **Site language**, **site encoding**, and **Country** or territory for you. After verifying that they are correct, click the **Continue** button.

5. Our **Search Results** page needs style. The changes we make will appear in a dynamic sample box on the left side of the **Search Results Style** page. Select **Seaside** from the **Palettes** drop-down list. Change the **Border** color to (**#d1edbb**), the **Title** to (**#006600**), **URL** to (**#006600**), and the **Logo Background** to (**#ffffff**). Next, enter the **URL** path for your logo into the **Logo image URL** text field. The path for Georgia's smaller logo is **http://www.leesjordan.net/social/ffa_logoth109.jpg**. This optional step adds a professional look to the search results page. After you type in the path of the logo, the sample will be refreshed and displayed with a copy of the logo, as shown in the following screenshot:

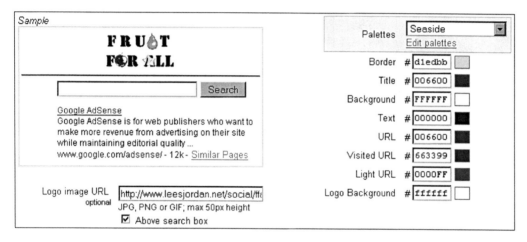

6. Look, it's our dear friend, the **More options** section. The **Opening of search results** page should be set to **Open results on Google in the same window**. The **Site-flavored search** should have **Customize the type of search results I get to my site content** checked. As there are no profiles on the drop-down list, click on **Add new profile** to create one. Type **organic** for the profile in the pop-up box, and then click the **OK** button. The new profile item will be added to the drop-down list. Put a check on the **Use SafeSearch** checkbox. We need to create a custom channel for our search box. Click the **Add new channel** link, and type **ffa search box** in the pop-up box. Click the **OK** button, and the item will be dynamically added to the drop-down list. Click the **Continue** button to move to the next step.

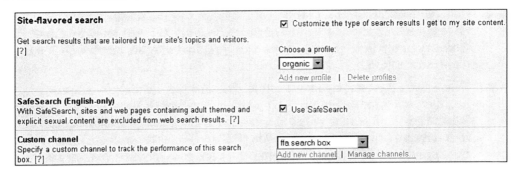

7. It's finally **Get Search Code** time! Copy and paste the code into an **HTML/ JavaScript** page element. Don't use the exact code given here, unless you want Georgia to enjoy the fruits of your site's search box ad revenue.

```
<!-- SiteSearch Google -->
<form method="get" action="http://www.google.com/custom"
            target="_top"><table border="0" bgcolor="#ffffff">
  <tr><td nowrap="nowrap" valign="top" align="left" height="32">
  <a href="http://www.google.com/">
  <img src="http://www.google.com/logos/Logo_25wht.gif"
                                        border="0"
  alt="Google" align="middle"></img></a><br/>
  <input type="hidden" name="domains"
  value="fruitforall.blogspot.com"></input>
  <label for="sbi" style="display: none" Enter your search
  terms></label>
  <input type="text" name="q" size="31" maxlength="255"
        value="" id="sbi"></input>
  </td></tr>
  <tr><td nowrap="nowrap"><table><tr><td>
  <input type="radio" name="sitesearch" value="" checked
  id="ss0"></input>
  <label for="ss0" title="Search the Web"><font size="-1"
  color="#000000">Web</font></label></td><td>
  <input type="radio" name="sitesearch"
  value="fruitforall.blogspot.com" id="ss1"></input>
  <label for="ss1" title="Search fruitforall.blogspot.com"><font
  size="-1" color="#000000">fruitforall.blogspot.com
  </font></label></td></tr></table>
  <label for="sbb" style="display: none">Submit search
                                        form</label>
  <input type="submit" name="sa" value="Search" id="sbb"></input>
  <input type="hidden" name="client"
        value="pub-7228537097350713"></input>
  <input type="hidden" name="forid" value="1"></input>
  <input type="hidden" name="channel" value="4474446872"></input>
  <input type="hidden" name="ie" value="ISO-8859-1"></input>
```

```
<input type="hidden" name="oe" value="ISO-8859-1"></input>
<input type="hidden" name="safe" value="active"></input>
<input type="hidden" name="flav" value="0000"></input>
<input type="hidden" name="sig" value="BSNIkd2tTVMlE0xC"
                                             ></input>
<input type="hidden" name="cof"
value="GALT:#006600;GL:1;DIV:#d1edbb;VLC:663399;AH:center;BGC:
FFFFFF;LBGC:ffffff;ALC:006600;LC:006600;T:000000;GFNT:0000FF;
GIMP:0000FF;LH:50;LW:95;L:http://www.leesjordan.net/social/ffa_
logoth109.jpg;S:http://;FORID:1"></input>
<input type="hidden" name="hl" value="en"></input>
</td></tr></table>
</form><!-- SiteSearch Google -->
```

8. After adding the new search box widget, we need to check the blog for any display issues. When we view the blog, we can see that the search box fits neatly into our sidebar.

What Just Happened?

When you selected the **Google WebSearch + SiteSearch** type, you set the variable control to allow users either to choose search the web, or perform the search on the site.

Next, you changed how the items within the search box widget were arranged in relationship to each other. The Background color could have been set to black or grey to match a template with a dark theme. When changing the Background color to black or white, the text color should also be changed. Otherwise, the text will not be visible. As the sidebar on our template is narrow, changing the length to a longer width would not have helped.

Customizing the appearance of the search results page was the next major step. Adding a custom logo gave visitors a reminder that they were using search from your site. When you entered a URL path for the logo, you told the form to follow the path to the image, and replace the placeholder logo with the provided logo image URL. If the path contained an error, the image would not display in the preview window. We also had the option to display the logo below the search box, instead of above it. Displaying the logo above the search box keeps it from being mistaken for an ad.

More options contained advanced settings for the search box widget. Setting the search results to open in the same window made it possible to avoid opening additional browser windows. However, the disadvantage is that users can then navigate away from your blog, instead of having it available in another window. Checking the checkbox in the **Site-flavored search** section sets a flag in the code to return results matching the topics on the blog, making them more relevant to your audience. Creating a new profile made it possible to organize pages or sites with the same type of content together to increase the relevance of results. You can find out more about it by reading this detailed article in the AdSense Help Center: `https://www.google.com/adsense/support/bin/answer. py?answer=35784&ctx=en:search&query=profile&topic=&type=f`.

Setting up Referral Ad Units

Referral ads have been around for a while. They work when someone clicks on a referral ad, downloads an application, or signs up for a service. Only then do you receive the money in your AdSense account. You decide which categories and products to show in the ads. It is common to see referral ads for the Firefox browser, and Google services. Traditional advertising categories such as *Home & Garden* have not proven to be popular choices.

Time for Action!—Adding a Referral Ad Unit

It's time to prepare and place a referral ad on our blog. This service may not be available in all the areas of our blog. We will configure the ad, grab the code block, and then add it to our blog using a **HTML/JavaScript** page element.

1. Log in to AdSense. Click on the **Referrals** link on the **Get Ads** page. The **Description** screen will then be displayed. Click the **Get started now!** button to continue to the set up page.

2. Select **Ad format** for you referral block. We want to use this ad unit in our sidebar, so choose the **180 x 60 button** ad format. The **Categories** are listed in a tree menu structure. Clicking the plus symbol [+] next to a category name will show the list of ad products underneath the main category. Click the **view products** link next to an item to see if there are actually any ad products available for that product group.

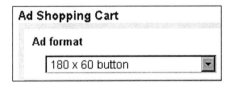

Once you start adding a product to your cart, you will not be able to change your ad format.

3. If ads are available for a product group, you will see a list of ads below it on the **view products** page. To restrict the referrals to those that match the **Ad format** size, select the **Restrict** checkbox. You will see a list of available ad formats. Put an ad in your cart by clicking the **Add product to cart** button.

4. The ads will be listed in the cart product. We can decide whether we want to display only those ads with the best performance record, or if we want to display image-based ads, below the product list. Put a check on the **Pick best performing ads** checkbox.

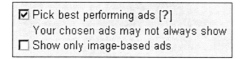

5. Click the **Advanced options** link to add a **Custom channel**, making it easier to identify the ad block. You can either group your current referral ad block with an existing channel, or create a new one. Adding a new channel involves the same process as that for other ad products. Click the **Add new channel** link and enter a name for your channel. We will type **Google and Firefox referrals** in the pop-up window. Click **OK** and you will be taken to the main configuration page. The new channel has now been added to the **Custom channel** drop-down list.

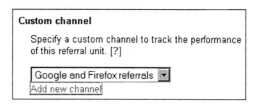

6. The final configuration step in AdSense is to choose an **AdSense unit name**. This is the title that will appear on the **Manage ads** page. Let's leave it set to the default name, **180 x 60, created 1/11/08** for now. We will change it later, when we work on managing our ads. Click the **Submit and Get Code** button to activate the ad unit and grab the code for our blog.

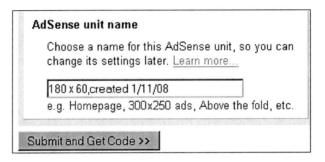

7. Copy the code from the **Your AdSense unit code** field. Log in to your blog, and click on the **Layout** link on your **Dashboard**. Paste the code into a new **HTML/JavaScript** page element on your blog. Click the **SAVE SETTINGS** button to finish adding it to your blog.

Your AdSense unit code:
```
<script type="text/javascript"><!--
google_ad_client = "pub-7228537097350713";
//120x60, created 1/11/08
google_ad_slot = "6957314601";
google_ad_width = 120;
google_ad_height = 60;
google_cpa_choice = ""; // on file
//--></script>
<script type="text/javascript"
src="http://pagead2.googlesyndication.com/pagead/show_ads.js">
</script>
```

8. It can take a few minutes for the ad unit to activate. So, go for a quick walk or take a short nap. When the referral ad unit is active on your blog, it should look similar to the following screenshot:

What Just Happened?

When you selected the ad format for the referral unit, AdSense set the value of the format size and saved it. Selecting a product and adding it to the shopping cart space locked the size of the ad and prevented any further edits to the ad format type.

The available products for the referral ad are based upon the chosen ad format. The larger the ad format, the more product choices you will have. While looking for available products, you can browse for an item by typing in a keyword and then clicking the **Browse** button. If you browse and don't like the results, you must click the **Back** button to return to the full list of referral categories.

We were able to add products for the Google pack and Firefox. Be sure to view the product you are interested in to check for available ads, as not every product has an ad associated with it. Once you choose a product, you will not be able to do this.

As with all other Ad products, you will see links to preview, edit, and create a new AdSense unit, directly below the code block.

Why Not to Use Referrals

Compared to the ease of setting up the other ad products, this one is torture. It's not up to Google's usually high user interaction standards. Seriously, this is no fun whatsoever. If you really are passionate about sharing the Google pack or Firefox browser with your visitors, go ahead and use referrals. I think I would rather go to the dentist myself. There are bucketful of usability issues you face when trying to set up referrals:

- Being slowly phased out and not available to all AdSense users.
- Convoluted set up process with too many clicks and not enough real product choices.
- Confusing terminology.

Referrals require users to drill down into a product category, and then visit an additional page to determine if there are any ads associated with that product. The referrals feature does not automatically disable products which do not currently have ads associated with them. Using the word, shopping cart, for a list of ad products gives users the assumption that they'll have to make a purchase. How about a different term, like *Referral group* or *ad queue*? Referrals is painful to use and takes too long to set up.

Getting the Most Out of AdSense Ads

There's more to making money with ads than placing them on our blog. We also need to check their progress regularly and get the most out of our ads by:

- Managing ads by editing settings
- Using reports
- Filtering out competitive sites

Now that we've installed AdSense Ads, let's take a look at how to manage them in AdSense.

Managing Ads in AdSense

When you select the **Manage Ads** page in AdSense, you will see a screen similar to following one. You will see a list of all active ads, the date they were last edited, the content types, ad size, status, and channels. You can edit the settings of each ad under **Actions** by clicking the **Edit settings** link. Clicking on the **Code** link will display the code box for the ad or the products page in the case of Referrals. AdSense Content ads can be edited by changing the color scheme of the ad, the name, and the content format of the ad.

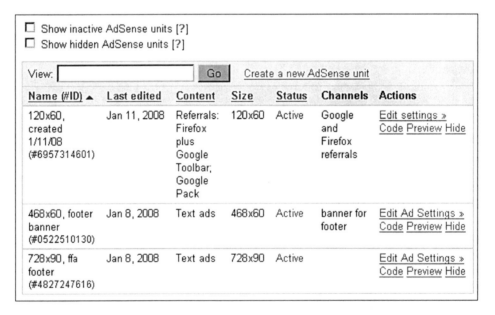

Using Advanced Reports

AdSense generates periodic reports on the first day of every month and once a week on Mondays. We want more than that. We want to see reports with customized date ranges, selected channels, and a choice of views. AdSense gives us the freedom to create advanced reports with many features. We can also export any report as a CSV file (Comma Separated Values) and view it in a spreadsheet program.

 You will see your custom generated reports and the periodic reports on the **Reports Manager** page under **Recently Generated Reports**.

You can view reports and export them as CSV files from the main **Reports Manager** screen.

Recently Generated Reports

Report name	Created	Type	Status	Get report
one-time report	Jan 12, 2008 4:22 PM	One-time	Ready	View	CSV
one-time report	Jan 12, 2008 4:03 PM	One-time	Ready	View	CSV
one-time report	Jan 12, 2008 4:02 PM	One-time	Ready	View	CSV
one-time report	Jan 12, 2008 3:48 PM	One-time	Ready	View	CSV
one-time report	Jan 8, 2008 7:33 PM	One-time	Ready	View	CSV

Generating Reports

First, select the product. Choose **AdSense for Content** from the **Choose product** drop-down list under **Show select Channel data**. Then, place a check next to all active channels you wish to include in the report. We have clicked all three **Active Custom Channels**.

Setting the date range on the left to the **Last 7 days** will give us an idea of our performance for the last week. Note that when we make our selection from the drop-down list, the custom date range selection is populated with a one week time period. Finally, choose **Page** from the **Show data by** drop-down list.

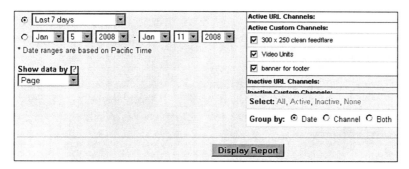

Now that we've generated our report by selecting the date, channels, and data display, we are ready to view our report.

Viewing Reports

The report will be generated and then displayed at the bottom of the screen. It will show the **Totals** and **Averages** for all selected channels based on the date range. The following report has been generated for the active ad channels. The ads were created recently, so we won't see any big money yet. The first column displays the **Date**. Under **Page impressions** we see only a few from the first two days, followed by a big increase in the next two days. Sadly, there have been zero **Clicks** on our ads so far.

The **Page CTR** (Click-through rate) percentage is calculated as the number of clicks for an ad divided by how often the ad is shown. **Page eCPM** (Cost Per thousand impressions) helps you calculate the amount of earnings versus the number of page impressions .The **Earnings** column will display our earnings for the listed dates, if we are lucky enough to have any.

Save as Custom Report: ⊙ [   ] [Save]

January 5, 2008 - January 11, 2008

○ [Replace report...   ▼]

CSV

Date	Page impressions	Clicks	Page CTR	Page eCPM [?]	Earnings
Wednesday, January 9, 2008	6	0	0.00%	$0.00	$0.00
Thursday, January 10, 2008	6	0	0.00%	$0.00	$0.00
Friday, January 11, 2008	37	0	0.00%	$0.00	$0.00
Totals	49	0			$0.00
Averages	16	0	0.00%	$0.00	$0.00

We can easily generate and view reports. Let's save this one as a custom report we can set to repeat automatically.

Time for Action!—Scheduling an Automatic Custom Report

Scheduling a report is relatively easy and saves your time. It also impresses anyone you need to send the report to. Let's schedule the custom report we set up earlier to be sent out automatically by email.

1. First, enter a unique name for the report in the **Save as Custom Report** field, above the report results. The text **Active channels week** is entered in the following example. It describes the report as one for all active channels over a one week time period.

2. Click the **Save** button. You will be taken to the **Report Manager** screen to continue setting up the report schedule.

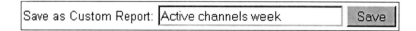

3. Now we are going to schedule a time for AdSense to generate the report and then mail it to a specific email address. Scroll down to the **Saved Report Templates** section on the **Report Manager** page. Click the checkbox next to the report name. Set **Weekly** from the **Frequency** drop-down list. The **Send to** drop-down list designates which email addresses the report will be sent to. You can add additional email addresses by clicking the **edit addresses** link.

4. The **Format** for the report is the final choice. Select **CSV** or **CSV-Excel** from the drop-down list. **CSV** will work in all types of spreadsheet programs. Alternatively, it can also be saved as a plain text file. The **CSV-Excel** format works best in, you guessed it, Microsoft Office Excel. The **Saved Report Templates** options are shown in the following screenshot:

What Just Happened?

When we created and configured our custom report to be distributed automatically by email on a weekly schedule, we instructed AdSense to save our preferences and send copies of the report to every specified email on a weekly basis.

So far, we've focused on configuring and placing ad blocks in our blog. Whenever we use programs such as AdSense, there is the risk that a competitor's ad may show up in the ad box or in the search results that our visitors see. We can block many competitive ads using filters provided by AdSense.

Using AdSense Filters

Georgia became worried when she saw a competitor's ad displayed in an AdSense ad on the blog. She asked us to filter their web address out. Ripetoyou.com was advertising for fresh fruits. We can block that URL and many others we want, using the filters within AdSense. Let's set up filters to do just that.

Time for Action!—Blocking Competitive Ads with Filters

If you already have an idea of who your competitors might be, you can add them all at once. Every time you see another competitive domain, follow these steps to block them:

1. Write down the competitive domain (`www.ripetoyou.com`) and log in to your AdSense account. An example of the competitive ad that appeared in the ad block is displayed in the following screenshot:

   > **Buy Fruit Online**
   > Fresh Delicious Fruit From our Orchard to your Home.
   > www.RipeToYou.com
   >
   > **Pancake Recipe**
   > Recipes, Menus, & More Search, Savor, & Share Now!
   > www.MyRecipes.com

2. Navigate to **AdSense Setup | Competitive Ad Filter**. The **AdSense for Content** tab should be active above the filter box. Type the domain name, without the www in front, to set the filter wide enough to catch as many variations of the URL as possible. The text `ripetoyou.com` should now be displayed in the **AdSense for Content Filters** box.

3. Click the **Save changes** button to finalize the addition of the URL.

```
ripetoyou.com
```

Save changes

What Just Happened?

When we entered the text string `ripetoyou.com`, we instructed AdSense to block all ads with a URL matching the text that we entered. We could have also typed just `ripetoyou`, to block any other domain such as `.net`, which our competitor might have. We could also have tried variations such as `fruittoyou` or `fruitshippingtoyou`.

We've worked our way through four of the ad products currently available to AdSense users. Google's purchase of FeedBurner, in the summer of 2007, is opening up new ways to bring ads to your blog.

Monetizing Blog Feeds with FeedBurner

We worked on publicizing and analyzing our blog with FeedBurner in Chapter 6. FeedBurner also provides additional ways to turn your blog feed into a source of revenue. The recent acquisition of FeedBurner by Google can only mean more choices for you.

Ways to Monetize

There is more than one way to monetize your blog feeds. Here are some ways you can do it:

- **FeedBurner Ad Network**: Qualified sites can take advantage of the established FeedBurner ad network to serve ads.
- **Google AdSense for feed content**: Ads targeted at the content of your blog and then your feeds.

If you already have FeedFlare, you've noticed the social networking tags on the bottom of each of your feeds. FeedBurner does have plans to place ads in the footer of feeds sent to feed aggregators, such as Google Reader. Right now, while I'm sitting on the couch in my living room, it is not yet a reality. You should also be aware that using the services under the **Monetize** tab is not free. Currently, FeedBurner receives 35% of its ad revenue by serving ads through them.

FeedBurner Ad Network (FAN)

The FeedBurner Ad Network (FAN) is currently invitation only. If you are eligible for the FAN, you will see a message on the **Monetize** tab in the **MyFeeds** section of FeedBurner. You can review, approve, or deny ads offered to you by the FAN service. When the FAN ads are active on your blog, they will look very similar to Google AdSense Content ads. They are rectangular text-based ads:

Advertise With FeedBurner

Advertising copy is inserted here for viewing. FeedBurner is the largest feed advertising network. Begin advertising with FeedBurner today.

www.feedburner.com   ADS BY FEEDBURNER

They can even be like the slick rich media box ads we are all familiar with by now. FeedBurner's own ad for the FAN is a perfect example, as we can see in the following screenshot:

My prediction is that Google will keep the FAN service as a premium, preferred advertising service. The networks that FeedBurner has built with huge companies such as NewsWeek, AOL, Geffen, and Circuit City are too valuable to throw away.

How can you prepare for that happy day when you would be able to offer FAN ads? If you already have FeedFlare code installed in your Blogger template, the hardest part is done. All that is left is to accept and activate service under the **Monetize** tab. Let's get a head start by adding an AdSense ad block using FeedBurner.

Displaying AdSense Ads with FeedFlare

Way back in Chapter 3 of this book, we added a FeedFlare code snippet to our Blogger template to serve up social networking tags under our blog posts. Now, as an added bonus, you can also display Google AdSense ads, if you want.

The ads will be tied directly to your AdSense account. As soon as you activate the feature under the **Monetize** tab in FeedBurner, the ads will begin making their way to your blog, merrily. They will display under the first post on your blog.

Time for Action!—Setting up AdSense Content for Feeds

You should already have a FeedBurner account before you begin. We will configure an ad starting with FeedBurner, and then add it to our blog using the FeedFlare template code that we added earlier. The ads will appear below each blog post.

1. Log in to http://www.Feedburner.com, and then click on the **MyFeeds** link. Select the **Monetize** tab and log in to AdSense from that screen. It will ask for the email address, and either a phone number or postal code associated with the Google AdSense account. Click the **Sign In** button. You will be reminded to check your email to verify and grant FeedBurner access to your AdSense code.

2. Check your email and click the authenticate link to allow FeedBurner access to the code and performance information. Return to FeedBurner.com and click the **Monetize** tab under **MyFeeds**. Now, you will be able to configure an ad block specifically for your feed.

3. Check the box next to **Display Ads from AdSense for Content**. Click the **Edit Channels** button to ad a new custom channel to track our feed. You will be redirected to the AdSense site. Click on the channels submenu item under the **AdSense Setup** tab. Type **300 x 250 clean feedflare** as the name of the channel. Click the **Add Channel** button and then return to FeedBurner. Select the highly effective **300 x 250 format** from the Ad Size drop-down list. Now, your selections should look like the following screenshot:

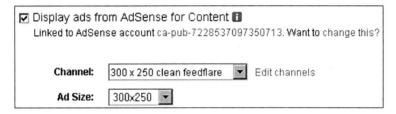

4. We will use the **Open Air** color **Palette**, since it is very neutral. Set the **Border** to white (**#ffffff**), and leave the **Title** to the standard bright blue ink color (**#0000ff**). The **Background** should be set to (**#ffffff**), the **Text** to black (**#000000**), and the **URL** links that appear below the ad information should be set to a medium green, (**#008000**). We can see a preview of our ad block in the lower right corner, under the **Palette** drop-down box.

 Save a custom palette by clicking the **Edit custom palettes** link. You'll be taken to https://www.google.com/adsense/colors. Enter a name for your custom palette and click the **Save Palette** button. You can also opt to replace a palette.

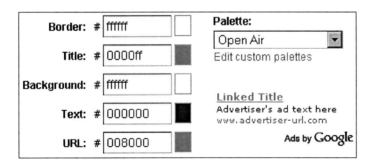

5. Click the **Activate** button at the bottom to activate the feed. It is hard to miss, being surrounded by red as it is. Now we have a lovely feed active ad block. We still need to grab the ad code and save our settings.

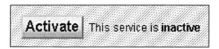

6. The page will reload once the ad block is activated. Scroll back down to just above the **Save** button and select **Blogger** from the drop-down list if you have not already added FeedFlare to your template. A new window will open up with instructions on adding the FeedFlare code to the Blogger template. We had looked at it back in Chapter 3. Click the **Save** button to save your settings. Want to see what the code snippet looks like? Here it is:

```
<script expr:src='"http://feeds.feedburner.com/~s/fruitforall?i="
  + data:post.url' type="text/javascript" charset="utf-8"></script>
```

7. We can see the ads served by the FeedFlare code snippet by looking below the top blog post.

What Just Happened?

When you checked the **Display ads from AdSense for Content** checkbox, you were prompted to create an AdSense account or sign in to an existing one. A message was sent from FeedBurner to AdSense notifying it of your request. You were then sent an email from AdSense to verify whether you really wanted to allow your AdSense information to be shared with FeedBurner.

You were then able to set up your ad block. Creating a custom channel made it possible to easily track your FeedBurner ads. Choosing between two optimal format sizes for displaying below the blog posts, we settled on **300 height x 250 width**. The format choices are severely limited compared to what is available directly from AdSense. When FeedBurner activates advertising from within feeds, the two format sizes currently provided will be the largest that will easily fit with most feed reader services.

Customizing the colors of the ad block did not change the appearance of other AdSense ads on our blog. The FeedFlare ads filter through the color settings on FeedBurner, overriding any other settings in AdSense.

When we activated the feature and saved our settings, we were able to grab a custom code snippet just for the Blogger users. FeedBurner provided a short and simple code snippet to display ads, below the first blog post, as part of the FeedFlare service.

Managing AdSense Content Ad Units in FeedBurner

Any time you uncheck the **Display ads...** box on the **Monetize** tab, the whole section below it is disabled. Deactivating the feature requires you to click the small **Deactivate** button in the bottom right corner of the screen. You can reactivate the feature again by clicking the **Activate** button.

You can change your AdSense publisher id anytime in FeedBurner by clicking the **Change this** link under the **Display ads...** check box.

Discovering Other Advertising Programs

Google AdSense is not the only game in town, but is the best known. There are many other advertising networks around. A quick Google search will bring up over 32 million results, at least 20 of which are actual advertising network sites.

You don't want to invite just any advertising program onto your site. They could turn out to be an obnoxious relative, tracking dirt into your home, and scaring away your visitors. The best ways to discover new advertising programs is through word of mouth, that is from other bloggers, or by visiting blog sites that you trust. In the meantime, there are several good resources available for you to try.

Amazon Affiliate Ads

Amazon has a great reputation and a wide selection of products for visitors to choose from. Their Affiliates program gives you the ability to sell products from your site, without keeping an inventory, or any other retailers' hassles.

Time for Action!—Adding a Customized Recommended Product Ad

Let's take part in the Amazon Affiliate program and recommend products to our visitors that tie in with the topic of our blog. We will build our product widget and then add it to our blog using the reliable HTML/JavaScript page element:

1. Log in to the Amazon affiliates page and then click on the **Build Amazon Widgets** link. Scroll down until you find a widget that you like. We will add the **Recommended Products** ad widget. Click the **Add to your Web page** button.

2. The **Recommended Product** links page will appear. Our choices will be made in the **Choose Content** box. First, select the product **Gourmet Food** from the **Select a Product Line** drop-down list. Next, select the **Enter Keywords** radio button and type **Baking Supplies, Fruits**, and **Vegetables** into the text field below it. You can click on the **See a full-size, live example** link to view the ad as you build it. Click the **Continue** button to move on to the **Select Size** screen.

3. Now it's time to select a size for your ad. You can scroll down to browse the different choices, or click a size link to jump down to a display size sample. Click the **Select this size** button for the **120 x 240** size display.

4. You can choose the default HTML code and keep the ad as it appears, or you can customize its appearance. Let's take a little time and customize the ad. Clicking the **Customize Link Appearance** link will cause it to expand. Leave the **Link Behavior** set to **Opens in New Window,** from the drop-down list. Leave **Price Options** set to **Display All Prices**. Change the **Background Color** to light grey (**f2f1f1**). Leave the **Text Color** set to black (**000000**). Change the **Link Color** to dark green (**054C07**). Click the **Update HTML** button. The page will refresh and close the **Customize Link Appearance** box.

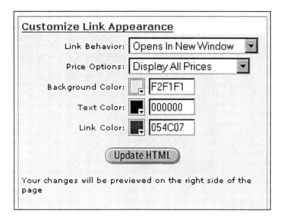

5. The **Change Link Content** box gives you another chance to change the keywords or to select a different subcategory. Let's leave that alone and focus on getting our HTML code. Click the **Highlight HTML** button and then copy the code. Log in to your blog and paste the code into a new **HTML/JavaScript** page element. Don't click the save button yet.

6. We need to tweak the code a little as the ad widget might appear too far to the left, and the top edge might be flushed against the header section of the blog. We need to add a little padding around it and move it over to the right. Set the `marginwidth="10"`, and the `marginheight="2"`, then change the style tag to `style="border:none;padding:10px;padding-left:40px;"`. A copy of the code with changes can be viewed below:

```
<iframe src="http://rcm.amazon.com/e/cm?t=fruforall-20&o=1&p=8&l=
    st1&mode=gourmet&search=Baking%20Supplies%2C%20Fruits%2C%
    20Vegetables&fc1=000000&lt1=_blank&lc1=054C07&bg1=F2F1F1&
    f=ifr" marginwidth="10" marginheight="2" width="120"
    height="240" border="0" frameborder="0" style="border:none;
    padding:10px;padding-left:40px;" scrolling="no"></iframe>
```

7. We now have a rotating Amazon product ad on our blog. Now, we've added a showcase of other products our visitors might be interested in, though it does look a little skinny.

What Just Happened?

When you chose the **Recommended Products** widget, a request was made in the background to send you to the recommended products setup wizard. Choosing the product line and keywords on the **Choose Content** screen determined the type of products pulled to populate the ad from Amazon's product database. Selecting an ad size determined how many products could be displayed at once, and allowed the system to generate the correct attributes for the code.

Customizing the widget was done on the final screen. The code contained a long search query string wrapped in an iframe tag. The tag displays even with JavaScript turned off. When the **Update HTML** button was pressed, the query string was updated each time in the code box. If you look closely, you will see the hexadecimal color codes within the query string. The box was positioned too far to the left, when pasted into a Blogger page element. Adjusting the code allowed us to manipulate the location of the widget without touching the blog's template. The widget can be edited later, just like any other page element.

Project Wonderful

Project Wonderful (`http://www.projectwonderful.com`) has a business model, different from most advertisers. It pays site owners based on the daily value of an ad, which fluctuates based on demand, called Cost per Day (CPD). They determine the cost by advertising auctions. Advertisers search for the sites where they want their ads to appear , either by category block or by targeting individual sites. They then bid for ad space on the site.

The advertisers and site owners tend to be web comic artists, young entrepreneurs, and small businesses aimed at the people in the 18-30 age band. If you have a blog that you think will interest a younger, more progressive audience, give Project Wonderful a try.

BlogAds

BlogAds (`http://www.blogads.com/publisher_html`) is an advertising group for bloggers, by bloggers. Their cooperative method of pairing niche advertising blocks with high traffic blogs has formed a strong network for bloggers. Instead of passively accepting the ads that come their way, bloggers have an active role in deciding which ads appear on their site. BlogAds is currently invitation only. Don't despair; email to `signup@blogads.com`, and they will let you know when a sponsor that fits your blog's niche is available.

There are many other ad programs out there to choose from, such as the e-commerce widget newcomer Lemonade (`http://www.lemonade.com`), a service already popular with MySpace (`http://www.myspace.com`), and Facebook (`http://www.facebook.com`) users. Try Lemonade or one of the other services mentioned above as an alternative to the traditional online ad revenue.

Summary

Earning additional revenue through advertising is a standard practice among bloggers. Now you know different ways to set up advertising on your blog. Your options include:

- Adding Google Adsense to a blog.
- Earning revenue from blog feeds.
- Using other advertising programs.

We will explore fun ways to analyze how our blog is doing using Google Analytics in Chapter 8.

8

Measuring Site Performance with Google Analytics

You want to know more about your visitors. Knowing where they come from, what posts they like, how long they stay, and other site metrics are all valuable information to have as a blogger. You would expect to pay for such a deep look into the underbelly of your blog, but Google wants to give it to you for free. Why for free? The better your site does, the more likely you are to pay for AdWords or use other Google tools. The Google Analytics online statistics application is a delicious carrot to encourage content rich sites and better ad revenue for everyone involved. By the way, in this chapter, we'll be using the names *Google Analytics* and *Analytics* interchangeably, since Google considers them to be the same thing.

Georgia comments, "Google Analytics sounds great, but can it really do more than just tell that my blog had visitors? Can it generate reports and integrate with AdWords?"

Google Analytics is a very powerful tool that has many features with easy to use visual interfaces. We will explore ways to improve site performance with Google Analytics including:

- Setting up Analytics
- Tracking site performance
- Managing reports
- Improving your site with Analytics
- Integrating with Adwords

There are many other free site statistic applications out there. Google Analytics stands out from the crowd with slick graphical reports, customizable settings, and profound answers for the fundamental question all bloggers want to know the answer to—is this site working?

"So where do we start from," asks Georgia, "do I need to install a bunch of software, or configure Google Analytics for me?"

Google Analytics is hosted by Google. There is no software to install, just a short code block to add to your blog to begin tracking its performance. Configuration of individual sites on Google Analytics is done in a friendly, easy way. No obscure log files or time consuming tasks. Let's go ahead and get ready to help Georgia set up Google Analytics for her blog.

Setting up Analytics

Analytics isn't rocket science, but it is a feature rich web application. Before climbing up the high cherry tree, that is Analytics, we will pick the low hanging fruit off the nearest branch. First, you need a Google account. You do have one after all we've been through together, right? Activating your Google Analytics account will make it possible to start collecting data on your blog right away.

Time for Action!—Activating Google Analytics

Activating your Google Analytics account will involve signing up, customizing settings, then installing a tracking code block on your blog.

1. Navigate to the Google Analytics site (www.google.com/analytics), and enter your Google username and password. If you are already logged into Gmail, you only have to enter your password as your Gmail username will be fetched automatically. On the next screen, click the **Sign Up** button.

2. You are now on the **New Account Signup** screen. Enter the URL of your blog (http://fruitforall.blogspot.com). The form will automatically suggest an **Account Name**. If you are planning to add multiple sites, keep in mind that you would want to keep them apart. Let's stick to the suggested name for now.

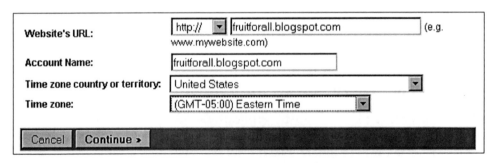

3. Your **Time zone country or territory** is already selected for you. Go ahead and correct it if it's wrong. Click the **Continue** button.

4. Accepting the user agreement is simple. Scroll down the agreement and take a good look. When you are satisfied, click the **Yes, I agree to the above terms and conditions** checkbox and click the **Create New Account** button.

5. You have a choice between the **Legacy Tracking Code (urchin.js)** and the **New Tracking Code (ga.js)**. The new tracking code is the best. Click on the **New Tracking Code** tab.

6. Sign in to your Blogger account at `www.blogger.com`. If you have more than one blog under your Blogger account, select the blog that you'll be tracking. Click the **Template** tag.

7. In the HTML code box, scroll down to the bottom of the code. Paste the Analytics tracking code directly above the closing </body> tag.

```
<script type="text/javascript">
        var gaJsHost = (("https:" == document.location.protocol) ?
        "https://ssl." : "http://www.");
        document.write(unescape("%3Cscript src='" + gaJsHost +
        "google-analytics.com/ga.js'
        type='text/javascript'%3E%3C/script%3E"));
</script>
<script type="text/javascript">
        var pageTracker = _gat._getTracker("UA-3394333-1");
        pageTracker._initData();
        pageTracker._trackPageview();
</script>
```

8. Click the **Save Template** button. Go back to Analytics and click the **Check Status** link, as shown in the following screenshot:

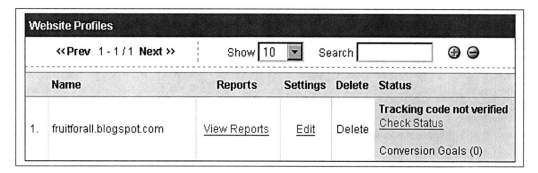

9. The **Status** box will change color as the status changes. Once the box is yellow, it should have a message noting the code is successfully installed. Click the **Finish** button.

What Just Happened?

When you activated your Google Analytics account, Google added Google Analytics to your list of Google MyAccount applications. It made the domain you added the default profile for your Analytics account during activation. You were then able to add a block of tracking code from Analytics to your blog. The tracking code began gathering data about your blog, including the posts, the content, and site metrics such as page views.

It can take a long time, anywhere from a couple of hours to several days for the tracking code to be fully activated. It's hard to be patient during the process. Deleting the profile will not help anything. It took over three days for the fruitforall. blogspot.com profile to become fully active.

Which tracking code should you use? If you are new, go for the new code. The new tracking code has additional features including event tracking and outbound link tracking. The legacy code urchin.js will not be updated.

 Google firmly believes in using colors as clues to success or failure. A yellow box means "waiting" or "in progress", a green box indicates "success", and a dark pink box means "watch out", just like a red traffic signal.

Adding Tracking Code without Editing Your Template

You can also add the code to your page without editing your template. From the **Layout | Page Elements** screen, click the **Add a Page Element** link in one of the sections. Choose an **HTML/JavaScript** page element and paste the code into the content area of the page element form. This method makes it easier to maintain your site, since you won't increase the risk of something horrible going wrong by messing directly with the template code.

Now that we have installed our tracking code, it's time to learn how to administer Google Analytics.

Administrating Google Analytics

Having administrative privileges in Analytics involves many of the same actions as other administrative consoles. You will be able to add and restrict user access, add websites, and maintain the information in Analytics.

Managing Website Profiles

A **profile** is an individual website or section under that website domain. This is what makes profiles so confusing. Just like all rectangles are not squares, a profile is not the same thing as a website. Profiles can represent different areas of an existing site, like a sub domain. You can have multiple profiles for the same site, as long as they are for different areas of the site.

Adding Additional Profiles

Georgia wants to track the progress of her company site this year using Analytics. Her marketing guru wants to see reports from the company site and the blog. Before she gives the guru access to see reports on that area, she needs to set up the correct profile.

Time for Action!—Adding a New Profile

We will add a profile from the **Analytics Settings** page. Adding a profile for a specific user will enable us to customize what they see when they log in to Google Analytics.

1. Log in to Google Analytics. Click the **Add Website Profile** link on the **Analytics Settings** page. The **Create New Website Profile** screen will appear.

2. Select **Add a Profile for a new domain** from the **Choose Website Profile Type** section.

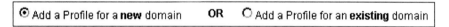

3. Now, we need to tell Google Analytics the domain for the profile. Select **http://** from the drop-down list, and then type the URL (`fruitforall. googlepages.com/`) into the text field, as shown in the following screenshot. Click the **Continue** button.

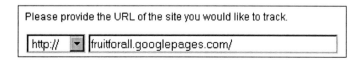

4. We've made it to the **Tracking Code** screen. Select the **New Tracking Code (ga.js)** tab. Copy the code and paste it into the pages of the new domain. This is the same code that we used for set up in the earlier section, except for the tracking code id. It is UA-3394333-2 instead of UA-3394333-1. Click the **Finish** button once you have a copy of the tracking code. You will be re-directed back to the **Analytics Settings** screen.

What Just Happened?

Every time you add a profile for a new domain, it can take as long as 48 hours for the tracking code to be verified and for data collection to begin. They say it only takes 24 hours, but from my own impatient experience it is often longer than that. Bloggers who host their own Blogger blog will find the ability to add additional profiles very useful. You will be able to view reports and use all the other features of Analytics with the new profile, and so will everyone else who is assigned to the site's profile.

 Not sure about what sites you have worth profiling? Use Google's Webmaster tools (https://www.google.com/webmasters/tools/) to pull URLs of your internal and external sites.

Managing Users with Access Manager

You can set it up so that users have access to view reports belonging to a profile. Alternatively, you can give them full administrative access. In cases where you want to restrict users to viewing reports on specific campaigns or areas of a site, you will want to create a unique profile for that area before granting anyone else access.

Preparing to Add a User

Before you add a user to Analytics, they must have a Gmail address. Google Gmail is a "free" ad-based email system. A Gmail account is also required for the Standard version of AdWords. Users can create an account at http://Gmail.google.com.

Time for Action!—Granting Access to Users

We will be working in the **Access Manager** to add and configure the access of individual users to Google Analytics.

1. Click **Access Manager** and then click on the **Add User** link. You will be re-directed to a screen with a form to add the new user.

2. Enter the user's Gmail address, last name, and first name. Select the **Access type** for the user from the drop-down list: View reports only or Account Administrator. The Account Administrator setting will give them access to everything and not just reports. Give administrator access out carefully.

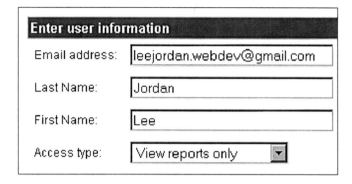

3. Now, we move down to the **Allow access to** area of the form. Click on a profile in the **Available Website Profiles** list to highlight it. This will give the user access to all the reports on this profile.

4. Move all the highlighted profiles into the **Selected Website Profiles** list by clicking the **Add** button. Did you get a little highlight happy? You can remove a profile from the **Selected Website Profiles** list by highlighting it, and clicking the **Remove** button.

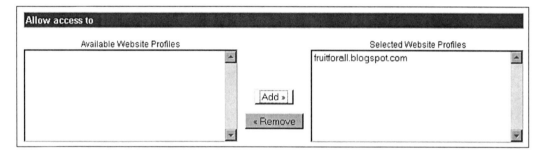

5. Click the **Finish** button. Your new user now has access to Analytics, and the profiles you chose.

What Just Happened?

When our user was created, we gave them the ability to view all reports associated with the website profile. This is the ideal access for an executive or other person who needs to be able to see reports but not make changes to the settings. Users will see only the reports of each profile they are given access to. If we wanted to, we could have added many more website profiles for the user to access.

When the user logs into Analytics, they will see the profiles available to them on the **My Analytics** drop-down list on the long orange menu bar at the top of their screen. Selecting a profile from the drop-down list will take them to the areas of the profile they have been granted access to.

Editing Existing Users

Sometimes we need to change the access a user has to Analytics. They may have taken on a new role needing administrative access, or maybe they just need access to reports now. Let's edit current users' access to our default profile.

Time for action!—Changing Access for Current Users

The access of current users in managed in the **Access Manager**. We will upgrade a user from viewing reports, to being an administrator.

1. Log in to Google Analytics. Navigate to the **Access Manager**. Locate the user in the **Existing Access** list table and click the **Edit** link.

2. Select **Account Administrator** from the **Access type** drop-down list to change the user from **View Reports Only** to an administrator.

3. To add additional profiles, highlight the profile on the **Available Website Profiles** list and click the **Add** button to move it to the **Selected Website Profiles** list. You can also remove profiles they are allowed to access by highlighting a profile in the box on the right and clicking the **Remove** button. If you remove the profile from their **Selected Website Profiles** list, they will not be able to see reports or administrate the profile. Click **Save Changes** to save the new settings for the user.

What Just Happened?

When we changed the user access from viewing reports to an administrator, we gave them administrative access to all profiles listed in their **Selected Website Profiles** list. There are no in-between settings. They can either read reports or see and make changes to everything on a profile.

If you host your blog on your own domain, you can create additional profiles for each individual sub domain. You cannot create new profiles for each area of your blog. The URL `http://fruitforall.blogspot.com/2008/` is invalid for profiles. Instead, you would need to use a filter. Georgia could create profiles for each additional blog she has. If she has an organic recipes blog and an organic gifts blog in addition to the *Fruit for All* blog, she could add each one to her Google Analytics account as profiles. Then, she can grant different user access to them by editing their user profile and granting access to that specific profile, removing any other profile from the selected website profiles on their user access form.

Deleting Users

Removing users from Analytics is a little too easy. To remove them and never look back, navigate to the **Access Manager** and click the **Delete** link next to their name on the **Existing Access** table. Deleting users is final. There is no setting to disable users at this time. Deleting a user removes them completely from Google Analytics. The Google Analytics site gives you a pop-up warning before the user is deleted. One accidental click on the **Delete** button and their access is gone. To restrict the profiles they have access to, remove the profiles that you don't want them to belong to from their access list as described above.

 You cannot delete the original administrator of the Analytics account.

Controlling Data with Filters

Filters in Google Analytics have the same purpose as other types of filters. A filter keeps out everything you don't want, and lets in everything you do, much like a bouncer at a trendy club. Analytics filters can block unwanted data, process chunks of data, and format how that data appears in reports.

There are two types of filters in Google Analytics:

- **Predefined Filters**: Blocks friendly IP addresses such as the one from your Internet connection or hostile ones from Phisher or copycat sites. They can also separate data from sub directories on your site into separate reports.

- **Custom Filters**: Data collected by Analytics affecting any Analytics report can be processed using custom filters. There is always someone coming up with a clever way to process data with a custom filter.

The easiest way to decide which type of filter to use, or whether to use one at all, is to ask yourself whether adding the filter will solve a problem being faced by your business or by you as a blogger. Use a predefined filter if you think the internal visits from your site to your blog are messing up your Analytics. Use a custom filter if you need an easier way to decipher long strings of ugly web addresses representing product pages for reports.

Setting up Filters

Multiple filters can also be set up for profiles to do a wide variety of tasks. They are applied to a profile in the order they are listed, in the filters table on the **Profile Settings** screen. We will start with adding a simple filter to keep out traffic from Georgia's personal IP address, then climb higher up the branch by applying a complex custom filter to a site profile.

Time for Action!—Adding a Predefined Filter

We will be adding a filter already created by the Google Analytics team to a website profile.

1. Starting at **Analytics Settings**, click the **Filter Manager** link. Then, click the **Add Filter** link in the **Existing Filters** table. The **Create New Filter** screen will appear. We need to enter a name for the filter to identify it among all the others we might add. Let's call it **companyip**. Type the name into the **Filter Name** text field.

2. We are keeping all traffic from the IP address out. So, select **Exclude all traffic from an IP address** from the **Filter Type** drop-down list.

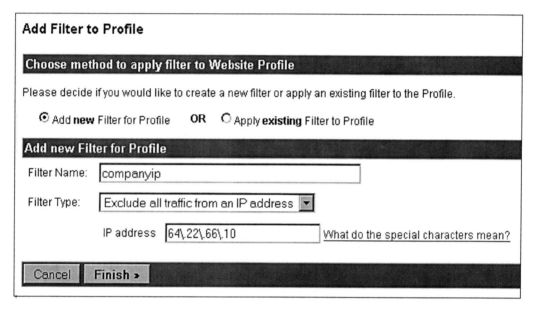

3. Type the **IP address** carefully into the **IP address** text field, leaving all the backslashes and periods in place. It should be in the same format as the example 64\.22\.66\.10. Confused! Type 64 then a backslash, then a period, 22, a backslash, a period, 66, a final backslash, a period, and 10. Click the **Finish** button.

4. The filter will be automatically applied to the default profile. To add the filter to another profile, go to the **Edit** screen for that profile and select the **Add Filter** link. Select the **Apply existing Filter to Profile** radio button, then select the filter, and add it. The process is the same as when you add profiles to a user account.

What Just Happened?

When you added the IP address as an exclusion filter, any incoming data from page clicks originating at that IP address were then excluded from reports. The filters in Analytics use special characters to control how the filter operates, called regular expressions. We applied a type of regular expression, wildcard set with a period symbol, and a forward slash symbol. That set of characters tells the filter to treat the period symbols between each set of numbers as actual periods instead of regular expression wildcards. We'll look at regular expressions and useful wildcard combinations next.

Filters are activated in the order they are created unless a different order is specified. When you have multiple filters, you can rearrange them to change the way incoming data is processed. A very common problem for Analytics users is to place their filters in the right order. Think of filters as a series of traps in a water pipe. The largest filter will let large rocks and debris pass. The medium sized filter will block the larger rocks and bigger debris. The smallest filter has fine mesh, letting only water and the tiniest particles through. The first filter listed is always applied first.

Understanding Regular Expressions

Did you notice the link by the IP address field referring to special characters? These character combinations are regular expression wildcards. Just like wildcards in a deck of playing cards, regular expressions perform special actions in filters. Of course, it's more complicated than wildcards. Regular expressions are much more powerful, with an extensive list of many types of wildcards instead of just the one in a typical playing card deck. You can take a quick run down of the main ones in the following table:

Wildcard/ Wildcard Set	Description	Example
.	The period symbol matches a single character, including letters, numbers, symbols, and spaces except for end of line characters such as carriage returns.	Can be equal to most characters including: a, 8, or @.
?	Matches zero or a previous item.	8? 88? Not 888?
[]	Isolate a list of characters to match.	1[23] Will match 12 or 13.
-	Dash creates a range of numbers, or digits.	[a-g] instead of [abcdefg]
|	The pipe symbol means "or"	Organic | healthy Tells the filter to match the string with organic or healthy.

Wildcard/ Wildcard Set	Description	Example
^	The carat symbol has two purposes. When used in brackets, it means "not". When used without brackets it looks for characters or strings only at the beginning of a line. It is used at the beginning of an expression.	[^0-9], anything but not a digit. ^How, finds any line that begins with the word "How"
$	This wildcard looks for characters and strings at the end of lines or fields. It is used at the end of an expression.	Fresh fruit$ will be matched only if it is found at the end of a field, or if there is a carriage return or line feed right after it.
\	The backslash symbol means "escape". When used with another wildcard, it converts the wildcard into a normal character.	\. Converts the period wildcard into a normal period: 64\.12\.34\.56
*	Matches zero or more of the previous item.	Z* is the same as zz, zzz, to an infinite number of z, or a blank string.
+	Matches one or more of previous items, but not an empty string.	Z+ will match z, zz, zzz, and all other groups of the same character but not a blank string.
( )	Stores part of a set, grouping it for a regular expression set.	(.xls|.pdf|.doc)

Regular expressions can be used to filter traffic for many types of data. You can use them to isolate keywords, filter out all monitor resolutions, except for the ones you specify, and the list goes on and on. We're going to use regular expressions to build a custom filter for our default profile.

Processing Data Using Custom Filters

We want to apply filter to more than just IP addresses, and subdirectories. Custom Filters give you incredible freedom to process data before you see it in a report format. Regular expressions are the secret ingredient to all custom filter recipes. We will go ahead and create a custom filter, then look at other ways we can use custom filters to harvest as much useful data as we can, from Analytics. Georgia wants to change the year, and month portions of the displayed page titles to a more readable format. We'll start with changing the date format on last year's blog posts.

Time for Action!—Creating a Custom Filter

We are going to create a custom filter using regular expressions to find, and replace the date format of our posts in Google Analytics.

1. Log in to Google Analytics. Starting at the **Analytics Settings** screen, click the **Filter Manager** link. Click **Add Filter** from the **Filter Manager** screen. The **Create New Filter** page appears.

2. Enter a **Filter Name** for this filter. Let's type **Replace year and date** so that we can easily separate it from other filters. From the **Filter Type** drop-down list, select **Custom Filter**.

3. Now click the radio button next to the custom filter you want to use. We are asking the filter to search for a string, and if it finds a match, to replace the characters in the string with the new ones provided in the replace box. Select **Search and Replace**.

4. Select **Page Title** from the **Filter Field**. Enter the following string **^/2007/12/** into the **Search String** text box, as shown in the following screenshot. We are telling the filter to search for all page titles starting with that string of data.

5. Enter **December 2007** into the **Replace String** text box exactly as shown in the following screenshot:

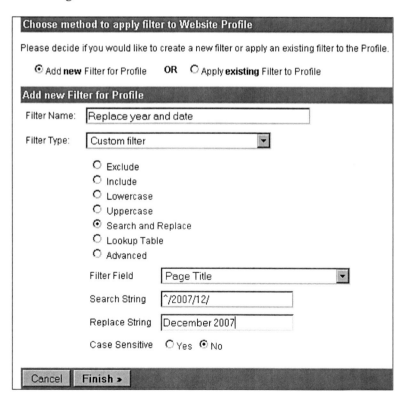

6. As the search does not need to be case sensitive, keep the **Case Sensitive** radio group set to **No**.

7. Click the **Finish** button to complete setting up the filter on the default profile.

What Just Happened?

When you create the custom filter, you told it to search for a string of characters matching the **Search String** field. If a string of characters matching the specified string was found, it would then be replaced by the string you entered into the **Replace String** box. After about a day, any new incoming data that was processed after the filter was created will begin to appear in the reports.

 Filters will have no effect on data that has already been collected by Analytics.

If there are already existing filters for this profile, your new filter will be applied after them. To change the order, visit the **Profile Settings** page and click **Assign Filter Order**. Click on a filter in the **Assign Filter Order** box to highlight it. Click the **move** button to change the order of the filter on the list.

 Want to learn more about using regular expressions with Analytics? Visit http://www.epikone.com/blog/2007/12/10/my-regular-expression-tool-box/.

Types of Custom Filters

There are many types of custom filters. It can be hard to decide which one is right for what you want to do. Just like a wrench or a hammer, they are tools you can use to help build structure for your reports. The following table will help you figure out which custom filter to use.

Filter Name	Purpose	Example
Exclude a pattern	Filter out information you don't want to see. The most common use is to filter out price codes or keywords.	Georgia has seasonal fruit baskets whose item codes begin with the character string, "Season". Choosing the exclude filter and typing ^Season* will exclude all seasonal baskets from her reports.
Include a pattern	Includes only data identified with the specified pattern marker.	If Georgia wants to only see data on her seasonal baskets, selecting the include filter and typing ^Season* will only include item codes with that character string in her reports for the selected profile.
Search & Replace	Includes data that needs to be searched, and then replaced automatically.	Referring to the example in the above section, Georgia wants to replace 2007/12 with December 2007. Using the search & replace filter Georgia can easily apply the format.
Lookup Table	Use a specified xls file to replace strings of item code digits, or URLs with descriptive names. This feature is not currently active.	Georgia can upload a tab delimited text file that matches her item codes, when the feature again becomes available.
Advanced	Combine, and process data from multiple filter fields.	Show full URLs of referral fields, process, and compare strings of data; then output them to a specified report.
Upper/Lower	Change text to all upper or all lowercase. Particularly useful for page titles, keyword reports, or anywhere manual user's error may cause inconsistencies.	Georgia has item codes that use different cases, and wants them all to show up as the same data: GolDel403, goldel403, GOLDel403

Have the desire to experiment with regular expressions, but don't want to risk causing problems on your live Analytics site? Visit the (unofficial) Google Analytics Regular Expression filter tester (http://www.epikone.com/tools/regular-expression-filter-tester). Are you looking for a tool that can handle complicated regular expressions? The Regex Coach is a desktop application for Windows and Linux for in-depth work with regular expressions. It can be downloaded at http://www.weitz.de/regex-coach/.

Managing Ad Campaign Metrics

We can view AdWord campaigns in rich graphical format, and add advertising campaigns from other sources to measure their success as well. Managing ad campaigns can be very complex, so we will be covering the basics. AdWord users should checkout the AdWords (`http://groups.google.com/group/adwords-help`) or Analytics (`http://groups.google.com/group/analytics-help-basics/`) groups for in-depth questions and answers. Don't worry; we're still going to have some fun digging into campaigns here. Let's start by discussing, how Analytics can help us track campaigns?

Tracking Campaigns

Analytics helps us track our campaigns with easy to understand reports. Before we begin viewing those reports, we need to prepare our campaign items with code snippets made of special words that together uniquely identify the ads, known as tags. These tags enable Analytics to gather data on their performance, similar to how gardeners stick a label on plants, which describes the type of plant, how much sun it should have, and any other details. Tracking campaigns with Analytics requires a unique set of tags for each ad.

Tagging Campaign Items

Google automatically tags AdWords being used for a campaign. Manually tagging keywords tied to advertising campaigns can be done for all other campaigns. Typing the link tags by hand can lead to mistakes. Google has a special tool that will create the tags for you. All you have to do is type in the information about the ad into a simple form.

Experiencing URL Builder

URL Builder is a Google Analytics tool that reduces link tag formatting errors, and makes it possible to create tags for multiple ads quickly. Before you use the tool, gather all details about your ad campaign. You will need, at the least, details of the website URL, campaign source, medium, and name to complete the form.

Time for Action!—Creating Links with URL Builder

We're going to create a tracking link for an ad on a specific page of our blog.

1. Log into Google Analytics, and go to the URL Builder (`http://www.google.com/support/analytics/bin/answer.py?hl=en&answer=55578`). Type the full URL of the website in the **Website URL** field, as shown in the following screenshot. We are going to track an ad on `http://fruitforall.blogspot.com/holidaycitrusbasket.html`.

Step 1: Enter the URL of your website.

Website URL: * http://fruitforall.blogspot.com/holidaycitrusbasket.html

(e.g. *http://www.urchin.com/download.html*)

2. Enter **citysearch** as the **Campaign Source**. Type **banner** as the **Campaign Medium**, and leave **Campaign Term** blank. The last two fields are **Campaign Content** and **Campaign Name**. In the following screenshot, **holbasketpic** uniquely identifies the ad for the campaign.

3. The **Campaign Name** is filled with text related to the product. **Campaign Source** and **Campaign Medium** cannot be left blank. You should have that information ready, before you begin building a tag with URL Builder.

Step 2: Fill in the fields below. **Campaign Source** and **Campaign Medium** are required values.

Campaign Source: *	citysearch	(referrer: google, citysearch, newsletter4)
Campaign Medium: *	banner	(marketing medium: cpc, banner, email)
Campaign Term:		(identify the paid keywords)
Campaign Content:	holbasketpic	(use to differentiate ads)
Campaign Name*:	holiday_citrus_basket	(product, promo code, or slogan)

4. Click the **Generate URL** button to create the URL link. Our example link is:

```
http://fruitforall.blogspot.com/holidaycitrusbasket.html?utm_
        source=citysearch&utm_medium=banner&utm_
        content=holbasketpic&utm_campaign=holiday_citrus_basket
```

5. Paste the link into your ad to begin tracking your campaign.

What Just Happened?

When you created a link, based on an ad campaign with Google URL Builder, the form captured up to five key variables to identify the campaign. Pasting the link into an ad activated the tracking, and reporting of the ad using the campaign tag variables. You are then able to view reports based on the data collected from the ad campaign.

The values for campaign source, medium, and name are the required fields in Analytics and AdWords. It's an integration thing.

Identifying Campaign Tags

Each campaign tag serves a specific purpose. Use tags to measure the success of your non-AdWords campaigns. The following table identifies each tag, specifies whether it is required, and also states the purpose it serves. You don't have to use all the non-required tags every time.

Tag Name	Required?	Purpose
Campaign Source (utm_source)	Yes	Identifies a search engine, newsletter name, or other source. Example: utm_source=google
Campaign Medium (utm_medium)	Yes	Use utm_medium to identify a medium such as email, or cost-per-click. Example: utm_medium=cpc
Campaign Term (utm_term)	No	Used for paid search. Enter keywords for the ad here. Example: utm_term= eco-friendly + organic
Campaign Content (utm_content)	No	Used for A/B testing and content-targeted ads. Use utm_content to differentiate ads, or links that point to the same URL. Examples: utm_content=logolink or utm_content=textlink
Campaign Name (utm_campaign)	Yes	Used for keyword analysis. Use utm_campaign to identify a specific product promotion, or strategic campaign. Example: utm_campaign=holiday_citrus_basket

Now that we have explored how Google Analytics can help us track any ad campaign, we can take a closer look at how AdWords can be used with Google Analytics.

AdWords Integration

Why do AdWords users like Analytics? AdWords does give data about the ads, users have placed, but it is presented in boring old tables that are hard to analyze. Reading a big table of text is boring. Zooming through interactive graphs and charts is almost like a game. Since Analytics is free as well, it is very popular with AdWords users. Integrating AdWords with Analytics is easy.

If you already have an AdWords account and it uses a different email address, you can link it to Analytics by giving that email address administrator access to a website profile in Analytics.

You will need to create an AdWords account at `https://adwords.google.com/` before you can integrate it with Analytics. Use the same email address as you did for your Analytics account.

Time for Action!—Integrating Google AdWords

Google Analytics and Google AdWords are an ideal match. We will integrate them to make tracking and managing easier in both.

1. Log into your AdWords account at `https://adwords.google.com`. Click the **Analytics** tab on the navigation menu.

2. You've already created an Analytics account, right? Click on **I already have a Google Analytics account** link.

3. Now, its time to choose the Analytics account you want to link to. Select the name of the Analytics account you'd like to link to, from the **Existing Google Analytics Account** drop-down list. All the checkboxes on the list should be checked. We want our AdWords automatically tagged for us.

4. Click the **Link Account** button to finish the integration.

What Just Happened?

When you logged into AdWords, Google already had a tab prepared so that you could quickly visit your Analytics information without even leaving AdWords. The setup wizard did not assume that you wanted to link automatically to a particular Analytics account. It presented you with a list of Analytics accounts that you could access, based on your email address. When you clicked the **Link Account** button, you gave Google the final verification it needed to formally link the two applications together under your email address.

Analyzing Keyword Effectiveness

You've paid for keywords in AdWords and you've integrated AdWords with Analytics. Now, you need to track your keywords, and see if they really are paying off for you. Analytics has a number of graphical reports that make it easy to track the effectiveness of your keywords. We'll get comfortable with the layout of the **Dashboard** screen, and explore the different types of reports available to us.

Driving the Reports Dashboard

Analytics places all your available reports in the **Dashboard**. You can reach the **Dashboard** by clicking on the **View Reports** screen from the top menu of Analytics. You have a lot of control over what you want to see in the **Dashboard Overview** of the main dashboard.

We will explore the main areas of the **Dashboard** and different ways you can use it to analyze your site performance, email reports, and also have fun doing it. First, you need to get used to where everything is. The **Dashboard** has a lot of reports, and information hidden under each section. We won't cover every report; we could spend a whole book doing that. Instead, we will focus on the main reports you will care for as a blogger.

Navigating the Dashboard

The **Dashboard** navigation is different from the rest of the Analytics site. It contains a left menu with all the main report areas, a central dashboard section to give you an at-a-glance big picture look at how your site is doing, and special function buttons to export, email, and customize your dashboard view.

Using the Left Menu of the Dashboard

The left menu of the **Dashboard** is the same for every report screen. You will see the **Dashboard Overview**, called by the nickname **Dashboard**. It will take you back to the overview screen. There you will find a link to **Saved Reports**, and then the other dashboards: **Visitors**, **Traffic Sources**, **Content**, and **Goals**. Each dashboard has its own special icon. Clicking on one of them will cause a submenu to appear, which is very long in some cases.

They are followed by a **Settings** section with an **Email** submenu link. Clicking on the **Email** link will take you to the **Manage Scheduled Emails** screen within the dashboard area of Analytics. The **Help Resources** section is the last group of links on the left menu. It contains links which will display a small box with tips, and links about each topic, except for the **Report Finder** link. The **Report Finder** is a relic of the old Analytics dashboard, and will open a new window with outdated information about the left menu.

Exploring the Main Dashboard Overview Section

The **Visits** graph is the first graphical report that we see when we navigate to the **Dashboard** area of Analytics. Below it are quick overviews of three popular report sections: **Site Usage**, **Visitors Overview**, and **Map Overlay**. Clicking on the reports under **Site Usage**, or on the **Visitors Overview**, or **Map Overlay** report sections will take you to their respective report pages.

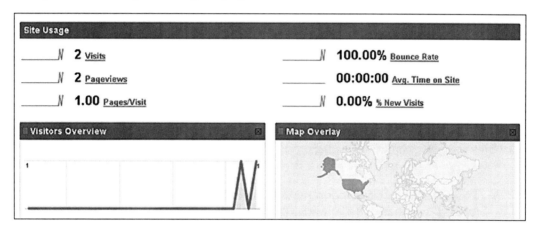

Customizing the Dashboard Overview

You can change what you see on the **Dashboard Overview**. Reports can be added, deleted, and rearranged. Note that at the top of every report screen, including the **Dashboard Overview**, is a default date range. You can change it with a click. You can also change the subject of most overview reports by selecting the legend icon for the graph in the upper right corner just above the graph itself. Let's get to work, adding the **Top Landing Pages** report to the **Dashboard Overview**.

Time for Action!—Adding a Report to the Dashboard Overview

Changing the reports seen on the **Dashboard Overview** makes the page more relevant for you, and any other member of your team.

1. Click the **Content** section on the left menu. A list of all reports available under the **Content** section will appear. Click on the **Top Landing Pages** link to view the report.

2. The **Top Landing Pages** report will appear with a visual graph metric on top, and a table with additional details below. On each of the dashboard reports, there is an **Add to Dashboard** button located near the top of the screen. Click on this button to add the report to the **Dashboard Overview** screen.

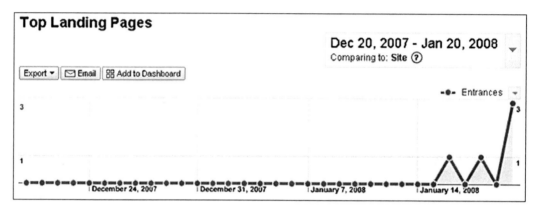

3. You will see a confirmation message telling you the report has been added to the **Dashboard Overview** screen. From there, you can move it around the portion of the screen below the main dashboard overview report.

4. You can remove reports from the overview by clicking the 'x' symbol at the top right corner of the title box for each report.

5. Reorganize the report boxes by dragging and dropping them on the **Dashboard Overview** screen. Hover your mouse over the grey title section of a report box until you see the mouse cursor turn into a black crosshair symbol, as shown in the following screenshot:

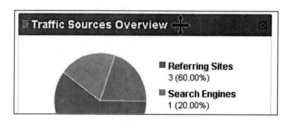

6. Once you see the crosshair symbol, press down the left mouse key, and drag the box to the new location. The box content will be hidden and the box will change to a light grey square while you move it. It will look similar to the following screenshot when it is being moved:

What Just Happened?

Looks weird, doesn't it? It is fun to play around with the report boxes, getting everything arranged just so. If you remove a report by accident, you can always add it again by going to the individual report page, and clicking the **Add to Dashboard** button.

When you chose a report to add to the **Dashboard Overview**, the Google Analytics site responded by adding a thumbnail image of the report to the **Dashboard Overview** screen.

Viewing Reports

The reporting interface is deceptively simple. Exploring the different toggle boxes, graph nodes, and other areas of the report screens will reveal many more details, and information to drill deeper on. Let's take a look at a hidden piece of functionality that beginners might not notice — viewing multiple metrics on a graph.

Time for Action!—Viewing Multiple Metrics on a Graph

Viewing multiple items on a report allows you to compare them at a glance from one location. This saves time and can reveal surprising trends. We will change the view of a report to show multiple items, also known as **metrics**, in a line graph format.

1. Log in to Google Analytics, and navigate to the **Reports** section. Open up the **Graph Mode** box by clicking on the subject icon in the legend portion of the report, shown in the following screenshot as a blue circle with a short line through it, next to a toggle arrow. Now, the **Graph Mode** box is revealed. We have three options available. When you select an option, it will appear to fade in color.

2. Select **Compare Two Metrics** for the mode; then select **Visits** as the blue line, and **Avg. Time on Site** as the orange line. Click anywhere on the white space above the box to close the **Graph Mode** box and return to the main report screen.

3. You will now see a line graph showing the two metrics we selected. We can now see a glance of the report in the following screenshot, and how they compare with each other.

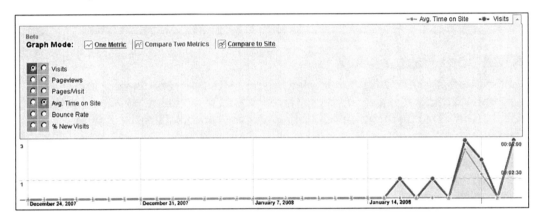

What Just Happened?

When we changed the mode of the line graph, we were able to compare multiple metrics t each other. This enabled us to examine whether two metrics might be related to an issue surrounding our blog. When we choose different metrics from the **Graph Mode** box, we will be able to see relationships between them.

Changing the mode of a report can reveal more details. Glancing at reports is not enough. We need to analyze the information of a report, and interpret it so that we can take an action. Let's take a look at the popularity of the page titles to see if any subjects stand out.

Analyzing Reports

Dissecting the data contained in a report is much easier with a choice of graphical report formats. We will use the pie chart view to quickly see which pages are the most popular with visitors according to the **Content by Title** report. The **Content by Title** report tells you which sections of your site and which pages are the most popular with your visitors.

Time for Action!—Understanding the Content by Title Report

Every report within Google Analytics follows a similar format. By understanding this report, you will also be able to analyze other reports within Google Analytics.

1. Log in to Google Analytics. Go to the reports area for the URL of your blog. Click on the **Content** section, and then the **Content by Title** report link, or navigate to the report from the report box on the **Dashboard Overview** screen. Select the small pie chart icon next to **View**. We can change our graphical view of the report any time by choosing a different view button.

2. We can see right away that the main page is the most popular. Either there is too much content in the form of full articles to read on the home page, or visitors are not finding the types of subjects they are looking for. Hovering our cursor over each section of the pie reveals the actual view in percentage for each page. We can change to other reports within the **Page Title** dashboard by selecting them from the drop-down menu above the pie chart. An example is shown in the following screenshot:

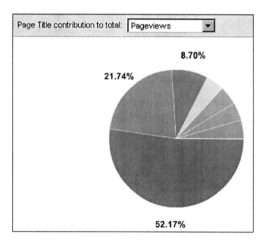

3. Drill down into the individual pages by clicking on the title links to see how they were located, and how they factored into reported issues such as page exits.

What Just Happened?

When we navigated to the **Content by Title** report, Google Analytics changed the view of the report data according to which report format we selected. The deeper we went, the more detailed information we found. When we want to send this to a marketing or web design guru to help us analyze the data further, we need a quick and an easy way to get the reports to them. Luckily, reports can be emailed to other people in a variety of formats.

Emailing Reports

The ability to schedule, and email reports is a must have feature for enterprise users. Bloggers can benefit from scheduled reports sent to them via email by saving time, and avoiding repetitive tasks. You'd rather be blogging than digging through Analytics, gathering up reports, right?

You can add any report to an email queue by clicking the email icon on its report screen. You are then taken to a screen with three separate email setup forms. You can email a report once, schedule a report to run at specified dates and times, or add a report to an already scheduled group. Let's schedule a report to run weekly while we are at the coffee shop or better still, sleeping in.

Time for Action!—Sending Reports by Email

To send a report, we will fill out a short series of tabbed forms. You need to have the email addresses of the people you will be sending the reports to, ready.

1. Log in to Google Analytics. Navigate to the **Content Overview** screen, and click on the email icon. The **Set Up Email** screen will appear with three actions tabs to choose from: **Send Now**, **Schedule**, and **Add to Existing**. Click on the **Schedule** tab to select it.

2. Enter the email address of each person you want to send the report to, followed by a comma. Click on the **Send to Me** checkbox, to also send a copy to yourself. That's right; you don't have to type in your own email address.

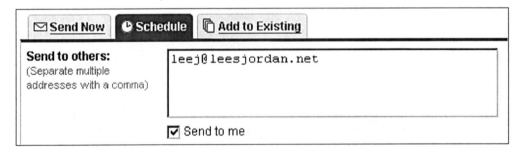

3. Enter a descriptive title into the **Subject** of the email form. Try to avoid any words that might activate a spam filter. Next, type a **Description** of the report. Consider your audience while deciding just how detailed you want your description to be.

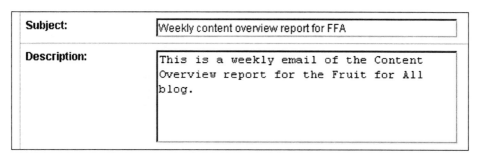

4. Now, for the interesting part. You have the choice of four widely accepted formats for your report: **PDF**, **CSV** (Comma Separated List), **XML**, and **TSV** (Tab Separated Value). Select the **PDF** radio box, since we are sending it to a person, and not processing it or storing it in an application.

5. Choose the **Date Range/Schedule** for how often the report should be sent out. Unless you have someone eager to digest daily reports, stick to weekly or monthly status reports. Select the **Include date comparison** checkbox, if you require that information to be included in the report. Click the **Schedule** button to save the form. It will now be accessible from the **Settings** box on the left menu of the reports screen. You can now also add other reports to this one with the third and final **Set Up Email** tab.

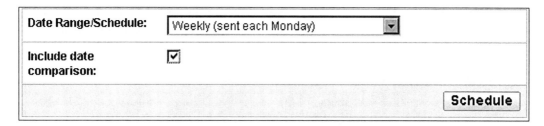

What Just Happened?

When you chose to schedule an email report, the subject and description information you filled out on the form was used to store an email message for later use. The format choice for the actual report was stored. Later, when it was time for the report to be sent as an attachment in the scheduled email message, the data was processed and sent as your chosen file type.

The format in which the report is sent, who the report is sent to, and all the other information you entered into the email setup form can be changed at any time by clicking the **Email** link under **Settings** in the **Reports** section of Analytics. Your data won't change; just the email and the format will be different.

Evaluating Performance with Goals

Goals in Analytics are used to measure an activity that represents a core purpose of the site. Georgia will want to set up goals to measure user interest in surveys; recipe downloads, ordering items, and the sharing of site widgets. Goals help you measure the success of your site. They answer the question "Are our visitors responding to the content on the site we think will interest them?"

Analytics can't pick your goals for you. You have to decide how much of a visitor response, also known as a conversion, is equal to success. Picking the right goal to measure may take a little practice. Start with the simplest, and the most obvious choices that are most closely tied to your site's purpose. You heard me. Put that ten page survey away for later, and join me for a journey with a purpose.

Tracking Performance with Goals

So how do you decide what to measure with a goal? Goals can be any action a visitor takes on your blog. Examples include finding a link, downloading a podcast, taking a poll, leaving a comment, or signing up for an RSS feed. We know we should start with something simple. Let's track visitors who create an RSS box of the blog feed using Springwidgets. Every time a user visits the Springwidgets site using the **Subscribe to reader** link on the blog, it will show up on Analytics.

Time for Action!—Setting up a Goal

To track the performance of a specific area of our blog, we can set up a goal. It will tell us how many visitors completed the task we are interested in tracking.

1. Log in to Analytics and click on the **Edit** link next to the blog profile to bring up the **Profile Settings** screen. Click the **Edit** link on the **G1** row in the **Settings** column.

2. Now you're on the **Goal Settings: G1** screen. The new goal is set to active, by default. Turn the goal **On.** This selection decides whether Google Analytics should track this conversion goal at this time. Generally, you will want to set the **Active Goal** selection to **On, and** not **Off.**

3. Select **Head Match** from the **Match Type** drop-down box. We'll talk about when you should choose one over the other, after we set this goal up.

4. Type: `http://www.springwidgets.com/widgets/view/23/false/true?param=http://feeds.feedburner.com/fruitforall` in the **Goal URL** text box.

5. Enter a name for the goal in the **Goal name** text box. We're using the name **Create RSS Box** to identify this goal.

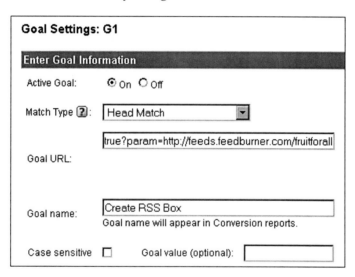

6. Jump down to the **Funnels** section. You don't have to fill this out, but if you have any other steps towards the goal, such as a checkout process, you can track the progress through it here. Click the **Step 1** box, and enter the URL of the first page on which users will land, on their way to the goal: `http://feeds.feedburner.com/fruitforall`

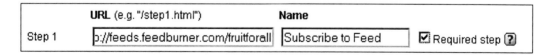

7. Click the **Finish** button to save your goal. You will see it listed in the **Conversion Goals** box the next time you visit the profile settings page.

What Just Happened?

When you set up a goal for your profile, you instructed Analytics to monitor a designated page for visitor activity. Be very careful while setting the match type for your goal. The three match types address three situations for processing Goal URLs.

- When **Exact Match** type is selected the URL entered as the goal must match perfectly with the one the visitor encounters. If it does not, Analytics will not track it as a valid goal conversion. Keep in mind that dynamically created URLs will not work with this match type. This doesn't mean you can't use regular expressions. For example, if we want to track how many visitors reach the post, `http://fruitforall.blogspot.com/2007/11/apples-fall-fruit.html`, we do not have to list the full URL. We can use a regular expression and type "**^/2007/11/apples\-fall\-fruit\.html**" without the quotation marks.

- When **Head Match** type is selected, it will match the portion of a URL, which is not dynamic. Copy the goal URL into a text editor, and then delete any dynamic session identifiers, or query parameters. Google uses a lot of these. The Analytics URL looks like this with a dynamic session identifier included: (`https://www.google.com/analytics/home/admin?vid=1234&prid=1234567`).

  When we remove the dynamic portion of the URL, it looks like: (`https://www.google.com/analytics/home/admin?vid=1234`).

- The **Regular Expression Match** type is the last and the most powerful match type. This is used when visitors are coming from multiple domains or sub domains, or there are query parameters scattered throughout the URL.

Creating a funnel of any intermediate page or pages a visitor must go through to reach the goal made it easier to track any points where a visitor abandoned the process. A high abandonment rate on a funnel page indicates user frustration, and a block towards them reaching your goal. Funnel pages do not have to be the only way for a visitor to reach a goal page. If a visitor could reach the goal from different sources, the required step checkbox should be left empty.

You can either enter a single step for the funnel, or up to ten pages. Remember not to include a landing page, or a product page as a step. The shopping cart view page or other activity page is a better choice.

 If you have more than four goals to add to your site, copy the site profile, and then add the other goals to that profile.

Editing Goals

You are given four goal slots for each website profile. The finishing page link for a goal may change, or you may decide to reuse a goal slot after the usefulness of the old goals have expired. Editing an existing goal can be done quickly from the **Profile Settings** screen. You can change the goal URL, name, and set the goal to an active or inactive state.

Time for Action!—Changing a Current Goal

We can edit current goals easily on the **Profile Settings** page.

1. Log into Google Analytics. Navigate to **Profile Settings** from the **Analytics Settings** page.

2. Click the **Edit** link next to the goal number you wish to change. Clicking the **Edit** link next to **Goal G1** will enable us to change it.

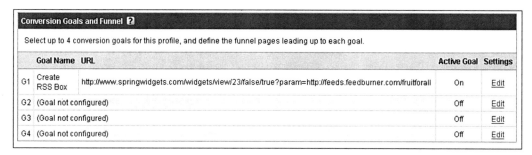

3. Make changes to the URL, name, or active state using the form. Note that you can edit the **Match Type** settings too. Click the **Save Changes** button to make your edits final.

What Just Happened?

When you change the settings of a goal by editing it, Google Analytics saves the changes, and begins reporting on the new conversion goal.

We want to do more than just capture information about what visitors do to our blog. Improving our blog based on the information we can gather from Google Analytics is the most fruitful goal for us. Google knows that this is the best way to keep you coming back to their analytics tool. They have many ways to help you.

Improving Your Blog with Google Analytics

Analytics gives you an overwhelming amount of data to use for measuring the success of your sites, and ads. Once you've had time to analyze that data, you will want to take action to improve the performance of your blog, and ads. We'll now look at how Analytics can help you make decisions about the design, and content of your site.

Analyzing Navigation

The **Navigation** section of the **Content Overview** report reveals how your visitors actually navigate your blog. Visitors move around a site in ways we can't predict. Seeing how they actually navigate a site and where they entered the site are powerful tools we can use to diagnose where we need to improve our blog.

Exploring the Navigation Summary

The **Navigation Summary** shows you the path people take through your site, including how they get there and where they go. We can see from the following graphical representation that our visitors entered the site through the main page of the blog most of the time. After reaching that page, over half the time, they went to other pages within the site.

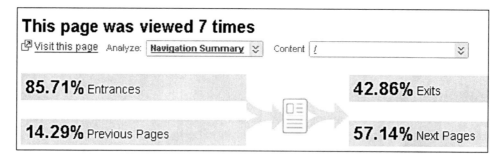

Entrance Paths

We can see the path, the visitors take to enter our blog using the **Entrance Paths** report. It will show us from where they entered our site, which pages they looked at, and the last page they viewed before exiting. Visitors don't always enter by the main page of a site, especially if they find the site using search engines or trackbacks.

The following screenshot displays a typical entrance path. The visitor comes to the site home page, and then goes to the full page of one of the posts. It looks like our visitors are highly attracted to the recipe posts. Georgia may want to feature more posts about recipes that tie in with her available inventory.

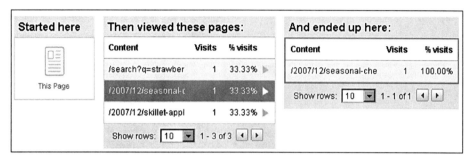

Optimizing your Landing Page

The **Landing Page** reports tell you where your visitors are coming from, and if they have used keywords to find you. You have a choice between viewing the source visitors used to get to your blog, or the keywords. Knowing the sources will give you guidance on the areas you should focus your marketing or advertising efforts on.

Examining Entrance Sources

You can quickly see how visitors are finding your site, whether through a direct link, or a search engine, locally from Blogger, or from social networking applications such as Twitter.com. In the **Entrance Sources** graph shown in the following screenshot, we can see that the largest among the number of people are coming to the blog using a direct link. Blogger is also responsible for a large share of our visitors, which is over 37%. There is even a visitor drawn to the blog from Twitter.com, where Georgia has an account.

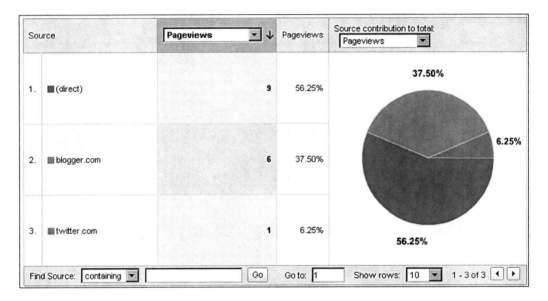

Discovering Entrance Keywords

When visitors arrive at your site using keywords, the words they use will show up on the report. If they are using words in a pattern that do not match your site content, you may see a high bounce rate. You can use this report to redesign your landing page to better represent the purpose of your site by the words, and phrases that you use.

Interpreting Click Patterns

When visitors visit your site they show their attraction to links, and interactive content by clicking on them. **Click Patterns** are the representation of all those mouse clicks over a set time period. Using the **Site Overlay** reporting feature, you can visually see the mouse clicks represented in a graphical pattern. Much like collared pins stuck on a wall chart they will quickly reveal to you, which areas of your site visitors clicked on the most, and which links they avoided.

Understanding Site Overlay

Site Overlay shows the number of clicks for your site by laying them transparently in a graphical format on top of your site. Details with the number of clicks, and goal tracking information pop up in a little box when you hover over a click graphic with your mouse.

At the top of the screen are options that control the display of the **Site Overlay**. Clicking the **Hide Overlay** link will hide the overlay from view. The **Displaying** drop-down list lets you choose how to view mouse **Clicks** on the page, or goals. The date range is the last item displayed.

The graphical bars shown on top of the page content indicate where visitors clicked, and how many of them did so. You can quickly see what areas of the page interest your visitors the most.

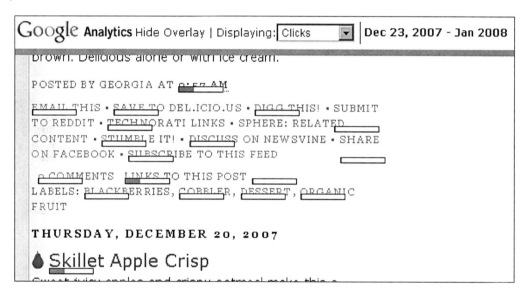

Based on the page clicks you see, you will have an idea of the content, and advertising that is most interesting to your visitors. Yes, **Site Overlay** will show the content areas of the page the visitors clicked on, and the advertisement areas. It will also help you see which links are tied to goals, and whether they are enticing your visitors to click.

Summary

We can now track the performance of our blog, and advertising efforts, using Google Analytics. There was a lot to learn in this chapter about measuring site performance, analyzing reports, and managing ad campaigns. Google Analytics gave us powerful tools to track site, and advertising data.

Using Google Analytics we were able to track:

- Who was visiting our site
- What they were doing
- Where they came from
- How long they stayed
- How effective the ad campaigns were

We've done a lot of hard work designing, publicizing, and measuring the performance of our blog. Now we're ready to attract more people to our blog. Coming up in Chapter 9 we will work on optimizing our blog for search engines. We will use suggestions from Google Analytics, Webmaster tools, and Blogger to improve the search engine ranking of our site. Improving our search engine ranking will increase exposure to our blog.

9

Search Engine Optimization

You want people to find your blog when they perform a search about your topic. The painful truth is that search engines have to find your blog first before it will show up in their results. There are thousands of new blogs being created everyday. If you want people to be able to find your blog in the increasingly crowded blogosphere, optimizing your blog for search engines will improve the odds.

We've covered many ways to increase the visibility of your blog in earlier chapters, but one thing we haven't explored until now is optimizing your blog for search engines. Why wait until now? It's a big topic. There is a lot of information out there on the Internet about it, but much of it may harm the reputation of your blog, the exact opposite of what you want, right? We are focusing this chapter on search engine optimization techniques that work best for blogs. But what is good for the blog is good for all websites.

We're going to spend this chapter working on:

- How search engines see blogs
- Examining your blog with search engines in mind
- Planning and prioritizing improvements
- Optimizing the blog to work well with search engines

Vincent Flanders, self proclaimed "Marketing Weasel" and host of `http://www.webpagesthatsuck.com`, loves to say *"Google is God, don't upset her"*. He isn't trying to offend anyone's religious faith. What he means is that when it comes to finding content on the Internet, Google search is the most popular way to do it. Preparing the settings and content of your blog with Google and other search engines in mind is the top priority for anyone trying to achieve search engine optimization.

Seeing a Blog through Search Engine Goggles

Not "Google's" but goggles the kind people with sensitive eyes like to wear while swimming. Search engines don't see your site the way you do. Knowing how search engines see your blog will help you optimize your blog to get the best possible search page result ranking naturally. You don't have to use crazy or expensive strategies that will scare away your actual visitor's.

 Find out how Googlebot sees your blog. Log into Google webmaster tools (`https://www.google.com/webmasters/tools/pageanalysis`), and then add your URL. Finally, navigate to **What Googlebot Sees** under the **Statistics** section.

We're going to start by seeing which blogs rank high, what tools we can use to evaluate our blog, and preparing to examine our blog for search engines using a checklist.

Performing a Search—Which Blogs Rank High

Blogs are ranked differently by search engines compared to other sites. Posting frequency, friendly URL paths, descriptive keywords, RSS feeds, external links, internal links, and how long your blog has been in existence are all factors that affect your blog ranks in search results. Let's perform a search for "organic fruit blog" on Google to see what comes up.

Open up Google (`http://www.google.com`) in your browser window. Typing in the phrase **organic fruit blog** brings up the search results page similar to the following screenshot:

Georgia is disappointed that she is not listed in the top ten results. Although, she is pleased to see her favorite cooking blog, `http://cookingwithamy.blogspot.com`, is listed as the top result. "How did Amy manage to get listed so high in the results," Georgia asks thoughtfully, "If she can do it with a blogspot blog, so can I."

What is Amy doing right with her blog to be listed so high in the search results? Let's examine her blog from a search engine's point of view.

What High Ranking Blogs Do Right

Amy is doing a lot of things right with her blog. She uses many different types of text content to attract traffic to her blog. Looking at the following screenshot, we can see she uses multiple types of navigation to lead visitors and search engine crawlers to archives, external links, and additional resources. Her post titles are descriptive. She uses an image in every post, but pairs it with articles rich in keywords. She also uses Feedburner to serve bookmarklets and a subscription to her RSS feed.

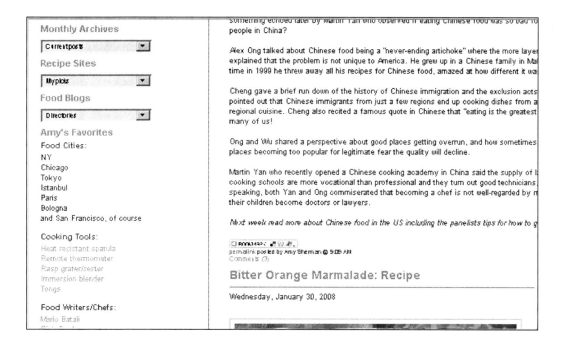

When we evaluate her blog using the URL checker provided by NetConcepts (`http://www.netconcepts.com/urlcheck/`), we see Amy's blog has great visibility with most of the major search engines. Yahoo!, Google, Ask, and Windows Live Search have indexed pages of her blog.

URL Check of cookingwithamy.blogspot.com/	
Search engine	**Pages found**
Google:	734
Yahoo!:	1980
Google Directory (DMOZ):	1
Ask:	276
Live Search:	84

Her deepest penetration is with Yahoo!, followed by Google. Amy has put a lot of careful planning into how her blog is seen by search engines. We can sweeten our own search rankings after checking our blog for key areas to improve. There are many different tools available online to help us evaluate our blogs.

Using Tools to Evaluate a Blog

There are many tools out there you can use to analyze your blog. You don't have to buy fancy software packages or pay expensive consultants. Optimizing your blog can be done with the help of freely available tools and a little elbow (and brain) grease.

Popular tools used by search engine optimizers include:

- **Google Trends** (`http://www.google.com/trends`): Do a comparison search of two sites or two keywords.

- **Google toolbar** (`http://toolbar.google.com/`): Shows the search result page ranking of any site, on a scale of 1-10.

- **NetConcepts SEO Tools** (`http://www.netconcepts.com/tools/`): Includes multiple tools such as a URL and a keyword checker.

You can find many other tools out on the Internet by doing a Google search for "free SEO tools". The most important tool is the search submission guidelines for each of the major search engines. The guidelines for Yahoo! search can be found at `http://searchmarketing.yahoo.com/srchsb/ssb_gl.php`. Let's dig into checking the current page rank of a site using the Google toolbar.

Time for Action!—Using a Toolbar to Check Site Rank

Whenever you visit a website, you can easily check the site rank it has been given by Google using the Google toolbar. We will install the toolbar and use it to test the rank of a website.

1. Go to the Google Toolbar page (`http://toolbar.google.com/`) to download the toolbar for your browser. Click the **Download Google Toolbar** button. You will be taken to a license agreement, click the **Agree and Install** button.

2. A **Software Installation** confirmation box will appear. It will look different on different Internet Browsers. The Firefox **Software Installation** window lists the name of the extension (**google-toolbar-win.xpi**) at the top of item window in bold text. The name of the company, **Google Inc,** is in italic text in the upper right corner. The URL the file is being downloaded from is displayed below the name of the file. Click the **Install Now,** or **OK** button, to proceed with the installation.

3. An Installation progress box will appear. It may take several minutes for the toolbar to be installed. You will be prompted to restart your browser to complete the installation and activate the toolbar.

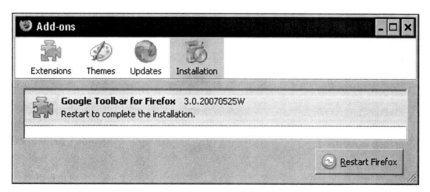

4. When your browser is opened again, you will be greeted with a window thanking you for installing the toolbar. This **Google Toolbar** window contains important settings for the toolbar. Google has helpfully placed a red box around the **PageRank** feature choices. Select the **Enable PageRank** radio button. Click the **Finish** button.

What Just Happened?

Installing the Google Toolbar gave you quick access to the PageRank of any site you wanted to visit. When you downloaded the Google Toolbar, you gave Google permission to attach small applications called `plug-ins` or `extensions` to your browsers' toolbar area. The PageRank mini-application was displayed in the browser toolbar area as an icon with a visual progress bar. The higher the rank of the page, the fuller the rectangular progress bar appeared to be.

PageRank is an important tool in researching and evaluating the success of a site within Google's search engine. It is a quick way to view the results of a complicated set of evolving algorithms used by Google to calculate the ranking of a site within it's own search results. Now that we have the tool installed, let's get comfortable using it.

Using the Google PageRank Button

The PageRank extension displays a dynamic icon, which changes depending on the site currently active in the browser window. When you hover your cursor over the PageRank icon, the message `PageRank is Google's view of the importance of this page (n/10)`. The letter "n" represents the PageRank score Google has given the page. Amy's blog (`http://cookingwithamy.blogspot.com`) has a Google PageRank of 6 out of 10. Every site you visit has a Google PageRank. Sites not yet listed with Google will have an extremely low PageRank. When you visit a site, you can quickly eyeball the PageRank by looking at the amount of green area displayed on the PageRank icon.

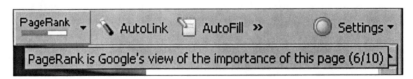

Yahoo! also has a toolbar. If you're ask me, the thought of cluttering up your limited browser window with multiple search engine toolbar widgets is not pleasant. There is another way to estimate the perceived value of your site according to search engines. Finding out which search engines have indexed the pages of your site tells you which search engines aren't offering your site to their users as search results.

Discovering Search Engine Reach Using Tools

We can easily find out the reach of our blog in the most popular (at the moment) search engines by using the URL Checker tool provided by NetConcepts. This free tool is easy to use and provides an overview of the search engine reach of any URL. The *Fruit for All* blog is relatively new, but checking its current reach will help us decide which search engines to submit the blog to, and whose guidelines we need to take a closer look at.

Time for Action!—Checking Search Engine Reach with NetConcepts URL Checker

Checking your search engine reach using the URL check tool will help you figure out which search engines aren't crawling your blog. We'll type a blog URL into the form and then examine the results.

1. Open up your browser window. Type the URL, `http://www.netconcepts.com/urlcheck/`, into the address bar of your browser. The **URL Checker** screen will appear. Enter your full URL into the text field and click the arrow button, as shown in the following screenshot:

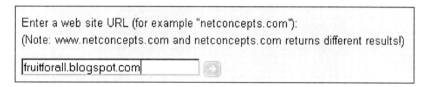

2. The tool will process your request and then display the number of pages from your URL found on each search engine. The results will be different depending upon how you enter your URL. If you submit multiple requests over several days, you will see groupings of results by date. We can see the results in the following screenshot:

URL Check of fruitforall.blogspot.com

Search engine	Pages found
Google:	15
Yahoo!:	0
Google Directory (DMOZ):	0
Ask:	0
Live Search:	0

What Just Happened?

When we entered the URL of our blog, the URL Checker tool performed a specialized search within each major search engine. The returned results told us two things: which search engines had not yet indexed our blog (and also those which had), and how many pages of our blog they were able to crawl.

Using the tool over a period of several days or every few weeks will show you whether your optimization efforts are resulting in improved spidering of your site by search engines. It can take time for search engines to add site pages to their indexes. It is worth taking the time to submit your site to all major search engines showing zero pages found. If you have video or other specialized content, search engine sites such as Yahoo! have special submission processes for your rich media content.

Improving Search Engine Rank with Web Standards

Search engines now expect most sites to use site mark up tags in predictable ways that are used by most web professionals, often called web standards. Practicing web standards when you edit the template of your blog makes it easier for search engines to index, more accessible to visitors who are using screen readers, and prepares your site structure for any future changes in web design.

Web standards are set by the World Wide Web Consortium; a group composed of designers, developers, and technology companies. Visit `http://www.w3c.org` for more details.

Validating Your Blog Template

Taking the time to validate your blog template with the World Wide Web Consortiums Markup Validation Service will open your eyes to any bugs or code hiccups hidden in your template. Blogger sites with the top Blogger navigation bar will show many errors. Most Blogger blogs do not naturally validate as XHTML Strict. We can improve our search engine rankings by changing the DOCTYPE from strict to transitional.

Time for Action!—Validating Your Site with W3C

The World Wide Web Consortium has created a handy validation website where you can check your blog template against established web standards. This can help you spot errors you might miss after wasting hours trying to diagnose them on your own. It saves you time, effort, and frustration.

1. Open your browser and type the W3C URL into your address bar, `http://validator.w3.org/`. The **Validate by URI** tab is selected by default. Type the full URL of your site into the **Address** field, as shown in the following screenshot:

2. You can perform a variety of advanced tasks by clicking on the **More Options** link. The space below the link will expand to display more ways to filter results, see the source code, view the outline of the site markup, fix common issues, and control how result messages are displayed. Select the **Group Error Messages by type** radio button.

3. Click the **Check** button to begin the validation. A large amount of errors will appear. Don't panic! One of our first optimization tasks will be to clean up the template and change the document type to XHTML Transitional. We will work on resolving the crucial errors in the optimization section of this chapter.

4. You can see details about the document type of the blog in the following screenshot. The **Result** row displays the number of validation errors. Looks like it found plenty. The **Encoding** row contains the nickname for the encoding format of any characters being used for the blog, **utf-8** is known as **8-bit UCS/Unicode Transformation Format by Internet Engineers**. The **Doctype** displays the document type declared in the template of the blog. We can see it is currently set to **XHTML 1.0 Strict**, the default for most Blogger templates.

5. Scroll down the list of errors and take a look. Many of the errors are related to the use of the Blogger toolbar at the top of our blog. We aren't supposed to remove it, so changing the **Doctype** to **Transitional** should eliminate many of these errors. Notice the way the error is listed. The title of the type of error is displayed in bold with a red **x** to the left of it. In the following screenshot, we can see the error title, **XML Parsing Error**, displayed. The line number where the error is found is listed. It also offers a suggested reason for the error. A snippet of the markup is displayed below the line listing of the error. If there are multiple errors of the same type, they will all be listed under the title of the error type.

XML Parsing Error
 • *Line 70, column > 80*: XML Parsing Error: EntityRef: expecting ';'

   ...ogger.com/comment.g?blogID=23876822111306986798postID=6707628459787307333' on...

6. When we make changes to the template of the blog, we will return to the validator option and see the type of results we manage to get.

What Just Happened?

When we entered the URL of our blog into the W3C's Validate by URI service, we asked it to check our site for markup errors based on the document type. Markup here refers to any tags or other elements used to form the site page. These are usually contained in the template. The W3C has guidelines for each document type, detailing what types of tags can be used. You can learn more about DOCTYPE and the guidelines at `http://www.w3c.org`.

What you really need to be concerned about is the actual results of each validation check. These are displayed in a lengthy list. The line number for each item helps you find errors quickly when using an HTML or code editor. Clicking the **revalidate** button caused the validator to check our blog for errors again. Every time you make a correction to your template go back to the validator tool and run it again to see the results.

Many of the errors that were displayed were unfortunately within the Blogger code. The only way to resolve many of those is to turn off page element widgets. We will examine the reasons for the errors later in the chapter and look at potential solutions to improve validation against the DOCTYPE.

Blog SEO Checklist

We want an efficient way to analyze our blog and track any optimizations we make. Using a checklist will give structure to the issues we need to consider. We will use the checklist below to determine which areas of the blog need to be optimized.

Start with this checklist when you are ready to evaluate your blog. Put a **yes** or **no** in the "Optimized" column for each issue. When you are done working your way through the checklist, you will be ready to plan the improvements for your blog.

Issue	Description	Optimized?
Blog Title and Description	Title and Description use Keywords, even if an image is displayed instead of text.	
Alt text used for images	Blog posts and site images have keyword text in the alt portion of the image tag.	
Text used more than images in Posts	Posts are a minimum of 250 words with keywords within that first block. Images are paired with text describing them.	
Post URLs are Search Engine Friendly	Blogger settings convert any URLs to readable search engine friendly ones.	

Issue	Description	Optimized?
Inbound links from higher profile sites	Inbound links is a good option to have. A "link to this site" or "subscribe" link is visible.	
Keywords used relate to the topic and purpose of the blog	Figure out which keywords are most popular and closely match your topic. Visit `http://www.wordtracker.com` or `http://inventory.overture.com` and research the cost of AdWord keywords.	
Keywords match phrases people use to find my blog	Ask other people how they would search for my topic. Do experimental searches. Talk to a librarian or other bloggers.	
Google Blog Search lists my blog	Blogger settings allow Blog Search and others to find me.	

Now that you have a firm grasp of the many tools and techniques available to you to make your site more attractive to search engines, you are ready to plan improvements to your blog.

Planning Improvements

Optimizing a blog for search engines should be done in a methodical way. This will save us time, and give us documentation to use when we need to compare future results with how things are now. We are going to:

- Create a list of improvements.
- Develop strategies for on-site and off-site optimization.
- Prioritize our improvements for maximum results in the shortest amount of time.

Creating a List of Improvements

We have a general idea of the types of improvements we want to make. We've used the checklist to evaluate our blog. Now we need to make a list of the improvements that will be necessary to attract search engines. A list can be created by preparing a checklist from the earlier sections of this chapter and penciling in additional ideas, like those found in the following list:

Ten Ways to Optimize a Blog for Search Engines

Here are ten proven ways to optimize your blog for search engines:

1. Experiment

2. Consistently provide quality content focused on a narrow topic

3. Hone your writing style

4. Update your blog and post on a predictable schedule

5. Stick to one subject per post

6. Fill your posts with content. Aim for 250 or more words per post. Beef up your image and video posts with additional descriptive text.

7. Make every post unique.

8. Use the Ping settings on Blogger to automatically notify blog networks

9. Set your blog up with an RSS tool such as `www.feedburner.com` and then submit your feed URL to big syndication portals such as MyYahoo! (`http://publisher.yahoo.com/rssguide`).

10. Submit your blog URL to search engines where it isn't listed yet. Popular search engines include Google, Yahoo! (`http://search.yahoo.com/info/submit.html`), Ask (`www.ask.com`), and Windows Live Search.

The items on the top ten lists repeat several of the ideas listed in the checklist. These ideas are supported by major search engines. They are often referred to as "white hat" techniques, evoking the image of the good law abiding cowboy from the Wild West.

Wearing a White Hat

It can be very tempting to try a few "black hat" SEO tricks. The downside is that search engines, especially the folks at Google, are constantly updating algorithms and making other adjustments to how they evaluate and rank sites. Do the right thing and focus on long term results. Most promises of high page rank in a short period of time are scams.

Developing Improvement Strategies

There are two types of search engine optimization strategies. There is the type you do to your own site, called "On-site" by search engine gurus. Then all the things you or other people do without touching your blog, known as "Off-site" techniques. Divide your list into those two groups. We can use the following chart to organize our list into the two strategies:

Improvement Strategy	On or Off Site
Keywords in blog title & description	On-site
Alt text used for images	On-site
Inbound links using keywords (use widget)	Off-site
Blog settings allow spiders to crawl site	On-site
Content focused on core subjects, one per post	On-site
Adwords or other advertising with keywords	Off-site
Submit blog to major search engines	Off-site
Add a sitemap using Google webmaster tools	Off-site
Edit template for better DOCTYPE validation	On-site

Think of it this way, if you can make the improvement while logged into your blog, then it is an "On-site" strategy. Any improvements made using other sites or resources are "Off-site" strategies. You've got a list of all the improvements you want to make to your blog. You're ready to start right now. Before you rush off and try to do it all in one day, take a deep breath, sit down, and look at your list again.

Prioritizing Improvements

If you could only do one thing today, what would it be? Trying to do all possible improvements in one day can cause optimization burn out. We already have the list of things sorted out into On-site and Off-site techniques. Now, we have to decide where each item on the list ranks in priority.

There are complicated factors that need to be considered. You have to weigh the time involved, the risk, the level of difficulty, and the potential benefit. Sounds like a matrix to me! If you have a business, or you are considering hiring someone to help you, the cost will also be a factor. To keep things simple, a sample improvement matrix has been filled out for you in the following example:

Item Type	Difficulty level (1-10)	Time to complete	Potential benefit (1-10)
Header & Description	1	5 minutes	9
Blog Settings	4	10 minutes	9
Template	6	30 minutes	7
Content	2	Every time a post is created	10
Add a sitemap	2	5 minutes	8

We can quickly see immediate benefits from updating the header and description of our blog. When visitors use a search engine, the title of the blog and description will often display in the search results. The greatest benefit also takes the longest to ripen. Creating content takes time, but has enormous long term benefits.

The search engines, their interests, and what we can do to attract them have been explored. We've gathered our lists of improvements, and know that editing our template and blog settings will yield the best immediate benefits. We're ready to tackle optimizing our blog for search engines.

Optimizing Your Blog for Search Engines

We are going to take our earlier checklists and use them as guides on where to make changes to our blog. When the changes are complete, the blog will be more attractive to search engines and visitors. We will start with changes we can make "On-site", and then progress to ways we can improve search engine results with "Off-site" improvements.

Optimizing On-site

The most crucial improvements we identified earlier were around the blog settings, template, and content. We will start with the easiest fixes, then dive into the template to correct validation issues. Let's begin with the settings in our Blogger blog.

Seeding the Blog Title & Description with Keywords

When you created your blog, did you take a moment to think about what words potential visitors were likely to type in when searching for your blog? Using keywords in the title and description of your blog gives potential visitors a preview and explanation of the topics they can expect to encounter in your blog. This information is what will also display in search results when potential visitors perform a search.

Time for Action!—Updating the Blog Title and Description

It's never too late to seed your blog title and description with keywords. We will edit the blog title and description to optimize them for search engines.

1. Login to your blog and navigate to **Settings | Basic**. We are going to replace the current title text with a phrase that more closely fits the blog. Type **Organic Fruit for All** into the **Title** field.

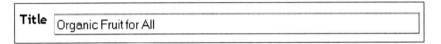

2. Now, we are going to change the description of the blog. Type **Organic Fruit Recipes, seasonal tips, and guides to healthy living** into the description field.

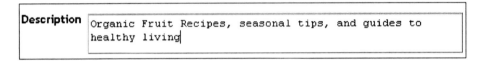

3. Scroll down to the bottom of the screen and click the **Save Settings** button.

 You can enter up to 500 characters of descriptive text.

What Just Happened?

When we changed the title and description of our blog in the Basic Settings section, Blogger saved the changes and updated the template information as well. Now, when search engines crawl our blog, they will see richer descriptions of our blog in the blog title and blog description. The next optimization task is to verify that search engines can index our blog.

Allowing Search Engines to Find Your Blog

Blogger prevents search engines from crawling your blog, by default. Why? Blogger assumes that most people are creating blogs as online journals and may not want search engine exposure. You can easily change the settings in your blog to allow search engines to find your blog.

Time for Action!—Activating Blogsearch and Ping Access

Activating blogsearch and ping access will cause each blog post to be available for search engines and will notify blog services when the blog is updated. This will increase the chances of a potential reader finding the blog.

1. Log in to Blogger and click on the **Settings** link next to your blog. The screen will reload with the **Basic** section already selected under the **Settings** tab as shown in the following screenshot:

2. Scroll down the page until the option **Add your blog to our listings** appears. Select **Yes** from the drop-down list.

3. Continue scrolling to the next item on the page. **Let search engines find your blog** is the next option displayed. Select **Yes** from the drop-down list. Scroll to the bottom of the screen and click the **Save Settings** button.

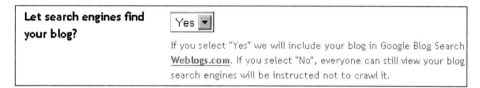

What Just Happened?

When you selected **Yes** for the **Add your blog to our listings** option, you increased the chances of your blog being discovered by other Blogger users, making them more likely to create inbound links to your blog. The second setting allowed search engine robots to crawl your blog. Your blog will now be indexable by search engines, including Google Blog Search. We will get technical in the Off-site optimization section and view the actual `robots.txt` file to better understand the areas of our blog where the robots crawl.

Fertilizing Content with Keywords

Choose one focus keyword for each content post. You should be able to use it naturally about five times during the post. For example, the keyword "eco-friendly" for an article on natural cleaning supplies. You can see a list of all labels used for posts and can edit active posts by clicking on the **Edit Posts** sub menu option under the **Posting** tab.

Try not to use the same keywords for every post. Make the keyword phrases as unique as possible. Do this by being as specific as you can. The phrase **Fresh organic fruit basket** could be a better keyword phrase than **fruit basket**. Rich keyword phrases will interest search engine robots and readers.

The title for each post should be as unique as possible. Remember, it will become the title of the individual page of the post. Think of it as a magazine headline, brief and focused on your post topic. To change the title of a post, click the **Edit** link.

Optimizing Image and Video Posts for Current Searches

Whenever you add a video or image to a blog post, try to add a descriptive message with it. Use an RSS feed or an alternative content service such as `www.feedburner.com` to package your content into different formats for visitors and other interested parties to enjoy. At the same time, you will be creating additional information about your content. Useful! Let's add a new post to practice optimizing image posts for search engines.

Time for Action!—Getting Descriptive with Image Posts

You can increase the accessibility of your blog and improve your chances of a post containing images showing up in search results by adding alternate text to the tag of an image.

1. Log in to Blogger and click the **New Post** link under your blog. Start by creating a new post as you normally would. Enter a descriptive title for the post. In this example, we are typing `Star Fruit adds Exotic Thrill to Winter Romance` as the title.

2. Next, we need to create content for the post. I recommend typing content before adding images to posts. It makes positioning the images easier. The full content for the post is available online at `http://fruitforall.blogspot.com` and also in the code download section of this book's companion website, `http://bloggerbeefedup.blogspot.com`.

3. Now, it's time to add the image. Before you click the upload button, check the name you gave the image. The name should be descriptive and formatted to be search engine friendly. The star fruit image for the post is named `exotic-star-fruit.jpg` for optimal indexing by search engines.

4. Upload the image using the Blogger post image icon. Select the size of the image to display and its location in relation to the text content. We are setting the image size to `small` and the layout to `center`. Click the **UPLOAD IMAGE** button to add the image to the post.

5. We are almost ready to publish our post. Before we do, let's take a look at the HTML code of the post and add alt text to the image. Select the **Edit Html** tab on the post editor. Don't be confused by the long strings of Blogger identification attributes in the image tag. We notice right away that the alt attribute is an empty string: `alt=""`. We're going to fill it with useful keywords and make it more accessible to visitors using screen readers at the same time.

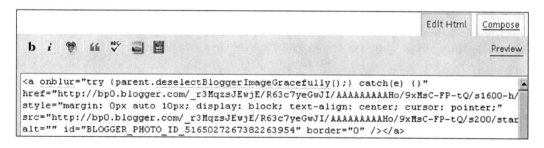

6. Type the following phrase between the quotes of the alt tag: `Juicy yellow organic Star Fruit on a romantic pink satin background`. The alt tag should now look like this:

   ```
   alt="Juicy yellow organic Star Fruit on a romantic pink
                                       satin background."
   ```

7. Click the **Compose** tab and enter the following keywords into the **Labels** field: `Star Fruit, organic fruit, romance, valentine, exotic fruit,` and `exotic fruit recipe`. Now, click the **PUBLISH POST** button.

[Google robots prefer dashes "-"for parts of a title or file name, where a natural space would go.]

What Just Happened?

When we created an image post with descriptive image names and rich keywords in the alt attribute, we increased the chances of the post being properly indexed by search engines. We also made the post more accessible to visitors using screen readers.

Submitting Rich Media Content for Indexing

You can submit media feeds to the Yahoo! media content stream (`http://search.yahoo.com/mrss/submit/`) or place videos on YouTube (`http://www.youtube.com`). You can also opt-in to Google's Enhanced Image Search on the Google Webmaster Tools site in the **Tools** section (`https://www.google.com/webmasters/tools/imageoptin?`). Photographers and original image creators will want to take advantage of labeling their work with metadata using tools such as Adobe Photoshop.

Improving Template Validation

Blogger has placed a low priority on changing the template and the surrounding code to be fully compliant with the XHTML 1 doctypes. Using third-party templates that are created with iframe tags and the Blog Archive page element can cause numerous validation errors. If validation is important to you, weaning yourself from widgets is necessary. We can easily improve matters by changing the **Doctype** of the template from XHTML 1.0 Strict to XHTML 1.0 Transitional.

Time for Action!—Editing the Template Doctype

Changing the doctype of our Blogger template will enable it to be correctly analyzed by the W3C validation tool and will improve its processing by web browsers.

1. Log into Blogger and click the **Layout** link next to your blog. Navigate to the **Edit HTML** section under the **Layout** tab. Download a full copy of your template to back it up before any changes are made.

2. Select the Doctype tag in the **Edit Template** text area box. Copy and paste the following document type declaration to replace it:

```
<!DOCTYPE html PUBLIC "-//W3C//DTD XHTML 1.0 Transitional//EN"
    "http://www.w3.org/TR/xhtml1/DTD/xhtml1-transitional.dtd">
```

3. Click the **SAVE TEMPLATE** button to finalize the changes.

4. Time to visit the **Layout** screen and remove several page elements that are causing validation errors. Click the **edit** link on the Blog Archive page element or any other page elements such as the third-party widget from Amazon that display validation errors. Click the **Remove page element** button on each, one by one.

5. Let's revisit the W3C validation tool to see how well the blog template validates now. We can see real progress towards a more valid site in the following screenshot. We are still 62 errors short of complete compliance.

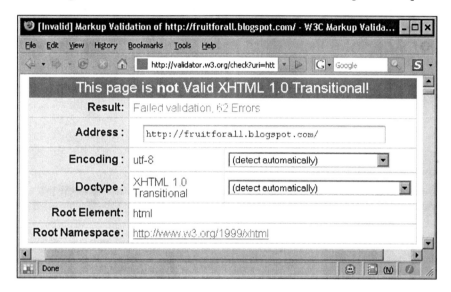

What Just Happened?

When we edited the template to change the Doctype, we instructed browsers and other user-agents such as robots to examine and process our blog using the guidelines established for the Doctype. A Doctype acts as a roadmap for browsers and other user-agents when they visit a site. XHTML 1.0 Strict would require removing the FeedBurner flare tags in the template and turning comments off. We could use a third-party comments system such as Haloscan (http://www.haloscan.com/) instead.

Optimizing with Off-Site Techniques

Some "Off-site" improvements as quality inbound links take time to build, while others can be done right away. Google webmaster tools has a full array of features to help you optimize your blog. These features include sitemaps, robots.txt testing, and viewing your site the way a search engine does.

Adding a sitemap to Google's webmaster tools will make it easier for search engine robots to crawl your site. We will do this as soon as we have added the blog to Google webmaster tools and verified it.

Adding a Blog to Google Webmaster Tools

Google webmaster tools has a Dashboard where you can manage multiple websites. Once you've added a site, you can upload a sitemap, run diagnostics, and even add a Webmaster tools gadget to your iGoogle home page. Before you can add a sitemap, you will need to verify your blog address. Then, we will add a general sitemap that will work for Blogger users who have redirected their blog feed using FeedBurner.

Time for Action!—Verifying Your Blogger Blog Using a Meta tag

Adding a Meta tag to your template from Google Webmaster tools will indicate you have admin access and rights to the blog.

1. Log into the Google webmaster tools site (`https://www.google.com/webmasters/tools/`). Type the URL of your blog to add it to the tools, if you haven't already. Click the **verify** link.

2. Now, select **Add a meta tag** from the **Choose verification method** drop-down list. Google will generate a special Meta tag. Select all the text and then copy it.

3. Open your blog in a new window. Navigate to **Template tab | Edit Html**. Paste the Meta tag just below the `<head>` tag of your template. It should look similar to the code snippet below:

```
<head>
<meta name="verify-v1" content="WfPbTvz7
                        +zlMyzH3zJXHf1ZwX3O1g2pgxo Ptgq9T4E8=" />
    <b:include data='blog' name='all-head-content'/>
    <title><data:blog.pageTitle/></title>
```

4. Click the **SAVE TEMPLATE** button at the bottom of the template screen. Go back to the Google webmaster tools site and click the **Verify** button. The page will reload, and a success message will appear similar to the one shown below:

> ✓ You've successfully verified http://fruitforall.blogspot.com/.

What Just Happened?

When you added the Meta tag to the head section of your blog template, Google webmaster tools was able to track the blog template and verify whether you had admin access to the blog. The addition of the Meta tag was proof to Google webmaster tools that you were the owner or an administrator of the blog, and therefore had the authority to add that URL to Google webmaster tools. Now that the blog URL is verified, we are ready to add a sitemap.

Adding a Sitemap using Google Webmaster Tools

Blogger users can add sitemaps of their blogs to Google Webmaster tools. Adding a sitemap makes it easier for search engines to index your blog.

 You can add multiple sitemaps to help Google spiders index your blog for multiple content formats, including mobile phones.

You do not have to do any coding or understand sitemap formats to upload a sitemap of your blog to Google webmaster tools. We will leverage the existing `atom` or `RSS feed` of our blog to provide a sitemap.

Time for Action!—Adding a Sitemap

Adding a sitemap to webmaster tools will increase the chances of all your blog posts being indexed by Google's web spiders.

1. Log into the Google webmaster tools site. Enter your blogspot URL, for example `http://fruitforall.blogspot.com`, and click the **Add Site** button, if the blog has not yet been added. If this is the first site you have added, you will need to verify the site instead. Click the **Add** link under the **Sitemap** column to add a sitemap to your blog.

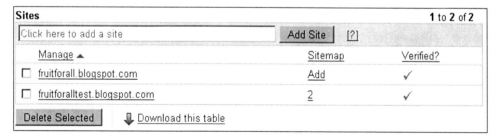

2. Select **Add General Web Sitemap** from the **Add Sitemap** type
    drop-down list.

3. Enter **atom.xml?redirect=false&start-index=1&max-results=100** into the
    URL box. Click the **Add General Web Sitemap** button.

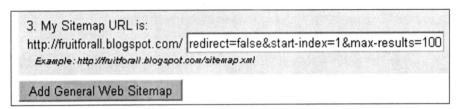

4. A success message will appear. The new sitemap information will be listed
    in a table, including the number of pages on the site that have been indexed,
    and the last time it was crawled. It may take a little while for the sitemap to
    be processed.

What Just Happened?

When we added a sitemap for the blog using the General sitemap format, we were
able to add parameters to the URL of the blog. Usually, only the last twenty-five
feeds are listed in a feed-based sitemap. Specifying the maximum post results gave
the Google spiders additional content to examine. We can currently set the maximum
posts to 500. This number may change in the future. If your main concern is having
Google index your freshest content, you can create a sitemap for a feed using `rss.`
`xml?orderby=updated`.

To create a sitemap for a Blogger blog that does not have the feed redirect feature
activated, type `atom.xml` in the **Sitemap URL** field.

 Taking advantage of your blog feeds is currently the only way to add
a sitemap.

We have added a sitemap to help search engines find and crawl our blog. How it is being indexed can be analyzed using **Crawl stats** under the **Statistics** menu at Google webmaster tools.

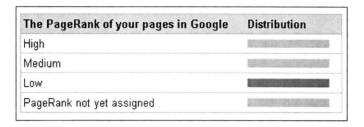

The PageRank of your pages in Google	Distribution
High	
Medium	
Low	
PageRank not yet assigned	

We can see the **PageRank** of the blog in more detail on the **Crawl stats** page, as shown in the preceding screenshot. The possible PageRank ranges from **not yet assigned** to **High**. It is possible for individual pages to have higher rankings, depending on popularity. In the future, we will see darker blue bars in the **Distribution** column for multiple PageRank levels.

 You can learn more about how Google indexes your blog by visiting the help topic: http://www.google.com/support/webmasters/bin/ topic.py?topic=8843&hl=en.

Unfortunately, there currently isn't a way to edit the robots.txt file for your blog directly within Blogger. Using the **Analyze Robots.txt** tool on Google webmaster tools gives us a view of our blog's robots.txt file and statistics surrounding how search engines are crawling our blog.

Communicating with Search Engine Spiders

Search engine spiders may seem mysterious, but they are your friends. You can view the commands within a robots.txt file to see how your site is setup to be crawled. Google webmaster tools make it easy for you to view your Blogger robots.txt file.

 You cannot currently edit your Blogger robots.txt file.

Time for Action!—Viewing Robots.txt

Knowing what is in the `robots.txt` file of your blog will give you a better understanding of how search engines are interacting with it.

1. Navigate to the Google webmaster tools site (`https://www.google.com/webmasters/tools/`) and click on the **Tools** menu item. Select **Analyze Robots.txt** from the **Tools** sub menu.

2. On the **Analyze Robots.txt** screen, you will first see a status table. It displays the URL the `robots.txt` file is set to, the time the file was last downloaded by a search engine crawler, and the status of the file in the table. Scroll down to view the text within the `robots.txt` file. It should currently look similar to the one shown in the following screenshot:

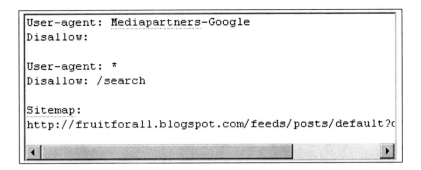

```
User-agent: Mediapartners-Google
Disallow:

User-agent: *
Disallow: /search

Sitemap:
http://fruitforall.blogspot.com/feeds/posts/default?c
```

3. Editing the file cannot be done directly. When you submit your blog to search engines or sign up and post AdWords on your blog, a change will automatically be made to the file. Search engine robots are commonly referred to as user-agents. Note that all user-agents are disallowed from following any search subfolder on the blog.

What Just Happened?

When we reviewed the `robots.txt` file for the blog, we saw that it was set to allow Google's special AdWords user-agent **Mediapartners-Google** to index all pages on the blog, but to prevent all search engine robots from indexing any files within the **search** folder. The location of the sitemap was also listed for all search engines as a result of adding the sitemap using the sitemap creation wizard.

 The `robots.txt` file does not prevent people or other programs from finding pages or files on your site. It is not a security measure.

It is easy to make a small error and unintentionally block all robots from your site. `Robots.txt` uses a set of rules and syntax meant to be read by programs, not people.

Understanding User-Agent Behavior in Robots.txt

Knowing how user-agents interact with `robots.txt` will help you analyze what is happening in your `robots.txt` file. A combination of wildcards (*), file paths, and keywords instruct robots where to go when they attempt to crawl your site. Specific robots can be told to go away or avoid specified areas of your site. The first keyword, "User-agent", names the User-agent(s) to whom the instruction set is addressed. This is immediately followed by the command portion of the instruction set, either an "Allow" or "Disallow" statement detailing which portion of the site is restricted.

Situation	Syntax	Results

Allow all robots to crawl on the site.	`User-agent: *`
	
	`Disallow:`
		The "*" is a wildcard, meaning "all". Its use invites all robots to your site.

Allow a specific User-agent full site access.	`User-agent: Mediapartners-Google`
	
	`Disallow:`
		The AdWords robot can crawl all areas of our blog.

Block all robots from crawling a folder of your site.	`User-agent: *`
	
	`Disallow: /search`
		Any file or folder coming after this statement will not be crawled by search engines.

You can find a list of common user-agents on the Web Robots Database located at `http://www.robotstxt.org/db.html`.

[Leaving the space after the `Disallow` statement blank tells robots that they can index the entire site.]

Measuring Optimization Success

There are many ways to measure the success of your search engine optimization improvements. One quick way is to keep an eye on your reports in Google Analytics. Over time, you should see more visitors from organic searches visiting your site. The number of comments, feed subscribers, and inbound links will also clue you in on how successful the changes have been. A third way to track success is your blogs Google PageRank number.

Evaluating the Impact of Improvements

I just told you that there are many ways to measure the impact your changes had on the search engine results for your blog. It will take time to accurately determine if the improvements worked. You don't like that answer, and neither do I. The longer your blog stays in good shape, the more its rankings will improve over time. We can and should take measurements using a variety of tools on a regular basis.

While we are waiting, we can use tools available online to continue analyzing our blog. Most of the tools are for free. They are provided out of goodwill or a desire to attract visitors.

Tools and Resources

There are many resources on the Internet you can use to optimize your blog. We could have spent a whole book just covering website tools. Since we couldn't fit all of them into this chapter, several additional ones have been included here. New tools are being added every day, but these should get you started.

Here are several of my favorite site improvement tools:

- **Access color**: Provides a quick way to improve how humans view your site, making them more likely to link to you, `http://www.accesskeys.org/tools/color-contrast.html`.

- **Google website optimizer**: Experiment with the effect changes to your blog could have on your marketing and search engine optimization strategies. You will need to have an AdWords account to use this tool, `http://services.google.com/websiteoptimizer/`.

- **Web pages that suck checklist**: Improve the appearance, accessibility, and attractiveness of your blog to search engines using this checklist, `http://www.webpagesthatsuck.com/does-my-web-site-suck/`.

- **W3C XHTML validator**: Take a deep breath and use this online tool to measure the validity of your site against current W3C guidelines, `http://validator.w3.org/`.

- **NetConcepts**: `www.netconcepts.com/tools/`.

They will give you suggestions on how to improve your site. Even making small improvements can have a big impact on your search engine rank.

Maintaining Your SEO Status

Keeping your blog optimized for search engines should be part of your regular site maintenance routine. There are always improvements being made to optimization tools, the Blogger platform, and search engines. Every season, there is fresh fruit to harvest.

Controlling the Destiny of Your Blog

If you write the content, they will come. We all know some really cool bloggers who barely make their first post and are instantly famous and sought after. The reality for most of us is it takes continuous effort to build an audience and achieve high search engine rankings. You can control the destiny of your blog.

You can continue to improve your blog by maintaining:

- The title and description of your blog
- The content of your posts
- The settings of your blog
- Who you link to, and who links to you

It can be an uphill struggle. People who don't blog think it is easy. Stick it out, and remember there are some things you cannot control about your blog.

You have no control over:

- How long your blog or domain has existed. The longer your blog exists with periodic updates, the higher it will rank. It takes patience for this optimization method.
- The past bad behavior of your domain or blogspot site. If it is really bad, consider using a different domain or blogspot site.

The Secret to Search Engine Attraction

There is a very popular school of thought right now which states that if you send positive thoughts out to the universe, positive things will happen to you. This applies to search engines as well. Create a blog that is rich in content and follows web standards, and you will attract search engines. Keep looking at what techniques other bloggers are using. Sign up for RSS feeds of the Google webmaster blog so you can be the first to know when changes are afoot. Check your site rank and keywords regularly and make adjustments.

Search Engines Crave Rich Media Content

Bloggers have unique issues when it comes to search engines. We have a lot of content over time, which makes search engines happy. We also face more difficulties if we primarily post images, video, and other multimedia files. Search engines are scrambling to catch up and accommodate searches for rich media content.

Why Search Engines Care about Rich Media Content

Video, audio, and image content are extremely popular right now, and search engine users are looking for better ways to find this content. The search engine that can successfully solve this problem for users will widen the opportunities for additional ad revenue. They will collect more revenue from site owners who mainly offer rich media content and want to be found, and from search engine users who are looking for this content. These changes are happening at a rapid pace. Expect big changes over the coming months. Wait till YouTube and FeedBurner services, acquired by Google, mature.

Summary

Like it or not, search engines are your biggest marketing tool. Play nice with the search engines, and your blog is more likely to prosper. In this chapter, we optimized our blog for search engines by using the following process:

- Find out where your blog currently is ranked on major search engines.
- Examine your blog for areas to optimize using our checklist and free tools on the Internet.
- Make a plan and set a goal for changes to the blog.
- Optimize the blog, one area at a time.
- Measure the success of optimization through searches and tools.

We've come a long way. Chapter 10 is where it all comes together. We'll be integrating the blog with a company website. This will involve adding links, a tab menu, putting cool RSS-based blog widgets on the company site, and other exciting things.

10
Website Integration

At some point you will want to add your blog to your website, add the navigation bar from your website to your blog, or make changes to your blog, so it looks like part of your own site instead of a separate site. Making these changes is often referred to as **integration**. Integrating your website with your blog opens up more opportunities to promote both sites, makes your sites more attractive to search engines, and gives you powerful ways to publish your blog.

We'll focus on the most popular ways sites are integrated with blogs, including navigation, fonts, colors, widgets, and publishing methods. By the end of this chapter, you will be able to take colors, fonts, and navigation code from your site and seamlessly integrate them into your blog template. You will also be able to make an informed decision on whether publishing to a custom domain is right for you.

We're going to spend this chapter working on:

- Adding website navigation to your blog
- Using widgets on your site to share your blog
- Matching your blog template to your website
- Publishing your blog to a custom domain

Georgia has a simple e-commerce site set up for her company. She wants to share her blog on her website and add the navigation from her website to her blog. She is also interested in adding RSS feed subscriptions, bookmarklets, and other cross-promotional widgets to her website. Georgia is not sure if she wants to publish her blog using a custom domain or FTP. She does want to explore those options with us to decide if they will work for her.

You can see the company site we have to work with in the following screenshot:

The changes we make to the blog and the website will range from simple copy, paste efforts to dynamic JavaScript programming tweaks. Let's jump right in to the most popular integration area, navigation.

Adding Website Navigation

Shared navigation unifies your website and your blog. It will also make it easier for search engines to crawl both sites. There are three different looks most site use for navigation:

- Text-based interactive CSS menus
- CSS driven drop-down menus
- Graphical tabbed navigation

Preparing to Add Navigation

Navigation can make or break a site. Here's what we need to do before we begin adding our new navigation.

- **Decide how the navigation should look**: We will start with a simple text navigation menu formatted with CSS, as seen in the preceding screenshot, and then add a dynamic drop-down menu once we get our feet wet. DynamicDrive.com (http://www.dynamicdrive.com/style/csslibrary/) has many different navigation blocks that are easy to add to any site.

- **Gather or create any images needed**: Save the images and upload them either to an existing domain or an image host. The images in the examples will be hosted on my own domain `http://www.leesjordan.net/images/`. I recommend using Google Pages, Photobucket, or your own domain to host images on your blog. You can upload an image in a post to Blogger and then set the post as a draft to use the image. Uploading multiple images can sometimes become time consuming.

- **Edit the code to fit the blog**: Save a backup copy of your code. Prepare the size, links, formatting, CSS for the blog. Change any relative URLs or image links such as `/images/ffa-mini-logo.gif` to absolute URLs like `http://www.leesjordan.net/images/ffa-mini-logo.gif`. Remove any margins or padding from the navigation, so that you can add it back and custom fit it to the blog.

Time for Action!—Adding CSS Text Menus to a Blog

We're going to add a text menu styled with CSS by editing our blog template, and then the HTML portion of the code to a page element.

1. Log into Blogger. Go to **Layout | Edit HTML** and check the **Expand Widget Templates** box. Begin by changing `maxwidgets='1'` to `maxwidgets='3'`. The attribute `showaddelement='no'` should be changed to `'yes'`. Now you should have:

   ```
   <b:section class='header' id='header' maxwidgets='3'
                                showaddelement='yes'>
   ```

2. Save the template, and go to the **Layouts | Page Elements**. We can now see the page elements link we were hoping for. Click the **Add a Page Element** link.

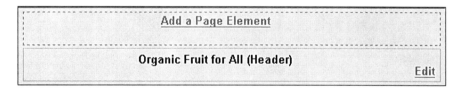

3. Open up your web page and copy the navigation content block. Paste it into a text editor or website editor. Check the links in the navigation block. They should point to absolute URL paths such as `http://www.leesjordan.net`. Here's a simple text menu block that you can use:

   ```
   <div id="navigation">
    <ul>
     <li><a href="http://www.leesjordan.net/fruitforall/store.html"
         target="_blank">Buy Fruit</a></li>
   ```

```
<li><a href="http://fruitforall.blogspot.com"
        target="_blank">Read the FFA Blog</a></li>
<li><a href="http://www.twitter.com/fruitforall"
        target="_blank">News</a></li>
<li><a href="http://www.leesjordan.net/fruitforall/about.html"
        target="_blank">About FFA</a></li>
</ul>
</div>
```

4. Select the **HTML/JavaScript** page element and paste the navigation code block into the **content** box of the page element. Leave the **Title** field blank. Click the **SAVE CHANGES** button. Drag the new page element navigation block below the **Header** page element block, as shown in the following screenshot:

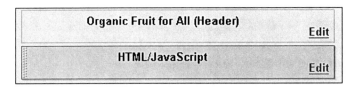

5. Now we need to add the CSS to the blog template. Go back to **Layout | Edit HTML**, and scroll down the template to the CSS section. Paste the following code after the last tag in the #header block, before the beginning of the Outer-Wrapper CSS block.

```
/* Top menu navigation -- edited for Blogger */
#navigation
{
  display:block;
  float:right;
  margin: 2px 0 0 2px;
  padding: 2px 2px 0 2px;
  text-align:left;
  border: none;
  z-index:199;
}
#navigation ul
{
  background: none;
  width:400px;
  padding: 0;
  margin: 0;
  float:right;
  font: bold 80% Verdana;
```

```
}
#navigation ul li
{
 margin: 0;
 padding: 0;
 display: inline;
}
#navigation ul li a, #navigation ul li span
{
 float: left;color: #990000;
 font-weight: bold;
 padding: 8px 5px 5px 6px;
 text-decoration: none;
 background: none;
}
#navigation ul li a:hover
{
 text-decoration:underline;
 color: #cc0000;
}
#navigation ul li a:visited
{
 text-decoration:none;
 color: #ff6600;
}
```

6.   Click the **SAVE TEMPLATE** button, and then view the blog. An example of the same is shown in the following screenshot. We now have a nice top menu on our blog!

What Just Happened?

When the `maxwidgets` is changed from 1 to 3, the number of widgets allowed in the header increases. Changing `showaddelement` from `no` to `yes` instructs Blogger to show an `Add a page element` block in the header area of the blog.

If you do not move the navigation page element below the header page element, the navigation will be hidden behind the header image, and the header will be set to hide the title and description text, if you have one uploaded.

You may have to adjust the margin, width, and padding of the CSS for your navigation block to fit properly. Remember that the CSS will treat the page element as its own container and ignore its relationship to the top, bottom, left, and right of the blog template. Note that the default link color of the navigation text was changed from brown (#693f15) to dark red (#990000), to be a closer match to the template.

You can also add a footer navigation bar to the blog using the same content block. You may want to create a separate CSS block for footer navigation or build on the existing footer styles. Don't forget to change the id of the content divs from "navigation" to "footer".

The CSS can be added in the same page element by placing the CSS styles within opening and closing <style> tags, as shown:

<style type="text/css">

CSS code

</style>

See the BetaBloggerforDummies blog for more details.

http://betabloggerfordummies.blogspot.com/2008/03/
free-css-navigation-menus-in-blogger.html.

Now that we've added a simple menu, we are ready to add a more complex drop-down menu to the blog.

Creating a Multi-Level Menu for a Blog

Way back in 2003, the online web design magazine Alistapart.com published an exciting, revolutionary article by Patrick Griffiths and Dan Webb titled *Suckerfish Dropdowns* (http://www.alistapart.com/articles/dropdowns/). It gave designers new ways to look at lists and menu navigation.

If your blog or any of your other sites have been around for a while, they have a lot of content to share. Using a drop-down menu navigation system will enable users to quickly dive deeper into your site. We'll be taking a menu from Dynamicdrive. com and customizing it to fit our blog. You can grab the original code files directly from the site at http://www.dynamicdrive.com/style/csslibrary/item/ suckertree-menu-horizontal/.The customized code will be available on the companion site of this book.

Time for Action!—Adding a Drop-Down Menu to a Blog

We're going to add a drop-down menu using one of the many menu scripts available from www.dynamicdrive.com. We will edit the CSS so that the menu fits and displays properly within our blog. We will then customize the menu with our own links.

1. Download the images and code from the companion site of this book. They will also be available at http://bloggerbeefedup.blogspot.com. Click the **Layout** tab on your blog, and then click on the **Edit HTML** tab. Scroll down inside the template of your blog until you reach the closing curly brace tag for the last header style, usually `header img{}`. Paste the following CSS code:

```
/* Top Menu Navigation*/
/* Credits: Dynamic Drive CSS Library */
/* URL: http://www.dynamicdrive.com/style/ */
/* Adapted by Lee Jordan for Blogger users. Added
background images and adjusted colors.*/
.suckertreemenu ul
{
 margin: 0;
 padding: 0;
 list-style-type: none;
}
/* Top level list items* /
.suckertreemenu ul li
{
 position: relative;
 display: inline;
 float: left;
 background-color: #F3F3F3
 url(http://www.leesjordan.net/fruitforall/suckerfish/images/
          bg_out.gif)repeat-x;
}
/* Top level menu link items style* /
.suckertreemenu ul li a
{
 display: block;
 width: 90px;
/* Width of top level menu link items */
 padding: 1px 8px;
 border: 1px solid black;
 border-left-width: 0;
 text-decoration: none;
 color: #990000;
 background:#f0f0ff
```

```
url(http://www.leesjordan.net/fruitforall/suckerfish/images/
          bg_out.gif)repeat-x;
}
/* 1st sub level menu */
.suckertreemenu ul li ul
{
 left: 0;
 position: absolute;
 top: 1em;
/* no need to change, as true value set by script */
 display: block;
 visibility: hidden;
}
/*Sub level menu list items (undo style from Top level
                                        List Items)*/
.suckertreemenu ul li ul li
{
 display: list-item;
 float: none;
}
/*All subsequent sub menu levels offset after 1st level sub menu*/
.suckertreemenu ul li ul li ul
{
 left: 159px;
/*no need to change, as true value set by script*/
 top: 0;
}
/* Sub level menu links style */
.suckertreemenu ul li ul li a
{
 display: block;
 width: 160px;
/*width of sub menu levels*/
 color: #990000;
 text-decoration: none;
 padding: 1px 5px;
 border: 1px solid #ccc;
}
.suckertreemenu ul li a:hover
{
 background:#009900
 url(http://www.leesjordan.net/fruitforall/suckerfish/images/
          bg_over.gif)repeat-x;
 color: #006600;
```

```
}
/*Background image for top level menu list links */
.suckertreemenu .mainfoldericon
{
 background: #F3F3F3
 url(http://www.leesjordan.net/fruitforall/suckerfish/images/
         arrow-down.gif) no-repeat center right;
}
/*Background image for subsequent level menu list links */
.suckertreemenu .subfoldericon
{
 background: #F3F3F3
 url(http://www.leesjordan.net/fruitforall/suckerfish/images/
         arrow-right.gif) no-repeat center right;
}
/* Holly Hack for IE */
* html .suckertreemenu ul li
{
 float: left;
 height: 1%;
}
* html .suckertreemenu ul li a
{
 height: 1%;
}
* html .suckertreemenu ul li ul li
{
 float: left;
}
/* End */
```

2. Save the template. Now the CSS styles are in place. It's time to add the
    `JavaScript`. The best way to do this is to save the `JavaScript` as an external
    file, either on a domain you already own or on a free hosting site. The file
    should be named `suckermenu.js`. Paste the following code into an empty
    text file and save it as `suckermenu.js`:

```
<script type="text/javascript">
//SuckerTree Horizontal Menu (Sept 14th, 06)
//By Dynamic Drive: http://www.dynamicdrive.com/style/
var menuids=["treemenu1"] //Enter id(s) of SuckerTree UL menus,
separated by commas
function buildsubmenus_horizontal()
{
   for (var i=0; i<menuids.length; i++)
```

```
{
  var ultags=document.getElementById(menuids[i])
              .getElementsByTagName("ul")
    for (var t=0; t<ultags.length; t++)
{
    if (ultags[t].parentNode.parentNode.id==menuids[i])
{
//if this is a first level submenu ultags[t].style.top=ultags[t].
parentNode.offsetHeight+"px"
//dynamically position first level submenus to be height of
    main menu item
ultags[t].parentNode.getElementsByTagName("a")[0]
                                        .className="mainfoldericon"
}
else
{
//else if this is a sub level menu (ul)
ultags[t].style.left=ultags[t-1].getElementsByTagName("a")[0]
                    .offsetWidth+"px" //position menu to the right
                    of menu item that activated it
ultags[t].parentNode.getElementsByTagName("a")[0]
                                        .className="subfoldericon"
}
ultags[t].parentNode.onmouseover=function()
{
    this.getElementsByTagName("ul")[0].style.visibility="visible"
}
ultags[t].parentNode.onmouseout=function()
{
    this.getElementsByTagName("ul")[0].style.visibility="hidden"
}}}}
if (window.addEventListener)
  window.addEventListener("load", buildsubmenus_horizontal, false)
else if
    (window.attachEvent)window.attachEvent("onload",
                                        buildsubmenus_horizontal)
</script>
```

3. The content for the menu now needs to be added. If you have already worked through the previous example, edit the **HTML/JavaScript** page element located below the header page element. Otherwise, add a new **HTML/JavaScript** page element. Paste the following menu content code into the content section of the page element:

```
<script type="text/javascript"
        src="http://www.leesjordan.net/fruitforall/suckerfish/
            suckermenu.js"></script>
<div class="suckertreemenu">
<ul id="treemenu1">
<li><a href="http://www.leesjordan.net/fruitforall/store.html"
```

```
                target="_blank" style="border-left: 1px solid black">
                Buy Fruit</a></li>
<li><a href="\">Blog</a>
<ul>
<li><a href="http://fruitforall.blogspot.com/2007/11/5-ways-to-go-
                green-with-lemons.html">Eco-Friendly Cleaning</a></li>
<li><a href="http://fruitforall.blogspot.com/search/label/recipe">
                Recipes</a></li>
<li><a href="http://fruitforall.blogspot.com/search/label/
                organic%20fruit">Organic Fruit</a></li></ul>
<li><li><a href="http://fruitforall.blogspot.com/search/
                label/recipe">Recipes</a>
<ul>
<li><a href="http://fruitforall.blogspot.com/2007/12/banana-nut-
                pancakes.html">Banana Nut Pancakes</a></li>
<li><a href="http://fruitforall.blogspot.com/2007/12/seasonal-
                cherry-stuffing.html">Cherry Stuffing</a></li>
<li><a href="http://fruitforall.blogspot.com/2007/12/skillet-
                apple-crisp.html">Skillet Apple Crisp</a></li>
<li><a href="http://fruitforall.blogspot.com/2008/02/star-fruit-
                adds-exotic-thrill-to-winter_09.html">
                Star Fruit</a></li>
<li><a href="http://fruitforall.blogspot.com/2007/12/wild-
                blackberry-cobbler.html">Wild Blackberry Cobbler
                </a></li></ul>
</li><li><a href="http://www.twitter.com/fruitforall"
                target="_blank">News</a></li>
<li><a href="http://www.leesjordan.net/fruitforall/about.html"
                target="_blank">About FFA</a></li></ul>
<br style="clear: left;" /></div>
```

4. Save the page element and view the blog. Notice how the menu items with multiple sub menu items show them in a drop-down list.

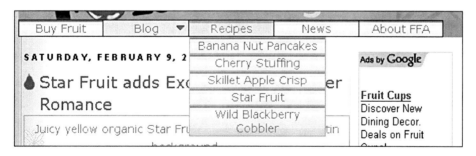

What Just Happened?

When we used lists within lists to create drop-down lists for menu items, we were able to give visitors a quick way to go deeper into our blog and our parent website. Using a combination of CSS styles and external JavaScript, we have created a powerful, attractive, and interactive menu structure that will work well with screen readers and search engines.

If the color of the text on your drop-down menu is not showing up correctly, check to see if the **Title** color or **Description** color of your blog is overriding the color set for the navigation. This happens as the CSS styles cascade over each other, like layers in an onion, or sheets on a bed. The style applied last, having the same name, wins.

Using Widgets on Your Site to Share Your Blog

Widgets promoting your blog add fresh content and give your site a dose of coolness. We'll look at two cool widgets you can add to your site. They can be placed anywhere on your site, and come in different sizes and colors to match the look of your site.

The widgets we will add are:

- **Headline Animator from Feedburner.com**: Displaying the article titles from your blog as teaser headlines in your website is easy using the Headline Animator widget from Feedburner. Your blog headlines will rotate on your website, attracting people to visit your blog.

- **Express Widget from SpringWidgets**: Integrating your blog directly into a page with SpringWidgets shares your blog with visitors to your website. SpringWidgets gives you the flexibility to control the size and look of the blog.

You can use the widgets on any part of your site, as long as they are between the starting and ending body `<body></body>` tags. Let's start by adding a slick animated blog headline.

Publicizing Blog Articles with Headline Animator

The Headline Animator displays recent blog article titles in an exciting scrolling format. It encourages visitors to try other articles on the site.

Time for Action!—Installing Headline Animator on Your Site

We'll grab the code for the Headline Animator widget from Feedburner.com and then add it to our blog using a page element.

1. Log into `Feedburner.com` and click on your blog feed. Select the **Publicize** tab from the main page of your feed. Click on the **Headline Animator** link on the left menu. The **Headline Animator** setup screen will open with a form to customize the widget.

2. First, choose the **Theme** of the widget by selecting it from the drop-down list. Select **234 x 60 White** for a widget that will be 234 and 60 pixels wide. This size will fit in the side bar of most websites.

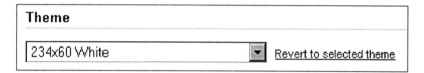

3. Now, type the title you want to be displayed on your widget. It can be different from the actual title of your blog. The text Organic Fruit for All blog will be the title for this widget. The **Width** should be set to 172 and the **Font Size** should be set to 11. You can change the color of the title by choosing from one of the color boxes, or by entering your own custom color, if you know the hexadecimal code. Type the hexadecimal code #339900 into the **Color** box. The **Title** will appear as medium green.

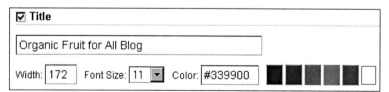

4. The **Headlines** section of the widget can now be customized. The **Wrap long headlines** checkbox should be empty. Keep the font size set to default and select a dark color. The following screenshot shows that the **Headlines** text is set to black, whose hexadecimal code is #000000.

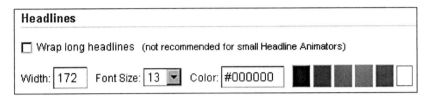

5. The last item to be customized is the **Dates** section of the widget. Choose your preferred date format from the drop-down list. You can also set the font size and color for the text. The standard is to make the date a smaller font size and a lighter color as compared to the rest of the sections. The **Width** is set to 172, the **Font Size** is set to 10, and the **Color** is set to #666666, dark gray, as shown in the following screenshot:

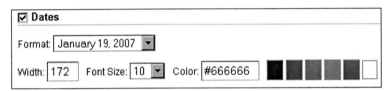

6. We've customized all the sections of the widget. Quickly, type a label for the widget in the text field next to the **Activate** button. The text 234 x 60 White is entered there by default. Now, it's time to click the **Activate** button and begin the installation process.

7. You will see a success message at the top of the screen once the widget has been activated. Now, select Other from the **Add to...** drop-down list. Click the **Next** button for the code screen.

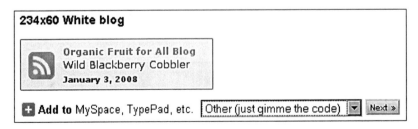

8. A new window will appear with the title, **Grab this Headline Animator**. It contains a preview of the widget, a checkbox, and a code box. Place a check in the **Include a Grab this link** checkbox. Click your cursor in the code box to select the code and then copy it. The code should look like this:

```
<p style="margin-top:10px; margin-bottom:0; padding-bottom:0;
      text-align:center; line-height:0">
  <a href="http://feeds.feedburner.com/~r/fruitforall/~6/2">
          <img src="http://feeds.feedburner.com/fruitforall.2.gif"
      alt="Organic Fruit for All Blog" style="border:0"></a></p>
<p style="margin-top:5px; padding-top:0; font-size:x-small;
      text-align:center">
  <a href="http://www.feedburner.com/fb/a/headlineanimator/install?
      id=1383454&amp;w=2" onclick="window.open(this.href,
      'haHowto','width=520,height=600,toolbar=no,address=no,
      resizable=yes, scrollbars'); return false"
      target="_blank">&uarr; Grab this Headline Animator</a></p>
```

9. Paste the code into your website anywhere after the opening `<body>` tag and before the closing `</body>` tag. To place it at the top of a sidebar with an id of sidebar2, paste it directly after the opening `<div id="sidebar2">` tag.

You can drag and drop the different sections of the Headline Animator to re-arrange their order on the widget.

What Just Happened?

Headline Animator is a cool widget. When we added the widget, it used the article titles from the blog post feed to display dynamically animated titles that visitors could click on. The JavaScript within the widget code caused a special **Grab This** window to open whenever the **Grab this** link on the widget was clicked.

We've added slick animated titles but there are no summaries included to help visitors decide if they want to read the full article. We'll need to add a different widget to share that information across multiple sites and web platforms.

Publicizing Your Blog with SpringWidgets

When you want to show more than just the headline of a blog article, you need an express widget with custom styling. It gives the user a preview of your blog's content and promotes your blog with a viral "grab this" feature that encourages visitors to put the widget on their own sites. Since it can be used on any site, you can re-use the same widget across multiple sites once it is created, and also share it easily with others.

Time for Action!—Displaying Blog Previews with SpringWidgets

We will add our Feedburner blog feed to an express widget on the SpringWidgets site. Customizing the widget will give us control over the appearance of the widget. We will then add it to one of our websites.

1. Go to the SpringWidgets site at `http://www.springwidgets.com/`. Click the **Express Widgets** button on the left side of the screen. The **Express Widgets** page will open with a fancy form to be filled out.

2. On the **Express Widgets** page, enter your feed URL. The *Fruit for All* blogspot feed is `feeds.feedburner.com/fruitforall`. Don't click the **Submit** button. See the pretty **Use Feedburner? Click here** button? Click it and you will be prompted to sign in to Feedburner.

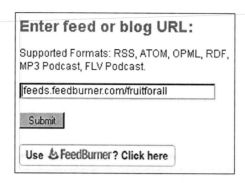

3. You are then taken to the **myfeeds** page. Click on the title of your feed and then on the **Publicize** tab. The **SpringWidgets Skin** link is on the left menu. It should look similar to the following screenshot:

    SpringWidgets Skin

4. You will need to have a place to host your image. This can be done on Blogger by uploading an image to a post and keeping it in draft format, uploading images to Picasa, using Google pages, or your own domain. I'm using my own domain. (`http://leesjordan.net/images/ffa-big-logo.jpg`)

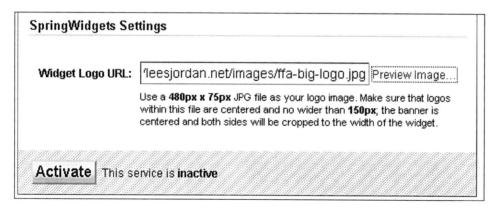

5. Click the **Preview Image...** link to see how the image will look once it is added to the SpringWidget. This is your chance to check whether the logo is centered. It will not tell you if the logo will be cut off at the bottom. Even though you can use a logo with a **height** of 75, the logo within the banner should be no more than 50 pixels high, to avoid being cropped. I'm using a simple logo with a blank background. Feel free to get fancy with your own. An editable psd file has been included in the code folder at the companion site for the book.

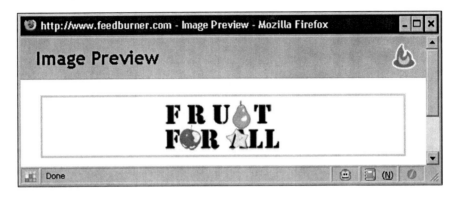

6. Now, it's time to activate the widget. Click the **Activate** button. The page will reload, and a success message will appear on the FeedBurner **SpringWidgets Skin** screen. Click the **Save** button below the preview image of the widget.

7. We can customize the size and color of the widget. Click the big link, **Get your SpringWidget for "Fruit for All News"**. You will then be redirected to the SpringWidget site. Change the **width** to 600, the **height** to 500, and then click the **enter** key on your keyboard. Let's change the border color by clicking on the color chip. Select a color say, #33cc00. The sample of the widget on the right side of the screen will change in size and color in response to your choices.

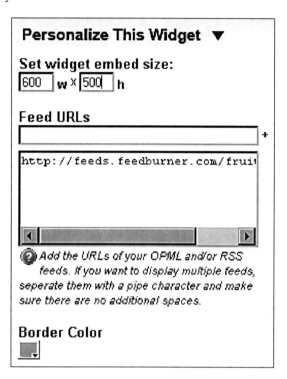

8. Now, it's time to grab the widget and put it on our site. Scroll down the screen and copy the code from the box labelled **Get the Code here**. Paste the copied code into your website. The code should look similar to the one below:

```
<object allowNetworking="all"
        allowScriptAccess="always"
        allowFullScreen="true"
        type="application/x-shockwave-flash"
        id="springwidget_0"
        codebase="http://fpdownload.macromedia.com/pub/shockwave/
                  cabs/flash/swflash.cab#version=7,0,0,0"
        width="250"
        height="318"
        align="middle"
```

```
                data="http://downloads.thespringbox.com/web/wrapper.php?
                  file=RSS Reader.sbw">
     <param name="movie" value="http://downloads.thespringbox.com/web/
                  wrapper.php?file=RSS Reader.sbw" />
     <param name="flashvars" value="param=http://feeds.feedburner.com/
                  fruitforall&param_style_borderColor=0x33CC00&
                  param_style_brandUrl=&partner_id=0&wiid=0" />
     <param name="quality" value="high" />
     <param name="wmode" value="transparent" />
     <param name="allowNetworking" value="all" />
     <param name="allowScriptAccess" value="always" />
     <param name="allowFullScreen" value="true" />
     <param name="bgColor" value="0x000000" />
     <embed bgColor="0x000000" allowNetworking="all"
                  allowFullScreen="true" allowScriptAccess="always"
                  src="http://downloads.thespringbox.com/web/
                  wrapper.php?file=RSS Reader.sbw"
                  flashvars="param=http://feeds.feedburner.com/
                  fruitforall&param_style_borderColor=0x33CC00
                  &param_style_brandUrl=&partner_id=0&wiid=0"
                  quality="high" name="0" wmode="transparent"
                  width="250" height="318" align="middle"
                  type="application/x-shockwave-flash"
                  pluginspage="http://www.macromedia.com/go/
                  getflashplayer" /></object>
 <div style="font:11px/12px arial;width:250px;margin-top:2px;"><b>
   <a href="http://www.springwidgets.com/widgetize/23/?
            param=http://feeds.feedburner.com/fruitforall
            &param_style_borderColor=0x33CC00&param_style_brandUrl=
            &width=250&height=300&wiid=0&partner_id=0"
            target="_blank">Get this widget!</a></b></div>
```

9. Open up the file of the company site and paste the code into the sidebar. Save the changes to the file and upload it to the server. We now have an easy way to share previews of our blog posts with visitors to our company site.

What Just Happened?

When you activated the **SpringWidgets Skin** feature on Feedburner.com, Feedburner combined your feed link data with the widget code snippet to create a customized item for your website. After activating and saving the widget, you were able to choose the size and look of the widget and add any additional feeds.

Visitors to your site who want to grab the widget will be redirected to a page just like the one we visited while building our widget. They will then be able to add the widget to their blog or web page. Editing and customizing the widget for their own site will be an additional option they have as well.

Adding Twitter Updates to Your Website

We want to reach out to as many people as possible. Adding a Twitter badge to your website gives visitors quick updates on what is happening. They can also interact with your tweets by responding to them. Placing a badge on your site as well as on your blog strengthens the connection between your blog and your website.

Time for Action!—Creating and Installing a Twitter HTML Badge

We will create our own custom HTML badge for use on our site. Adding our own background image, font format, and color scheme will give us control of how the badge looks and fits on our site.

1. Navigate to the Twitter site, and sign in. Go to the badges page of the Twitter site located at `http://www.twitter.com/badges/`. Select **Other** from the list of locations for your badge. You will be automatically redirected to the next step.

2. Now, it's time to choose which type of badge to use. Pick the **HTML/ JavaScript** badge, the third, plainer looking one on the page. We can always jazz it up using `CSS`.

3. The final screen of the badge wizard will display two steps: **Customize** and **Grab the Code**. Customizing the settings of the badge is what we will do now. Select the **Number of updates** from the drop-down list. You can display between 1 to 5 updates at a time on the badge. Next, type the **Title** for the badge in case you decide to display it. Click on the **No Title** checkbox to select it. We do not want to display a title for the badge on the company website. The **Customize** section should now look similar to the following screenshot:

4. Click on the **Grab the Code** box to select the code. Copy the code. It should look similar to the code shown below:

```
<div id="twitter_div"><ul id="twitter_update_list"></ul></div>
<script type="text/javascript"
        src="http://twitter.com/javascripts/blogger.js">
</script>
<script type="text/javascript"
        src="http://twitter.com/statuses/user_timeline/
            fruitforall.json?callback=twitterCallback2&count=2">
</script>
```

5. Choose the page you will be adding the Twitter badge to and open it in an HTML or a text editor. Paste the content portion of the badge in the body of your code.

```
<p>A paragraph of your web page content</p>
    <div id="twitter_div"><ul id="twitter_update_list"></ul></div>
      <h3>Grower Spotlight</h3><p>Peggy has been growing organic
          strawberries...</p>
```

6. Paste the `JavaScript` portion of your code just before the ending body tag on the page. The script portion of the badge should look like this:

```
<script type="text/javascript"
        src="http://twitter.com/javascripts/blogger.js"></script>
<script type="text/javascript"
        src="http://twitter.com/statuses/user_timeline/
        fruitforall.json?callback=twitterCallback2&count=2"
                                        ></script>
</body>
```

7. Viewing the Twitter Badge without any styles will show a plain looking list item. It doesn't look like an exciting badge at all. Let's give it some extra pizzazz with a little CSS.

> • We now have fresh organic strawberries from Florida ready to ship out! 59 minutes ago

8. We will add the CSS for the Twitter badge between the opening and closing head tags `<head></head>` of the web page. You can always copy the CSS located between the style `<style></style>` tags and add them to an external stylesheet. Copy the code below and paste it after the opening head tag `<head>` of your web page and before the closing head tag as shown here.

```
<head>
   <title>Your web page title </title>
     <style>
       #twitter_div
       {
         width:85%;margin:5px 5px 5px 10px;
         padding:0 3px 3px 3px;
         background:#ffffff url(images/ffa-mini-logo.gif)no-repeat;
         border: #008000 3px solid;
         text-align:left;
       }
       #twitter_update_list
       {
         font-weight:bold;
         display: inline;
       }
       #twitter_update_list ul
       {
         float:left;
       }
       #twitter_update_list li
       {
         list-style:none;
         padding:0 2px 2px 2px;
       }
     </style>
   </head>
```

9. Save the page, and upload it to your server. It should now show the Twitter badge as seen in the following screenshot:

We now have fresh organic strawberries from Florida ready to ship out! about an hour ago

What Just Happened?

When you selected the HTML/JavaScript version of the Twitter badge, Twitter grabbed your username. It then combined it with a simple code snippet customizing the number of updates, the title, and whether the title should display set flags for the badge code on the server associated with your username.

 You can reuse the code above by replacing the text fruitforall within the second JavaScript tag with your Twitter username.

The HTML portions of the Twitter badge were made up of a list tag wrapped in a div tag. Both tags contained id attributes that identified them to the JavaScript portion of the badge. The ids also made it possible to uniquely style the look of the badge.

Adding CSS styles to the badge gave it a nicer appearance. It also stood out from the page. Using a background image and a border in the #twitter_div class, the badge could be given a shaded background, a decorative border, or any other looks you could think up. A high contrast dark border was used with a white background for the badge in the example, to make it easier to see in the screenshots.

The JavaScript portion of the badge contained two separate JavaScript tags. The first tag contained a call to the badge script controlling the behavior of the badge. The second tag identified the Twitter user by username, "http://twitter.com/statuses/user_timeline/fruitforall" then called JSON, an AJAX toolkit, and requested it to return the two most recent Twitter updates posted by the user. Placing the JavaScript tags just before the ending body tag preserved the Twitter badge in case the Twitter server experienced any down time.

 You can install the same badge on your blog using a Blogger page element.

We've done a lot so far to integrate our site and our blog. Visitors to a site look for similar fonts, colors, and layout as they navigate to different links within the site. You want to create a standardized look across your blog and website, tying them together with colors, fonts, and other visual clues.

Integrating the Look of Your Blog & Website

Users are most comfortable when they are on the same site. Consistency builds trust among your visitors. There are many ways you can give visitors visual clues that they are still on the same site.

These methods include:

- Using the same fonts
- Choosing the same colors for backgrounds, content, and navigation
- Offering the same navigation bar on each page
- Matching the title of the new page with the navigation link they clicked
- Providing the same layout structure on every page

We've already taken care of the navigation. In this section, we are going to match the colors and fonts of Georgia's main website to her blog for a more consistent feel. We are going to do this by copying the CSS styles from the website. We will then transfer them to the template of the blog.

Using the Same Fonts

There are two ways the fonts can be transferred from a website to your blog. The first method involves no coding or template editing. You can set the font on different areas of your blog template using the **Layout | Fonts and Colors** page. The six potential fonts are Arial, Courier, Georgia, Times New Roman, Trebuchet, and Verdana. These are all proven web fonts.

When you want to use a different font, such as Myriad Web, you will need to specify it in the template of your blog. Let's edit the template in order to transfer the font from Georgia's site to her blog.

Time for Action!—Transferring Fonts from a Website

We will add a new font variable tag to our template that can then be edited from the **Fonts and Colors** section under the **Settings** tab of our blog.

1. Open up the external CSS file of your site or look for an inline style tag or a font tag. The style tag or class for a font should look similar to this: `font-family:"Myriad Web"`. A font tag will look like this: `<font face="Myriad Web">`. Carefully copy and paste the name of the font, also known as the font-family or font-face into a text file. Georgia's website is using "Myriad Web", a web safe font that is not one of the font choices in Blogger.

2. Navigate to **Layout | Edit HTML** to open up your blog template. Wherever you find the current font in the blog, replace it with the new font. For example:

```
Replace:
<Variable name="bodyfont"
    description="Text Font"
          type="font"
        default="normal normal 100% Georgia, Serif"
          value="normal normal 109% Verdana, sans-serif">
With this instead:
<Variable name="bodyfont"
    description="Text Font"
          type="font"
        default="normal normal 100% 'Myriad Web', Serif"
          value="normal normal 109% 'Myriad Web', sans-serif">
```

3. Continue replacing the font in the variable tags and the CSS styles. Save the template and take a look. The titles are now easier to read and have a modern look.

What Just Happened?

When you replaced the font values in the template, Blogger saved the new font and then displayed it on the blog page. You could have also specified a different font for each area of the blog. Fonts have more impact when you don't use more than three different ones. Too many different fonts will make the blog difficult to read and distract a visitor from your content.

While your cursor is in the blog template box, do a Find (Ctrl + F for Firefox browsers and Windows users) and type in the current font used in the blog to quickly locate all the places where it appears.

Now that we've added a font not specified in the Blogger **Fonts and Colors** administration page, let's match the colors of our blog and our website.

Choosing the Same Colors

Colors quickly tell a visitor if the page is an extension of the main website. Using the same color palette on your website and blog gives your site a consistent and a professional look. Matching the colors can be done easily using tools available for the Firefox browser. You can also use an image editor such as Photoshop, to take samples of the different areas of your website for color values.

 The PaletteGrabber extension for Firefox (`http://www.gusprevas. info/palettegrabber/`) will save the color palette of any web page for you with a quick click of the button. You can then load the palette into any image editor that accepts `aco` files.

Let's check the sites to make sure that our colors are consistent. Changing the colors in our blog will visually tie the blog and the website together.

Time for Action!—Transferring Colors from a Website

We'll synchronize the colors on our website and our blog to keep them consistent across both sites.

1. Open up the external CSS file of your site or look for an inline style tag or a color declaration. The companion site of this book has the `ffa_company.css` file available for you to use. Text colors are set in stylesheets using the format `color:black`, or `color:#000000`. Carefully copy and paste the color into a text file for reference. Download the `website_colors.txt` file for a quick list of all the main colors on the *Fruit for All* company site.

2. Navigate to the **Layouts | Fonts and Colors** section. Select the **Page Background Color** and then type #92d660 into the **Edit color hex code** box. Scroll down the select box to **Post Title Color**. Select it and type #339900 into the **Edit color hex code** box. Click the **SAVE CHANGES** button.

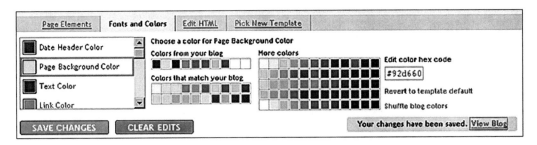

3. View the blog and then return to the **Fonts and Colors** screen to make any additional changes.

What Just Happened?

When we edited the colors of the blog template, we matched them to our main site. Blogger saved each color choice in the template as a value in the corresponding variable tag. We discussed this in detail, back in Chapter 2 of this book. You can revert to the default color and font choices by clicking the **Revert to template default** link located just below the hex code box.

Our blog is now visually integrated using fonts, colors, interactive widgets, and navigation. If you've had some experience using Blogger, you may be ready to move out of blogspot.com, Blogger's equivalent of your parent's basement, to a more professional custom domain address. It's a big step to use Blogger with a custom domain. The next section focuses on common issues and methods for using Blogger with a custom domain.

Using Blogger with a Custom Domain

There are many ways to use Blogger to publish a blog. You can use Blogger's blogspot domain, provide a domain for Blogger to redirect your blog to, or use a classic template and manage your blog using FTP. Each method has its pros and cons, good points and negative points that you should be aware of.

Deciding How to Publish Your Blog

Do you feel like you have outgrown your blogspot domain? Want the more professional feel of a custom domain or want to use your blog content to send visitors to your site?

Publishing Method	Pros	Cons
Blogspot.com	Free Blogger code updates automatically. Part of Blogger community. Easy to change templates. Easy to add additional blogs.	Not as "professional" looking as a custom domain. Cannot make full domain search. engine friendly. No control over image management.
Custom Domain for blog	Content still hosted by Blogger, pay only for a domain. More professional looking than a free account. Blog has a more descriptive domain name. Ideal for advanced users or companies.	Not free, must pay for the domain. Domain could have a negative past (see chapter on SEO for details). It takes several days to register the DNS settings across all servers.
FTP publishing	Control of domain and content. More professional looking than a free account. Ideal for expert users.	Pay for hosting and domain. Requires knowledge of FTP, or the ability to learn it really fast. Some Blogger features are not available, such as drag and drop layouts. Feed URLs have to be reset. Must use a Classic template. Difficult to keep up with Blogger code updates.

The most adventurous method is to publish using FTP. The biggest drawback is not having access to the latest templates and Blogger page element widgets. FTP publishing is best because you control the way your blog is published and can modify it to your heart's content.

Publishing to a Current Domain Using FTP

Setting up FTP for a current domain can be completed in 10 steps. If you've already examined the Pros and Cons and own a domain, you're ready to publish using FTP.

Time for Action!—Setting up FTP for a Current Domain

Setting up FTP for your Blogger account is a big step. Be sure to review all the steps before actually trying them on a live site. We'll backup our template, revert to a classic template, and then change our Blogger publishing settings to reflect our new domain and FTP settings.

1. Go to **Settings | Permissions** within the blog. Under **Blog Readers,** set **Who can view this blog?** to **Anybody.** Save the changes.

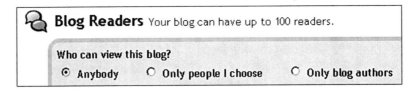

2. Navigate to **Layout | Edit HTML.** Click the **Download Full Template** link to backup the current template. Scroll down below the template.

3. Click the link **Revert to classic template.** Click **OK** on the pop-up alert box.

4. The blog has now reverted to a classic template. Go to **Settings | Publishing** to choose the publishing method. Click the **FTP** link.

> ## You're publishing on blogspot.com
>
> **Switch to:** • Custom Domain (Point your own registered domain name to your blog)
> • FTP (publishing on your ISP server) • SFTP (secure publishing on your ISP server)

5. Enter the domain used for the FTP server. If you are hosting the blog in the root files of your domain, enter the full server domain, for example `organicfruitforall.com`. If using a sub domain as shown in the following screenshot, enter the sub domain name followed by the domain, for example `blog.organicfruitforall.com`.

Blog URL	http://blog.organicfruitforall.com

6. Type the **FTP Path** of the blog. Many servers have a root public html folder called `public_html` as shown below, or `httpdocs`. Using an FTP client such as CoreFTP LE, or a control panel such as CPanel, which is provided by most ISPs will reveal to you which folder type is used.

FTP Path:	public_html

7. Enter the name of the main page used for the blog. The default is **index.html**.

Blog Filename:	index.html

8. Enter **atom.xml** or **rss.xml** into the **Feed Filename** field.

Feed Filename:	atom.xml

9. Time to add the username and password for logging into the FTP server of your domain. **FTP Username**: enter your username provided by your ISP. **FTP Password**: enter your password provided by your ISP. The example username **organicffa** is shown for reference in the following screenshot and the password is shown as a series of asterixes.

FTP Username	organicffa
FTP Password	**********

10. Click the **Save Settings** button to complete the form and set the blog to publish by FTP. You should now be able to publish posts using FTP.

What Just Happened?

When you decided to publish the blog using FTP, you were required to set the blog to a classic template. All current template settings and page elements were not applied to the classic template once the **Revert** link was selected. Blogger backed up the template you were using before you reverted. You were then able to change the publishing settings to FTP or SFTP. The main difference between the two choices, from a user's perspective, was the ports used for connecting to the servers. The FTP port is set to 21, by default. The SFTP server is set to 22, by default.

The FTP form was then filled out. The host domain name was entered, then the actual URL of the blog, and finally the default path for the blog was entered. Any index.html file in the same folder as the blog was overwritten when the form settings were saved.

FTP Errors and Solutions

Bloggers with their own domains and FTP access face unique issues while using Blogger. Given below are six common issues faced by users. The Error column describes each error. The Cause column explains why the error usually occurs, if it is known. The solution lists the current suggested solution to the issue.

Error	Cause	Solution
reason: 530 Login authentication failed	Some hosting providers are not allowing login to the Blogger service.	The Blogger team is currently working on the issue. Visit http://knownissue.blogspot.com for updates.
500 error on label feeds	Label contains spaces Example "Organic Fruit"	Create labels with hyphens instead of spaces. Example: "Organic-Fruit"
FTP blog feed not publishing in rss format.	Unspecified. Only Atom feeds were available initially.	FTP blogs now publish an rss.xml file and an atom file.
Cannot drag and drop Layout template items on Layout screen.	Layouts drag and drop functionality is closely tied to Blogger's method of serving up dynamic pages.	No current solution, due to the way Blogger pages are served. FTP users will need to edit their blog template.
Post pages are served even if the "Publish post pages" setting is set to "No".	Unspecified.	Delete the pages manually in the year/ month/ subfolders of the blog. Check http://knownissues.blogspot.com for updates.

Using a New Custom Domain

When you want Blogger to continue hosting the blog for you, purchasing a custom domain and associating it with your blog is an ideal solution. You get the benefits of having your blog hosted on Blogger without the hassle and expense of hosting the blog application yourself.

Purchasing a New Custom Domain

Purchasing and activating a custom domain to use with a Blogger blog is a procedure with multiple steps. It can take several days for the process to be completed, so plan ahead to minimize any potential problems.

Here's the process:

1. Purchase a domain, through Blogger, Google or any other registrar. To purchase from Blogger, visit the **Settings | Publishing** tab and select the **custom domain** link. The **Publish on a custom domain** screen will appear.

Publish on a custom domain

Switch to: • <u>blogspot.com</u> (Blogger's free hosting service)

Hint: If you want to publish to an external FTP server , you will need to <u>Set 'Blog Readers' to 'Anybody'</u> and use a <u>Classic Template</u>.

---

2. Enter the new address of your blog in the address box. The domain name address **organicfruitforall** is shown in the following screenshot. Select the type of domain (**.com**, **.net**, or **.org**) you want it to be. The **.com** option is selected from the drop-down list in the following screenshot. Click the **CHECK AVAILABILITY** button.

3. You will be redirected to the **GoogleApps** page if the domain you entered is available. A confirmation message will appear similar to **organicfruitforall. com is available**. Click the **Continue Registration** button and follow the steps of the domain registration wizard to complete your purchase.

4. Visit your domain registrar to verify whether your Domain Name Server (DNS) has the correct categorical name and a nickname for the domain name server called the **CNAME**. The **CNAME** for Blogger is **ghs.google.com**.

5. Visit your Blogger address and follow the instructions below to publish your custom domain to finalize the change.

[The CNAME steps for several major domain name registrars can be found at the Google Help Center: `http://help.blogger.com/bin/` `answer.py?answer=58317&topic=12451`.]

It may take several days for the CNAME information to be shared with other servers on the Internet. After the other servers have received your CNAME information, they will properly route visitors to your blog. Now that you have a custom domain that is active, you are ready to point your blog to the custom domain.

Time for Action!—Publishing with a New Custom Domain

After you've purchased a domain and the domain is active, it is time to point your blog to the custom domain.

1. Log into Blogger and select your blog. Click on **Settings | Publishing**. You should see a message on the **Publishing** screen asking you if you want to use a custom domain. Click the **custom domain** link.

2. You will now be prompted to enter your new domain. It can be a full domain (`www.leesjordan.net`) or a sub domain (`blog.leesjordan.net`). Click the **Save Settings** button to save the change.

Your Domain http:// `organicfruitforall.com` (Ex: `blog.example.com`)

Your domain must be properly registered first. (setup instructions)

What Just Happened?

Once the Domain Name Servers have finished resolving the domain, Blogger will automatically forward all content and links to your domain from your old blogspot address. If you don't see a change after several days, report the issue to the Known Issues team.

A common issue I see on the Blogger Groups is people having problems with their domains. A typical post reading `xxxx.domain.com` works, but `www.xxxx.domain.com` does not. They are either impatient or haven't taken the time to understand the process. The world is a big place, and the Internet is all over the world. It takes time for domain name servers to resolve domains. Remember, the domain you see is the nickname of your site, not the full IP address.

Georgia finally has a blog she can use to promote her business and share her passion for fruits. Integrating her blog with her company site has given her more ways to offer fresh content and interact with her customers.

Summary

We've integrated our blog with our website by adding a top menu navigation bar. Changing the fonts and colors of our blog to match our site tied them together visually. Cool interactive widgets were added to our site to promote our blog and attract new readers. We also explored our options for publishing our blog in different ways.

Our blog and our website are now "beefed up" beyond the ordinary. Blogger constantly rolls out new features and tweaks current ones. Now we can confidently use those features to keep our blog sharp.

Index

A

Ad campaign
campaign items, tagging 246
campaigns, tracking 246
campaign tags, identifying 248
links creating, URL builder used 246, 247
managing 246
AdSense
account, linking to YouTube account 203
ads, blocking with filters 220
Ads, managing 216
Ads creating, with blogger page elements
194
AdSense Ads, designing 199
advanced reports, using 217
custom AdSense Ad block, creating 199-202
custom AdSense Ads, using 198
filters, using 219
for search blog, adding to blog 207-211
options 198
page element, using 194-197
referral ad unit, adding 212-215
referral Ad unit, setting up 212
referrals, disadvantages 215
search block, adding 207
setting up 194
video unit players, managing 206
video units, adding 204-206
advertising programs
Amazon Affiliate Ads 225
BlogAds 229
project wonderful 229
recommended product Ad, adding 226-229
AdWords
about 248
account, creating 249
integrating, with Google Analytics 249
keyword effectiveness, analyzing 249
Analytics. *See* **Google Analytics**
Atom Syndication Protocol. *See* **Atom**

B

backlinks
about 107
activating 108
advantages 109
blogger feature 109
configuring 107
creating, to blogs 112, 113
disadvantages 109
Haloscan trackback service, adding 114-116
maintaining 111, 112
multiple backlinks, viewing 110, 111
need for 108
trackbacking, Haloscan used 116-119
trackbacks, adding automatically 110
trackback service, using 113
working 109
blog
AdSense, setting up 194
CSS text menu, adding 299-302
drop down menu, adding 303-308
multi-level menu, creating 302
optimizing ways, for search engines 278,
279
publicizing, with headline animator 309
publicizing, with SpringWidgets 312
publishing ways 325
website, integrating 297

blog, fruit for All
  access, granting to users 236, 237
  add recipes widget, creating 153-157
  AdSense page element, using 197
  blogger template, modifying 27
  blogging ways 8, 10
  blog previews displaying, SpringWidgets
    used 312-316
  Blogs of Note 10
  BoingBoing blog 14, 15
  book marking 18
  bookmarks, adding to blogs 83
  colors, transferring from website 323, 324
  community, building 22
  Cooking with Amy blog 11, 12
  CSS text menu, adding to blogs 299-302
  current users access, changing 238
  custom AdSense Ad block, creating 199-202
  custom domain, publishing with 330, 331
  custom filter, creating 243, 244
  customizing 10, 17
  Digg, linking to 20, 22
  drop down menu, adding to blog 302-308
  Facebook, linking to 18
  Facebook badge, customizing 139-143
  Feedburner 23
  feed post URL, obtaining 169, 170
  feed URL, in Safari 171
  fonts, transferring from website 322, 323
  goals, defining 16, 17
  Google Analytics 23
  Google Analytics, activating 232-234
  Google gadget, adding to draft.blogger.com
    160-164
  improving 23
  Innocent Drinks blog 15, 16
  integrating 18
  layout, selecting 49
  link bait content 18
  links, adding 102
  Meeblog 12, 14
  navbar, navigation bar 10
  PayPal storefront widget, adding 146-151
  photo slideshow widget, adding 129-131
  predefined filter, adding 240
  profile, adding 235, 236
  readers attracting, with links 102

  Reddit, linking to 20
  RSS feeds 18
  sales, increasing 22
  SEO 18
  social bookmarking, working 77
  social networking 18
  tagging 102
  template code, pruning 51
  theme, selecting 25
  twitter HTML badge, installing 317-321
  users, deleting 239
  website, integrating 297, 298
blog, optimizing
  improvements, prioritizing 280
  improvements list, creating 278
  off-site optimization 287
  off-site strategy 280
  on-site optimization 281
  on-site strategy 280
  strategies, developing 280
  ways 278, 279
  ways, for search enignes 278, 279
blog, publishing ways
  blogspot.com, cons 325
  blogspot.com, pros 325
  current domain publishing to, FTP used
    326
  custom domain, publishing with 329-331
  custom domain for blog, cons 325
  custom domain for blog, pros 325
  FTP publishing, cons 325
  FTP publishing, pros 325
  FTP setting up, for current domain 326-328
blog and website, integrating
  about 321
  same colors, using 323
  same fonts, using 321
blog feeds
  monetizing 221
blog feeds, monetizing
  AdSense Ads, displaying with FeedFlare
    222
  AdSense content Ad units, managing in
    FeedBurner 225
  AdSense content for feeds, setting up
    222-225
  FeedBurner Ad Network 221, 222

blogger
custom blogger widgets, creating 152
feed management 171
FTP errors 328
page element widget, adding 129
site feeds, working 167
widgets 129
widgets, planning for 159
widgets, selecting 158
blogger blog
Blogs of Note 10
feed post URL, obtaining 168, 170
feed, types 168
navbar, navigation bar 10
blogger feeds
managing 171
blogger feeds, managing
about 171
advanced feed settings, configuring
173-175
basic feed settings, managing 172
blogger feed, adding to FeedBurner 176,
177
blogger feed adding to FeedBurner 177
FeedBurner chicklets, adding 178-180
feed publicizing, FeedBurner used 180
feeds, offering by label 183
feeds, redirecting 175
feeds, specifying by label 184, 185
Google sitemaps, updating 182
headline animator, adding 180-182
label specific feeds 183
SmartFeed 183
subscription links widget 189
blogger template
blog, creating 27
customizing, page elements 27
modifying 27
blogger widgets
about 151
blog improving, Google Analytics
click patterns, interpreting 264
entrance keywords, analyzing 264
entrance path, exploring 263
entrance sources, analyzing 264
improving 262
landing page, optimizing 263

navigation section, analyzing 262
navigation summary, exploring 262
site overlay 265
blog network
working 125
blog optimizing tools
access color 294
Google website optimizer 294
NetConcepts 294
W3C XHTML validator 294
web pages that suck checklist 294
Blogosphere
about 107
blogrolls
about 119
blogroll widget, adding 121-124
setting up 120
blog SEO checklist
about 277, 278
Blogs of Note 11
blog template, validating 274, 277
BoingBoing blog 14, 15
bookmarks
adding, as text link 86, 88
adding, to blogs 83
bookmark buttons, addding to posts 90-92
bookmark link scavenger hunt 89
dynamic counters, adding to bookmark
links 94
dynamic links, adding with counters to post
95, 96
multiple bookmarks, AddThis used 92-94
multiple bookmarks, with one button 92
multiple counter scripts, adding 96
multiple counter scripts, adding with
Feedburner flare 96-101
selecting 83
services, selecting 85
social bookmark button, adding 89
social bookmarking sites 84, 85
text link bookmark, using 86

C

causes, errors 328
Cooking with Amy blog 11, 12
current domain, blog publishing

FTP, setting up 326-328
publishing to, FTP used 326

custom blogger widgets
add recipes widget, creating 153-157
creating 152

custom domain
publishing with 331
purchasing 329, 330
using 329

customizing, page elements
about 27, 28
blog templates, customizing 37-41
colors, changing 41, 42
font, matching to blog 45
fonts, changing 41, 42
header image, replacing 33
header page element, manging 30
header text, changing 30-33
high contrast text colors, choosing 43
image, adding to header 33-36
Navbar page element, editing 29, 30
page elements, manging 29
template font, changing with colors editor 45-49
text color changing, hexadecimal code used 43, 45

D

dashboard
about 250
dashboard overview section, customizing 251
dashboard overview section, exploring 251
left menu, using 250, 251
navigating 250
report, adding to dashboard overview 252, 253

Digg 20

E

errors
causes 328
solution 328

F

Facebook 18
FAN 221
feed
adding, blogger page element used 187-189
advanced settings 173
basic settings 172
specifying, labels used 184, 185
success, measuring 185

FeedBurner
blog feeds, monetizing ways 221
blogger feed, adding 175
feed, publicizing 180
FeedBurner chicklets, selecting 178
PingShot, activating 183
SmartFeed feature 183
versus subscription links widget 191

FeedBurner Ad Network. *See* **FAN**
feed protocol
about 168
Atom 168
feed post URL, obtaining 168, 170
feed URL, in Safari 171
multiple icon 168
RSS 168

feed redirect
configuring 176

feed success
measuring, FeedBurner stats used 186
measuring, FeedCount used 185

feed syndication
about 167
ways, for handling content 167

filters, Google Analytics
about 239
custom filters 239
predefined filters 239

FTP, blog publishing
current domain, publishing to 326
setting up, for current domain 326-328

FTP errors 328
FTP solution 328

G

goals, Google Analytics
  about 258
  current goal, editing 261
  editing 261
  performance, tracking 258
  setting up 258-260
Google
  PageRank used, site rank checking 272
  toolbar used, site rank checking 271, 272
Google Analytics
  access, granting to users 236, 237
  activating 232-234
  Ad campaign 246
  administrating 235
  campaign, tracking 246
  current users access, changing 238
  custom filter, creating 243, 244
  custom filters 239
  custom filters, types 244, 245
  dashboard 250
  data processing, custom filters used 242
  filters, setting up 239
  filters, types 239
  goals 258
  integrating, with Google AdWords 249
  links creating, URL builder used 246, 247
  predefined filter, adding 240
  predefined filters 239
  profile, adding 235, 236
  regular expressions 241, 242
  reports 253
  setting up 232
  tracking code, adding 234
  users, deleting 239
  users, managing 236
  website profiles, managing 235

H

Haloscan trackback service, adding 114-116

I

improvements, search engine optimization
  improvements, prioritizing 280
  list, creating 278

strategies, developing 280
Innocent Drinks blog 15, 16

L

layout
  sample sketches, creating 50, 51
  selecting 49
  usual suspects 49
linkbaiting bloggers
  about 124
  complex topics, writing 125
  content, creating 125
  readers, attracting 124
  serial articles, creating 125
links
  adding 102
  article, creating 103, 104, 105
  post schedule, developing 105, 106

M

Meeblog 12, 14

N

Navbar page element, editing 29, 30

O

off-site optimization
  blog, adding to Google webmaster tools
    288
  meta tag, adding 288
  robots.txt, analyzing 292, 293
  search engine spiders, viewing 291
  sitemap adding, Google webmaster tools
    used 289-291
  user-agents, robots.txt 293
on-site optimization
  blog description, updating 282
  blogsearch, updating 283
  blog title, updating 282
  content, changing with keywords 284
  image post, text adding 285
  media content, submitting 286
  ping access, updating 284
  template Doctype, editing 286, 287

P

page elements
  customizing 27
  managing 29
PageRank 272
pingbacks
  about 107
  advantages 109
  blogger feature 109
  disadvantages 109
  working 109
planning, widgets 159

R

Really Simple Syndication. *See* **RSS**
Reddit 20
reports, AdSense
  automatic custom report, scheduling
    218, 219
  exporting 217
  generating 217, 218
  using 217
  viewing 217, 218
reports, Google Analytics
  analyzing 255
  analyzing, by content 255, 256
  emailing 256-258
  multiple metrics, viewing 253, 254
  viewing 253
robots.txt, search engine
  user-agents 293
  viewing 292

S

search engine. *See* **also search engine**
  optimization
search engine
  attracting ways 295
  blog, optimizing ways 278, 279
  blog, searching for 268
  rank improving, with web standards 274
  reach checking, NetConcepts URL checker
    used 273, 274
  rich media content, need for 296

search engine optimization. *See* **also blog,**
  optimizing
search engine optimization
  blog, searching 268, 269
  blog checklist 277, 278
  blog optimizing, ways 278, 279
  off-site strategy 280
  on-site strategy 280
  site rank checking, toolbar used 271, 272
  strategies 280
  success, tracking 293
  tools 270
search engine optimization, status
  maintaining
  blog, updating 295
  rich media content, need for 296
SEO. *See* **search engine optimization**
site
  improvement, tools 294
  rank checking, toolbar used 271, 272
  validating, W3C used 274-277
site feeds
  advanced settings, configuring 173-175
  basic settings, managing 172
  working 167
SmartFeed 183
social bookmarking
  bookmarks, adding to blogs 83
  bookmarks, selecting 83
  bookmark services, selecting 85
  dynamic counters, adding to bookmark
    link 94
  links, sharing with friends 77
  logging in 78-81
  multiple bookmarks, with one button 92
  multiple counter scripts, adding 96
  online bookmarks 77
  post, submitting without bookmarks 78
  posts, sharing by email 81-83
  sites 84, 85
  social bookmark button, adding 89
  text link bookmark, using 86
  types 77
  user generated views 77
  working 78
solution, errors 328
subscription links widget

using 190, 191
versus FeedBurner redirect 191
success tracking, search engine optimization
    293

T

Technorati
  exploring 109-127
template
  backgrounds, adding 65, 67
  borders, adding 65, 67
  code, pruning 51
  current template, modifying 68
  custom variable tag, adding 53, 54
  footer styles, editing 61, 62
  header image width, editing 72, 74
  header styles, editing 63-65
  image, adding to post title 55, 57
  images, adding to post text blocks 57
  modifying, with styles 65
  post text styles, editing 57, 58
  sidebar styles, editing 59, 61
  three-column template, creating 67-71
  visual look, designing 52
theme
  presentation 26
  selecting 25
  uses 26
third-party widgets
  about 152
tools, search engine optimization
  Google toolbar 270
  Google trends 270
  NetConcepts 270
trackbacks
  about 107
  adding automatically 110
  advantages 109
  blogger feature 109
  disadvantages 109
  Haloscan trackback service, adding 114-116
  trackbacking, Haloscan used 116-119
  trackback service, using 113
  working 109

V

validating, site 274-277
visual look designing, template 52

W

website and blog, integrating 321
website integration
  about 297
  CSS text menu, adding to blogs 299-302
  drop down menu, adding to blog 303-308
  navigation adding, preparing for 298, 299
  website navigation, adding 298
website navigation, adding 298
widgets
  amazon affiliate widget, adding 143-146
  blogger widget form tags 157
  e-commerce, with blogger 143
  experimenting 160
  Facebook badge, customizing 139-143
  Google gadget, adding to draft.blogger.com
      160-164
  MeeboMe chat widget, adding 136-139
  page element widget, adding 129
  PayPal storefront widget, adding 146-151
  photo slideshow widget, adding 129-131
  planning for 159
  product sales widget, using 143
  selecting 158
  social network badges, adding 139
  third-party widgets, adding 132
  twitter badge, adding 133-136
  types 132
widgets, selecting
  about 158
  matching, to blogs 158
  matching matrix 158
  ways 159
widgets, using on site
  blog previews displaying, SpringWidgets
      used 312-316
  headline animator, from FeedBurner 308
  headline animator, installing 309-312
  SpringWidgets 308
  twitter badge, adding 317-321

About Packt Publishing

Packt, pronounced 'packed', published its first book "*Mastering phpMyAdmin for Effective MySQL Management*" in April 2004 and subsequently continued to specialize in publishing highly focused books on specific technologies and solutions.

Our books and publications share the experiences of your fellow IT professionals in adapting and customizing today's systems, applications, and frameworks. Our solution based books give you the knowledge and power to customize the software and technologies you're using to get the job done. Packt books are more specific and less general than the IT books you have seen in the past. Our unique business model allows us to bring you more focused information, giving you more of what you need to know, and less of what you don't.

Packt is a modern, yet unique publishing company, which focuses on producing quality, cutting-edge books for communities of developers, administrators, and newbies alike. For more information, please visit our website: www.packtpub.com.

Writing for Packt

We welcome all inquiries from people who are interested in authoring. Book proposals should be sent to authors@packtpub.com. If your book idea is still at an early stage and you would like to discuss it first before writing a formal book proposal, contact us; one of our commissioning editors will get in touch with you.

We're not just looking for published authors; if you have strong technical skills but no writing experience, our experienced editors can help you develop a writing career, or simply get some additional reward for your expertise.

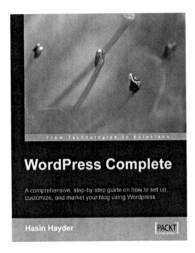

WordPress Complete

ISBN: 978-1-904811-89-3   Paperback: 272 pages

A comprehensive, step-by-step guide on how to set up, customize, and market your blog using WordPress

1. Clear practical coverage of all aspects of WordPress

2. Concise, clear, and easy to follow, rich with examples

3. In-depth coverage of installation, themes, syndication, and podcasting

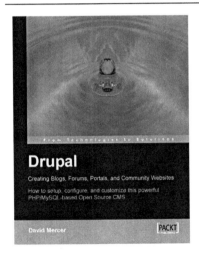

Drupal

ISBN: 978-1-904811-80-0   Paperback: 267 pages

How to setup, configure and customise this powerful PHP/MySQL based Open Source CMS

1. Install, configure, administer, maintain and extend Drupal

2. Control access with users, roles and permissions

3. Structure your content using Drupal's powerful CMS features

4. Includes coverage of release 4.7

Please check **www.PacktPub.com** for information on our titles

LaVergne, TN USA
05 November 2009
163058LV00004B/45/P